Jonathan Dee is the author of five novels. He is a staff writer for the *New York Times Magazine*, a frequent contributor to *Harper's* and a former senior editor of the *Paris Review*. He teaches on the graduate writing programmes at Columbia University and The New School. *The Privileges* was published by Corsair in 2010.

Also by Jonathan Dee

St Famous
The Liberty Campaign
The Lover of History
The Privileges

Palladio

Jonathan Dee

corsair

Constable & Robinson
55–56 Russell Square
London WC1B 4HP
www.constablerobinson.com

First published in the US by Doubleday,
a division of Random House Inc., 2002

First published in the UK by Corsair,
an imprint of Constable & Robinson Ltd., 2011

Published in this paperback edition by Corsair, 2011

A copy of the British Library Cataloguing in
Publication data is available from the British Library

ISBN 978-1-84901-992-7 (A Format)
ISBN 978-1-78033-097-6 (B Format)

Printed and bound in the EU

1 3 5 7 9 10 8 6 4 2

What if the old love should return?
—Horace

1

A TOWN CALLED Ulster in central New York – west of the Hudson, but still closer to Albany than to Syracuse or Buffalo – prospered briefly in the 1960s and 70s when IBM opened a regional sales division on the site of an old dairy two towns away. Ten minutes off the thruway, the abruptly thriving area wasn't long removed from its earlier life as farm country; most of the old sagging barns were bought up and knocked down to make way for new construction, but a few of the better-preserved ones were left on the vistas to go about the picturesque business of their own slow decline. They stand there today, swaybacked, holes punched in their steep roofs by years of snowfall; and the regional sales division has shut down. Roger Howe was offered a job there, a job that effectively represented the promotion which had not been forthcoming in his four years at the office in Westchester. He and his wife, Kay, with a small relocation allowance from the company and what remained of her inheritance from her father, moved upstate in the fall of 1970, when their son Richard was three years old, and Kay, though she didn't know it at the time, was pregnant with Molly.

The older homes in Ulster were well separated from one another, built for the most part on the apexes of the rolling, stony hills that had led its earliest settlers to hit upon livestock farming as their path of least resistance. A number of the IBM families, though, including the Howes, bought into a new development called Bull's Head, laid out at the wide end of a valley which narrowed toward the bald mountain that gave the venture its name. Roger and Kay, who were both twenty-eight and had never owned a home before, first saw Bull's Head on a Saturday in June, at an open house their realtor had scheduled from the hours of eleven to one. By the end of their first winter, when they had seen how the sunlight disappeared behind the mountain at around two in the afternoon, how the open end of the valley funneled perfectly the noisy, persistent winds that rattled the windows and leaked freely through all the casings, the house itself had become something of a sore subject, any mention of which seemed freighted with recriminations. Kay turned up the thermostat the moment Roger left for work in the morning; if she forgot to turn it down again before he came home, as she sometimes did, there were words. Downtown Ulster was an unplanned bloom of small enterprises – the gas station next to the drugstore next to the bank next to the IGA – which grew out of the town's main intersection but tapered off quickly to open land in every direction. In the evenings, a few minutes before each hour, the television antennas turned silently together like slow propellers atop the roofs in the valley.

A new building had to be erected one summer to hold the lower four grades of the burgeoning elementary school. From her first-grade classroom Molly could watch her brother Richard for forty-five minutes every day through the windows that faced on to the playground, unless the weather was too severe for recess outdoors. Her teacher noticed her staring out the window from time to time, though she didn't guess what the girl was staring at, and when it got too nettlesome she would make Molly bring her desk up to the front of the room for the rest of the day. It was a more effective punishment than she knew, for Molly was not a child who courted attention. She did not like her teacher, who seemed to feel so sorry for herself. The people Molly admired then were the members of her family, and her admiration often took the form of a kind of watchful daydream that she *was* one of them. At home she could sometimes be found, if Kay was on the phone or otherwise not to be disturbed, staring sleepily into the mirror above her mother's dressing table, or standing in the walk-in closet with her feet in a pair of her father's impossibly wide leather shoes.

Her room was painted white, with white blinds over the window, and a small bright bullseye throw rug on the cold wooden floor beside her bed. One wall was painted with a nursery design, the cow jumping over the moon, the laughing dog, the dish running away with the spoon; Kay had meant to stencil the whole bedroom that way, but she had gotten that far and no further. It was one of those subjects the children knew without being told was best not brought up. There was a nightlight shaped like an old gas lantern in the baseboard outlet in the hallway.

Molly was out of school more than most kids, sometimes because she was sick and sometimes only because she felt she might be; it was never difficult to persuade her mother to let her stay home. Kay preferred her daughter's company to the treadmill of housework: and beyond that she was cultivating Molly, dreaming of the day her daughter would be old enough to rely on as a kind of ally of perception, to see as her mother saw the great unfairness which lived behind the wasting mundanity of everyday life in that house, in that town; this, Kay believed, was what would save her from going crazy.

Molly's eyes were a pale blue, and their lashes, darker than the auburn shade of her hair, were unusually long. Kay Howe's few Ulster friends, who dropped by in the late mornings to slander their husbands for bringing them there, would stare at Molly in a way which was so invasively adoring that it didn't feel friendly at all, and say to Kay: "The girl is such a beauty. You shouldn't waste it. You shouldn't. She should be on TV."

"You think?" Kay would say, looking at her daughter with a skepticism intended as modesty.

"Oh my God yes. What is she, six? Put it this way. A girl that gorgeous now, in ten years she'll be making your life miserable. Every boy in this town will have his face against that window. So you might as well get some advantage out of it while you can!"

They all laughed, without softening their aggressive faces; Molly played quietly or turned the pages of a book, accustomed to being talked about in her presence. Later, when they were gone, she would climb into the chairs and look for the mysterious pale pink outlines the women's lips had left on their cigarettes.

Then one winter afternoon Kay fanned a dozen photographs of her daughter across the kitchen table, lit a cigarette, and moved them around like a puzzle. There were phone calls in which Molly's name was used, and spelled, and later there would be a trip to Mahoney's for a new dress. Kay wore an odd expression during those phone calls, a reactive, polite, charming expression, as if whoever was on the other end of the phone could see her face. "Auburn," she said into the receiver, suddenly returning Molly's stare. "Blue. Five/thirteen/seventy-one."

A week later, Kay watched from the front porch until the school bus had come for Richard, then went back into the house and began putting on makeup. Molly observed from her parents' bed. When Kay's face was perfect – though there was nonetheless something unsettling, for Molly, in seeing this glamorous nighttime rendering of her mother at eight-thirty in the morning – she turned from the mirror and focused her attention on the girl. An hour later they were driving much too fast to the train station, Kay looking testily from the road to her watch to Molly's rouged, pouting face.

"Other girls love to get all dressed up," Kay said, not in a conciliatory way. "When I was a girl, I begged my mother to help me get all dressed up. I liked looking pretty for other people."

It was true that Molly hated being out of play clothes, and especially hated having her hair manipulated and powder put on her face. But perhaps it was also true what her mother told her – that she was unlike other girls – because when the two-and-a-half-hour train trip was finally over and the secretary at the casting agency opened the door to the room in which they were to wait, there were thirty other girls sitting nicely in pretty dresses with ribbons or bows or combs of some sort in their hair. It was a larger group of girls her own age than Molly had ever been part of before; even birthday parties in Ulster couldn't convene this many children. The room was crowded with folding chairs. The secretary shut the door behind them. There was a good deal of friendly talk in the waiting room – girls to girls, mothers to mothers – but no one moved from her seat. Molly found an empty chair; Kay silently made her get up to smooth out her jumper properly before sitting down again.

Mothers and daughters were called from the room, one pair at a time, and none of them returned. It had never been explained to Molly why exactly she had been brought there – that is, to do what. She grasped only that there was some sort of vague premium placed on looking pretty. Of course, her mother didn't understand the task in much more specific terms herself.

The secretary who had greeted them an hour earlier stuck her head in through the open door.

"Mrs Howe?" she said, looking all around the room.

They were led down a long hallway and through a door which had taped to it a paper sign reading *Maypo*. Three men were seated around a small round table covered with papers and photographs; two of them stood to shake Kay's hand. The third, whose left arm was in a sling, just sat and looked discouraged. At one end of the room was a white backdrop with all sorts of large lights pointed at it. The lights had fans blowing on them. Molly had expected to find in this room all the other girls whose names had been called; but she was the only girl there. She began to worry.

"Now, Molly," one of the men said. He was much taller than her father; he squatted down and held her hand. "We're going to take a picture of you. You've had your picture taken before, right?"

She stared at him. He had long sideburns, and his tie was loose. He straightened up, still holding her hand, and began leading her toward the white backdrop, in front of the lights.

"Well, this is a special kind of picture," the man went on. He was kind, but he spoke quickly. "You have to stand here for it to work. Right here. See that bit of tape on the floor? That's perfect, sweetie. Now," he said, backing away from her, "in a few seconds I'm going to say some things, and I want you just to repeat what I say. But you know what? This is all just practice. Just practice. So do your best, but you don't have to be scared. You can look at your mom if you want to."

He was back in his seat by this time. The second man had gotten up and was on one knee in front of the table, holding a big Polaroid camera like the one Molly's grandfather had. Molly was glad to be reminded to look at her mother instead of the strange men or the cameras. Kay stood near the back of the room, her arms folded, smiling weakly.

"You look gorgeous, Molly," the tall man said. "Molly. Molly, look at me for a second. That's it. Now, let's pretend a little. Let's pretend you've just eaten your favorite thing in the whole wide world. What's that?"

After a few seconds went by, Kay said from behind him, "It's pizza."

"Good, thank you," he said, without turning around. "Pizza. So you've just had some pizza, and it was delicious, the best pizza you ever had, but you didn't quite have enough of it. You want some more."

Molly found these difficult circumstances for pretending. She put her hand up to shield her eyes from the lights.

"Put your hand down, please, honey. We'll be through soon, I promise. Now, this particular pizza has a special name, kind of a silly name. It's called Maypo. It's a funny name to say, isn't it? Try saying it. Maypo."

Molly said nothing. She stood still and didn't cry, but for some reason she felt that even if she wanted to she couldn't say anything at all.

"Say, 'I want my Maypo.' You can say it to your mom if you want."

Ordinarily Molly found silence to be a preferred way of hiding, but this time silence itself was playing, quite inadvertently, as an act of disobedience, an accidental exercise of her will. She was only trying to do nothing; still, she saw in their faces and felt in the air of the room that she was doing something wrong. The man with the Polaroid took one more picture, then put the camera on the floor.

The man at the table with his arm in a sling sat back in his chair, crossed his legs, and looked sullenly at the window, which was covered by a shade.

"Okay, just say your name then," said the tall man, still very gentle. "Say—" he picked up a pile of papers – "Say, 'Hello, my name is Molly Howe.' "

Her mother took her for ice cream near Radio City afterwards but didn't say a word to her while she ate it. The train station was almost an hour from Ulster; Molly was hungry again in the car, but she had an intuition that it was not a good

8

time to ask for something. Outside her window, the hard limbs faded into the brown of the hillsides, and before long the headlights in the opposite lanes were all there was to see. Kay checked to make sure the heat was turned up all the way.

When they got home, it was after dark, and Molly's father and brother were watching television. Kay forgot to ask any of them about dinner; she left her coat on the chair in the vestibule and walked quickly upstairs. They all heard the bedroom door click shut. Roger massaged his temple for a moment and then stood up unhurriedly. He believed it was important not to express anger in front of the children; but whenever he was angry it was easy enough to see in his face the vague and upsetting outline of what was left unexpressed. Molly wandered into the living room and sat on the floor. Her parents' muffled voices floated down. After a few minutes, Molly got up, climbed onto the couch, and laid her head on Richard's lap.

"Where were you?" Richard said, still looking at the set.

Richard had his father's black hair and a serious expression that he hadn't inherited from anybody. Toward his younger sister he maintained a kind of benign detachment, responding to her questions with ostentatious patience, never cruel to her but never really emotionally engaged by anything she had to say. Like Molly, his main pleasures were solitary ones. He had, for instance, an electric football game he was given for Christmas; it developed that he would much rather play both sides of the game himself than invite a friend over to oppose him – or, indeed, to go outdoors after school and play football itself. He did well in school but not conspicuously so, was not unathletic, had no sort of stammer or blemish, and yet other children appeared to him principally as a source of hurt. His

9

threshold for this sort of injury was so low that his classmates and neighbors would have been genuinely surprised to learn about the humiliation they caused him. Kay and Roger, when they had run out of other things to disagree about, would disagree about whether there was theoretically a time when a parent should take a book out of a ten-year-old boy's hands and encourage him strongly to go socialize with other children.

The more the Howes argued, the more parties they went to. While Kay got dressed, Roger drove out of the valley to Sennett Hill Road and came back with the babysitter, whose name was Patty. Patty was a teenager whose mannerisms were an object of Molly's fascination: the first thing she did, the moment the door had closed behind Mr and Mrs Howe, was to kick off her shoes, wherever she happened to be standing, and go to the kitchen drawer where she knew the cigarettes were kept. Patty had long, perfectly straight blond hair, wristbands made out of some kind of braided rope, and a wardrobe of secondhand jeans she bought at the Salvation Army in Coxsackie. When she was bored, which was most of the time, she liked to draw on her own jeans with a ballpoint pen – peace signs and monochromatic daisies – an undreamt-of bit of disobedience which Molly regarded with esteem. Time in the house with Patty alternated between long periods of equable silence and occasional flashes of an overcompensating harassment: out of nowhere, she could suddenly insist on making brownies, or playing some old board game that Richard had already outgrown. Once she had been their regular babysitter for six months or so, she began to act differently around them, talking to them in a false voice that staked out a zone somewhere between sister and mother – asserting her authority over them, but in such a way that she wanted them to think it was all for their benefit, that their interests really superseded her own.

Often it had to do with what they watched on television. "Don't you think you're a little young for this, mister?" she would chide Richard, who sat Indian-style on the floor in front of the big TV, five minutes into a boring *National Geographic* special about life on the Nile.

"Aren't you sleepy?" she would say to Molly, right before *Dallas* came on. "You must be sleepy. I think it's time for bed."

Molly was almost eight by now, old enough that she didn't really need to be put to bed; all the same, it was different when the last face she saw was Patty's, and she often lay awake until she heard her parents come in, her father starting the car again to drive Patty home, her mother's stockinged feet on the stairs.

Outside the house were other houses in the development that looked just like theirs, divided in Molly's mind into those with children in them and those without; the yards were separated by identical brown split-rail fences. And in the town center, which was reachable by bike, the stores were all interesting in their way – the revolving shelves of wristwatches in the glass case at the drugstore, the velvet ropes at the bank – mysterious at least until you got a little older and the mysteries weren't explained so much as they just dissolved into intelligence. It was enough for her, at that age; but her mother seemed forever to be bringing Molly her jacket and telling her to get in the car, sometimes for a doctor's appointment or a haircut, more often for something that had nothing to do with Molly at all. The car itself was like an absence, the way sleep is an absence, the embodiment of in-between, the blank time and space that connected the events and routines in her life. Wherever they went, the same bare landscape through the cloudy window: pine trees, power lines, roadside gullies filtered by sodden leaves. Molly spent a lot of time in the car with her mother; in that rural setting you soon thought little, even with small children, of driving an hour each way just to visit a friend or to shop somewhere.

One summer Monday, Roger surprised them all by walking through the door, pale and secretive, at three in the afternoon; the whole office had been sent home early because Roger's boss, a man in his fifties, had had a heart attack while introducing the staff to a special guest speaker from Research and Development in Armonk. By the next morning he was dead. From scraps of conversation and tensely veiled references over the next few days, Richard and Molly picked up that their parents were fighting over the question of whether they, the children, should be forced to attend this man's funeral. In the end, Roger's concern for appearances (would his colleagues think him insufficiently respectful? Would they think of him as a man whose children could do as they pleased?) won out, and the kids were dressed up and driven to the funeral home in Oneonta. On the way their mother leaned her coiffed head over the seat and explained that what they were going to was not a funeral, strictly speaking, but a wake, and that they should try their hardest not to act shocked or to say anything at all when they saw their father's boss's casket at the front of the reception room with the lid open and Mr Murphy in it.

They both did as they were told. At a whispered signal from their mother, Richard and Molly walked slowly up to the casket and knelt on the little upholstered bench, as they had seen those ahead of them do, even though they then had to crane their necks to see inside. Molly was told she had met Mr Murphy before, but she did not remember it; in any case, the face before her, wearing makeup, smelling of perfume, lying in a frame of satin, with its strange concavity around the mouth, was not one she had ever seen before. She was aware of Richard next to her, his head down and his hands folded, looking very solemn, even close to tears. "Goodbye, Mr Murphy," he whispered. He was older than she and might well remember meeting this man, Molly thought, maybe even more than once; still, she was puzzled by this evidence of a feeling stronger than muted curiosity. He did not seem to be faking. She folded her own hands and lowered her eyes to the polished side of the casket, watching Richard as well to see when he would stop or what he would do next. She knew that their posture was that of prayer. But she wasn't thinking about anything but the posture itself, and she was still waiting for something to happen when her brother stood up and whispered sternly, "That's enough."

She was smart, and passively respectful, but she was also the kind of child who notices everything, who takes everything in and doesn't ask questions, and while that made some adults fond of her, others were discomfited even to the point of suspicion. Her teachers at school fell into these two camps as well. All of them were women; the only men she ever saw in her school building were the principal and the janitor. Her fourth-grade teacher, Mrs Park (who, like every teacher of Molly's, was wary of her at first, remembering the more temperamental Richard from three years ago), was the only one who said to herself that

13

there was clearly something more inside the girl than was getting out: she tried to befriend her, to find out what that something was, but Molly only felt the maternal heat of this interest as something contrived, something to be tolerated rather than understood, and nothing more than kindness ever came of it.

What did the other children see? Molly was not the kind of shy girl who took pains to keep from being noticed, but rather one who seemed not to notice herself, not to assert or even bear in mind her own presence in a group. Thus she was not offended when others did not recognize it either. Unlike her brother, though her pleasures were unshared ones, it didn't follow that she could find pleasure only in solitude. She could often be found in the band of children – children of all ages hanging out together, as happens in small neighborhoods – on their bikes on the aesthetically crooked roads of Bull's Head, on the expanse of tended grass just before the boundary line where the slope of the valley began. She was considered by adults a child who loved to read, and relative to others perhaps she was; still, in those years she spent no more time reading each day than she did in front of the television, usually sitting on the floor, occasionally scooting forward to turn the dial on the box which controlled the rooftop antenna, knowing it oriented toward New York City or Albany or Vermont but preferring to imagine an element of magic to it, watching happily as the rotor hummed and the lives of the families on the screen were retrieved from a purgatory of the unobserved, brought into focus through a kind of electronic snowfall, their voices growing clearer, along with the bodiless, ratifying laughter that enclosed them wherever they went.

Holidays were spent all the way up in Syracuse, where Kay's mother lived; Molly's other grandparents were in Illinois. Kay was from a large family, none of whom seemed to have gotten very far away from Syracuse: they were all there, along with Molly's cousins, at Christmas and Thanksgiving.

The snow drifted all the way up to the windowsills. The children ate at a card table set up for the purpose in the passageway between the kitchen and the dining room; an hour after dinner, the whole house still smelled like food. The heat was always up too high. Kay sat on the stairs, talking quietly and intensely with her sister. The six cousins still sat at the cleared table in a kind of limbo of parental circumscription: they couldn't play outside, and they couldn't watch TV, because Roger Howe and his brother-in-law had the football game on.

Kay had a maternal uncle whose own children were grown and lived far away; after a few beers, it always seemed, he couldn't leave the cousins alone. When they were having a good time at something, Great-Uncle Phil would come over and muss their hair and ask them if they were having a good time; when they were bored, his idea of entertainment was to find ways to extract from them declarations of their affection for him. Now, from his seat at the end of the kitchen table, he called the six restless cousins over to his side.

"You kids have been so good today," he said, "that your Uncle Phil wanted to give you something. Something for the holidays. I said to myself, I'm gonna give each of those good kids a dollar."

The children, Molly included, shouted in celebration. From the sink across the kitchen, their grandmother frowned at Phil, but said nothing.

15

"But you know what?" Uncle Phil said, pulling a sad face. "I just looked in my wallet, and I found out I only have one dollar in there. I just don't know what to do. I don't know how to decide who should get it. I guess I'm just going to have to give it to the boy or girl that wants it the most."

They whined and jumped in place and tried to make their voices heard over one another.

"Whoa, whoa," Uncle Phil said, amused. "I'll tell you something. I just hope nobody wants it so bad they're going to cry if they don't get it. I think if something like that happened, if somebody busted out crying, well, I couldn't stand that, I'd just have to give it to them."

The kids set about moaning and making pouty faces, saying "Boo hoo," and other sorts of received imitations of sadness.

Uncle Phil glanced all around the kitchen, smiling slyly, trying to catch the eye of one or two of the other adults so he could wink at them; but they were all looking away from him. He turned back to the cousins and shook his head skeptically. "I meant real crying. Real tears. Cheaters never prosper, you know. I don't believe you really are sad."

That silenced them for a moment: they wanted, as much as they wanted the dollar, to solve the puzzle of Uncle Phil. Molly stood a few inches from Uncle Phil's knee; she looked at his big head, at the pale tones of old age. Her face was still and unrevealing. Half a minute went by. Uncle Phil's eyebrows were too long; his upper teeth, which were false, were beautifully proportioned inside his loose mouth. Sadness is easy, Molly thought, though she wasn't sad at all just then. Uncle Phil shifted in his chair; "I think we've got something here," he said excitedly. Everyone turned to look at Molly; in another

16

few moments, she blinked, and two thin tears rolled down her face.

THE HARDEST THING was concentration. John Wheelwright got up from his desk and opened the door to his office a few inches so as not to miss the woman with the coffee trolley when she circled by. The oversized sketchpad on his desk had a ring on it from the coffee he hadn't finished yet. John's copywriting partner, Roman, was off this morning on some personal time involving his daughter's interview for nursery school. John had even come in half an hour early to take advantage of the uncommon solitude, imagining how he might surprise Roman after lunch with a brainstorm; but the solitude was doing nothing for him. He pushed up the sleeves of his shirt, with the felt-tip pen still between his fingers, leaving another hatch on the blue cotton.

Of course it was only a rough storyboard, whose eventual realization, even if it managed to win the signoff of the AD, would become some director's problem; but a rumor had begun circulating that the Doucette casual wear account was going to be put into review, so John was well aware that he and Roman and the other teams were being watched more anxiously than was usual there. And John took his work seriously in any case. Their first proposal, which Canning had rejected on Friday, was one continuous thirty-second shot of an urban intersection, say Eighth Street and Broadway: it would be shot in black and white with a deep-blue wash, except for those items of Doucette clothing – jeans, T-shirts, caps, shorts – worn by a few strategically placed pedestrians, which would show up in full color. John wanted to mount the camera on a waist-high pole in the middle of the intersection and spin it horizontally 360 degrees, as in a shot he remembered from Brian De Palma's *Blowout*. The soundtrack was a talky Altmanesque burble: Roman didn't even want to write it, he said, just edit it down from whatever ambient conversations the filming happened to pick up. Canning had liked the thought of it but said that it skewed too young, too hip for the room as he liked to say, too funky an image for an essentially conservative line like Doucette, whose whole appeal lay in the idea that it stood outside the exigencies of fashion. Roman offered to change the soundtrack from dialogue to music – something old and wryly cheesy, like Petula Clark, or something from *Saturday Night Fever*. Canning still wouldn't go for it: more precisely, he thought the client would never go for it, and if that was the case, then there was no point in any further compromising to make it real. Their only course was to come in Monday and start all over again.

But where was the starting point? John closed his eyes. The office they shared was personalized with three years' worth of imaginative detritus, little totems of an ironic sensibility: a framed photo of David Ogilvy with Roman's forged inscription; the old Farrah Fawcett poster from the 70s; a Frisbee with the Backstreet Boys' faces on it; an original *Looney Tunes* cel; several of those miniature football-player dolls whose heads bobbed when you tapped them; a typeface directory; Pee Wee Herman's mug shot, clipped from the New York *Post;* a vintage deck of pornographic playing cards; a Lyndon LaRouche for President bumper sticker; a huge Atlantic City beer stein filled with Magic Markers; a mounted ad for Chesterfield cigarettes featuring John Cheever; a three-foot-high, inflatable Monica Lewinsky doll, which Roman had ordered off the Internet; a dog-eared copy of *American Psycho;* a stuffed iguana; six packages of margarita mix and a blender. All around the windowsills and on top of some of the piles of magazines were samples of the Doucette clothes themselves, khaki pants, corduroys, loose V-neck sweaters. He could put the most gorgeous models money could buy in the clothes, but that had been seen. He could just show the clothes themselves, uncompromised by bodies; *that* had been seen. He could take the product off the screen and out of the ad entirely and replace it with something else; that was at least as old as Infiniti. In the comfortable office, with no partner to remind him of things like deadlines, John stared some more at his blank pad, wiggling his pen between his fingers and thinking about where newness lies.

There was a soft knock on his open door, and before he could even lift his head Vanessa had slipped in; without a word she sat down sideways in the low blue velour armchair perpendicular to John's desk, her legs over the arm of the chair that faced the wall, so that she almost had her back to him. John looked at her curiously but politely; she turned her head and smiled at him but said nothing, swinging her feet back and forth. She took a sweater off the coffee table and held it up against her shoulders. John pushed his long hair back behind his ear and leaned over the sketch pad again.

Vanessa Siegal worked at Canning Leigh & Osbourne as an account planner; she was wearing the sort of skirt only she would or could wear in the office, a short red tight synthetic garment that never seemed to wrinkle or to move in

19

disharmony of any kind with the way she moved. She was tall and angular and her hair was marcelled into a kind of fashionable helmet which followed the curve of her ear, and which never moved either. Her austere stylishness and its translation into other realms was a subject of great and admiring speculation among a particular type of man. John was not of this type; if anything, he was a little afraid of her. It was distracting to have her come into his office unannounced like this even though the two of them were certainly on friendly terms. She sighed loudly. John pretended to go back to work, not out of aloofness or to express annoyance but instead out of the exaggerated deference to women that still characterized him, that was his most exotic feature to Northern women like Vanessa. She looked furtively at him, which he did not miss, and bit at one of her nails.

"What are you working on?" she said.

"Doucette," John said, amiably; but when a few more seconds went by and she didn't seem to want to say any more, he started drawing again.

"Listen," Vanessa said, and she swung around to sit normally in the chair, in profile to him. "You like me, right?"

John felt himself start to blush. He sat back in his chair, but even as he struggled to find something to say, she waved her hands and frowned. "I mean, you like me as a person, a friend, am I right?"

"Well, of course I do," John said. His accent still crept defensively back into his voice at moments like this.

"And when you like a person," Vanessa went on – he could hear that there was some irony in her vulnerable, cautious tone, that she was acting something out – "you accept that they might have bad points as well as good points. That they may have flaws."

"Everyone has flaws," John said patiently.

"Or not flaws, so much. That they might make a mistake from time to time. They might blurt something out sometime, because, because that's what people sometimes do, right, in social situations? They blurt things out."

John put his pen down. He couldn't help smiling a little. Out in the lobby, the bell for the coffee trolley rang.

"What a word, right?" Vanessa said gaily. "Blurt."

"Is there something you're trying to tell me?" John said.

Vanessa grimaced and stood up. The skirt, John observed, never creased. What could it be made of? She went to the door of his office and shut it. Her long arms folded, she stood in front of his desk. *Striking* was the word that sounded in John's mind.

"So last week", she said in a lower voice, "was the MPA Awards dinner? You remember?"

"I remember people talking about it."

"Right, well, so, I went, and during dinner there was this—"

"Hold on," John said. He leaned forward and put his hands flat on the desk. "You *went*?"

Vanessa made an impatient gesture.

"That was three thousand dollars a table," John went on, enviously. "That was partners only. And you went?"

"I went," Vanessa said simply; her eyes moved all the way to her left in a manner that was simultaneously coy and uncomfortable.

"With whom?"

"Never mind."

"With whom?"

21

"Never *mind*. The point is that they had this dinner at MOMA, right, and so of course at some point the talk turns to the art, somebody says, like, Hey, have you seen the Francis Bacon show here, it's *monumental*. So then a couple of them start discussing Bacon, and Anselm Kiefer, and whether Basquiat could draw or not, and before long everybody's got their dicks out, you know how it is when those guys get together."

John had been lagging behind her narrative just a little bit, hung up as he was on the question of which of the partners Vanessa was secretly dating – though apparently it wasn't much of a secret anymore – but the affectless coarseness of her language brought him back to the present. He'd never really grown accustomed to women who swore so casually. His inclination was to hear it as a sign that the speaker didn't take John seriously in the masculine realm.

"And of course it dawns on me, while they're talking, the arc that this conversation is going to follow: at some point, they're going to patronizingly drag the women at the table into the argument. The 'feminine perspective,' you know? Like they care. I swear, put these guys, *any* guys really, into a tux and stick a cigar in their mouths and they turn into their grandfathers. I'm sure you're the same way."

John raised his eyebrows and pointed to his chest.

"So anyway." She sat down sideways in the chair again, facing him, her knees nearly as high as her chest; conscientiously he looked into her eyes. "This is the bad part. What I know about painting you could fit on the head of a pin. I mean, I know the *names*. But in this of all situations, you don't want to conform to their stereotype. Right? So when Canning finally asks me—"

"Was it Canning?" John said. "That took you?"

"No. When he asks me who are some of the living artists whose work I admire most – well, these are my bosses, in the end, and you don't want to look like an idiot in front of them. So I mumble something about how I used to like Julian Schnabel but you never hear about him anymore, and then about Keith Haring, because I forgot for a second he was dead, and I notice that the men are all looking at me in this way. In the way my father used to look at me when I came downstairs in my pajamas because the party was too loud. You know what I'm saying?"

"I think so."

"So," Vanessa said, looking at her nails again, "I sort of panicked. Here's what I said. I said, You know who'd be a good person to ask about this stuff, though, who really knows a lot about painting, is my friend John Wheelwright in the art department."

"Oh my goodness," John said.

"He's a very smart guy. In fact, he was an art major at Berkeley. That is right, isn't it?"

"Art history," he said nervously. "So did they know who I was?"

"Of course they know who you are," Vanessa said. "So anyway, I talked you up to these guys as a real expert. Your ears must have been burning something awful. It was just, like, anything to fill that silence, you know? Anything to get their interest off of me." She raised her eyes and looked directly at him again.

John leaned back in his chair and put his palms together. It was a little scary, to be sure, to learn that you had been bragged about in front of your superiors like that; but she had only been complimenting him – even if in an exaggerated way. So why would she worry that it would make him angry?

"Vanessa?" he said. "Have we reached the climax of this story?"

She shook her head no, with a meek, childish reluctance that still seemed to have an element of irony or performance in it. She began swinging her feet again. "He didn't say a word at the time," she went on, "but the guy at the table who I guess really picked up on what I was saying was Mal Osbourne."

John started. "Osbourne was *there?*"

"I know!" Vanessa held her hands in front of her face and pantomimed great fear. "Amazing, isn't it? He *never* shows up at these things. It was like seeing J. D. Salinger or something. Anyway, he's this big art collector, apparently, you probably know that but I didn't."

"Sure," John said. "My God."

"And apparently he has this thing where he spends one Saturday morning every month studio-hopping downtown, checks out what he wants to buy, what he might want to buy later on. So," Vanessa said, her voice getting a little shakier, "this morning I come in and there's this email waiting for me, sent, by the way, at two in the morning." She shut her eyes tightly to recall the exact wording.

"Oh, this is unbelievable," John said.

" 'Tell your friend in Art to meet me Saturday at 8.30 a.m. outside his building. I have his address from personnel. If he can spare a few hours, I would greatly value his expertise, and a fresh pair of eyes. Osbourne.' "

"*This* Saturday?"

"I guess. Why, did you have something planned?"

"Would it matter if I did?"

"Oh, please, please, don't be mad at me," Vanessa said, and John, mad as he was, was nevertheless abashed to see that she was actually in tears. The theatricality of her nervousness had been more for her own prompting than for his; real remorse was hard for her. "I had no way of knowing this could happen. I was just trying to talk you up. And besides," she said, trying to smile, "is it necessarily a bad thing? I mean, if you make a good impression on him, it could really help you out, don't you think?"

This was true, but John felt it would be immodest to let on that this had occurred to him; besides, the reverse proposition was equally obvious. "Osbourne is, what, forty? And he's already probably one of the ten or twenty biggest collectors in the city. In other words, he's a lot less likely to be bowled over by my expertise, such as it is, than you are, bless your heart. And if he decides I'm a moron, well, that's not going to give my career prospects here a big goose either. Oh, Vanessa, what have you done to me?"

She wiped at her eyes and nodded. "It's all so fucking *whimsical!*" she said.

Later, John called Rebecca at work, but she had a client in her office and had no time for a long conversation; so they arranged to meet for dinner at Mahmoun's, the Middle Eastern restaurant around the corner from their apartment in Brooklyn. They ate there often – neither John nor Rebecca liked to cook. Mahmoun's delivered as well, but lately the two of them felt that maybe they had been ordering out too much: the endless garbage, the white cartons with their metal handles which lingered in the refrigerator for days, could begin to seem like a small joke at the expense of their new home, as if they weren't really committed to the idea of it, as if they hadn't made up their minds to stay. Dining out was at least nominally social. The owner nodded contentedly at them when he emerged briefly from the kitchen and saw them in their usual booth by the window, in their wrinkled business clothes.

"This is scandalous," Rebecca said, though she seemed more annoyed than actually worried. "I can't believe Vanessa would do this to you. Put you on the line like that, just to look good. What's the matter with her?"

"She apologized," John said. He wanted Rebecca to focus on Saturday, but she seemed determined to extract from him a condemnation of Vanessa, whom she had met at a few parties and did not like or trust.

"So she crosses her legs and apologizes and that makes it okay. Not to mention that she's doing one of the partners. A real traditionalist."

"Well, whatever," John said impatiently, "it's done. I mean, I can't get out of it. I can't refuse to go."

Rebecca shook her head. "Of course not," she said.

He was disappointed, and somewhat alarmed, by the way she kept agreeing with him so completely when what he really wanted was for her to tell him he was making too big a deal of it. "Vanessa got my major wrong, too, which is a problem. Osbourne probably thinks I'm still painting, still going to galleries. Wait'll I tell him I wrote my thesis on Goya, and even that was eight years ago."

Rebecca, her mouth full, put her hand to her head as she

remembered something, and patted the leather tote bag on the seat beside her. She swallowed. "At the end of the day I did a Lexis search on Mal Osbourne," she said. "There's not as much as I would have thought. But there was one good article about him as a collector, talks about some of his recent acquisitions. Give you some idea of his taste. Where the hell is it?"

John smiled at her gratefully, even though she was no longer looking at him. Rebecca had an abrupt, distracted way of speaking, when he called her in her office, that sometimes left him wondering if she was paying attention to what he said. Even in the conservative, dark, A-line suits she wore to work she was dramatic-looking, with broad eyebrows, full features, a face that was somehow most naturally alluring when she frowned. Her fingers flipped a second time through a fat accordion file.

"Well, it's in there somewhere," she said, annoyed with herself. "I'll find it when we get home."

"No rush," John said calmly. He knew how she obsessed if she thought something was lost. "I've got five days."

They ordered two cups of the bitter Turkish coffee and watched each other in mannerly silence while their dishes were removed.

"So how much do you know about this guy?" Rebecca said.

"Not much more than anyone else. I met him when I was hired, just shook his hand really. I'm sure he wouldn't recognize me. He doesn't even come into the office anymore – just stays in touch by email, fax, messengers. Which I understand has pissed off the other partners considerably. Though I only hear that kind of stuff secondhand."

"From Vanessa, you mean. Hey – do you think Osbourne's the one she's sleeping with?"

"Well, that would be good and weird. I'm pretty sure he's not married. But it's hard to imagine. Osbourne's famous for hating parties; I heard a story that he RSVP'd no to Canning's daughter's wedding a couple of years ago. He did go to this thing at the Modern, but that must have been just because of the art connection – he's mostly kind of a hermit from what I understand. I can't see Vanessa going for that. She's out six nights a week. I mean, this is a guy who people in the office have disagreements about even what he looks like."

"He's a young guy, though, isn't he?"

"Relatively. I think he's forty-two, forty-three, something like that. The youngest partner, certainly." John shook his head. "He did some groundbreaking work, boy, when he was a writer. He was in on the Apple 1984 ad. He once got a client, a vodka importer, to use their whole promo budget to hire actors to go into trendy bars in New York, LA, Miami, and just order the stuff. Just order it. Performance advertising, I think he called it."

"Does he really know anything about art, or is it just one of those rich-guy affectations, so we won't think he's like the other rich guys?"

John cocked his head. "Beats me. A better question is whether I know anything about art, and if he decides not, do I start looking for another job."

"Oh, I'm not worried about you," she said flatly. "You're the real thing. I just don't know if you have it in you to be as fake as he is, if it comes to that." She fumbled in her bag for her purse. "Can we get out of here? I have to have a cigarette."

At home, a second-floor walk-up, Rebecca made straight for the bathroom without even turning on the light. John stood in the doorway for a few moments, looking at the silhouettes of the scarce, new furniture, the cocked squares of ambient city-light on the white wall, the patient, minuscule blink of the answering machine.

On Saturday morning, John, too nervous to eat, came down the steps of the brownstone a few minutes early to wait for Osbourne, but Osbourne was already there. At least that was the conclusion to be drawn when John saw the black livery car idling directly in front of his stoop, an opera light just visible through the tinted rear window, alien to the weekend quiet of the narrow side street. It wasn't an ostentatiously big car by any means. Still, uncertain about approaching it, John had halted instinctively on the brownstone's bottom step; the driver's door opened and a pale-complected man in his sixties in a shirt and tie walked briskly around the grille of the car, curtly nodded, and opened up the rear door for him.

Osbourne was all the way in the far corner of the back seat, leaning forward, examining with interest the house fronts on the opposite side of the street, where lights were just beginning to come on. He responded to John's weight in the seat beside him, turning quickly, his expression blank, his eyebrows raised inquisitively.

"John Wheelwright," John said meekly.

Osbourne nodded, and offered a brief, awkward smile, but didn't say anything – as unsure of the right pleasantries, John supposed, as he himself was feeling. He remembered that his first limousine ride had taken him to his high school prom. The car rolled on without any more instruction. Osbourne was wearing jeans, a denim shirt, and a floral tie; John felt he had miscalculated badly with his own blazer and linen pants, but he reminded himself that he had had nothing at all to go on. Osbourne had a beard, and small round glasses, neither of which John remembered from their only prior meeting three years ago. He had gone back to looking out his window. John noticed a folded *New York Post* and an empty Dunkin' Donuts bag at his boss's feet.

"I like your neighborhood," Osbourne said quietly, watching the four- and five-story row houses go by. "What is it called?"

"Cobble Hill," John said; and then, when nothing more followed, "My . . . my girlfriend and I bought our apartment here just a couple of months ago." *Girlfriend* seemed such a juvenile word, John thought, but *fiancée* was not strictly accurate, and *lover* was just out of the question.

"Probably a real family neighborhood?" Osbourne said. "Lots of kids? That's why you chose it?"

This would have seemed almost aggressively intimate, except nothing in Osbourne's manner showed that he considered it anything but small talk. "Well," John said, "that wasn't – I mean, we've talked about that, and of course at some point—"

"Listen," Osbourne said earnestly, and turned to look into John's face for the first time. "I'm sorry about the car. I really don't ride around in limos, you know, especially not on my days off. I love to drive. I would have been happy to drive us around myself. It's not the driving, it's the parking; and where we're going, downtown, you can squander half an hour just looking for someplace to leave your car. So just in the interest of time, we engage Max here to circle. You understand, don't you?"

"Really," John said, "it's quite all right."

Max maneuvered across the empty lanes of the entrance ramp and on to the Brooklyn Bridge. It was mostly truck traffic at that hour. John looked up through the window at the rhythmic, cathedral wave of the cables. The sky between the lines was low and colorless.

They spent ten minutes traversing clogged Chambers Street; Osbourne said nothing but displayed no impatience either, content to stare out his tinted window at the pedestrians, who stared back inhospitably though they couldn't see him. Then the limo turned north and slowly nosed its way through the narrow lanes of Tribeca. Vacant sidewalks and shuttered buildings and their quiet limousine. John knew these street names but could never have given directions on how to find them, even after five years in the city. The strategy he had carved out for himself this morning was to manifest comfort in his role as a subordinate, to offer opinions only when asked directly, to patiently play himself down: but such a thorough-going silence had permeated the car again that John, remembering he was with one of the name partners, now wondered if it might not behoove him to ask a few questions, to show some initiative, whether he felt like it or not.

"Do you always have this same driver?" he said. "He seems to know the neighborhood very well. If you asked a cab driver to take you to one of these streets, odds are he couldn't do it."

Osbourne turned his head just long enough to smile indulgently and nod. He went back to watching the buildings. The modern elements – galleries, boutiques, sometimes a restaurant – fell like silt to the level of the street, while it was

31

easy to imagine the upper floors as abandoned, or occupying a different time.

Well, that was suave, John told himself witheringly.

They pulled up in front of an old six-story warehouse, unretouched on the outside since its days of commercial use; the outer door bore only a large, painted "76" on the frosted glass. "Here's our first stop," Osbourne said, unnecessarily. The driver stayed behind the wheel, and the two men let themselves out. The sidewalk was narrow and canted visibly toward the street. Between the outer and the inner door of the building was a graying patch of black and white mosaic tile, a few discarded post office flyers, and an amber St Ides bottle. Wheelwright pressed an unmarked buzzer. A few moments later, they were incautiously buzzed inside.

They walked upstairs in silence; John thought it would only have been polite of Osbourne to mention what floor they would be stopping at but resisted the urge to ask. His boss walked very fast, he noticed, eager to feel he was noticing something.

At the fifth-floor landing one door was left ajar; Osbourne knocked softly and pushed it open. Behind it was a vast, low-ceilinged space, one open rectangle easily twice the size of John's whole apartment. The air-conditioning was on full blast, and shades were drawn over all the windows. In one corner of the loft was a large kitchen area, with a stove and two refrigerators, and a young man making espresso or cappuccino. The woman who came to greet them was long-limbed and gorgeous, and John was guilty of assuming she had to be one of the artist's assistants; but no, she was the artist, though Osbourne introduced her to him only as Heather.

"Heather, this is my associate, my resident art expert, John Wheelwright." Ill at ease, John bowed slightly; Heather gave him her hand, then hung it casually on Wheelwright's near shoulder and left it there.

By that time one of the assistants had completed his walk across the broad floor to ask if the visitors wanted any sort of coffee. "By all means, bring us a couple of espressos," Osbourne said. He seemed energized since walking into the loft. "I could use something to warm me up in here." He and Heather both laughed, then turned to walk deeper into the room; and John, wondering more than ever if his presence was really wanted, followed a step or two behind them.

The first sculpture they stopped in front of was easily recognizable as a nude self-portrait of a seated Heather, but it took a few moments more for John to identify the medium: dark chocolate. It certainly explained the need for the air-conditioning and the window shades, which he had assumed were merely eccentricities. The chocolate figure, a little less than life-sized (though he could tell that only from having the model herself standing unself-consciously nearby), was seated with its hands clasped around one knee. Bending forward a bit in the dim light, John could see, on the figure's elbows, toes, one breast, and again just at the end of the jawline beneath the ear, teethmarks, as if the sculpture had been gnawed at by someone. Well, not *as if,* John realized; it *had* been gnawed at, and he wondered whose job this was – the artist herself, or one of the male assistants. He couldn't decide which answer presented the more arresting mental picture.

While John was gazing at the self-portrait, Osbourne and Heather moved a few feet away to a large, perfect cube, also made of chocolate, also with one of its sharp corners degraded by someone's having eaten at it. They stood before it, talking softly. John was about to trail after them when one of the assistants appeared with his espresso.

"Shocking, isn't it?" the man said, glancing discreetly at the nude. He himself was young and somewhat potbellied, with hair brush-cut to a kind of tennis-ball fuzz; he wore an oversize black turtleneck.

John wanted to ask about the gnawing – not just who initiated it, but whether it was meant as the start of a process, whereby the work of art was distorted and eventually consumed entirely by the owner, or the artist, or the museum-goer – but, even though he had a hunch that these were the very questions the chocolate sculpture was meant to excite, he was worried about inadvertently coming off as mocking or contemptuous.

"She's found the perfect medium here, for the expression of her themes," the assistant went on, in a soft voice. "The degradation of women, the violence inherent in our culture's images of women, the whole *consumer* idea." He made quotation marks with one hand; the other still held John's espresso. "And of course the fragility of the work of art, its impermanence, its vulnerability."

John was reminded by this speech that the casually dressed young man was at work, and that he himself was seen now as a prospective buyer, or at least assistant to a buyer. Unable to ask the questions he most wanted to ask, about technique – they seemed at once too simple and too intimate – he asked instead, "Tell me, how do you – if one buys the sculpture, say – how does one warehouse something made out of chocolate?"

The assistant smiled wickedly. "Well, that's the genius of it,

isn't it? It becomes valuable, it *becomes* a work of art, simply by
virtue of the great effort and expense necessary to maintain it,
to keep it intact. A lovely bit of irony. You know, when
Guernica last came to this country – in the seventies I think it
was? Twenty years ago at least – it was shipped for flight in a
special crate which was not only built to withstand the most
enormous impact in case the plane crashed but had its own
automatically inflated life raft, complete with radio signals and
flares." He laughed. "I find that the most heartwarming story.
Though I wonder what the pilot felt about it!"

Suddenly Osbourne was ready to go. Heather, standing a step
behind him, looked neither upset nor surprised – apparently
she was used to his quick visits. "I'll talk to Mary this week,"
he said. At the door, he kissed her hand.

"It was a pleasure meeting you," she said to John. "Please
come back anytime." He felt himself reddening.

Back on the landing, Osbourne said nothing to John and
skipped down the steps ten feet ahead of him; then he stopped,
on the ground floor, and held open the front door. The car was
idling at the curb when they emerged from the building. The
morning haze had begun to burn off. As they drove, Osbourne
fell again into a private, unselfconscious silence, benignly
antisocial, though it was clear from his face that his spirits were
lifted somehow. John wondered if his boss had just bought
anything; he kept waiting for some question about the work
they had just seen. He wondered, too, if all the young artists
they were visiting that morning would be as comely and
familiar as Heather had been. That would explain a few things.
Though it would also obscure more than ever Osbourne's
reasons for wanting John there in the first place.

"Pleasant woman," John said finally. Osbourne just nodded, without any special enthusiasm that John could see.

The second studio they visited was more crowded with outsiders like themselves, though that may have been due merely to the later hour. An extroverted young man with a long goatee met them at the door; John could tell from Osbourne's reserve that the two had not met before, though the young man behaved as if they knew everything about each other.

"*So* good to see you, Mal," he said. "David is overjoyed you could make it."

David? Osbourne saw the confusion on John's face as he realized they were in the company of another personal assistant; lagging behind for a moment, he caught John's gaze and discreetly inclined his head toward a perfectly miserable-looking man in his fifties, bald, sitting across the windowsill with one foot on the fire escape, holding a squeeze bottle of water, looking as if he were about to burst into tears of humiliation and worry. He did not glance their way.

They spent a few minutes circulating through the studio. The assistant stayed out of their sightline but was never more than six feet away. David's latest work, as they saw, was concerned with the recontextualization of familiar images (whether from the history of art or from contemporary pop culture), shaking them up, violating their accepted meanings through juxtaposition. Some of these wall-mounted works were done with intentional crudity, using just scissors and paste (though one such collage of perhaps a thousand tiny images of celebrities' faces, almost a pointillist work when seen from across the studio, must have taken a lot of effort); others employed some form of computer-printing technology to make the merger of the images perfectly seamless, as in a giant silkscreen reproduction of Vermeer's *Girl at Her Window* holding a Diet Coke, or a photograph of the distinctive geometric patterns of a computer circuit board superimposed over a copy of Constable's *The Hay Wain*.

Apparently the assistant didn't know Osbourne's reputation well enough not to be agitated by his silence. "David sees this reorientation of images as a way of empowering people," he whispered to them. "In the age of mechanical reproduction, in a culture that's absolutely drowning in images, it's simply hubris to go out and create your own, to add to the static – it's self-defeating. The only revenge is to appropriate what's out there for your own purposes, to subvert the corporate mindset that anesthetizes these endless copies. Images, more than reality, are our true environment now, and hasn't that always been the task of art – to skew representation just enough to get you to look at your environment in a new way?"

Listening to this in the wake of his experience at Heather's, John understood that he was observing the practice of a specialized profession – the explainer, the pre-critic, whose task was central to the meaning of the work itself and not a commentary on it. In fact, maybe that was where the appeal of art like this – touched, at least, by David's hands in some cases, but untouched by his own invention – was supposed to lie: in ceding to the interpreter the satisfaction of creation. After a while, John found, you couldn't even look at these recombined pictures without hearing the goateed assistant's voice in your head. Personally John didn't have a lot of patience with this kind of work, but he kept his mouth shut and his expression thoughtful, not knowing how Osbourne felt about it. After all, some of the images drawn from advertising, some of the reproduced text, might even have been his.

"What's this?" Osbourne said suddenly, pointing to the back of the studio, where several people were gathered. A full-scale reproduction of Rodin's *The Kiss,* cast in some sort of lightweight orange polyurethane and evidently hollow, was suspended upside down by what looked like fishing line so that it hung about eight feet off the floor, wavering slightly. The familiar couple looked as though they were holding each other tightly as they plunged to their deaths. To leave the studio by its freight elevator, one had to walk under it.

The assistant looked momentarily embarrassed. "It's a reappropriation of Auguste Rodin's *The Kiss,*" he said, "cast in—"

"No, I can see that," Osbourne said, a little impatiently. "I mean that notepad there or whatever it is."

The assistant beamed. John finally noticed a clipboard hung on a nail next to the elevator, underneath the suspended sculpture. "Part of the same piece," the goateed young man said. "It's a pad on which visitors, if they're willing to linger underneath the sculpture itself, answer a series of printed questions about their impressions of the work. It's really drawing a great deal of positive attention, this piece."

And suddenly, Osbourne turned to look expectantly at John, the look that had been so long in coming John had stopped waiting for it. Alarmed, he tried to think of something perceptive to say about the upside-down *Kiss,* something astute but noncommittal. A few seconds crept by.

"Interactivity?" John said. The assistant nodded his head vigorously.

Back in the car, Osbourne appeared bothered by something; he sighed twice and kept tapping his fingertips on the knee of his jeans. John feared of course that the source of this displeasure was himself – that whatever Osbourne's unfathomable hopes might have been in mandating the companionship of an unknown employee in the first place, they weren't panning out. But in fairness to himself, John thought, not a word had yet passed between them on the subject of what exactly it was that John was supposed to do, what sort of aid he had been commissioned to provide. His exasperation was that much greater for being, under the circumstances, inexpressible. Another sort of person – Vanessa, certainly, and probably Rebecca as well – would have been indignant or curious or bored enough by this time to ask Osbourne straight out what the deal was; but John found this course of action too confrontational to think about seriously. His demurral went beyond the uncomfortable fact that Osbourne was his superior, with a power over his career which may have been hard to define but couldn't be entirely discounted; it just wasn't in John's makeup to be the one to break the compact of civility, especially not with a virtual stranger.

When they were dropped off at the next address, over toward Alphabet City, they found no one at home: at least no one answered the intercom. Osbourne looked at his watch and pressed the button again. Several business cards had been stuck in the door, presumably by other would-be visitors with similar appointments. The name above the intercom, printed and stuck there with one of those old blue label-tape guns familiar from John's own childhood, was Jean-Claude Milo. John followed the fashions of the art world, as he came across them by chance in magazines or newspapers, more closely than the average person, even the average person in New York: still, not one of this morning's names was remotely familiar to him. That was the rule, though, he supposed: by the time you heard of something, it was gone, divided up, absorbed. And therein lay much of the appeal of being a collector – not the buying or the speculating but the way the money permitted you to look for the source, to experience the art unmediated, or to try to.

In another minute Osbourne gave up on Mr Milo. They went back down the steps and waited for the car to circle around again. Osbourne's mood, strangely enough, seemed improved by their having been stood up like that. He took a pair of sunglasses out of the pocket of his denim shirt, put them on, and turned to look at John, smiling.

"A shame you couldn't meet Jean-Claude," he said. "He's doing some interesting work. The last time I was there, he was doing spin-paintings with his own blood." He shook his head fondly.

"And you liked his work?" John said blandly. He didn't want to let Osbourne's burst of relative gregariousness pass him by.

"I liked him. Something very genuine about him. Even his pretensions are genuine, if that makes any sense. I really enjoy the company of artists, especially young artists. I find them all so . . ." He didn't finish. The car reappeared around the narrow corner and slowed to a stop in front of them. *"Determined,"* Osbourne said. Max, his eyebrows registering concern, jumped out to open the rear door. Osbourne waited for him and then got in without a word; John followed suit.

It was nearing lunchtime when they made their next stop, this time at a gallery whose windows looked down on the

Hudson River. The walls were white and empty; the works stood in a haphazard arrangement on the floor. Each one was enclosed in some sort of glass booth or tank. Within one booth was an empty suit of clothes, with shirt, tie, underwear, socks, shoes lying crumpled on the floor. Another contained a large pile of bricks. But there was something in a darkened back room, separated from the main gallery by a thick curtain, that seemed to be drawing the interest of most of the morning's visitors. John parted the curtain for his boss, and they joined other strangers surrounding a large glass tank, lit from within in the otherwise dim room, which contained an actual tiger shark, suspended some six feet off the ground either by invisible wires or within some perfectly clear element, in a position to suggest swimming. It had been formaldehyded somehow, John supposed; its dull gray skin was unmarked. Everyone was very quiet as they circled around it. The power of the curled tail, the uneven, crowded rows of teeth in the slightly parted mouth, and the eyes – stone dead, and looking all the more alive because of it. At any point in one's journey around the tank, of course, one could see through to the solemn faces of the viewers on the other side.

Later, while waiting for the elevator, Osbourne said genially, "I think that's all I feel like seeing for today."

This time John was aware of the stares their car drew, as they retraced their path past City Hall and across the bridge. He was very hungry, but grateful just the same that Osbourne had not extended his trial by asking him along to lunch. He still had no better idea why he had been drafted for this excursion than he had had yesterday. At the same time, he had a rising sense of vague failure. He felt he had to try again to say something, that perhaps his very capacity for acquiescence was what was being tested here. This in spite of the fact that Osbourne had never once even alluded to the fact that they had a weekday, working life in common, that they were anything but friends, as if friends were like prospective jurors, who could abruptly be summoned to appear. The silence between them was indeed, John thought squeamishly, like the silence between old friends. It was inappropriate and perverse.

"So," John said – maybe a little too loudly, for his boss seemed startled. "Did you see anything you liked today?"

Osbourne cocked his head. "I saw some people I wanted to help," he said. Then, halfheartedly, as if rousing himself to converse, he said, "And what about you?"

John took a deep breath. He was mad at himself now for having stifled his real opinions all morning, when he didn't even know for sure why he was doing it: that's just like me, he thought. "I have to admit," he said, "I liked the shark." Osbourne smiled. "Even though – well, maybe I shouldn't say it."

"Even though what?"

"Well, a dead shark in a tank: what is that? It's a canvas for clever interpretation. And so reacting to it at all makes me feel a little foolish. Do you suppose that's the intent of it? Does everything have to be ironic?"

Osbourne said nothing.

"And who caught that shark?" John went on animatedly, forgetting, for once, to worry about the impression he was making. "Who preserved it? Who built that tank? Who installed the lighting? I don't know for sure but I'd be willing to bet that the artist's own hands have never been anywhere near it. I apologize if he's a friend of yours or anything. But this whole premise that the work of creation should consist of putting your name next to something: I just keep getting hung up on that. I still have a bias about . . . I still think of art as *making* something. Not causing it to be made. I know I shouldn't admit that, I know it's totally reactionary of me."

"And yet," Osbourne said, interested, "you liked the shark."

"And yet I liked the shark. However it got there. When I was in that little room, I felt I was in the presence of something powerful."

Osbourne laid his head back against the leather seat. "Me too," he said, just audibly.

They were turning on to John's block in Cobble Hill, the sidewalks alive now with children and dogs and sunlight, when Osbourne said suddenly, terrifyingly, "So John: are you happy working at CLO?"

John silently cursed his own uncontrollable blush. "Yes," he said, straining to sound sincere even though he was in fact telling the truth. "Yes, I like it very much."

Osbourne nodded thoughtfully. He looked out his window again, and then rested his forehead against it.

"I hate it," he said.

All the verbal pleasantries of goodbye were left to John; Osbourne remained in the back seat, listening with interest as John labored to thank him, but not saying a word. He took John's hand when it was offered. The limo disappeared around the corner and John still stood there, listening to the traffic sounds and the screams from the playground over on Kane

Street. He didn't want to go inside yet. He hoped Rebecca wasn't watching him from the window, insane with curiosity, wondering what was the matter with him. It was just that, once he went in, he was going to have to start talking about everything he had seen and heard that morning – the odd rift between the artists and their art – and about Osbourne himself, his appearance, his cryptic ignorance of John's desire for any sort of explanatory remark, his strange and somehow charismatic uneasiness around those who only wanted to please him. And maybe it was just a matter of his own poverty of expression, but John found that anything truly interesting usually became less interesting, even to him, when he heard himself trying to explain it.

IN A LIFE such as Molly's – in the life of a place such as Ulster, unwatched, forgetting itself, animated now mostly by the remote hand of late-century technology – the world outside the world you knew reached into your life now and then in a way that was not imaginary. These points of contact were a mixed blessing, for they served both to connect you to the larger vitality you dreamed of and to remind you at the same time how cut off from it you were. For Molly, the tool of this insinuation was music. Music was as private as it was international. It was everywhere you went but at some point around the age of twelve or thirteen it suddenly began speaking to you directly.

The Howes owned a fancy Bang & Olufsen stereo, seldom used except at parties, which was wired into a large cabinet beneath some built-in bookshelves in the living room. After dinner, when her father read the newspaper in front of the TV, her mother sat at the kitchen table with a cigarette and a stack of magazines, and her brother Richard had shut himself like a lodger in his room for the evening, Molly would drag a chair from the dinner table and listen to the radio for hours with the headphones on. The reception was sometimes poor because they lived in the valley, but she could pick up a college station from Albany if the night was clear. She sat with her back to the room, the cabinet door open and her feet propped on the shelf inside it, her head on her hand, her eyes closed. Gay boys in London, scarified New York City punks, patiently righteous black men in Jamaica: on the one hand she believed she understood their feelings, *felt* their feelings, with an un-improvable clarity; but then the lives they lived were so improbably romantic, so taken up with the painful drama of themselves, that when the song was over and she opened her eyes she couldn't believe she lived where she was living. Every few weeks she would ask her father if she could just move the stereo into her room, since no one else ever used it, but he was helplessly mindful of the value of the thing and couldn't stand the thought of damage to it. To salve his guilt over saying no to her he wired the radio to the rooftop antenna, so that her reception was no longer dependent on wind or the weather.

She came to know the DJs from that college station in Albany by name. They mumbled, they forgot when their microphones were off, they made private jokes to their friends, because they couldn't imagine that anyone who wasn't a friend of theirs would be listening. Their absence of a talent for what they were doing only impressed her further, because it seemed like the purity of the amateur. No news, no commercials, seldom even a mention of what time it was. They loved the music they played, and they hated the music they didn't play. Molly too conceived a scorn for whatever too many others liked. She thought that this was what college would be like – a place of tacit understanding, a little republic of sensibility.

Though she herself was often silent, silence was less and less a part of her waking life; anytime she found herself alone was by definition an opportunity to hear music, loud, without others to spoil it by rousing her anesthetized self-consciousness. She never once had the ambition to learn to play an instrument or to form a band herself. Music was not something you made but something you listened to; listening well was the act. The nearest she came to this creative boundary was to copy especially pithy song lyrics into her school notebook, during biology class or in the minutes before tests were collected, so that they might seem to her more like original thoughts of her own.

> *Home is where the heart is*
> *Home is so remote*
> *Home is just emotion*
> *Sticking in my throat*
> *Let's go to your place*

Records weren't the same. It was a moot issue because any record Molly might consider worth owning was not likely to be found at the Rexall in Ulster or anywhere near it; but even so, a record, which you could hear whenever you wanted, as many times as you wanted, skipping the bad songs and hearing your favorites as many times in a row as you liked, could never produce the same satisfaction because it lacked that element of providence. When a song you loved – a song you felt protective of, because you were hearing things in it that no one else seemed able to hear – came on the radio, it was an event, a small blessing conferred by randomness, a reason to believe in waiting at all, when the rest of your life brought you nothing with any power to surprise, no reason to expect much from the passage of time.

It didn't cost her anything, this type of modest self-estrangement from whatever was most popular; if others took it the wrong way, she didn't notice. The word most often applied to her, in discussions among her peers which did not include her, was "intense," which in the way of teenage vocabulary meant nothing specific but stood for a great deal: a sincere demeanor, a reputation for intelligence, an abstention from any of the self-mockery or regressive foolishness which insulated most kids her age from the things that really bothered them, a quietness which was not exactly shyness but more like patience, a face that did not smile much but did not turn away or look down either, that held your eyes until you forgot that you were the one doing the observing. And she was looked at more and more. All the children in Ulster knew one another too well, and yet as they passed through the onset of adolescence they watched each other more or less reborn, at least in some cases – visually and socially reestablished. Molly emerged as one of the prettier girls, certainly, if not one of the three or four prettiest, but she had a kind of physical charisma that made her seem older than she was, an ease within herself expressed in the slowness with which she moved and spoke – an indolence that was easy to make fun of but that also seemed construable into sensuality. Her languor, her inattention to the stare of others, introduced many of the boys her age in that town to the agonizing interplay between desire and sexual fear. Among themselves they included Molly in all their contemptuous fantasies of conquest, but this was partly an effort to talk away their private images of her, which were less definite; they drifted more toward those girls who they felt might be more naturally dominated.

There were forty-seven students in Molly's freshman class – the graduating class of 89 – at Ulster High School. Three or four would drop out before graduation, if the past was any guide; they would go to work for their fathers, or join the military, or, once every few years, disappear into some other eventuality which children couldn't get their parents to discuss. Such a small circle was of course more oppressive than a larger one would have been, for there is no question of finding a place to hide, socially speaking, in a class of forty-seven. Still, like teenagers anywhere, they found themselves quickly stratified by the ruthlessness of fortune; and Molly was welcomed into the circle of the fortunate just by virtue of her looks and the relative wealth of her family, and in spite of the renowned weirdness of her older brother. She made no effort to be attractive, but that didn't mean she was unmindful of her appearance or embarrassed by it: in fact she was greatly interested in the idea of changing her looks, and the consequences of that. She even flirted with the idea of a tattoo, but Richard refused – on the basis of a simple risk/reward calculation, he told her – to drive her anywhere to get it.

One afternoon at school, by arrangement, Molly cut math class and waited in the girls' bathroom for her friend Annika to get out of social studies by complaining to her teacher of menstrual cramps. These words tended to produce a kind of magical effect upon adults who worked at the school, particularly the men: Annika claimed her older sister had gotten the school doctor to send her home early complaining of cramps three different times in the space of six weeks. In the girls' room, undisturbed, in the muddy light from the one opaque, sealed window, Annika helped Molly to dye her auburn hair jet black in the sink. One of the reasons the two girls were becoming so close was that it never took more than thirty seconds to talk Annika into anything. She came home with Molly after school; they walked in the front door just as Kay Howe was emerging from the downstairs bathroom. She stopped in her tracks. They all stood there wordlessly for a few moments, before Kay, to both girls' amazement, actually burst into tears. She turned and hurried upstairs, and they heard the sound of her bedroom door closing.

"I guess you saw that one coming," Annika said, trying to recover her customary apathy.

But Molly hadn't done it to get this reaction, or to rebel in any way; and though she knew that if she had spared a thought for it she could have easily guessed what her mother's reaction might be, the truth, which she wasn't proud of, was that she hadn't considered it at all. Her mother was capable of attaching a crazy significance to Molly's most prosaic decisions – what to eat, whom to befriend, which shoes to wear with which pants – and her feelings could be hurt by the smallest manifestations of Molly's autonomy. But like the town itself, Molly's home, though intimately familiar to her and in some particulars even quite dear, lately seemed to her not so much where she

49

belonged as simply where she found herself. She loved her family but not in the sense that their problems seemed in any way like her problems. A year ago, her father had been promoted to supervisor at IBM, and eight months after that he was ordered to lay off more than a third of the managers who had formerly been his colleagues, some of whom were still his friends. Molly watched her father react to this trial at work by becoming, at home, even more congenial than usual, more gratingly optimistic not only about his own prospects but about hers, everyone's, as if constant expressions of enthusiasm could call some reason for enthusiasm into being; at the same time she saw the expression of injured dignity on his face at the end of the evening when he was watching TV and thought no one was looking. He did his best not to talk at all about his own guilt and fear, in part because he didn't want to be reminded that his wife had long ago stopped caring about his problems outside the home. Molly was interested in all this, genuinely sympathetic to him, and yet at the same time it all seemed to take place on a sort of stage. It all managed to seem less like something that was happening now than like something she knew she would want to remember someday.

In the summer after her ninth-grade year, her brother Richard enrolled in an intensive course at the community college in Herkimer in conversational Japanese. Roger and Kay gladly paid for it, trying to take in stride the idea that a child of theirs would volunteer to go to school in the summer; but before long they had reason to debate whether Richard's growing fascination with the East ought to be encouraged or treated as a symptom of some sort. It was the ascetic, ancient, somewhat brutal side of Japanese culture which interested him.

He bought a complete set of the works of Mishima and beginner's tracts on various martial arts. He moved all the furniture out of his room into the attic and brought in a tatami mat. At dinner, if Kay mentioned that he didn't look well, he might reply gamely that he hadn't eaten since dinner the night before. The thing Molly couldn't figure out was how all this Eastern self-denial squared with the fact that Richard was still smoking prodigious amounts of dope and even dealing it to friends out of the closet in his otherwise purified bedroom. At the tail end of childhood, he was still trying to forge a personality for himself – to find an identity that felt true to him, that might harden him against the world – but it seemed to be made up, at this early stage anyway, of an unstable compound.

A few months later he surprised his father at dinner by asking if he was a member of the local Rotary Club. Roger smiled somewhat condescendingly and said he was not. "Would you consider joining?" Richard asked him. The Rotarians, it came out, ran a worldwide student exchange program; a friend at school whose father was treasurer had mentioned that they were having trouble finding a local teenager willing to take a year off and see another part of the world, which, in turn, was holding up the application to spend a year in Ulster of a high school student from Sapporo, Japan. Roger and Kay argued for a month about whether to send their only son abroad for a year. Neither of them felt sure what was best, really – they just took turns being goaded into different positions by each other's unreasonableness. By the time they went to Mr Darwin, the Rotary Club treasurer, to ask formally if Roger could join their organization, the spots in Japan were all filled (though the boy from Sapporo, whose name was Tsuney, still planned to come to Ulster). The only place left open was with a family in West Germany, in the countryside near Bonn. Right there in the office, without waiting to be asked, Richard surprised them all by saying he would take it. He left Labor Day weekend from the Albany airport, where Tsuney, who was to live with the Darwins, arrived three days later. All year long Molly would pass him in the hallways at the high school, looking polite, genially confused, and above all cold. She admired his mask of good cheer in the face of all this strangeness, but she also couldn't help feeling like he was in some way the ghost of her displaced brother, and for that reason she found it too hard to talk to him.

Patty, their old babysitter, was married now but still lived in town. Molly ran into her once a month or so, usually at the IGA. She was old enough herself now to recognize that Patty was usually stoned. She would lean over her cart full of soda and frozen food, until her small breasts were mashed against the handle and her hair fell around her face – as if Molly were still four feet tall. "Hey, gorgeous," she would say lazily. "Are you staying out of trouble?"

It stayed in Molly's mind because she herself was babysitting now, on Friday or Saturday nights, sometimes for families she knew well, sometimes for other families to whom she had been referred, people who had up to then been strangers to her because they had no children nearer her age. She was good with kids, but what interested her more was the sudden access to the insides of other people's homes. A sinkful of dishes, a profusion of flowers, an unmade bed seemed to her so deeply revealing (especially within Bull's Head, where the housefronts were all nearly identical), so intimate; and the little quarrels, the odd customs, the pasts hinted at within her hearing were so compellingly unlike her own home that it was hard for her to be discreet about it. She sometimes had a strong impulse to steal things she found – nothing of any real value, just small personal items, especially photographs – but she was afraid to follow through on it.

She helped out a few families but soon became the regular sitter for a family called the Vincents, who lived in one of the converted farmhouses on the other, older side of Ulster, five miles from Bull's Head. Mr Vincent was the president of the bank; Mrs Vincent also worked full-time, in one of the town's three real estate offices. They had two children, Kevin and Bethany, he in the third grade and she in the first. Once or twice a week after school Molly got off at the bus stop nearest the Vincents' house, knocked on their door, and waited to be let in by Mrs Vincent, who then drove back to her office for a few hours. Molly stayed with the kids, usually just doing her homework while they sat in front of the TV, until both parents had returned from work, and Mr Vincent could drive her home.

The Vincents were in their thirties, though she looked older than he did. Molly's own parents often tried to leave each other alone but just couldn't seem to do it; whereas in the Vincents' house, everything seemed, for better or worse, to have been worked out a long time ago, and the daily life of the house ran as if in accordance with some amicable contractual arrangement. Molly was sometimes invited at the last minute to stay for dinner. The little girl, Bethany, had a cute round face and you could already see how someday, with luck not until full adulthood, she was going to grow right into her mother's stout

53

physique. Though Molly was not the type to invent new activities or otherwise take it upon herself to stimulate the children, her compliant good will toward them was so reliable – she would get up to do them any favor they asked, play any game they brought to her – that they came to accept her unguardedly as a part of the home, though Kevin's face, she noticed, did darken just a bit on those afternoons when he watched his mother in the front hall putting on her coat again as Molly took hers off.

Mr Vincent was a trim, youthful-looking man with fair skin and small, sharp features; he was neighborly enough but the most extroverted thing about him, whether he was aware of it or not, was his surprisingly expressive taste in clothing, at least for work: double vents, broad Jermyn Street stripes, neckties much more modishly colorful than one might expect from a small-town bank president. His voice was softer than his wife's and he was obviously the pushover of the two parents where the children were concerned. The house he had grown up in was just four miles away; his parents had moved to Florida in 1981 but couldn't bring themselves to sell the place, so he still forwarded them the monthly rent checks from their IBM-employed tenants, and he paid the local plumber when the tenants called up and complained in their unfriendly New York City way that the pilot on the hot water heater was out again. He still kept the longish sideburns he had had in high school, not out of fashion or nostalgia but because to change his own appearance in the mirror in any way would have struck him as a worrisome vanity in a man like himself, a sign of creeping pathos in a husband and father approaching middle age. He thought more about such questions than was useful or even healthy, for the truth was he felt like a much younger man than his years but he was too young yet for this feeling to be a source of pleasure or pride to him; on the contrary, it was more like a source of shame, even if no one else knew anything about it. Eight years after the birth of his son he still thought of himself much more readily as a child than as a father, and he was worried that the death of his own parents, whenever it came, was going to find him unprepared. Every night he stood at the far edge of his lawn, just beyond the reach of the house's light across the grass, and smoked a cigar. He pretended this was because his wife had prohibited cigars in the house, when the truth was she disliked them but didn't really care if he smoked them as long as the children were upstairs. He asked Molly to please call him Dennis. Molly knew what Mrs Vincent's first name was too, but she was never invited to use it.

It would be six or eight months yet before anyone in Molly's class was old enough for a driver's license; and since the owners of the few stores within walking distance of the high school were experts in a kind of saccharine harassment of loitering teenagers, most often they would all just take turns going to one another's homes, preferably a home where the mother held a job so that they could have the place completely to themselves for a few hours. It was a tough experience for the girl whose house it was, for she knew the gimlet eye with which her friends regarded the fripperies of adults, whether they happened to be your parents or not. The girls lounged or paced around the strange living rooms, absentmindedly opening cabinets and drawers, trying the father's brand of cigarettes, talking ironically about the world as they found it, defining themselves through the instrument of their contempt.

Annika liked this way of marking time more than Molly did, maybe only because she had more to fear from going straight home. When she could she prevailed on Molly to hang out with them. They were sophomores by then, and they understood that they were living in the clumsy intensity of the male gaze.

"I had lab yesterday," a girl named Tia said, flipping through a stack of mail addressed to her friend Lucy's parents, "and Mr Hinkson comes over to show me how to work the titration tube. Like it's that complicated. And he puts his hand on my arm and he leaves it there for like nine hours."

"He wants you to work his titration tube," Lucy said.

"You are so fucking disgusting," Tia said. Even in disgust, her boredom was imperial. She ran a hand through her hair, which Molly thought of as perfect – long and shaggy and almost two-toned.

Molly spoke up. "Imagine being Mrs Hinkson," she said. She had a soft voice, the kind you had to lean closer to hear, which some people found annoying or assumed had to be some kind of careful affectation. They turned to look at her. "I mean have you ever noticed how much he sweats? In the middle of winter? Just imagine what he—"

"*You* imagine it," Tia said. "You are both so disgusting I can't even deal." She tossed the stack of mail down, not where she had found it. "Does anybody have a Chap Stick or something?"

None of it was real. Or rather, something was hardening around whatever was real, taking the place of it, strangling it. It would be very hard to call what had happened to her peers since grade school unnatural, for Molly felt sure that neither Tia nor

Annika nor any of them had even the remotest worry that the way they acted now in all their waking hours was in any way at odds with something within them that was more true, more personal. What was personal in them simply seemed to have given way. The social was what was real. And while any group – whether you were speaking of the whole of the town or the whole of the school or merely the five or six ascendant girls who made up the set which sometimes incorporated Molly – had its hierarchies and its leaders, the organizing principle of life as a teenager was that all your beliefs, your tastes and standards, were now a communal matter. You had to agree on which were the cute boys, you had to agree on how to act around the cute boys, you had to agree on what constituted an acceptable item of apparel, what the good movies were, what the simple transgressions were, like smoking or shoplifting cheap cosmetics from the Rexall. Conformity was not a limitation but a stage of development.

But Molly did feel that, just by virtue of being aware of it, she was protecting something private, though she couldn't have said what that something was – perhaps just protecting that space where something private might theoretically exist. Something that was more authentic than the sarcasm of the fortunate teenager, something less accessible, less easily defined.

Their culture was no longer local, as a child's culture was; its reference points were celebrities and brand names: Dynasty, Levi's, Elvis Costello, Paulina, Richard Gere, Nicole Miller, Duran Duran. Yet alongside this worldliness was a premonition that they were living in a place so remote that they might never be found. The high school building from the 1950s with its flagpole scratched by thousands of keys; the half-light of the closed stores at night; the farms which looked abandoned but were not; the evenings spent in front of the television or on the phone or looking out the bedroom window at the one or two visible lights; the damp, deadly quiet in the moldering woods across the road as you waited at the end of your driveway for the bus. Withering judgment of all these things, even if expressed only to yourself, was one way to make certain you were still alive.

Mr and Mrs Vincent didn't go out much on their own initiative, not even to the movies, but between their two careers and their positions as Rotarians they were kept busy with functions they felt it was prudent to attend: whenever they called the Howes and asked for Molly, it seemed to her, it was because there was somewhere they had to be, never somewhere they wanted to be. What with their evening calendar and the fact that they both felt better about working late knowing Molly was with the children, they began asking for her services two or three times a week. Though Kay constantly objected – she couldn't stop herself from taking as personal attacks things which really had nothing to do with her – Molly didn't mind it at all; she could do her homework as easily in one place as in the other, and there was something liberating, something anonymous, about feeling so at home in a place that wasn't your home at all, where the stakes for you were just about non-existent. Sometimes he would be the first one home from work, sometimes she would be: in either case Molly had to wait for both parents to return so that Mrs Vincent could be present with the kids while Dennis drove her home.

One spring Saturday they went to a nephew's wedding all

the way up in Loudonville and didn't return home until past midnight. While his wife slipped her heels off and tiptoed into the children's bedrooms, Dennis went straight to the living room and found Molly sound asleep on the couch. He stood in the doorway, just on the edge of the rug. She lay on her side, with a textbook open on the floor near her head. In the last moments before sleep she had pushed off her sneakers, and they rested, the heels still flattened, against the arm of the couch by her feet. It was April, and the evenings were still cool. She had on a pair of thick wool socks that might have belonged to her father or brother, green fatigue pants – she always wore pants – and a gray V-neck sweater with the sleeves pushed up. Everything was too big for her, twisted in her sleep – it was almost as if she were trying to hide; but she could not be hidden. One of her knees was drawn up near her stomach. Molly had a delicate face, round without being full, small-lipped, and her eyelashes were so long, so much darker than the auburn hair which was cast around her in her sleep as if she were floating on water, that you might even take them for false if you didn't know that she never wore makeup of any sort. Of course he had noticed all of these things before. Her left arm was folded against her chest, and her right was straight out beneath her head, fingers bent: the impossibly taut, impossibly reposed long arm of a teenage girl.

He heard his wife coming into the room behind him. "Molly, we're home," he said.

Molly's eyelids fluttered, and then she started upright, embarrassed to have been discovered asleep. Dennis too felt embarrassed all of a sudden, thinking she must have known she was being stared at; but really she was only worried they would be angry at her for sleeping on the job when one of the children might have been whimpering quietly in bed or calling to her. He smiled and held out his hand to try to settle her. She rubbed her face slowly with both hands.

Dennis looked from the girl to his wife and back again; Molly could see that he wanted to ask his wife something but couldn't work out how to do it discreetly. Finally he went ahead and said, "You know, Molly, it's so late, you were sound asleep, if you want it's perfectly okay to stay over here and I can drive you back in the morning. Right, Joyce?"

Joyce Vincent nodded immediately, briskly almost, as if to say that the iron reputation of her hospitality was not open to dispute.

Molly saw her sneakers still lying on the couch cushion and quickly swept them on to the floor. Dennis didn't come any closer; he stood in the doorway, hands in his pockets, on his face an expression of care that wasn't at all exaggerated, just outsized for the situation. It was a face her father sometimes made.

"No, thank you," she said hoarsely. "My parents would freak if I wasn't there in the morning, and I wouldn't want to call them now and wake everyone up. If it's okay, Mr Vincent, maybe you could just drive me home, if you're not too tired yourself."

"Dennis," he said.

He watched protectively to see if she would fall asleep again in the car, but she did not. The moonlight seeped through heavy clouds as they drove through the center of Ulster, past the closed gas station, the closed supermarket; the rooftops glinted in the valley. Richard was still up, watching an old movie on

TV with the lights out. Just from the way he rolled his head on the back of the chair to see her, Molly could tell that he was stoned.

Nowhere was the chasm of understanding between parents and children greater than when it came to the subject of drugs. Roger and Kay had no idea that their son had ever tried marijuana, much less that he smoked it habitually. He sometimes wore sunglasses inside the house, and all they did was roll their eyes at each other as if it were some amusing teenage affectation. You had to wonder how they could look so hard and see so little. The word *drugs* didn't even mean anything very specific to them; it was more like a way of not looking at other, less material sorts of damage that might be done within the controllable climate of home. And yet if they had ever figured it out, they would have overreacted, screaming at him, grounding him, cutting him off from his friends, wringing their hands about college. His grades were fine – he had it all under control in that sense.

Richard had only received half-credit for the time spent studying in West Germany, though, so he and Molly were still in the same high school. At some point during his months in Europe, it seemed, his samurai phase had passed without fanfare, and on the day he returned home he brought all the furniture and wall hangings from the attic back into his room, without a word to anyone about it. His old friends, many of whom had graduated by now, came over in the afternoons and joined him in his room. Molly knew some of these friends were checking her out, though others, more single-minded about getting high, just smiled absently at her on their way to the bathroom or the kitchen. One or two would urge her, with a great pretense of

61

subtlety, to come smoke with them. Molly could well imagine how these boys talked about her behind the closed door of Richard's room, beneath the boombox accompaniment of *Eat a Peach* or *Europe 72,* but she knew Richard was the type who would just change the subject rather than get offended. He had some friends who, as long as they had to put minimal effort into it, would like to fuck his sister: it would never happen anyway, so why waste energy getting all macho about it? Was his sister supposed to be different somehow from every other good-looking girl in the school, or in the world?

There were periods, though, when the Howes' place was unavailable after school, because Kay had stopped working again and was back to roaming through the rooms of the house with a sweater on, insisting that the place wasn't properly insulated. She went through stints as a bookkeeper at the clothing store, assistant to the principal at the elementary school, secretary to the town's one lawyer, who worked out of his house and handled mostly wills and real estate sales – Kay had no professional secretarial skills, but neither did anyone else in town. She took tennis lessons, and joined some of the other IBM wives in establishing a charity for the children of some of the poorer families in the county. Roger praised this sort of activity so indiscriminately that even his children could see the element of condescension in it. Occasionally, when she seemed most depressed, he would raise the possibility of Kay's going back to school part-time for a graduate degree, in some indeterminate discipline. But she could have done this years earlier if she wanted, certainly since the time Molly entered junior high. She felt it was too late, though she wouldn't explain what she meant by that. She was not yet forty-five.

She wanted to believe that there was something in her life besides fear and maybe vanity that made her regret the passing of the days, and for long spells she did believe it: but always some small frustration or thoughtless remark would tear down the curtain that separated her from this vista of pointlessness and waste, and when that happened, she would quit what she was doing, quit doing anything really, preferring to martyr herself to the decision that first brought her here.

Dennis Vincent came home one Thursday at quarter past four, to find Molly doing homework in the dining room while Kevin and Bethany played Trouble on the floor beneath the table, next to her feet. Molly looked at him quizzically, wondering if anything was wrong, if she had gotten the dates mixed up somehow. "Easy day at work," he said simply. "I thought I could knock off a little early." He went to the kitchen, got himself a beer, and sat wearily at the table, at the end perpendicular to Molly. His thin yellow tie was loosened, and when he crossed his legs there was a small pale strip of skin between his pant leg and his red argyle sock. She waited to see if he would say anything more – or if he would suggest putting the kids in the car and taking Molly home now, since his wife wouldn't be back for another two or three hours – but he just seemed to be unwinding, glad to be there at his ease, staring into space and drinking, far too at home to give a thought to being sociable. Molly picked up her highlighter and went back to reading her history textbook, *Our Living Heritage*. She could feel his eyes stray on to her when her head was over the book. He didn't say another word. It was a domestic little scene, even, it seemed, to the children, who went on with their game, popping the little bubble where the

JONATHAN DEE

die was contained, counting out loud, sociably taunting each other, comfortably fenced in by the adult feet and the table legs.

Whenever Molly's friends got together the subject might stray in a few worldly directions but it always came around to boys. Since their opinion of the boys they actually knew was so quickly recapitulated (and when opinions did change, they changed at a glacial pace), the girls tended to discuss good-looking celebrities, especially musicians – their best qualities, their sexual virtuosity, the downsides of relationships with them – with just as much of a sense of reality as they picked over the faults of the boys with whom they had gone to school since age five. In a larger, suburban school, it would have been possible to move from set to set, it would have been possible for a girl to start dating someone about whom her friends could tell her virtually nothing. But at Ulster High there was nowhere to disappear to after a bad breakup; and the boys were simply recycled from girl to girl because there was no other way to do it. If you started dating a guy your friend had dated briefly six months ago, you knew all his bad points, you knew everything intimate about him, and he knew that you knew it; you had no choice but to take a chance that your friend might be lying to cover her own shortcomings or that maybe the boy had somehow rehabilitated himself.

One of the few, though, about whom no one could offer much in the way of personal detail was a tenth-grade boy named Ty Crawford. He was in Molly's math and English classes; everyone knew who he was. When Ty was six his older brother had accidentally set their bunk beds on fire with his mother's Bic lighter. A neighbor saw the flames through the window and called the fire department. The burns had left scars all across Ty's upper body, which his clothing, if his sleeves were rolled down (as they always were), nearly covered up; some of the grafted skin, though, was noticeable advancing up his neck just above the collar of his shirt. In spite of this anomaly he was unguarded in his friendships, and no one had a bad word to say about him. His classmates were certainly past the age where anyone would dare to tease him about his physical difference, or refer to it at all; but given the renewed primacy of the physical in their lives, it was still hard to pretend to forget it.

"No one's gone out with him?" Molly asked. Today everyone was at her house; her brother was alone in his room with music on.

"No, as it happens," Tia said defensively.

"I mean, it's so sad," Lucy said. "It's sad and everything, because it's not his fault, but wouldn't you – I mean wouldn't it just, when the time came, make you—"

"Why?" Annika said. "What, do you like him or something?"

The true answer about Ty, who had a nice, fine-boned face and wore flannel shirts and tan work boots every day, was "I don't know"; the most attractive thing about him, after all, was that element of the concealed, and she was mindful of the possibility that he might turn out not to be that interesting after all, except to the extent that such an obvious form of damage made anyone interesting. But Molly knew well enough that whatever she said here – despite her friends' demeanor, which suggested that it was an act of great forbearance for them even to stay on the subject – might, if it was unusual enough, get back to Ty within a day. She liked the suddenly available role of the aggressor, even if it was an abstract sort of aggression; already she had had enough of guys putting their hands on the wall beside her head at parties, which was how these things usually started. And she wasn't unaware of the looks Tia and Lucy and even Annika were exchanging, which suggested that Molly might have stumbled on a way to shock them, a way of demonstrating that she wasn't really one of them.

"I never really thought about it before," Molly said. "It's . . . intriguing."

She was fluent in the language of the group she was in. Similarly, there was a language of home, a kind of anti-language in which the sentiments expressed were not true ones, and the facts were really encoded sentiments.

On the weekends, for instance: everyone's goal was either to get out of the house or, what was sometimes better, to wait for the others to get out and then have the house to yourself for a while. Play music through the speakers rather than the headphones, use the kitchen phone and not be overheard, just breathe easier for a while, open up the windows and let the air of sensitivity and cross-purposes blow out of the place.

"I thought I might go over to the courts," Roger would say, as if it had just occurred to him. Tennis courts and a nine-hole golf course had sprung up in an old cow pasture shortly after the IBM branch office came to town twenty years ago; the place billed itself as the Ulster Hills Country Club but Roger for some reason was prudish about referring to it by its name, whether out of some sort of high-class modesty or simple embarrassment at such pretension, Molly was never sure. "Want to come, Molly? There'll be other kids there."

"No thanks, Dad," Molly would say, as if this conversation were improvisatory. "I have a test."

"Richard?"

"Gee, I'd love to, Dad" – edging perilously close to sarcasm, but never all the way there – "but I should work on my college essay some more."

"And Kay, you have things to do today too, probably."

"Things to do," Kay said.

"Which car do you need? Do you need the Ford?"

"Either one. Take the Ford if you want it."

"Well, looks like I'm on my own, doesn't it?" Roger said, laughing.

Or at the dinner table – on a weekday, when they had to see much less of each other as it was: heavy silence, then Roger would say with a strained sort of joviality, " 'How was work today, Dad?' Well, thanks for asking, gang. The quarterly report comes out in two weeks, and if it's as bad as it's supposed to be, the rumor is they're going to start shutting down some of the Northeast offices entirely."

"Can I be excused?" Richard would say. "I have a test."

"Well, now, not so fast. Didn't you have a meeting with your college adviser today? See, you think Dad's not paying attention, but he is."

"Would anyone like anything more?" Kay said, departing for the kitchen without waiting for an answer.

"It went fine," Richard said, not at all impatiently. "The list is still Berkeley, Amherst, Williams, Connecticut College, Reed, and Tulane, with SUNY New Paltz as my safety." Again, the bright tone of his voice walked right on the edge of mockery; Molly knew that he thought this sham attitude effectively excused him from the conversation itself, but his strategy was less different from the others' than he thought. His ironic manner was over the head of no one; but as long as nobody called attention to it, things went on just as before.

Kay stayed in the kitchen much longer than was necessary. When she returned, the children had already gone up to their rooms. She looked into her husband's faltering smile. She found herself perilously close to expressing what she felt: that she was thrilled to imagine that Roger's office might be shut down, that he and indeed most of the people they socialized with might suddenly be jobless, ruined, that they would lose the house and not be able to send their son to college, that existence would become the wreck she had long dreamed of and to which she felt temperamentally better suited than the infuriating haze of life as a middle-class wife and mother.

"Well, that was delicious, as always," Roger said. "If you don't mind excusing me, I think I'll go catch the start of the news."

Molly never felt any sort of teenage scorn for the outright bogusness of all this, nor any lament for the absence of the genuine in every look, every word exchanged within her family. Of course it was false, but there was no true language that she knew about in any case; every place had its idiom, and this was the idiom of home.

Word filtered quickly back to Ty that Molly had mentioned his name in conversation in a nondismissive way; he began turning up in places she knew he had no reason to be, never saying more than "Hey," though he let his eyes stay on her longer now – nothing aggressive about it, just a loosening of his self-restraint. She did nothing different, and this, apparently, was all that was expected of her. Even though she had initiated whatever was going to happen, even though he had by all reports never been in this position before, he seemed to take it for granted that he would assume the role of the pursuer. A week went by. Then one evening Molly was in her room when Kay yelled upstairs to her that she had a phone call.

"Some boy," she heard her mother saying as she came down the stairs.

"And so it begins," said Roger.

Ty sounded dull, disaffected; with no preamble at all he asked if she wanted to go to the playground next Friday night. The elementary school playground after dark was always full of teenagers, smoking or surreptitiously drinking: it was a place Molly might well have gone on Friday anyway, alone or with Annika; there was nowhere else to go in town that you could make belong to you that way, unless you had a car. But Molly was not confused, because Ty, like any sixteen-year-old boy, was so easy to read: he wanted to make sure that if he was wrong about Molly or if the whole thing was some sort of mistake – the two of them had never really spoken for more than a few minutes – he would learn this in a place where he could easily pretend, in front of others, never to have thought otherwise at all. They would be in a group, and whatever might set it apart from any other Friday evening when they ran into each other there would be a matter only of an understanding between the two of them. She said she would do it.

"That's excellent," Ty said, with a little more animation.

The next afternoon Molly went to the Vincents', and when

she knocked it was Dennis who opened the door. He was not dressed in a way that suggested he was going back to the office. Her first sensation was annoyance. If she wasn't needed, she couldn't imagine being paid, and there were other things she could have been doing with her time.

"Have I made a mistake?" she said, though in fact Dennis was smiling at her as if he'd been expecting her.

"No, no," he said softly, absently, "I'm sorry, I ought to have called you, to give you the choice, I didn't know I'd be home so early. But I'd like you to stay. The kids are in the yard playing. I need you here. They're so attached to you."

Something was wrong with him. He seemed upset, though he was trying to hide it – the way a parent will try to act as if everything is normal in order to avoid transferring fear to the children. He was staring at her. It was strange that he was still standing in the doorway.

"So how are you?" he said, too loudly.

This was interesting, in the way that misfortune is interesting, to the point where it was hard to take her eyes off him; she wanted to stay in the room, to see what would happen next, but at the same time not to be in the room, not to be a part of whatever was taking shape. She remembered the two children, and that decided it for her, for the moment.

"I'll just get a soda," she said, stepping forward, "if that's okay, and I'll go make sure Kevin and Beth are all right."

"Oh," he said, finally backing out of her way. "Okay."

A few hours later Mrs Vincent came home. Molly had dinner with the kids and then Dennis drove her back to Bull's Head. His face was red. He didn't say a single word to her on the way, not even when she opened the door and said goodbye to him.

At home there was something of a celebration: Richard had been accepted to Berkeley, and though Kay and Roger made several plaintive jokes about his getting as far away from home as possible, mostly they seemed relieved to know that now the worst-case scenario still had him going to college somewhere. Roger even let Molly have a glass of wine. While they were all still downstairs, Molly went up to her parents' bedroom and looked at herself for a minute in the big semicircular mirror above her mother's dressing table.

Friday night she told her mother she was going to Annika's house; she met Ty outside the Bull's Head sign. He acted just like any other boy on a date, bluff and nervous, and she felt a little disappointed in the first few minutes. There were eight or ten other kids at the playground, mostly boys. The girls sat on the swings, pushing off gently with their feet; the boys hung on the jungle gym or walked up the slide. When the sun went down they all became shadows, and one or two pairs moved off into the darkness. Ty produced a joint, which he and Molly shared. The leaves shivered in the wind, and whenever a car slowed down on the road in front of the school, they all stopped what they were doing for a moment and turned their heads to listen like deer.

Ty walked Molly back to the sign, and they kissed, taking a moment first to throw out the gum Ty had brought to mask their breath for their parents – not that his parents would ever notice, he said, but he didn't know what hers might be like. It struck her then how much thought he had given to tonight. All of his tentativeness, which she had been waiting for all night, was in his kiss. She held her hands still on his back, wondering where under his shirt the unseen, damaged skin

71

was, wanting to avoid touching it not out of squeamishness but simply out of a fear of offending him. She let him put his hands on her breasts over her sweater, but when he tried to pull out the tails of her shirt his hands were cold and she gently pushed them away. He didn't pursue it. He counted on being stopped, maybe not right at that point, but at some point.

"See you," he said curtly, trying to behave a certain way, but he had to turn his back in order to hide the fact that he was smiling.

Monday at school he asked if she wanted to go to the movies in Schenectady with him – he had his license and had pledged an unspecified future favor to his older brother in return for one evening with his car. Molly's parents had a rule against unchaperoned dates involving cars, but the important thing to them was the rule itself, not its vigilant enforcement; so she told Ty to meet her in front of Annika's house on Route 3, where she would spend the night. It was a deception that meant nothing to her, but she could see Ty's confidence swell as she related the plan.

That Wednesday at the Vincents', Dennis wasn't there when she arrived, and in fact when Mrs Vincent came home at quarter to eight he still hadn't been heard from. She insisted that Molly must be starving and that she stay for dinner. When Dennis came home at nine, his tie loosened, he seemed surprised to see Molly at the table, doing her homework.

"There you are," his wife said, coming out of the kitchen. "Listen, I know you must have had a horrible day, I hate to ask you, but it's Bethany's bedtime now. Can you give Molly a lift home?"

He nodded somewhat glumly, turned and went back to the car without a word. Molly got in beside him. They were approaching the center of town when Dennis suddenly said – a little hoarsely, as if he had not spoken in quite some time – "Nine minutes, it takes, to drive from our house to yours."

Molly looked at him. She wondered if she ought to be afraid of him, but he seemed so weary, so beaten, it was hard to feel any sort of tangible danger at all.

"You don't say much," he went on. "It's hard to get a word out of you. It's hard to figure out what you're thinking about."

He seemed to be in some kind of distress, and Molly felt genuinely chastened by it; she wanted to say something reassuring to him now but she had no idea what to say.

Then when they reached the intersection, instead of going straight through toward the valley, he turned left.

"I thought we could take the long way this once," he said quickly. "I hope that's all right. I just thought we could talk a little. We never really get to talk."

They drove on the empty road, past the drugstore, the school, the silhouetted barns.

"Is that all right?" he said gently.

"Sure," Molly said, and she was telling the truth. Whatever was happening now, in the car, surely it was not something she had ever seen before. She knew him well enough to be certain that whatever trouble she might be in now was not imminent, not physical, deferred.

"We'll just go up to Route 2," he said needlessly, "and then into the valley the other way. Maybe ten extra minutes at the most."

73

"It's fine," she said quietly. Then, after a moment, she added, "I'm not scared or anything."

But that remark seemed to scare him; he took a deep breath and flexed his fingers on the wheel. Maybe she had said the wrong thing, maybe he wouldn't have minded her being scared – scared enough to demand he turn the car around, so scared that she would then tell her mother or his wife about it, and so bring an end, even a disastrous one, to something he had given up on ending himself.

It was important to the current of Dennis's desire that Molly was so good with the kids. It meant that he could go on fantasizing for himself an alternate life, however far-fetched, without the guilt of imagining the kids away as well. He was not made to be anybody's mentor; Molly's youth, to him, represented not something to be exploited but something indomitable, even frightening, a seat of power; and the pull of the thought of sex with her had to do, strangely, with the certainty that somehow, quite apart from any question of experience, she would be in control of it, above it all, above him, knowing the physical authority she had over him. A matter of decades, really, since sex – just the thought of it – had that power to make him feel panicked, ungoverned.

Molly may not have sensed all of this, but she did grasp right away that in this situation, where by rights he should have had all the power, he was clearly powerless. He was in the grip of all he had to lose, her approbation, the approbation of everyone he knew.

"A girl like you," he said, "must really dream a lot about getting out of this town. You probably can't wait to leave here."

The headlights showed them nothing, just fresh blacktop and the broken line and the lit surface of the woods at every curve. She felt incapable of asking him what he wanted. She just had to go where he took her. Already she could see some of the lights of Bull's Head at the bottom of the slope out her side of the car.

"I guess so," she said. "It's pretty boring here. Unless you want to go work for IBM, I guess."

"Well, it looks like even that won't be an option a whole lot longer," he said casually, relieved to get on to a less dangerous topic, forgetting for a moment who her father was. He kept his eyes on the road.

"Let me ask you something," he said. "Do I – I mean, I must seem really old to you. Not even real, somehow, in a way. I remember what it was like being your age, what parents appeared like. I hate to think that's how I look now to people, to you. But you know, you've got it all going for you, everything serves you, the world is set up to be at the service of a beautiful young woman. As it should be. As it should be."

Molly said nothing.

"Didn't I start that out like I was asking a question?" he said, and laughed. "Well, I don't know what the hell I'm talking about, I guess that's pretty apparent by now."

She didn't want to cut him off, and she didn't want to do anything to bring it all to a resolution: she wanted to keep it going, not because she enjoyed being the object of it but because for these few minutes everything that was unreal seemed to have been scraped away, everything was vital and true only to itself.

"You're a very secretive girl," he said as they started down the hill. He was crying a little. She could not have been more amazed. He spoke as though to himself: "You keep it all private. You don't say anything to anyone. You keep it all inside." Suddenly she could feel the truth of this. Not only that, it became more true the more he said it; the more he showed of himself, the further he came out of his own self-control, the further she withdrew into mystery, without even trying to, without doing anything at all.

He stopped the car and turned it off just around the corner from the Howes'. She turned to look right into his eyes, which may not have been smart, she knew, but she couldn't help it, she didn't want to miss anything.

"Can I," he said, and he had to clear his throat. "Can I just give you a hug?"

She couldn't figure out what saying yes meant, and she was afraid of what saying no meant, so she just continued to look at him, helplessly, and he took this helplessness for assent: he turned from his waist and reached out with his hands – abruptly, cheerfully, as if making one last effort to convince himself that everything that was happening could be taken two ways. But he couldn't fool anyone. His suit felt beautiful under her hands, against her neck. He was shaking. They couldn't really see each other in the green light of the dashboard. Suddenly it no longer seemed possible to hold what was happening in abeyance. Molly pulled away from him and opened her door; when she did so the dome light came on, and Dennis, his lips apart, his skin pale, flinched.

I don't have to sell my soul
He's already in me

Weeks before it was necessary, Richard started packing for college. He had quit his summer job in early August so he'd have time, he told his startled parents, to reflect and prepare himself mentally for the big challenge ahead of him. He didn't feel inclined to share these reflections with anybody. When the day came for him to leave home – his flight to California was the following morning – Roger drove him to New Jersey with all his luggage in a van borrowed from a friend at work. They would stay that night in a motel near Newark Airport and Roger would drive back the next day, once he was satisfied, as he said in his stylized but peculiarly unevocative Dadspeak, that his son was "squared away." Molly and Kay had the house to themselves. Molly had chosen to stay home that evening; she felt that something was happening which, while not momentous exactly, might be worth trying to mark in some way, even if just with a conversation which was contextually larger than they were used to.

"So Richard's gone now," Molly said. "It's weird."

"One down," Kay said. She looked at Molly and smiled fondly.

"Soon it'll be just the two of you."

She nodded. "That's what he thinks," she said.

There came a weekend afternoon when Molly knew where each of her parents was and when they would return. She watched out the leaded-glass windows framing the door until Ty appeared, on foot, around the bend in the road. He knew why he was there. He had probably never been so eager for anything in his life and yet he chose this moment to be polite, accepting her offer of a soda, asking how her classes were, mentioning his admiration of her house, which he had never been inside of before. Finally she went up and kissed him, her hands at her sides but taking his fingers in hers. She could feel him trembling. It was what she was hoping to feel.

She took him into Richard's room; it was a room which, for the most part, her mother never entered anymore, and so she could feel less paranoid about leaving behind any sort of unintentional evidence. Ty did exactly as he had done before, only this time things kept going past the point where they usually stopped, the way a dream often stops at the same point. The burn scars went all the way up his arms and shoulders, on to his neck, halfway down his back, and in a more random pattern – as if embers had fallen on him – on his chest and stomach. The healed skin was hairless and looked almost like bubble gum. He started to shiver, and kept shivering even after she ran downstairs in her underwear and turned up the thermostat. But it was important to her that he was completely naked; she knew all along that that's how she wanted him, even stopping him when he tried to enter her before all their clothes were off. It wouldn't have occurred to him to insist on anything or to contradict her at any point. A hard-on like that had to hurt, she thought, and it did seem to be hurting him in some way. The more exposed he became, in the daylight with the blinds half-open, the more his confidence eroded. You could see it. He couldn't stay on top of the desire that he felt when he saw her, her breasts, her stomach, her hips, her hair. When he tried, in vain, to close her eyes with his fingertips, that was the moment she came closest to feeling sorry for him.

"You're so beautiful," he said, and though he meant it, it didn't sound at all spontaneous – as if he were saying it in some other language, knew what it meant in a general way but still needed to take a moment to translate it from the language in which he thought.

She didn't know what she was doing either but he was so clearly looking to her the whole way. When he lifted first one knee and then the other so that his legs were finally between hers, he was so scared, so in thrall, that she thought she had never seen anything more worth looking at in her life. He couldn't pretend, he couldn't hide anything from her, nor from himself, there was nothing interposing itself between the two of them and what was real. It had nothing to do with any feeling that she might have had for him.

"I love you," he said.

Of course he didn't love her. He was just looking for something to borrow that would approximate what he felt. It was as if, having stripped away all the outer layers of his self – the ingratiation, the fear of ridicule, the sense of his misfortune, the layers which *were* himself, the rest of the time – in order to discover what was essential in him, it had turned out that there was nothing there: he still said what he thought he was expected to say. Nothing at the core of him – at least not yet. That was okay. He was sixteen years old.

She didn't have to do anything, really, not in the physical sense nor in any other. Just by fucking him she could get him to agree to show her everything about himself while she showed him nothing. The private space within her was maintained, it was defined, by this act of withholding it from him. Here he is, inside me, she thought, and I couldn't be more of a mystery to him. The whole game, as everyone else she knew seemed to understand it, was the boy's endeavor to solve the puzzle of the girl, to unlock the riddle, to find the trick that would make her vulnerable enough to him that she would agree to have sex with him. And often that was the end of it; once the riddle was solved, the boy's interest evaporated. But that's not how it is with me, she thought – triumphantly; that's not how it is right now. She could see it in his face. It was the fucking that provided the riddle.

It was all over, at least from his perspective, in less than a minute. In his face, at the moment which was supposed to define pure sensual thoughtlessness, was shame, weakness, loss of control. He turned away from her to take the condom off. She sat up, her legs still framing him, and ran her fingertips gently, proprietarily along the tight scar tissue on his back. Belatedly she thought that the pain really wasn't as bad as she'd been led to expect.

She had to ask him to leave pretty shortly after that, but he was obviously glad to. His face was still burning. He didn't appear exultant or relieved or any of the things he might have expected to feel. No part of him was invisible. Molly knew it wouldn't last long. It would last just as long as he could keep from telling his friends about it, for in the telling it would change, and soon the public version would harden over the real one and he would forget the way he felt right now. He would sacrifice her in the telling and go back to life as part of the group, go back to his popular identity. She didn't care. So much the worse for him. Or maybe it was better, the way it was sometimes said to be for the better when a dog was put to sleep.

IN SEPTEMBER, THE phone call came to announce officially that the Doucette casual-wear account was going into review. Five agencies had been selected by a search committee and granted the opportunity to pitch the account; Canning Leigh & Osbourne was one of those five, a courtesy not always extended to a dissatisfied client's incumbent agency, but generally and pessimistically viewed as a courtesy nonetheless. The account, which CLO had held for five years, was worth thirty-five million dollars in billings each year.

The call came on a Wednesday. On Thursday morning, Canning walked into John and Roman's office and told them the same thing he had told the other three teams previously assigned to Doucette: to take the work they had heretofore done on the new TV spots and shred it. Everyone was to come in first thing Monday morning and start all over again with, Canning said unhumorously, a new vision and a new attitude.

John did indeed have a new attitude: dread. "Doucette has had problems for years," he told Rebecca, who sat sideways on the couch, her legs folded beneath her, and ran her finger along the hairline at his temple. "And I've only been on it since spring. Still, if they lose it, that's got to mean cutting some jobs, at least in the short run. And the first people to go are going to be the people with that stench coming off them, the people who got lazy and let Doucette out the door. You know it."

Rebecca looked at the side of his face – the thin Waspy nose, the strong chin. "Well, I know that won't happen," she said soothingly. "But just to try to dispel your fears, let's say it did. How long would it take you to find another job at an agency in this city, with a book like yours? Four minutes? Five minutes? A better-paying job, too, probably."

John shook his head gloomily. "The point is, I want to stay," he said. "You have no idea what some of those bigger Madison

Avenue agencies are like. No idea. Guys in suits with pipes, guys telling you how they learned everything they need to know about advertising doing point–of–purchase ads for P&G in 1958. Bosses who will tell you in all seriousness that there are only two angles you're allowed to shoot a car from, or there are only three different typefaces you're allowed to use, because those are the three the dead founder said he liked in his memoirs. I can't go back there. It would be like grave–digging, compared to the work I get to do now."

The sun had gone behind the townhouses across the street. From the apartment upstairs they heard the sound of the neighbor's boy riding a tricycle across the wooden floor.

"I want to stay," John said simply. "I'm too used to the freedom of it. And if I want to stay, then I just have to come up with something. It's my fault as much as anybody's. It's my fault for not being creative enough. I have to come up with something new."

Rebecca said nothing more. But the next day she called John at his dead–calm office and told him she had rented a car, and made ferry reservations, and found an inn that was still open, and they were going to Martha's Vineyard for the weekend. She had just decided, she said, that this was something he needed and deserved. She had taken care of everything – even packed for him after he had left for work. He agreed to meet her downstairs at five on the dot, and hung up, smiling bashfully. It was the form their love always took, in the moments when love needed to reassert itself: she would act for him, and he would put his pride in her rather than in any thought of resisting.

When the ferry came in sight of Vineyard Haven, they went

up on deck and watched, hands jammed in their pockets, chins tucked down into their collars, as the low lights approached. They weren't alone, in spite of the wind and nocturnal cold; a half-dozen other passengers braved the open air as well. The late September days still held the warmth of summer, then the nights stole back with frost: the lure of the off-season.

Their hotel in Oak Bluffs was a Victorian-looking ginger-bread affair, with tight staircases and low ceilings. It was closing up for the winter the day after John and Rebecca were scheduled to leave. When they came downstairs Saturday morning to search for some breakfast, they saw the owner, a robust woman in her fifties or sixties with a long gray braid, atop a stepladder outside, looking in at them through the windows; she was putting up the storm panes. They drove out to the cliffs at Gay Head, and descended to the hidden beach where people of all ages went naked and covered themselves with the thick, comic, unguentous mud. John stood in the clay and looked out to sea and quite managed to forget himself for a while. He thought about how some beautiful women looked better clothed than naked and how Rebecca was not one of those women. The others must have seen that too. But something about the envelope of mud desexed what might otherwise have been a lusty atmosphere – they were all more like children, like statues, purely bodies, for that interlude when the sun was high.

When they came back to their inn the owner had left a space heater with a note outside the door to their room. John showered while Rebecca used the lobby phone to check which restaurants were still open for dinner this time of year. They drove on the beach road in the twilight out to Edgartown. By the time they had had a drink and ordered dinner, all John's worries had retaken possession of him, but out of consideration for Rebecca he kept it inside. She ordered a second bottle of wine.

"You know," she said, "in another few years, we'll probably have a baby, and we won't be able to do this kind of thing anymore." She said this neither excitedly nor with regret; but she seemed happy enough now.

John had to drive back much more slowly than he had come on the beach road, because he was drunk. There were stretches where the road dropped off to water on both sides. In their cold room, they took off each other's clothes quickly, laughing, and jumped into the noisy old bed. Soon she was holding his hair tightly between her fingers. Her eyes had a way of seeming to blur, and, seeing this, he stopped for a moment and moved his hands so that her legs bent over his shoulders. He tried to transmit to her some of the passionate honesty, the defenselessness, with which his fear inspired him.

When the work week began, the atmosphere at the agency was one of forced carelessness, a mask of cheerful fatalism gradually swallowed up, as each day progressed, in a fog of lost revenue, lost jobs. It didn't take long for the tension to inform each close working relationship. That was no problem – creativity learned to thrive on such pressure. The problem was that Roman, a born and bred New Yorker, wanted to resolve that tension by arguing in loud voices, while John was too thin-skinned, even with a good friend, for that kind of approach to be fruitful.

Roman had a theory as to why the previous year's Doucette campaign had failed: in fact, it was the same overarching theory he offered to explain the failure of any ad campaign, anywhere. People, he said sternly, hated advertising. They hated being spoken to like idiots, they saw five hundred ads a day in some form or other, they knew all the tricks that had been refined in order to sell them things they needed and things they didn't. The more you smiled at them, complimented them, sang to them, the wiser they were to what you really thought about them. And yet, he said. And yet they had not let go of their innate compulsion to be amused – not to consume or to have their self-image stroked, but purely and simply to be amused – and they would still agree in effect to subsidize that amusement by purchasing the product associated with it. So the answer, according to Roman – a burly, sloppy man in his mid-thirties, with two unpublished novels in his desk at home, a man whose imagination was powered by a deep conflation of passion and irony – was anti-advertising, advertising that looked nothing like it was supposed to, that looked – if you were willing to go all the way with it – like it was trying to subvert its own purpose. His idea, which he defended with gusto, was this: find the ugliest, most misshapen, unintelligent, comic-looking faces and bodies imaginable (he even brought in videos of *Amarcord* and *Stardust Memories* to show what he was talking about), put them in the Doucette khakis, bathing suits, lambswool sweaters, pocket T's, and photograph them. At the end of the TV spot, a title, or a voice-over, would deliver the tag: "Be honest. If we'd gotten Cindy Crawford, would you have noticed the clothes?"

"It's brilliant," Roman said. "With the right music for the dummy spot, it'll save the motherfucking day. Right now I'm thinking either Sinead O'Connor singing 'You Do Something to Me' or Robert Palmer's 'Simply Irresistible.' "

John, though, found this whole proposal too theoretical, too self-referential, and anyway the more attention it garnered, the more of a link it would create in the public consciousness between wearing Doucette's clothes and looking like a dateless outcast. He, too, had a pet theory, which ran like this: in a market glutted with products of every sort, where the selling itself was no longer a person-to-person transaction, the only way to make one product rise above its competitors was to find a way to link that product, however paradoxically, with the notion of individuality, nonconformity, the assertion of self. His idea was a black-tie wedding at which the groom emerges wearing a long-sleeved T-shirt and black jeans, smiling coolly, while his future in-laws look on in horror. He thought Roman could come up with some line about how the truly well-dressed man is comfortable at any occasion.

"I know it's kind of conservative," John said, as Roman, eyes squeezed shut, held his head between his hands as if trying to keep it from exploding, "but let me just remind you that this is a pitch, that we have to sell this idea not to a bunch of your East Village film-studies-major friends sitting on a couch watching television but to the marketing director from Doucette, who lives in Wilkes-Barre for God's sake, who's a member of the Christian Coalition for all we know."

Variations on this argument and on the ideas behind them took up a week. Then on Monday morning John arrived to find Roman holding a pink memo he had found pinned to the door of their office, signed by Canning. "To the Doucette teams," it read. "Effective immediately, the upcoming account pitch is placed under the supervision of Mal Osbourne. All communications with the client go through him, all ideas are to be approved by him, including the final presentation. Mal will run the pitch in Philadelphia personally. He'll be in touch with all of you directly. That is all."

The four teams met for lunch at Zen Palate.

"What does this *mean?*" Roman said. "I wasn't sure this guy was still alive. He hasn't done any creative work I know about in three or four years. Is he coming out of retirement or what?"

"Maybe that's it," said Andrea, an artist. About to turn thirty, she was lately enamored of a kind of schoolgirl look she couldn't quite bring off; she wore her hair that day in two pigtails tied with pieces of yarn. "I think it's kind of exciting, actually. It sure jazzes up the idea of working on this account. Mal Osbourne is one of the big names in all of advertising – maybe not lately. He's one of the reasons I came to this agency in the first place."

"But why the note?" said her partner Dale, a copywriter, a pallid young man just two or three years out of college. "Isn't this the kind of thing Canning might normally take the time to explain to us personally, instead of coming in on Sunday to leave us a note? I heard he wasn't even in the office today."

"He can't be too happy about it," Andrea said, "if he refuses to talk about it like this." The way she began speaking before Dale was quite finished brought back to John the memory of his own brief and unhappy working partnership with her, when he first started at the agency almost four years ago. "It must have been forced on him somehow."

"Jesus," Dale said, "I feel like one of those – what did they call those people, back in the eighties, those people you'd see on like *Nightline,* talking about what it meant that they were playing funeral music on Radio Moscow, or who stood next to who at the May Day parade?"

Roman finished chewing hurriedly. "Kremlinologists," he said. Everyone nodded.

John was the only one not saying much. He was embarrassed by a premonition he had that all this was related to him in some fateful way. He had never told anyone, not even Roman, about the morning he had spent looking at art with Osbourne last spring – the real genesis of their meeting was so unlikely that John felt certain no one would believe he hadn't engineered it himself somehow, and he had decided to keep it a harmless secret rather than risk being doubted and gossiped about. Right after it happened, Vanessa had of course demanded to know everything: he began by swearing her to secrecy, but with no real faith in Vanessa's word, he had then lied about it anyway, downplaying every interesting thing about it. Now he was newly nervous that it would get out. If the story circulated even in the most watered-down version that John had spent four clandestine hours one Saturday in the back seat of a car with Mal Osbourne, everyone on the Doucette account, everyone in the agency, would surely start assaulting him with questions about Osbourne's tastes, Osbourne's nature, and when he couldn't answer, they would accuse him of protecting some mysterious access of his own.

Over the next three weeks, Osbourne never once appeared in the CLO offices. He left no procedural instructions for any of the creative teams and no word on how anyone might get in touch with him. The portion of the staff charged with saving the Doucette account was near mutiny. Dale and Andrea were delegated to go to Canning's office and demand that the pitch be handed over to someone else. Canning was a man of strong, ephemeral passions, and this year it was fishing; fly rods leaned against the glass wall behind his desk, through which the bend of the Hudson just beyond the George Washington Bridge was barely visible. Slumped at his desk, speaking with his eyes closed and his fingers massaging his forehead, Canning told them wearily that since Mal Osbourne was technically a full partner, he couldn't be removed from a particular project if he didn't want to go, any more than Osbourne could kick Canning off an account if he had a mind to. All Canning could do was to repeat Osbourne's assurance that he would be responsible for the final presentation in Philadelphia – which did, yes, include his actually showing up for it. Canning had Mal's email address, and he promised to send another desperate message, though if the response to his prior desperate messages was anything to go by, he said, he might as well put it in a bottle and drop it in the cyber-sea.

The teams were more dejected than ever when this conversation was relayed to them. Something in the tone of Canning's promised message to his partner must have changed, though, for the next morning there were email messages for all of them, informing them of a specific date on which a messenger would appear at CLO to pick up all their final storyboards, artwork, magazine copy, videotapes, and market analyses, and would take these packages to Osbourne for his final selection.

John, who had gradually forgotten about pleasing the client in his pursuit of the enigma of what might please Osbourne, gave in at least in part to Roman's vision of the anti-campaign: he hired a photographer ("Too bad we can't get Diane Arbus,"

Roman said), and asked bemused casting directors to send over glossies of the lumpiest, most unglamorous, least photogenic people they could find. "They don't even have to be clients," John said. "Maybe there's someone who works in your office . . ." John and Roman picked eight photos and then staged and filmed a fashion show, laying in music and the sound of wild applause for the dummy TV spot to be used in the pitch, if their idea was the one Osbourne chose in the end. Osbourne sent no further word. On the appointed day, the four teams came out to the lobby one by one with their packaged materials, and waited there, staring at the elevator door, unconvinced that the promised messenger would actually arrive. At around four o'clock he came, a teenager with a hand truck: he gathered up the bulky packages and immediately got back into the elevator, looking nervously over his shoulder at the eight strangers glaring at him resentfully, jealously. As soon as the door closed again, Roman bolted to the receptionist's desk and grabbed the receipt out of her hand. It had no destination address.

That was on a Friday. A week later, with the pitch in Philadelphia just three days away, Osbourne had not been in touch. Anxiety in the office had given way to gallows humor as the eight staffers faced the prospect of traveling together to Philadelphia and standing helplessly before the Doucette search committee with absolutely nothing to say. Roman bought one of those old desktop wooden labyrinths, with a marble one maneuvered around a series of holes, at a vintage toy store and played with it at his desk all day long. At two o'clock he announced that he couldn't take it anymore and went home for the weekend. So John was alone in their office when the phone rang.

"John!" The voice was so lively and forthcoming that he didn't recognize it right away. "How have you been? It's Mal Osbourne."

John glanced through the open office door to the empty hallway. "Fine, thank you," he said. "I . . . well, how are you, sir?"

Osbourne laughed. "I can really hear the South in your voice, on the phone," he said. "Listen, I won't keep you, here's why I'm calling: I'm driving down to Philadelphia for the thing on Monday, and I wanted to know if you needed a ride down."

John swallowed. "Well," he said, "that's extremely kind of you. But the others are going down together, on the Metroliner, including my partner, and I already made plans to meet them. I don't . . ."

"Sorry?" Osbourne said.

"I don't think it would look right, for me to cancel on them, and arrive with you. I mean thank you for the offer, I'm sure I would prefer it. But just in terms of . . . decorum."

"Ah," Osbourne said. He sounded embarrassed. "You're probably right. I hadn't even thought about it. You're right. Very thoughtful of you, very . . . Well, I guess I'll see you at the Nikko on Monday then."

"Sir?" John blurted out.

"Sir?" Osbourne repeated, with gentle mockery. Perhaps he was one of those people who were most themselves on the telephone, like Glenn Gould. "Mal."

"Mal, I just wanted to ask quickly, while I had you on the phone, if you, which of the approaches, the four approaches, you decided to go with for Doucette."

"Oh, yes, of course," Osbourne said. "Right. None of them."

"None of them?"

"That's right. Well, see you Monday then? Have a good weekend."

Within a minute John realized that he had made a mistake by even asking: for, no matter what the answer had been, he would now have to ride with his seven colleagues on the train to Philadelphia knowing something they didn't know. He couldn't tell them what he had learned without explaining how he had come to learn it, and in the process estranging himself from their trust, through no real fault of his own.

They made the trip on the crowded Metroliner, sitting together in two adjacent double seats, empty-handed, plotting revenge for what they saw as their impending humiliation. Mick, a bald copywriter who had been at CLO longer than any of them – his work for Doucette had actually won a Clio three years ago – showed them a list he had made over the weekend of the most expensive restaurants in Philadelphia, where they might all go for an obscene blowout lunch on the company dime. The meeting was scheduled for 11 a.m., but since none of them had anything to say, they didn't imagine that making a noon lunch reservation would present any problem.

A Daily Event Schedule in the lobby of the Nikko directed them to a tenth-floor conference room. It was ten-thirty when they pushed open the door and saw Osbourne standing in the center of the white, thickly carpeted room, at the head of a rectangular conference table. Behind him were arrayed four large easels, each covered by a black cloth. Osbourne wore black jeans above a shiny pair of cowboy boots, a blue silk shirt, and the same light floral tie he had worn that summer morning in Soho with John. He had shaved off his beard and mustache.

"Welcome, everybody!" he said brightly; and then, incredibly, "John! Good to see you again!"

"Mr Osbourne," John said, horrified.

"Will you take care of the introductions?" Osbourne said.

Dry-mouthed, John introduced his seven colleagues to their boss, each of whom was staring at John in wary amazement.

"I'd like you all to sit over here, on either side of me," Osbourne said, pointing to the side of the table opposite the windows. "We have a few minutes before the Doucette people arrive, so there's coffee and bagels over in the corner if you like." John wouldn't have believed, from their only other encounter, that Osbourne had it in him to be so upbeat, so socially attentive. "Roman Gagliardi," Osbourne said meditatively, and Roman, who was already seated with his head in his hands, looked up at him warily. "You're the guy who did those excellent spots for Fiat, do I remember that right?"

"What the fuck is under those sheets?" Roman said.

Everyone turned to stare, but Osbourne either did not catch the impolitic hostility in Roman's voice or was able to ignore it. "Not something that any of you have seen before," he said genially. "Better it should be a surprise, I think."

"But what if we're asked questions about it?" Andrea said. "We'll be asked to defend it, that's the way these things work, isn't it?"

"Often," Osbourne said, "it is. But today I don't want you to worry about that. It's all taken care of. Your job today is simple: we all sit on the same side of the table and we project the unspoken impression that we're all on the same team."

Andrea frowned, but at the same time, John could see, she

and some of the others were visibly relieved. If anyone was going to be put on the spot today, it wasn't going to be them. Dale sat down in the swivel chair next to John and looked at him as if he had never seen him before.

"Oh, John!" Osbourne said suddenly. "I meant to tell you. I bought the shark!"

John smiled wanly.

At five of eleven a group of young men and women in unfashionable suits entered the conference room, and fanned out uncertainly by the door. The nine CLO representatives stood politely behind their chairs. This was the fourth of the five presentations the Doucette marketing executives would hear in this same conference room in a two-week period: John was unsure why they should seem so nervous. Behind them walked in two older men. The younger of the two, who was nearly bald and wore small, round, horn-rimmed glasses, went straight up to the table and extended one hand to Osbourne, holding back his necktie with the other.

"Mal, I presume?" he said. "We appreciate your coming down today. This of course is Mr Harold Doucette."

John had trouble suppressing a smile at that sycophantic "of course": but then he realized that to these junior executives at a family-owned company, and to their own employees, that stony, white-haired, large-featured, clear-eyed visage was probably as scarily omnipresent as a portrait of Mao.

Osbourne walked around the table to shake Mr Doucette's hand. "We're honored by your presence here today, sir," he said.

Doucette nodded curtly. "I was surprised to hear your request," he said, taking a seat. "If request is the word. This is the only one of the five presentations where my presence was considered necessary."

Everyone was seated now except Osbourne, who continued talking as he made his way back around the table. None of the Doucette people had touched the food, or even poured a cup of coffee; no one wanted to be seen ingesting in the presence of the old man himself. John saw their surprised expressions and discreet nudges and could overhear some of their critical whisperings about the absence of any slide projectors, any TV and VCR, any sound system. Just the four black–draped easels, like a high school science fair. It was not uncommon for agency spending on a pitch for a major account like this to go well into five figures. In the last week or so, John knew, these same marketing people must have beheld some sweaty, script-holding ad execs wearing lots of Doucette clothing and otherwise making clowns of themselves in this very same conference room.

"I wanted you here," Osbourne said, "because we have some very serious issues to discuss, issues that are at once fundamental to doing business in the *fin de siècle* and also somewhat of a departure in terms of past strategy, past ideas; and, with due respect to Mr Gracey here, I didn't want you to hear these ideas filtered or secondhand." He sat down across from Mr Doucette.

It was not lost on John that he alone might have reason to find Osbourne's assured, charismatic manner, his easy command of the room, strange or even ominous, given the amazing contrast it presented to his moody, insular silence when they had last met. All that was strange about it, though, was how connected the two states seemed. It was as if Osbourne were emerging from a sort of chrysalis of personality: developed, brilliant, natural, and inexplicable.

"Doucette's sales have gone up," Osbourne said, "in each of the three years since Canning Leigh & Osbourne took over its national advertising account. However, that's not good enough for you. I understand that. I understand that, at your level, competition, more than money, is the nature of the game. You blame CLO's advertising for the plateau Doucette seems to have reached in terms of its growth percentage. Well, such cause-and-effect relationships are notoriously hard to prove, but I will agree with you on one thing: our advertising for Doucette stinks. It's lousy. I can hardly stand to look at it."

He rose and walked over to the first easel. Pulling the cloth on to the floor, he revealed a blowup of a six-month-old magazine ad for Doucette's Oxford shirts. It featured a black and white Bruce Weber-style photo of a well-known young movie actress, wearing the shirt with most of the buttons undone, and with the tails tied into a knot at her midriff. "Wear What You Like," the copy began. John recognized it right away as Dale and Andrea's work. He didn't look over at them.

Osbourne stood there gazing at the sample ad for as long as a minute – an expansive silence, as if he had forgotten the others were waiting for him. Then he looked back at Mr Doucette.

"Let me tell you something about myself," he said, in a softer voice. "I hate advertising."

John felt his heart racing. He wondered if what he was witnessing was going to cross the line from humiliating failure into a kind of larger-than-life disaster, a Hindenburg of ad pitches.

"I hate it so much I want to kill it. Have you ever hated anything that much, sir?"

Mr Doucette wasn't sure where to turn his eyes. No one said anything.

"I see something like this, and . . . and you have to multiply it by like a billion, that's the problem, to get an idea of the cultural noise, the *mental* noise, advertising like this creates, you have to look at this ad and then close your eyes and imagine a billion images just like it, all speaking at the same time, all of them saying nothing. A huge, overwhelming, stupefying nothing. Images like this open their mouths and nothing comes out, and yet the noise they make is deafening."

Jerry Gracey, who had lured Mr Doucette to this meeting with the promise of meeting one of the legendary geniuses of the ad business, had made a tent out of his hands and was looking inside it.

"What I'm proposing today," Osbourne said, unruffled, "is not advertising."

"It's not?" Doucette said, with the indulgent air of a man who is holding his wrath for later.

"No, sir. Not as the word is understood. Because I don't want to speak in that language anymore. Not that I don't know it. Christ knows I'm fluent in it. But advertising, traditional advertising, is about nothing. It's about—" he gestured at the exposed ad – "it's about movie stars. Its great resources don't concern themselves with anything important. It's not about life and death. And I ask myself – why *can't* it be about life and death?"

"Death?" Doucette said skeptically.

"It's just a form, after all – advertising, I mean – and so the question of content is wide open. It's a form for the massive production and global distribution of simple visual messages; staggering, really, if you think about it. Why should it be limited to the perfection of titillating people sexually? Mr Doucette, you're a rich man. Because of that, and because of your position of power as the head of a large concern, you have the greatest means of communication in history at your disposal. How are you going to use it?"

"To sell casual clothing," Doucette said, a bit more animated now. "What the hell do you mean, how am I going to use it?"

Osbourne put his hand over his mouth for a few seconds. Then, saying something to himself the others couldn't hear, he marched over and tore the drapery off the second easel. The eighteen people at the table saw a large color photograph of a sparkling white beach, in the light of midmorning. At the left of the picture were two tanned, attractive couples, sitting in beach chairs, under a broad umbrella. One of the women had turned her head to the right, where, perhaps a hundred feet away, an inflatable life raft floated near the shoreline, filled to overflowing with a dozen or more dark-skinned, ragged, exhausted people, two of whom had climbed out to pull the craft the last few feet on to the sand.

"I submit," Osbourne said, "that the only effective way to use it is to show people something other than what they are bombarded with every second of their waking lives."

"What the hell is that?" Doucette said.

"It's a photograph of a boatload of Cuban refugees landing on a south Florida beach."

"Is it staged?" Gracey asked.

"The world's a stage. Our plan is to run this as a kind

of inaugural next spring in *Vanity Fair,* the *New Yorker, Elle*—"

"You do understand, young man," Doucette said, "that we're trying to sell a product here?"

"Yes, sir," Osbourne said patiently.

"And you understand the nature of that product? Casual wear, sportswear?"

"I understand it perfectly," Osbourne said. "I just don't think it matters."

Everyone on the CLO side of the conference table was watching Osbourne motionlessly, as if they were all having the same dream.

"With all due respect," Osbourne went on, "the product we're talking about here is not one that's unique to the market. The consumer knows, presumably, that Doucette's jeans or boxers or what have you are attractive and not cheaply made; but there's the Gap, there's Banana Republic, there's J. Crew and Lands' End. When you really think about it, what could possibly be unique or distinctive, in the common imagination, about Doucette clothing?"

He smiled and lifted his hands in a gesture of self-deprecation.

"The advertising," he said. "The advertising. Nothing else. Nothing but that."

He unveiled the third image: a photograph of a vast herd of cattle in a holding pen just outside a slaughterhouse. Rolling hills and a deep blue sky were visible in the background.

"Transgressive images," he said, "are your only viable strategy for rising above a market that's frankly overcrowded, for making yourself heard above the cultural noise."

One of the junior executives on the Doucette side of the table raised her hand; Osbourne nodded.

"I'm unclear on something," she said, very earnestly. "I would have thought we'd given CLO time enough to prepare some finished materials. But how are these photos you're showing us ultimately going to be incorporated into the finished ads?"

Osbourne raised his eyebrows; he looked behind him at the easels, then back at the young woman. "These are the finished ads," he said.

The woman laughed – then, embarrassed, returned her face to its businesslike cast.

Mr Gracey leaned forward and reexamined the photographs through his glasses.

"There's no logo," he pointed out, and sat back immediately as if regretting having made this observation out loud.

"That's correct," Osbourne said, unable now to keep some excitement out of his voice. "That, if you'll permit me, is the master stroke, I think, of the campaign we've devised for you. On one level, it's a way of acknowledging the truth that any powerful image, whatever its provenance, once it's released into the world, *belongs* to the world. There's no claiming authorship of a picture like this, and it would be unseemly to try to do it. I mean, my name isn't on it either. Imagine these photos you see here, two-page full-color bleeds, placed in magazines all over the world, with absolutely no attribution. It has a kind of guerrilla aspect to it, doesn't it? And of course the paradox is that people all over the world will forget the other five hundred ads they see that day in their frenzy to find out who's behind these anonymous images. Network news, the Internet, friends in restaurants, everywhere they'll be talking about it. I guarantee a buzz the likes of which your product could never generate by any other means. And it should also be said that this approach will insulate you somewhat from the inevitable, benighted charges that you're exploiting these images simply in order to sell more sweaters."

With that, he pulled the cloth off the final easel. Upon it was an enormous close-up of a woman giving birth. She was shown from knee to knee; the baby's head was fully emerged. The room erupted in gasps and oaths, and every single person twitched abruptly in his or her seat.

"My God!" Doucette yelled. "What is the meaning of this?"

"The most fundamental, most positive, most optimistic of human messages," Osbourne went on calmly, "and yet the one—"

"There are women in this room!" Doucette shouted, and he began to get to his feet. "Are you insane?"

Gracey jumped up and put his hands on his boss's shoulders. "Let's be calm, please," he said. "Mr Osbourne, if I could just return this conversation to the planet Earth for one moment, surely you know that no ad-sales department anywhere in the world would ever accept a photo like that for publication."

Osbourne smiled. "Well, I have to disagree with you a little bit on that. For one thing, this particular image has appeared in at least one magazine already – just not as an advertisement. For another, I can tell you that it's always possible to find two or three prominent print outlets who are willing to test the envelope a little bit. Because transgression – though it's getting harder and harder – transgression is still the engine of culture." He paused to let that sink in. "But your point, Jerry, is well taken. Most print outlets will indeed turn this piece down. That refusal, in itself, is news. And news is publicity. Of the free variety, I need hardly remind anyone. Again, I come back to the uncomfortable point that the best, in fact the only, way to associate a familiar product with the fashionable, the avant-garde, is for its advertising to establish that avant-garde."

"So let me get this straight," Gracey said. He still had one hand on his boss's shoulder. He himself was perfectly cool; perhaps he had reckoned that his own job would not survive this fiasco. "Your media buying plan for Doucette incorporates censorship?"

"In a culture of excess, censorship is an achievement in itself, a measure of success. And as for any negative publicity that might also be generated, from right-wing watchdog groups or what have you, I think that one of the self-evident truths in a competitive business like ours is that airtime is airtime."

John had forgotten his problems; he had forgotten that his own deception of his friends regarding his acquaintance with Osbourne had been exposed; he had forgotten whatever might have been going on outside that conference room. Doucette's face was so red that John wondered if he might be in any sort of dangerous distress. It was all so rarefied and silly: and yet, in a sealed room in a neutral city, where competing ideas seemed ready to bring men to blows, John was in the grip of a feeling that seldom came over him, which he couldn't have called anything more specific than an awareness that he was alive.

"Are there any other questions?" Osbourne asked amiably.

"Yes," Mr Doucette said, and immediately the other murmurings in the room hushed. "I have a question." His voice still shook a little; slowly he reached up and knocked Gracey's hand off his shoulder. "These . . . images, as you call them, they contain no picture or drawing of our product, no reference to our product. They don't mention the name of our product. So my question is, what, other than the fact that I pay you for them, makes these things advertisements at all?"

Osbourne nodded approvingly. "That's a very sophisticated question, sir," he said. "And I could go on about how those sorts of categories no longer exist: how economic and technological history has bequeathed us this network for the distribution of visual messages, a network so self-sustaining and efficient and culturally vital that it's frankly overwhelmed the whole idea of praising commodities that brought it into being in the first place. But I expect that's not what you're really asking. So all I can tell you is this. Your aim in launching an advertising campaign is to sell millions more pants, shirts, and sweaters. The campaign I've shown you today will result in the sale of millions more pants, shirts, and sweaters. I guarantee that. I guarantee it. If that's all our two ideas have in common, then that's all they need to have in common."

Doucette nodded, drumming his fingers on his leg. It was clear from his demeanor under stress that he had not been born into the class he now exemplified. He leaned forward and put his forearms on the table.

"You think I'm an idiot," he said quietly. "Don't you?"

"No, sir. I don't think that. And I understand your hesitation. The way I look at it, our relationship, yours and mine, is an ancient one. It's at least as old as the Renaissance. I am coming to you, in effect, to ask you to be my patron. As my patron, what glory accrues from my work will both reflect on you and, in indirect but very real ways, reward you. And you, of course, have something that I need, in order to do the work that I want to do. Which is why I thought it necessary that you and I meet here today. In order to obtain the opportunity to educate the public, it's first necessary to educate the patron."

The meeting broke up quickly after that. The junior people on each side of the table stared dumbly at one another for a few seconds before the Doucettes abruptly left as a group; Gracey said only that he would be in touch very soon. Osbourne seemed tired but well pleased; earnestly, he thanked his own eight staffers for their support, and without waiting for any reply, he gathered up the four boards, folded the easels, and left.

On the train back to New York, the stunned silence held for the first few minutes, before people began arguing tentatively about the exact nature of what they had just seen.

"He had to know what he was doing," Dale said. "I mean, he had to know that no client in the world would ever go for that. So why would he go all the way through with it?"

"As a joke," Andrea said. "As a kind of parting fuck-you. I mean, including CLO in the review process was a joke anyway. Does an incumbent agency ever win out in a review? No. Never. So he was just being vindictive, trying to make a fool out of old man Doucette instead of performing for him."

"I don't know about that," Mick said. "I just never got any kind of a sarcastic hit off his presentation today. Nobody's that deadpan. I think he was serious. And what he said was actually kind of brilliant in its way, I mean deranged, but brilliant."

"Or," Andrea said, excitedly. "Or. I mean let's remember that Osbourne doesn't even come into the office anymore. Hasn't produced an ad in years. He does no work at all, that I know about. And suddenly he decides to take over a major account pitch and then totally sabotages it?" She looked around the gently rocking compartment. "I think we just watched a guy self-destructing. Maybe he deludes himself that he's some kind of ad visionary, maybe not, but in fact he's just setting fire to himself, finishing up the ruin of what was once a really brilliant career."

"Good," Dale said. "That's what I was waiting to hear. Okay, any other votes for the guy's being clinically insane?"

There was a silence, in which John noticed Roman, across the aisle, studying him in discreet perplexity, as if to say, The others may have forgotten for a moment what happened in the minutes before the meeting, but I haven't. John felt himself reddening and turned his head.

"I mean, the fucking Renaissance," Dale said. "What's up with that?"

John went straight home to Brooklyn from Penn Station. He called in sick the next day. Wednesday afternoon, a staff meeting was called, at which Canning announced that, by mutual agreement, the agency's contractual relationship with Mal Osbourne had been terminated. Canning called the parting amicable, but he also apologized to the eight creatives whose hard work on the Doucette pitch had, he said, gone to waste. As for Doucette, they had signed that morning with Chiat/Day.

Osbourne's office email account had of course been closed; but it was just as well that his next message to John, months later, came to his home, in the form of a cramped but curiously formal handwritten note. "I am in the process of conceiving an exciting new venture," it read. "I'll be in touch with you about it in due course. In the meantime, I sincerely hope that you and your wife are well."

FIRST PERIOD MATH, second period US history, third period French, fifty minutes spent trying to find the facial expression that would discourage the teacher from asking you if you had a cat or if it was raining outside, and expecting you to answer. Lunch, the same long table in the corner farthest from the door with the same girls, Annika and Tia, Justine and Lucy, acting the way they thought people unaware of being looked at might act; the cafeteria tables seated eight and so they were always joined by two or three bold aspirants who did not join in the conversation but listened and laughed with great animation for the benefit of anyone at other tables who might be noticing them there. Fourth period free, fifth period bio; sixth period was AP English, where they were reading *One Hundred Years of Solitude;* it worked out well that this one interesting class was the last one, because it kept Molly from looking too frequently at the clock on the wall behind the teacher's head. Then straight into the parking lot, with everyone else, to get on the idling bus for home.

You never understood how diligently, in the common course of things, you were watched – how your absence from any of those places you were in every day, places in which you might have felt yourself thoroughly anonymous, could never go unnoticed – until you tried to get out from under it. Cutting classes was one thing, obviously possible only on an occasional basis before teachers and then parents got involved. But if for instance you weren't on the bus in the afternoon, people asked you about it the first time they saw you the next morning, and they had no doubt been speculating with each other about you before that – people with nothing more substantial to think about than what passed in front of their eyes. You couldn't have that kind of talk in the air. Miss a warm Saturday night at the playground behind the elementary school and Sunday your friends all phoned to find out what had happened to you. If you weren't at the dinner table, never mind the breakfast table, there were questions.

So what Molly did was to get off the bus at a stop before her own, near the center of town usually, telling anyone who raised an eyebrow that she had an errand to run or a babysitting job or that her mother was sick and had asked her to pick something up. Then, when the bus was gone, she would walk around the windowless back of the IGA, through a thin half acre of woods, and out the other side on to Route 2, where she would wait discreetly behind a tree, looking at the sky, until Dennis Vincent's car pulled up and she saw a smile flickering on his pained face through the window.

There was experience and there was learning, and Molly knew that the last several weeks had consisted much more of the former than the latter; still, one of the things she could say she had learned about herself in that time was that she was a marvelously gifted liar. She took this in without self-satisfaction, nor with a bad conscience – more in the spirit that any knowledge about one's self is a constructive thing. No one ever questioned her; no face showed any skepticism, no one ever caught her in a contradiction. She could only guess that Dennis was not nearly as persuasive with whatever lies he had to tell to get away from the bank at three-thirty in the afternoon, since he did such a poor job trying to convince her, when they were in the car together, that he was courageous, unconflicted, that his thoughts were only with her. It was touching, if also slightly condescending, that he should think she needed to be convinced of that.

The car trips, thirty minutes each way, were hard on Dennis. He tried to make conversation but it always tapered off into silence, and sometimes he looked through the windshield in such a way that Molly worried he didn't see the road in front of him at all. It would have made more sense for Molly to drive herself to Oneonta and meet him there, since she had her license now; but Roger and Kay, who thought little about it if they didn't see Molly over the course of an afternoon, were far more likely to notice if the car was gone for a few hours.

Sometimes she talked to him about trivial things, to try to cheer him up. Sometimes she too said nothing and they made the trip in a kind of considerate silence. And sometimes a very different feeling overtook her, and she would reach across and stroke his leg as he drove, unzip his pants and let him grow hard under her hand, watching as his face turned red, or undo a button or two on her own shirt and guide his hand inside the fabric under her breast. She'd see how far she could push him. This impulse was hard to describe, except to say that it felt closer to abandon than to excitement, less like lust than capitulation.

The motel in Oneonta was a long prefab rectangle, with an office at one end, and a brackish swimming pool behind a locked gate in the front. It was across the road from a strip mall. Parking and room entrances were in the back. Dennis always made her wait in the car while he went inside and paid. She looked around to see if there were any other cars in the lot; sometimes there were none. The best thing about those minutes in the car was the chance to savor the idea that no one in the world could have known where she was just then.

Inside, there was always some initial awkwardness, though some of that was dispelled by the fact that they needed to hurry, they were always so pressed for time. Dennis began by insulting himself, so reliably that Molly started to wonder if he wasn't getting some sort of erotic charge out of it; but that didn't seem to be the case.

"I don't know what's happening to me," he said. "You shouldn't be here. If anyone sees us, I'll be destroyed. How did I let this happen? Where will it all end?"

"It'll end when we end it," Molly said frankly, soothingly. "What, are you afraid I'm going to ask you to marry me or something?"

He seemed hurt by this; he wanted everything both ways. He would sit on the bed, looking lost, until Molly started to take her shirt off, or his. Then he would forget everything.

That October in Ulster the thing that had seemed to be happening so slowly happened all at once: the official announcement made its way from somewhere within the most rarefied precincts of IBM that the central New York regional sales office would be closed down entirely in twelve months' time. As it was, nearly half of all those who had moved to Ulster in the last twenty years to work for IBM were already unemployed; and most of those people were stuck in the town until they could find a buyer for their house or at least until their children's school year was over. There was no comparable work for them anywhere nearby. Much of what had been the town's new professional class now found themselves virtual deadbeats, late with the mortgage, having their credit cards rejected at the IGA. First the dry cleaner and then the Baskin-Robbins went out of business. Twelve months was considered a merciful notice, but nevertheless, life in Ulster had begun to take on a mournful, irritable, last-days quality.

The Howes, at least, were exempt from the harshest effects. Roger had achieved a position of such seniority within the doomed enterprise that he was promised that he could stay on at work until the very last day – he would be turning the lights off behind him, he joked. And he had also been offered a transfer to the office in Armonk, though there was at least a temporary hitch in that plan: Kay was refusing to go. She said she liked it here, Ulster was her home, the thought of organizing a move to another strange place was too stressful for her. It was the purest perversity – she would go to her grave in that town to punish him for bringing her there. No one in the family took her refusal seriously.

Sometimes Dennis was passive, sometimes he was forceful: he was trying to figure out what Molly liked, but what she liked, really, was to see him trying everything. The passive role certainly seemed most true to himself. He lay on his back, with his head to one side, while she straddled him with her knees up, her feet flat on the bed, so that she sometimes had to grab his shoulders for balance.

He had things that he liked. He liked her on her stomach, the wrong way across the bed, so that her arms hung down. He loved blowjobs, and Molly found them a lot less complicated than she had expected; but she discovered that she didn't really like it when he went down on her – it felt wrong, too intimate somehow, though she wouldn't say that aloud – and he was reluctant to let her do it to him if he couldn't reciprocate.

His body was small with just a few hairs on his calves and a sprouting right around his nipples that she found comically unattractive. He always took a shower afterward. While she waited for him, Molly peeked out behind the moldy curtain into the parking lot, or looked through the drawers to see if anyone else had left anything behind. Sometimes there were condoms, or pennies; once, a pair of black lace underwear.

He dropped her off a half mile from Bull's Head, on a stretch of road across from a cow pasture; before they parted they would schedule their next meeting, because it was not always possible to speak to each other on the phone. Like a child he looked both ways before kissing her goodbye, something she only let him do because he insisted on it – such were the ways in which he worked off, through a sporadic and self-devised romantic etiquette, the guilt he felt over treating Molly like a mistress. The car moved off, and Molly walked back home in the twilight, happy deep within herself like a spy, feeling the weakness in her legs. Her mother, in the chair by the TV, smiled with frail disapproval and got up to fix Molly a plate. With Richard away at college, and Molly keeping such unpredictable hours, the family had stopped dining together; Roger and Kay ate early, in front of the television, which did away with the silence between them. So Molly sat alone at the table, eating slowly, listening to the faint music and occasional laughter coming from the TV in the next room. And it was those moments – not the moments in bed with Dennis inside her, not the walks through the woods or the lies themselves – which were happiest for her, because she had escaped the world, it had lost her scent, she knew that she was not who anyone thought she was. The only way to stay pure in the world was to live inside a lie.

Richard didn't call much from Berkeley; he had moved off campus into a house with eight other people, none of whom, evidently, owned an answering machine. But he sent a letter with a copy of his grades in it, and from that it was possible to infer that he was doing fine. Molly now had a taste of what it might have been like to be an only child; her parents wanted to give her all the benefit of their attentions, but she made that difficult without really trying. She wasn't rebellious or unkind – merely self-sufficient. When she was thirteen, this independence, this casual unconcern with their opinion, had been worrisome to the point where Roger and Kay argued with each other about who was more to blame for it; four years later, Molly was in that respect basically unchanged, yet her mother and father now congratulated themselves, seeing in her comradely disregard of them evidence that they had succeeded as parents.

"So," Kay said unexpectedly, "there's nobody you're dating, no regular boyfriend?" It was a Thursday night, and Molly, who had come straight home from school that day, was emptying the dishwasher.

"No," she said. "Nobody regular."

Kay had stopped dyeing her hair recently; Molly thought it looked much better now, both more natural and more severe, but she never brought it up because the effects of time and age, even good ones, were understood to be an unpleasant subject. "Well, I have to say I can understand it," her mother said in a confiding, playful voice, "sorry as I might feel for you. A beautiful, smart girl like you, with so much on the ball, the boys around here must seem like real losers. I mean, not seem – they *are* losers. I see them too, you know. I notice things. Let's face it, they're hayseeds. I haven't met one who's good enough for you."

Some girls Molly knew spoke of being horrified by their mothers' attempts to gain their confidence by intimating that they were girls once themselves; Molly, though, found the idea of her mother's youth engrossing. "I mean, you've grown up here, too," Kay went on, "same as them, but let's face it, you're different. And that has to come from me. You don't belong here, any more than I do." She smiled. "One more year and you'll be out of here, in the wide world somewhere. You're smart to save yourself."

"I was talking to Mike Cavanaugh at work yesterday," Roger said. They were at breakfast together, more or less by chance, he in a gray suit and tie, his daughter in jeans and one of his own old tennis shirts with a bleach stain on it, a shirt he could have sworn he'd thrown out. "His son is a year behind you. And he said, Roger, I have to tell you, my son Stephen is just gone on your daughter. Talks about her all the time. Thinks she's a goddess on earth. I doubt she even knows who he is."

"I don't, actually," Molly said.

Roger laughed at this as if it were a joke. "See? And Bev whatshername, you know, who runs the market? She was telling me last time I was in there, your daughter Molly has grown up to be such a fine young woman. So mature, so polite. Never mouthing off like those others her age."

He reached out as if he was going to touch her shoulder but then pulled his hand back. He hardly ever touched her now.

"That's what I'm proudest of," he said. "Not that you're so

pretty, because that's just your mother's genes really, I can't take any credit there. Or even that your grades are good, though I am very proud of that. But you know how to conduct yourself. The Vincents, I'm worried they're going to steal you away from us, they adore you so much. Every time I see them they tell me how great you are. No one has a bad word to say about you. That's what I'm proudest of."

What unnerved her about these hagiographic speeches was not the mention of the Vincents but their strangely valedictory, summing-up quality, as if her father were preparing to die.

They hadn't been caught, but still, something so elaborate and time-consuming as a trip to Oneonta couldn't be attempted very often – eight or ten times in all. Sometimes a week went by when the only place they could safely be alone together was in Dennis's car itself. Molly still kept to the same babysitting schedule at the Vincents', so there were two or three nights a week when Dennis would take her home through the empty streets, driving too fast, pulling in behind the supermarket or down the dirt road where the train tracks had been torn up fifteen years before, turning off his lights. Undoing his safety belt but staying in his seat. His passivity, his desire for her to make the first move, was less a sexual instinct than a moral one: it let him feel that he was being acted upon. Molly leaned across to blow him if she felt for some reason they were in a hurry. There wasn't a lot you could do in a car but once in a while she liked it with her back to him, her hands on the steering wheel, listening for his gasps, looking through the windshield into the darkness and the noisy woods. For a few minutes everything was wrenched out of its usual context.

When she was alone in the Vincents' house with Kevin and Bethany, Molly could put it all out of her mind with a surprising ease, though sometimes the sight of a framed photograph or a glance into the darkened master bedroom would remind her of the position she was in. The Vincent children, partnered by shyness, happiest in their own home, reminded Molly more and more of herself and her brother; and they were just reaching the age at which Molly and Richard had begun to grow apart. Kevin was big for his age, and the other kids had made sport of his oversensitivity, teasing, enraging, and then running from him in well-founded fear. Molly stroked his head and told him that what other people thought or said didn't matter, but to him this was just one more adult maxim, the logic of which fell apart when you walked out your own front door.

With one or both parents at home, though, the atmosphere became a little more dense. Dennis was usually the first one home now. In part this was because the thought of Molly and his wife talking together outside the range of his hearing was torture to him; but it also had to do with Joyce Vincent's job. Half the people in Ulster and the neighboring towns were trying to sell their homes, and to sell them right away; for those in the real estate business it was like watching the stock market crash. No one wanted to move to the area now. The only potential buyers were longtime residents who were interested in trading up to a nicer, newer place, and those people would wait for prices to hit rock bottom — for foreclosure, ideally. Joyce was out of the house evenings, weekends, driving walk-ins thirty miles to look at places just so they could wrinkle their noses and say it felt too remote. Some of the people who were looking to her to save them from default were friends of hers, parents of her children's classmates, couples whose mortgages Dennis had approved. She had never worked harder in her life. It didn't do much good. Bull's Head, for instance, was now thirty percent empty.

The worse things got – and the guiltier she felt for working so much – the more Joyce needed to flank herself with the two children when she came home. She'd sit on the floor without even taking her coat off and join in a game of Chinese checkers; or she'd try to pull both kids on to her lap and get them to recount their day to her in exhausting detail. Kevin, who was ten, was beginning to shy away from his mother's affections a bit. Bethany, on the other hand, was drawing ever closer to her, even as they began to look more and more alike; the girl doted on these evenings in the circle of her mother's protective, guilt-driven attention, a mother who always seemed to be trying to make something up to her. Molly, meanwhile, would look at the waxy mask of normalcy on her lover's face. If his wife and children were in another room, she might fix him with a long look, or even touch his hand or his stomach. He hated it – he had not the least affection for risk. She didn't torment Dennis for fun, but she did find his torment interesting. Though she sometimes mused that a man who, in Dennis's situation, felt no remorse at all, who deceived and charmed and led two intersecting lives with perfect equanimity, might be interesting in his own way.

When, for example, the family that was renting Dennis's childhood home broke their lease and left town after the father was laid off by IBM, Molly thought the hardship of finding a place to meet was finally over for the two of them; after all, the heat and electricity were still on, and the house was furnished, nearby, empty, and not for sale. Dennis said that it was simply out of the question. He said he felt it would be tempting fate, and when she was impatient with that answer, he said that the idea of cheating on his wife with his babysitter in his parents' bed was such a psychic minefield that he doubted he would be able to perform at all. Molly thought that this was a little sentimental of him; she pointed out that the logistical difficulties of seeing him — walking through the woods, waiting behind trees, being dropped off by the side of the road — were very hard on her, hard enough that they might well outweigh some neurosis that he didn't even have yet but was only worried about developing. In the end, he was too afraid of her displeasure. When he finally consented, on the condition that they use only the guest bedroom, Molly felt simply that common sense had triumphed; though his distress — and her power to make him do something so rich in significance for him, so discomfiting — was not lost on her.

In the new, narrow bed, his obsession with variety continued; often he would want to change positions three or four times in the course of one encounter. At first Molly had thought this was a courtesy to her, an assumption that she would want to try new things (which she did) that she'd never had the opportunity to try before. But it went on like that, like he was trying to pose her for a deck of dirty playing cards or something; and it dawned on her that he was searching for a particular reaction from her. Not just trying to make her come — she did come, sometimes — but to find something that would make her lose control of herself, make her feel she needed him. He was a submissive man more by nature than by desire, because he still dreamed, apparently, of dominating her, of seeing her beholden to him, a dream that he couldn't make come true.

Of course it wasn't as cathartic now as it had been the first time – or the first time with Ty Crawford, when she couldn't imagine such a thing as a sexual routine and thought it would be that self-consuming, that final, every time. But a long sexual relationship introduced its own dynamics, the unromantic awakening of the senses, the grind of repetition, the powerful reduction of everything that attempted to make sex stand for something greater than itself. Passion as a kind of drug, in the sense that it granted you an absence from yourself. Besides, even to the extent that it did become boring, what was there in Molly's life to take its place? Sometimes she became depressed, but the remarkable thing, she found, was that the sex itself could also be used as an instrument of her depression, a way in which to negate herself, to lose faith in everything.

"Do you ever feel," she asked Dennis once, in the first few minutes on the bed when there was still room for talking, "like just a body?"

"What do you mean?"

"Just, like a body. Like all your thoughts or your feelings, everything you normally think of as being part of you, has just, I don't know, flaked off; but your senses are still there, and the truth is you're just this body that needs to be fed or that's food for somebody else."

He lifted his head. "Is that how I make you feel?"

"No. That's not what I meant. Never mind, it was stupid."

She wanted to say to him sometimes: You're screwing your seventeen-year-old babysitter; you'd be the envy of every male friend of yours, if they knew. Is this the real meaning of fantasies, that if they ever came true you couldn't enjoy them? But he wasn't the type to be able to enjoy it thoroughly – he worried too much. He even worried that if he ever took her too much for granted she might turn on him, expose him even if it meant shaming herself – everyone would think it was his fault anyway. But that was a fear based on nothing. Once Molly had waited for him by Route 2 for an hour and he never showed: she had had to walk three miles home. The next day at the Vincents' he came home early, in a panic to get her aside and apologize almost tearfully, imagining her furious and vengeful. But she knew what sort of thing must have gone wrong the day before. She would never let him get to her like that.

It was fall, then winter, of her senior year. College catalogues arrived in the mail for her, from all over the country, some by request, most not. The type was large, the words were vague, the pictures were a kind of gentle censorship: they looked like advertisements. It wasn't possible to learn anything from them. Molly thought optimistically about living in a big city, Boston or New York or San Francisco, but beyond that she had no idea where she wanted to go, when it was time for going.

"What about Michigan? I hear Michigan is great," Dennis said. He had traveled very little in his life and wasn't able to be helpful; but then he didn't really want to be helpful anyway.

"I don't know," Molly said. "I think I'd rather be in a city, but I'm really not sure about anything at this point."

"Of course, there are good schools right around here. Union is an excellent school. Bard's not too far, maybe that would be a good place for you, Bard. You could still come home a lot."

She looked at him.

"What?" he said. "Okay, maybe I would have a little stake in that."

"Really? But this will be over with before then, don't you think?"

Dennis agreed with her, but he winced anyway to hear her say it. Whether or not they were still lovers next fall, it would be hard for him to see her leave town. As ever, he treated it as something that would happen to him rather than something he might conceivably try to influence or prevent. He had imagined at the beginning that the whole affair would somehow run its course, end as inevitably as he believed it to have started; but lately the whole thing had taken on a different imagery for him, which was that when it ended, he would be old. Though he never said so, he was waiting for her to end it.

Molly spent a little less time with her friends now, but not that much; actually, the greater difference in the amount of time she now spent hanging out with Annika – giving her some pretext for putting off the return to her parents, though it was true that the longer she waited, the drunker they were – was due to the fact that Annika was going out with a boy in their class named Mike Lloyd, a short, strong, soft-spoken boy. Mike was on the wrestling team, and on every winter Friday he had to make weight for that weekend's competition, which sometimes meant spending Thursday night jogging in a rubber suit or spitting for hours into a can. He seemed so much less intelligent than Annika. But he was awestruck by her, given to writing poems about her which his friends would steal and shout aloud in the cafeteria; and Annika's own emotional longing for at least the appearance of constancy was not to be underestimated. Molly took a pleasure in their happiness which, though genuine, was nevertheless tinged with condescension toward the ordinariness of it.

The girls sat drinking in the TV room at Justine's house, on a Friday afternoon. "You should have seen this place," Tia said. "It's near the Albany airport. My brother said just giving me the name and address would cost me a bottle of one–fifty–one."

"Speaking of which," Lucy said, standing up unsteadily and heading for the kitchen.

"I don't know how it stays open – there must be some serious bribery going on there somewhere. Because it's all totally out in the open. They didn't even ask me for an ID. And then in the parking lot this kid, this boy who was like twelve *maybe,* came up and offered me five bucks to buy him a bottle of Bacardi. I should have told him I was a cop! Hey Moll, where were you yesterday?"

"Home," Molly said. "We had this thing where my father was bringing people home from work for dinner, and I promised my mother I'd help her clean up."

Her intimacy with a man her friends all knew, and addressed as Mr Vincent, was never a secret which she wished she could have told somebody. That would have tainted it. If you told someone, then thereafter, if, say, you were getting Dennis off with your hand while he drove, you might as well have been doing it for an audience, doing it for someone else's amazement.

As for the boys in school, they were a considerable nuisance. It seemed that the lesson Ty Crawford had drawn from his encounter with Molly (which was never repeated) was that he was more of an ordinary guy, more a part of the world, than he had allowed himself to think; ordinariness, in that sense, was what he had dreamed of since his accident. The only way to ratify this knowledge, though, was to make sure everyone else knew about it. And within a few weeks, they did: every boy had Molly Howe on his mental list of girls who would do it, girls about whom their fantasies had some small purchase on the real. The fact that she had let herself be deflowered by a sort of freak just hinted at a broad streak of perversion which they didn't understand but also didn't mind in the least. They asked her out constantly. They tried the three or four things they knew, things they had picked up from TV or the movies, mostly: one sent her flowers and a poem; one gave her a speech about how different she was from the other girls, how he had picked that up right away, how he would protect her from those who didn't understand her; one went up to her when she was at her locker and whispered in her ear that his cock was ten inches long. He didn't do it on a dare or for the benefit of any buddies snickering nearby – he actually thought this was what a girl like Molly wanted to hear. She turned them all down. It wasn't that she imagined she was too good for them now, or that she thought of herself as faithful to her older lover; but she knew what was going on, and she had no desire to put herself in a position where she was going to have to fight somebody off.

Frustrated, the boys began to make fun of Ty, saying that he must have been so bad in bed that he'd turned Molly into a lesbian. Ty didn't mind; it wasn't so long ago that nobody would have dared to make fun of someone as unfortunate as him, over anything.

In the evenings she sat in her room and read *The Stranger* or

Sister Carrie or whatever they were doing in Honors English that week; sometimes she read ahead. Her father was concerned that her grades in the subjects she cared about were so much higher than those in the subjects that bored her, like trigonometry; he thought this was going to prevent her from getting into a good college. And her extracurricular activities (at least as he would define them) were nonexistent. The school was putting on *Our Town* in April; why didn't she try out for it? Molly said no right away, so as not to get his hopes up, then went to her room and thought it over. The high school mounted two productions a year, three shows of each, and she had been to every single one since freshman year – *The Fantasticks, The Glass Menagerie, Godspell*. She admired people who could act, but that didn't mean she wanted to try it herself. She was a little afraid of it, actually – not of doing it badly but of doing it well. She wondered if she had that capacity to forget, even for a couple of hours, who and where she was.

In bed in his childhood home, Dennis would tell Molly the things he was privy to as a kind of civic figure in Ulster. He told her that the woman who had taught her kindergarten class was having an affair with the man who ran the hardware store, and who was just about to declare bankruptcy. He told her that the kid who used to work at the Mobil station had not joined the Marines at all – he had left town with money stolen from his parents, who made up the story to cover their shame. He told her how many times in the last month the town sheriff had been called out to Annika's house, to try to settle down her parents. He wasn't being insensitive; he had no idea Molly and Annika were friends, because she never mentioned her life at school, except for scheduling purposes, and he never asked about it, not wanting to have his sense of his own perversion stirred up by any reminder of how young Molly really was.

"You know what I wonder?" Molly said. She lay on her stomach, and Dennis sat beside her tracing with his fingertips the unflawed skin from her shoulder blades to the backs of her knees. "Has there ever been a day when you've come here, fucked me, and then gone home that same night and fucked your wife?"

The tracing stopped. "What would you want to know a thing like that for?"

"It wouldn't bother me, really. I was just curious about it. Don't you think it's an interesting question?"

"No."

"What, too intimate?"

He sighed. " 'Fuck' seems like such an angry word to me. Anyway, no. That's never happened. It's a pretty easy situation to avoid. She has a very exhausting life just now. I know it must be hard for you to imagine a life like that, but just wait."

That was the last time she ever saw him.

The golf course closed shortly after someone drove a car on to it at night and did doughnuts on the fairways. One of the officers of the charity organized by the IBM spouses was caught stealing from it to make her own mortgage payment; not long afterward the charity voted to dissolve itself.

On a Friday afternoon in March, misty and warm, Molly got off the bus at the stop nearest the Vincents' and walked up to the front door with her jacket tied around her waist. She knocked, and a few seconds later Joyce Vincent opened the door. She was not dressed in one of the smart, boxy suits that generally indicated she was going back to the office. Nor, Molly saw, was she wearing any makeup. In fact she had been crying, which made her silence now all the more unsettling. The children were not in sight behind her. She stood in the doorway staring up at Molly – who was now taller than she was – with a look of utter disbelief, as if the girl were someone she had been told was dead.

"I'm here," Molly said, confused.

Joyce's head pulled back slightly at the sound of Molly's voice. There seemed to be something she wanted to say but a few seconds went by and she couldn't get it out. The corners of her mouth turned down. Then she slammed the door in Molly's face.

Molly waited on the porch. There was no sound within the house. In a minute or two she turned to face the street, and the meaning of what had just happened began to bear down toward her as if on wings. She tried to figure out what had to happen now. For one thing, she had no way to get home. She knew a few shortcuts through the woods but it was still four miles at least. Lightheaded, she descended the porch steps.

As she grew more and more tired she really only wished that the trip were longer – that it would take her days of solitary hiking, sleeping under the moon, to get back home. She didn't have any idea what a woman in Joyce Vincent's position might do. All she knew was that she liked Joyce and was sorry she had been hurt. That hadn't been the intention. If there were two worlds to live in, then everyone's feelings could be spared, which is how Molly would have wanted it; but now the two worlds had fused back into one.

It was twilight when she finally walked through her own front door. At first she thought no one else was home because she heard no sounds from the television or the kitchen, no voices, no hiss from the dishwasher. But when she turned the corner into the living room, her mother and father were sitting there, Kay with her face turned away, Roger with his fist held up to his mouth. They sat in their chairs like two characters from the last act of *Our Town*.

The phone rang.

"Don't answer it," Roger said.

Instead she went up to her room. They didn't follow her. She stayed there most of the weekend.

It turned out that Dennis's parents' house was so ideally suited for secret trysts that within months of its vacancy it had been discovered by the high-schoolers in Ulster too; they used it to get high, or when it was too cold for the playground, or for the same purpose as Dennis and Molly. Someone must have seen them arriving, or leaving, or in the act. It could have been Annika and her boyfriend for all Molly knew. She never found out.

Monday morning Kay didn't come out of her room. Molly wanted to talk to her but she understood it would have to wait. She herself had slept a lot the last two days, at first as a refuge from depression but later out of a developing sense that the worst had happened and so there was really nothing more to worry about. Her father didn't say a word to her either. He tried to make his silence seem like punishment but she could see that the truth was he had no idea what to say. It was the sort of offense that made all his authority seem like a fiction, lighter than air. Then, as she was on her way out the door for school, Roger said to her, "Have you told any of your friends about this?"

"About what?" she said.

His nostrils flared. "Don't make me say it."

But that was what she wanted; if she was to be shamed, she had decided, she didn't want to be shamed by euphemisms. Still, she felt sorry for him then. "Of course I haven't," she said.

"Good. Don't. We have to figure out a way to keep this all under wraps."

But it was too late for that already. Joyce Vincent had considered the matter and had settled upon the course of public exposure as retribution for her husband. For one thing, she had thrown him out of the house and needed an explanation for it. Her defaming him, on the phone and then in person with all her friends and family, was mostly retributive, because she felt that he had disgraced her irremediably – that her home had been blown apart not by a sexual folly but by the proof it provided of his utter lack of regard for her, what she did and what she went through. Had he betrayed her with someone she had never met, or even someone she just didn't know very well, she might have found a way to put it behind her; instead, though, in the evenings, after the confused, tearful children were put to bed, Joyce sat up helplessly sorting through the memories of the hundreds of times she had welcomed Molly into her home, kissed the girl, gossiped with her, played the mother to her because her own mother was known to be unreliable, done small favors for her, entrusted her children to her. She heard the voice that said she was punishing the kids by kicking their father out – that a better person than her would find a way to forgive even this, for their sake – but Joyce was who she was and there was only so much that could be asked of her. She couldn't think which was worse: if the two of them, lying together, had smiled lewdly at their conspiracy to mock and degrade her, or if they had never even given a thought to her at all.

In school everyone cleared a path for Molly as if she were on fire. She felt the eyes on her at her locker, in the girls' bathroom between periods, felt the silence she created wherever she walked. At lunch she arrived early and sat at her usual table; when Justine and Tia got there, they coaxed each other with impatient glances for a minute before Tia finally said, in a whisper, "So is it true?"

Molly shrugged. "Yeah, it's true," she said.

They weren't really sure what to ask after that. Molly had found the limits of their apathy; in their eyes, she had gone too far – there were kids involved, after all – and for what? Dennis himself had never been considered one of the best-looking older men in town anyway. But they suppressed any desire to ask for details, sexual or otherwise. It was the hostility of the whole thing – the way Molly must have known all along, as they were finding out only now, that their own supposed intimacy with her was really just an indulgence, a lie – that surprised and, ultimately, estranged them. As for Annika, she never came to lunch that day at all.

It wasn't bad, Molly thought stoically as she sat alone on the bus at the end of the first day, this sort of amazed ostracism. Because all it signified was that she was not one of them. She had always known it. Now everyone knew it.

But she wasn't familiar with the other feelings that feelings of difference engendered. They were not about to esteem her for taking them all by surprise. They would not long be content to leave her alone. Whispers behind her back, which turned into accusations in her face: she didn't really care. Ridiculous pranks: someone poured a can of motor oil through the vent in her locker. Someone painted the word WHORE on her gym-locker door. Then one morning she opened the front door of their house and the word had been painted there too.

Roger called in sick to work that day, to think and repaint his door and try to find some safe point of escape for all the fury he felt inside him. If he could have he might have tried to find and beat Dennis Vincent – Roger had never beaten anyone in his life, but he had rage on his side, and Vincent was a small man; and even the alternative, which was taking the beating himself, was bound to be more cathartic than doing nothing. But Dennis had vanished: quit his job, left town with a car full of clothes; wherever he was he kept phoning his former home, asking to speak to his children, but his wife forbade it. She did not want Kevin and Bethany, if she could help it, to grow up with any version of the catastrophe other than her own. Dennis never tried to contact Molly; perhaps he was too afraid one of her parents would answer the phone. Or perhaps he had come around to blaming her somehow for the whole thing. In any case, he was probably not very far away; but when it came to such an exotic task as locating a man who was in hiding, Roger Howe had no resources at all.

A full week went by before he suddenly appeared in the doorway of Molly's room, finally seized by the courage to talk about it. Molly had had a lot of time to prepare and had decided that this conversation was at least going to have the merit of complete candor.

He stood with his back to the dresser, his hands behind him. Molly sat on the bed.

"I suppose the first thing I should ask you," he said, "is whether this, whether you were forced or in any way felt you were under duress, threatened . . ."

"No."

He nodded, neither pleased nor displeased, his lips pressed together. "Because I know that an adult can be a real figure of authority, and can trade on that—"

"No, it wasn't like that. No one forced me to do anything."

"You wanted to do it?"

"I did it of my own will."

"Whose idea was it, whose initiative?"

"His."

"And at some point he expressed this idea to you."

"Yes. But in a conversation. He didn't force himself on me or anything like that."

"How long did it go on?"

"About six months, I guess."

"You guess. Were you – was it your – well, never mind about that. I don't know why it matters. How long was it supposed to go on?"

"Sorry?"

"When was it going to end? When you went to college? Or was it going to continue after that?"

"Probably not."

"Probably not. So you just thought it could go on indefinitely. Did you really think you wouldn't get caught?"

"Yes, actually. I really did think that. Maybe that was stupid."

"You didn't want to get caught, on some level? Maybe to get Joyce out of the way? Or maybe to ruin Dennis's life, because you were really—"

"No, Dad. I honestly didn't think anyone would ever find out about it." She paused, and in the pause reminded herself of her resolve to leave nothing unsaid. "That was the whole point of doing it. To not get caught doing it."

Roger sighed, and walked to the window. "So you weren't in love with him."

"No," Molly said, and couldn't quite suppress a small laugh that went along with it. He spun around.

"Don't you laugh at me," he said, his voice shaking. "Don't you do that. You think I like asking these questions? The only reason I'm doing it is because I still think it's important for some reason that I know more about what's happened to my family than the woman at the drugstore or my secretary at work or your classmates at school."

Molly's strength wavered. She'd never seen her father like this – suffering beyond his ability to try to pretend otherwise. Still, while she was genuinely sorry for the pain she had caused him, she also couldn't help thinking that that pain was outsized, misdirected, that for some reason she couldn't figure out he was intent on making this an even bigger deal than it really was.

"But I couldn't expect you to give a damn about that," he said. "How you can sit there, with that blank expression on your face—"

"I can't help the expression on my face."

"—and just blithely ruin two families, and you don't even seem sorry about it."

"Ruin? How are we ruined?"

But he didn't pay attention to that. "Dennis Vincent was a friend of mine, you know."

"I never heard you—"

"I considered him a friend of mine. Which just makes the whole thing that much—" He stopped himself. "Well, this whole thing is my fault somehow, I won't run from that. But the point is I don't see how we can stay here now. I'm laughed at everywhere I go."

"Daddy, I don't—"

"I can quit work, of course. What are they going to do, fire me? But it'll probably mean turning down the job in Armonk."

"What are you *talking* about?"

"It's the worst possible time to sell the house, of course, but we'll have to take the hit—"

"We were ruined already!" Molly said. Her own calm was in pieces now. Roger, his eyebrows low, folded his arms and stared at her. She had found her way through his defenses, to the anger at her there, and she was no longer so sure that candor would be their salvation. But she pushed on.

"I mean, what is it you think you've lost? You're not friends with the Vincents anymore, that's true; and I'm not a virgin, that's true too, but if it makes any difference to you, I wasn't one before either. As for the rest of it, this town will be a ghost town in a year, everyone knows that. I really can't believe that all the people in Ulster who are going to be broke and unemployed soon, if they aren't already, are as concerned with your daughter's sex life as you think they are. What do they care? And this house is breaking up anyway. Richard's gone, I'm almost gone, you'll sell it in a year either way. There's not much left of it to break up. All these things were already happening. So why are you making such a big thing about me and Dennis?"

His arms were still folded, but the look on his face was now

132

more like fright. He couldn't believe, quite apart from the truth of anything she was saying, that she would have the disregard for him to say them at all.

"I'm very sorry that you and Mom are in such pain because of me, but I can't help it, I don't know why you care so much what everyone else thinks."

"All I care about," he said softly, "is you."

She winced at the onset of tears. He still can't say what he means, Molly thought. All I care about is you. He could have picked that up in any of a hundred places. She stood up and put her arms around him, carefully, as if he were much older than he was.

"I'm fine," Molly said earnestly. "I'm perfectly okay. Nothing bad has happened to me. So why can't that please be the end of it?"

The best reason to go to school, really, was to get away from this conversation, and from the problem of how far to go, out of pity for her family, in apologizing for things she didn't really feel sorry for. But school was breaking her down as well. She wasn't as impervious to their rejection of her as she had thought; not that she minded being an outsider, but why return day after day to a place just to show that you didn't belong there? To make matters worse, she was now constantly propositioned, in all sincerity, by the same boys who taunted her in public. There was little difference between the taunts and the come-ons: she was viewed as a source, as a locus of dreamily unfettered sex, and they were never going to leave her alone now, never going to stop trying to stumble on to the secret of something they had no hope of understanding. Finally one Monday just a month before exams she stayed home; she had her father call the principal's office to say she had mononucleosis and would like her homework assignments sent to her at home until further notice. They knew he was lying. They sounded grateful about it.

She had a fantasy that Annika would be the one to deliver the assignments to her: but it was only a freshman boy who lived at Bull's Head, drafted into this extra duty by the principal himself. The boy smiled nervously, involuntarily, whenever the Howes' door was opened to him, as if he were visiting the home of a celebrity.

When she couldn't take it any longer she went and presented herself to her mother, sitting patiently on the end of Kay's bed, staring searchingly at her, waiting to be spoken to. Her parents were more alike than she had ever understood. Barely speaking to each other, they had nonetheless between them frothed up this scandalous incident until it grew large enough to contain the explanations for all the damage life had done to them. The fundamental difference between them − which held their marriage together as effectively as a similarity might have done − was that Roger felt he must be responsible in some way for every bad thing that happened, while Kay felt that the whirl-wind of bad things around her was responsible for the wreck of her own early promise.

Kay lay on the bedcovers in a blue sweatsuit. Molly had never seen her dressed this way before: she must have decided that this was the garment of the woman who had been brought too low to care how she looked anymore.

"How could you do this to me?" Kay said wearily.

"I didn't mean to do anything to you, Mom. You can't take it all so personally. It's something I did, not something I did to you. I'm sorry if it hurt you."

"We're ruined in this town! Our reputation is destroyed!"

"But why do you care? I've never heard you say a good word about this town or the people in it my whole life. Why does their opinion mean anything?"

"Don't get smart with me! This is my home, that's why!"

"All my life all you've told me—"

"Don't tell me what I've told you!" she said, raising herself on her elbows. "All the hard work I put into raising you right, just so I could be the mother of the town slut?"

"Mom," Molly said, trying not to cry, "can't we forget everyone else just for a few minutes? If this is the last time you and I ever talk, can't we at least find a way to say what we mean?"

But Kay went on talking about how she had been victimized until Molly realized her mother wasn't even speaking to her anymore – she was speaking more to posterity. She never got it all talked out. She did not understand her judges.

On 17 April the mail brought Molly's acceptances to Bennington, Reed, and Tulane; she was rejected by Columbia and Stanford. A few more rejections came in over the next few days. Molly had no one to share the news with; she no longer knew what connection these letters had to her future anyway.

She passed all her exams, taking them unproctored on her dining-room table. No one cared if she cheated or not. She skipped graduation, getting her diploma in the mail. All they had taken from her was something she had never really valued anyway; still, it wore on her, and she didn't like the feeling of having nowhere to go.

In the middle of the night, in the darkened house, Molly came downstairs to the kitchen with a blanket around her shoulders and called Richard in Berkeley. He was home for once; it was after midnight there as well. Some sort of Indian music droned quietly in the background. She told him the whole story.

"I'm sorry to dump this on you," Molly said quietly, afraid of waking her parents, "but I don't have anyone else I can talk to. I'm stuck in my room in the middle of nowhere with these two lunatics who keep telling me I've brought a plague on our house. Okay, yes, I had an affair with a married man and maybe I shouldn't have done it, maybe I should have foreseen all this somehow, but still, I don't understand what they want from me. I don't know what to do. I know they want me out of here. I'm supposed to go to college in four months. Dad's out of work in another eight and they haven't even bothered to put the house on the market yet. I can just imagine going up to him right now anyway and asking him for twenty grand so I can go to Bennington or wherever."

"Do you want to go to Bennington?" Richard's voice was a lot slower and more soothing than she remembered it, like a voice on the radio. He didn't sound high, though. She knew she should take the opportunity to ask him more about how he'd been doing; but it was just such a relief to find someone who could talk calmly with her about the whole thing.

"No. I mean, no more there than anywhere else. I don't know. The most appealing thing about it is getting the hell out of here."

"So don't go. Take a year off. Take five years off. What's the law that says you have to finish learning things when you're twenty-two?"

"And do what in the meantime?"

"I don't know," he said. "Come out here and live with me for a while. Something different. Til you get everything else figured out."

At that, Molly started sobbing. One act of kindness was all it took now. Richard said nothing to try to quiet or comfort her; he waited patiently for her to get control of herself.

"Oh, right, that'll go over real big," she said, when she had settled down a bit. "I'd have to ask Dad for the money for that, too. A little vacation for me, I'm sure that's just what he's thinking about, a little gift he can give me."

"Ask him. I think I know him better than you do. Ask him."

When she asked him, his expression never changed. He waited until he was sure she had finished talking, and then he said, "How much do you need?"

A few weeks later, near the end of a hot June day, Molly walked aimlessly through the quiet, cool rooms of her house. Her parents were out. A cab was coming in the morning to take her to the airport in Albany. She was all packed. The narcissus and the daffodils Kay had planted years ago were browning in the sun; the paint was cracking on the vacant houses in the development; Molly went out on to the porch barefoot to listen to the sounds of the valley and to see if it all looked any less familiar to her now that she was relatively sure she would never lay eyes on it again.

On the road in front of the house a young girl was riding her bike. She rode in a lazy figure-eight right by the Howes, pedaling slowly, not looking where she was going unless she had to. She was overweight, and wore a big loose Little Mermaid T-shirt over pink bicycle shorts. She turned around to pass the house again and Molly saw that it was Bethany Vincent. When she noticed that Molly had seen her, she stopped circling and slid forward off the seat so her feet were flat on the road. Molly stood waiting for a minute or more, but Bethany's expression never clarified; the sun was right in the girl's face, and she held up one hand as a visor over her eyes. When Molly started down the porch steps Bethany hopped back up on to the seat of her bike and rode away.

JOHN WOULD HAVE felt at home in a world governed by an unspoken compact ordaining that anytime anything awkward or unpleasant happened, everyone involved would agree to forget about it and to go forward as if it had never happened at all. This may have been less a fantasy than a kind of vestigial memory of his childhood in Asheville, North Carolina, in particular of the houses of some of his older relatives, whose genuinely terrible secrets were held aloft by a magical understanding that any break in the chain of pleasantry would result in those secrets' crashing noisily to the floor in plain view of everyone. But John lived in New York now; and somehow he had surrounded himself with people who had no capacity for ignoring things that were difficult to explain – most conspicuously at work, where Roman spent the days immediately following the Doucette debacle glowering at him from across their office, ostentatiously awaiting some explanation for John's failure to mention his friendship with Mal Osbourne. John soldiered on as best he could, cordial and red-faced. On the subsequent Monday Roman didn't come in at all. Only by checking with the receptionist did John learn that his partner had decided to take a week's vacation.

Rebecca, too, tried hard to be supportive when he told her of the strain on his relationship with Roman; but she had trouble getting past the fact that he had never even said anything to his partner about that bizarre Saturday with Osbourne. It was kind of a funny story, she thought; certainly there was nothing embarrassing or shameful about it. Why keep it a secret?

"Don't you feel you guys are friends?" she asked gently. "I know we don't see them much outside of work—"

"We're friends," John said glumly.

"You trust him, right? Wouldn't he trust you as well? I mean, why *wouldn't* he?"

"You're probably right." He wanted to bring the conversation to a close by making every concession.

But she was too perplexed. "Aren't you assuming that he would think the worst of you? That he'd think you were lying, you were ambitious, you scheduled the whole thing because you somehow knew the Doucette review was coming up and then you lied about it?"

"I see your point," John said.

"Well, have you ever given him any reason to think that way about you?"

He sighed.

"Of course you haven't," she answered herself. "You should just have told him. Now you've turned nothing into something."

John didn't welcome being analyzed and so he agreed with her. There was a part of him, though, that held a more self-justifying view: We live in the age of directness, he thought; circumspection, the art of leaving things unsaid, is a lost one.

Still, he knew that no such formulation could answer the charge that his silence had been pointless, and he was desperate for things to go back to the way they had been. When Roman came back from his petulant vacation, John took him out to the Tenth Avenue Grill for drinks and told him the complete story of his dealings with Mal Osbourne, all its unlikelihoods intact, laced with apologies but pointing out also, in his own defense, how unbelievable it all seemed. He could tell that in Roman's mind, miffed though he was, the whole Doucette episode was already just about consecrated to the past, to the war-story pantheon, even though they were still less than three weeks removed from the trip to Philadelphia (which meant that John had not yet received his handwritten letter from Osbourne about his "exciting new venture," so he didn't need to worry about whether to throw in that detail as well).

Roman, though he struggled not to show it, gradually began to find the whole thing funny. He shook his head. "Chocolate sculpture," he said. "Well, as furious as I was the day of the pitch, I sure would have been sorry to miss it. It was one of the most demented things I've ever seen."

John, relieved, ordered two more drinks.

"I guess I can see why you didn't tell anyone," Roman said. "Still, I wish you'd told me a week ago, at least."

"Why?"

Roman smiled into his scotch glass. " 'Cause I went to Canning and said I wanted somebody else to work with, that's why."

Next morning they went together to Canning's office; with a viselike contraption balanced on his knees, the boss was trying to tie his own flies. "We kissed and made up," Roman said.

"Thank God," Canning said. "Now if you'll excuse me."

"So who were you going to partner me with?" Roman asked.

"I hadn't even thought about it. Things like this happen all the time around here. It's like a fucking junior high school. Now go and sin no more."

Everything became as it had been. The two of them came up with some spots for a fruit juice that won the account for the agency (now called Canning & Leigh) and led to Dale and Andrea – laid off in the wake of the Doucette disaster – being rehired. John and Roman even got to go to Malibu to oversee the production of the first two spots. It was a different world. Their director was about seventy-five years old, with a deep tan and long, chalk-white hair; he showed up on the set the first day scowling and waving a rolled-up copy of the script.

"Where's the cum shot?" he barked at them. "You left it out."

"Sorry?" said John.

"Fucking New York," the director said. "They think they invented everything. Do you know how many commercials I've directed?"

"Excuse me," Roman said, before the director could supply the number, " 'cum shot,' is that what you said?"

He looked at them murderously. An assistant was walking by with a tray full of unrefrigerated bottles of the fruit juice, to be used as props in one of the shots; the director grabbed one off the tray, unscrewed the top, tilted his head back, and poured the juice into his mouth from a height of about eight inches, so that some of it splashed off his perfect false teeth. He then lowered his gaze to Roman and John again, juice dripping off his chin.

"Idiots!" he said.

When they returned from the coast it was winter, just like that. The sun bounced off the roofs and the store windows. The plows came by after each snowfall to expose the streets, and the parked cars, up to their door handles in the resultant gray drifts, stayed half-hidden like cats in a meadow for weeks at a time. John wore his sunglasses on the walk to the subway in the morning, his breath steaming in front of him. The months that passed so quietly included his thirtieth birthday. He was less worried about growing old than he was consternated by the idea that thirty years – an enormous wedge of time – had now amassed behind him, without any correspondingly enormous sense of having lived.

He had never really stopped waiting for the promised communication from Mal Osbourne, though he wasn't certain of the tone of his anticipation: amusement, or genuine excitement at the prospect of a career change, or simple curiosity as to whether the "exciting new venture" his erstwhile boss was planning had any existence at all outside the broad boundaries of Osbourne's ego. Then one Saturday afternoon in April, John and Rebecca came home from the Twenty-third Street flea market with an oval mirror and a wall clock; by the time Rebecca had finished holding the mirror up in a couple of different places, hanging up her coat, and checking for phone messages, John had gone through the mail and had read the letter from Osbourne twice through. He held it out to her without a word and went to the kitchen, laughing soundlessly and shaking his head, to make them both some tea.

Dear Colleague:

In 1973 I entered the advertising business as an intern at Doyle Dane Bernbach in New York. The Creative Revolution, so-called, had carried the day — I remember there was a great big blowup beside the elevator of Bill Bernbach's great "Lemon" ad for Volkswagen, the ad that started it all — and a revolution seemed to be taking place outside the tiny confines of our office as well. In music, in literature, in radical politics, it seemed to me that what was happening was less a political movement than a movement to restore the idea of truth in language, of plain speaking — a kind of democratic speech to set against the totalitarian language of the times. "We had to destroy the village in order to save it" — I wonder how many of you reading this will even be old enough to remember that one. Anyway, advertising seemed like a part of this process. After a hundred years of the hard sell, honesty and plain speech was making its way into the unlikeliest place of all, the language of commerce. It was an exciting time.

Recently I turned on my television and saw another spot for Volkswagen — I don't even know who has the account now — which ended with the tag "Perfect for your life. Or your complete lack thereof." And it came to me at that moment that, thirty years after the "revolution" I thought I was a part of, our world seems to me to be held together right now by irony alone. Our culture propagates no values outside of the peculiar sort of self-negation implied in the wry smile of irony, the way we remove ourselves from ourselves in order to be

143

insulated from the terrible emptiness of the way we live now. That wry smile mocks self-knowledge, mocks the idea of right and wrong, mocks the notion that art is worth making at all.

I want to wipe that smile off the face of our age.

As most of you know by now, I have severed my ties with the agency which formerly bore my name. I have decided to devote the remainder of my working life to a new venture: I hesitate to call it an ad agency because that implies that it will be like other ad agencies for which you have worked, or are working. It will not. True, we will create advertising, and that advertising will be paid for by clients: but the advertising will be unlike anything the world has ever seen.

I am writing to you to ask you to join me in this venture. My letter will be postmarked from Charlottesville, Virginia, where I am overseeing renovation of the building which will house our activities. In other words, in order to join me it would be necessary to leave your current homes and relocate to this town, whose beauty and whose intellectual heritage (for those of you who have not visited before) are an integral part of the history of the United States.

By accepting this offer you will be on an automatic partnership track. In the meantime, though, I will do my best to make your salaries commensurate with the salaries you draw now. I don't want the sacrifice you're making to be any greater than it has to be. Besides, if our mission is to fail, then the fact that fair salaries may hasten that failure by a few months is by no means a negative prospect.

I will contact you upon my return from Virginia. Please take advantage of these weeks to talk over with your loved ones both the exigencies of this decision and the potential rewards of putting your unmatched talents toward a noble and original,

uncorrupted, ambitious purpose. The language of advertising is
the language of American life: American art, American politics,
American media, American law, American business. By
changing that language, we will, perforce, change the world.

Yours truly,
Malcolm Osbourne

"Dear Colleague?" Rebecca said, as John returned with the tea.
John smiled indulgently.

"He wants you to quit your job and move to Virginia, and
he sends a form letter?"

"He doesn't seem to be one for the social graces," John said.
"Anyhow, I can see it. He's busy down there overseeing all the
construction, can't sleep one night, he hammers out this letter
in one draft, takes it to—"

"Where does he get all the money, I wonder?" Rebecca said.
"The money?"

"To build this little Xanadu down there. It sounds like a big
undertaking."

"Maybe he has clients already," John said.

"Maybe he went to the bank," Rebecca said, deadpan.
"Maybe he went to the bank and said he needed a small-
business loan to wipe the smile off the face of our age."

Her sarcasm closed off any further conversation about it. John
was less cynical by nature. While Osbourne's plan might be a
crazy one, it never occurred to him that it was anything less
than sincere – that Osbourne was not set to try to do exactly
what he said he would do. You had to admire a man's sincerity,
John said (silently, to Rebecca who slept beside him), a man's

courage, even if he was doomed to failure. He lay awake and watched the shadow of the ceiling fan in their bedroom for what seemed like hours.

At the office Monday he found himself looking furtively into the faces of his colleagues, watching for some reflection of his own absentmindedness that might indicate someone else there had received a "Dear Colleague" letter too. But they looked as they always looked, poorly rested and unsurprisable. It might have meant that Osbourne had written to no one at the agency but him, or else that others simply had a better poker face than John did, which was certainly the case. Roman asked him once, when they were batting around ideas about the upcoming campaign for the Beef Council, if something was bothering him. He lied and said no.

He said nothing to anyone. It was easy to think of good reasons for his circumspection. For one, it might sound like he was lording it over his coworkers if he brought up the letter from Osbourne and no one else had received it: no one wants to be among the non-elect, even if the venture was one they would probably regard as insane. And there was no point in openly discussing another job opportunity, no matter how far-fetched, in your own office – it could only lead to repercussions, subtle or otherwise. Most of all, though, he had to admit, he was just reluctant to expose this whole idea to the kind of scorching cynicism he knew Roman and the others would unleash upon it. John knew they would react with jokes and insults, and would expect him to join in the mockery session, which he would eventually cave in and do.

A few days later they were still trying to find a way to help the beef sellers sell more beef. "Here's the thing," Roman said.

"At this point everybody knows beef is bad for you. It makes you fat, it clogs your arteries, it gives you cancer. It eats up the rain forest, cows fart and kill the ozone layer, blah blah blah. So you can't—"

"Everybody knows this?" John said.

"Well, maybe there are people in the Midwest who don't know it." The Midwest, for Roman, was more a psychic space than a geographic one, filled with conservative farm families who were virtual zombies of sincerity. "But those people are eating meat three meals a day already; they're not who the campaign's targeted at. They *couldn't* eat any more beef. We're aiming at the people who are trying to *cut down* on beef. They're doing it because it makes them feel smart. Stupid ads that show happy families barbecuing just reinforce their position. We have to beat them to the punch."

"By telling them that beef gives you heart attacks and causes global warming? *That' ll*—"

"By not pretending we don't know it. We know it and we're trying to get them to eat more meat anyway. We let them *know* we know it. That's the joke." He stood up and paced around the cramped office; as always when he was excited by an idea, he looked almost angry. " 'Six burgers a week. That's all we ask.' Just be up-front about it, and maybe give it that little extra sarcastic tweak, to let them know that we know. People really respond to that."

"Let them know that we know what?" John said.

Roman held out his hands. "That they know," he said.

John smiled uneasily, but he didn't say any more, intimidated by the force of Roman's confidence. He hadn't gotten into advertising in the first place to make any sort of statement, but rather to exercise, at something close to full capacity, his skills as an artist. If there were ideals in the service of which he wanted those skills employed, he might have become a painter, started a magazine, something in that line. But he had no specifically individual creative impulse. Nor did he care to spend the one life he was given in a state of righteous poverty – he didn't care about getting rich, but he also saw no reason to do without comforts that were easily within his grasp. So did his work then put forth the values, the beliefs, of whoever happened to hire him? On the contrary – in his experience, he and Roman were hired to do exactly as they pleased. The clients might be unhappy with the results, even to the point of withdrawing their business; but while he was working, John was left alone.

So what was behind the work they did? John knew that most people would have assumed that he himself was behind it, he and Roman and their other colleagues; yet he put nothing of what he believed into it. He felt much more like an instrument – an instrument of what seemed, especially after his we-know-that-they-know conversation with Roman, like a vast and powerful blankness, an opacity. Of course, maybe this was just a lie he was telling himself in order to displace his own responsibility (not for beef consumption, about which he couldn't have cared less, but for the blankness itself). Or maybe there was something substantive behind that opacity and he just wasn't astute enough to make out what it was.

He didn't say anything about all this, to anyone. He let Roman take the six-burgers-a-week idea to Canning, who loved it, and told them to come up with five more spots in time for the trip out to Omaha at the end of the month.

One Wednesday evening John got home before Rebecca and picked up the mail downstairs. Out fell a postcard of Monticello; it was addressed to him but had no other salutation. On it was written, "Cynicism is not useless – only we're conditioned to be cynical about the wrong things. Before it's too late let us try to reconnect with the better angels of our nature." It was unsigned. John felt his heart quicken as he stared at the Virginia postmark. He stuck the postcard under a magnet on the refrigerator door; but after looking at it for a few seconds he took it down again and hid it beneath some magazines on his bedside table, where Rebecca wouldn't see it.

He didn't know why he should be afraid to tell anyone what he was thinking. Still, he couldn't figure out an angle from which to approach the subject with his girlfriend. Then one night, as they were riding the subway home from the multiplex across from Lincoln Center, she brought up, for the first time in at least a year, the subject of marriage.

"I just would feel better," she said, holding his arm, "if there were some kind of plan about it, if we knew what we were doing."

"Feel better?" he said. "You mean you don't feel good right now?"

"I feel okay," she said. "Just, I don't know, a little sad. From time to time, not always. And not because I feel unfulfilled because I don't have a baby or any crap like that. It's just . . . time is passing, you know? Time is passing. And I don't even notice it. We're so busy that it's very easy not to notice."

They were in the front car, and as they rocketed through the darkness John could see each station, grimy white, floodlit, bracketed by thin pillars, turning into view a few seconds before the brakes' drawn-out screech.

"I think it's time," John said. Rebecca kept staring straight ahead. "I've been feeling sad, too, since you mention it. Sad about being stuck, you know? That's the sense I have, when I get a chance to look up from what I'm doing. Being stuck."

"Well, we shouldn't get married just to cheer ourselves up."

"Of course not. But I think our moods are trying to tell us something. It's time for . . . it's time for Act Two. Do you know what I mean?"

The train stopped at Chambers Street, and when it did she kissed him lightly.

"But when I think about it," he said, trying to keep his tone light, "I think about other things, too. Other changes I want to make."

"Like?"

"Like I don't think I want to raise a family in New York. I know that's one of the reasons we moved out to Brooklyn, but I've just changed my mind about it, what can I say. It doesn't seem sufficiently different, to me. Brooklyn, I mean."

"Well then where would you want to go?" she said softly. "Out to the suburbs, or what?"

"Oh there's no way—"

"Thank God, me neither."

"I was thinking of something more radically different. I mean it has to be a city, or near a city, because otherwise you and I couldn't keep doing what we do. Not a lot of ad agencies in small towns. But I wouldn't mind, to be totally honest with you, moving back down South."

His heart had begun racing.

"Back down South?" Rebecca said. "You mean like nearer your family?"

"That's not what I was thinking of, though there wouldn't be anything wrong with being a little closer to them than we are now, particularly if we have children."

"What are you thinking of, then?"

Suddenly they were there, and John hesitated, trying not to lose his nerve. "Actually," he said, "and I know you'll laugh, or have some reaction, but I've been thinking pretty seriously about—"

"Oh God," Rebecca said. "Not Virginia? Not the Mal Osbourne thing?"

His fear of crossing that threshold went beyond the fear of disagreement. Rebecca had a strong temper and a sharp style and thus won most of their arguments, arguments which John had little stomach for anyway: but the timidity he felt in those few seconds was more like a fear of sincerity, a reluctance to show himself even to the person closest to him in the world, and it infuriated him. "Yes," he said, feeling himself blush, "all right, god damn it, I'm thinking about the Mal Osbourne thing. I want to do it. I don't know why I should be embarrassed about what I want."

He had raised his voice to the point where others on the subway car turned to look, which was extraordinary for him; and Rebecca, seeing that he was upset, responded more gently. "You'd really just pick up and move to Virginia, just like that? Sell the apartment? I didn't realize you were that unhappy here."

"Well, first of all, it depends what you want to do. I mean

I'm not just telling you what I want like what I want is the only important thing. I know you have a chance to make partner, you've put in a lot of work toward that, and it would be hard to leave all that behind and start over."

They pulled into the Wall Street station. The doors opened on to the pale, water-stained mosaics and the dark vaulted ceilings. No one got on or off. When the train was moving noisily again, John resumed, his mouth close to her ear.

"But what I'm asking myself, the last few weeks, is why are we here? Why did we come here? It's the most expensive place to live in the country; we had to scrimp to buy a place we couldn't even raise children in, really. And would we want to raise kids here? Most of the children I meet here, teenagers, sons and daughters of my bosses or clients – they scare me. They're perfect and they know too much. Why did we come to this place? I think it's only because we were led here when we were too young to question it. If you want to work in advertising, this is where most of the famous agencies are. If you want to be a lawyer, this is where most of the famous law firms are. Well, now we know we're good enough to get those jobs. So is this still what we want?"

Rebecca was looking at him so intently she almost gave the impression of not listening to what he was saying. She was curious but not frightened. "Every couple over the age of twenty-five in New York has this same conversation," she said, "about why are we living here. I'm not so much interested in that. I'm more worried that you're not happy doing what you're doing. I was under a different impression all this time."

"Lately. Lately I'm not so happy with it. I'm asking myself questions about it. Not about selling out or serving big corporations or anything like that. More . . . aesthetic questions. About content."

"There are other businesses you could get into."

John shook his head. "It's not a bad business. It doesn't have to be. The stuff that Osbourne says about getting rid of the smirk, about saying something instead of finding new ways to say nothing – it touches some chord in me. I'm sorry if that seems silly. Trying to break that conspiracy between us and the audience, where everyone's scared to death to get caught taking anything seriously."

"Well," Rebecca said, still cautiously, "if you want to talk about having children: a certain desire for security goes along with that, you know? A certain anti-whimsy. Osbourne has no clients, no staff, no partners. You've only met the guy two or three times in your life. God knows how much money he has or what sort of facilities he's found down there."

John nodded. "Maybe it'll fail," he said. "Probably it will fail. But I'd like to be part of it. I'd hate to get to the end of my life and have to say that I did what I did because I never found out if there was any other way of doing it."

Rebecca nodded and sat back; she gazed at nothing, at their warped reflection in the window, for the rest of the trip. She was stricken by this conversation, as John had hoped she would be, yet he still felt guilty for unsettling her. "Just tell me you'll think about it," he said as they waited for the light to cross Atlantic. "If you don't want to do it, we won't, and everything will be fine. I'm really not unhappy with the life we have now."

Saturday another postcard arrived from Charlottesville, this one picturing the quadrangle at the University of Virginia. "What is a movie?" it said. "A work of art which owes its existence to men and women who are only interested in increasing the amount of money they make. And yet movies sometimes achieve true greatness, artistic greatness; and when they do, no one is shocked and amazed, no one declares that greatness and movies are incompatible. Why can't advertising, which comes into being via the same principle, occupy the same position in American culture?"

Weeks went by and John kept an eye on his girlfriend, who seemed to be keeping an eye on him as well. She was less talkative than usual – not angry or depressed, just preoccupied. He felt the same way. He didn't bring up Charlottesville again because he knew it was on her mind anyway. The fact that they weren't married, a fact which had seemed negligible to both of them for so long (when the time came for children, they had agreed long ago, they'd make it all official then), seemed suddenly to be gathering real weight. But John did his best not to think too much about contingencies. Instead he daydreamed a lot, though for some reason he caught himself reimagining his past much more often than his future. Other paths his life might have taken, other areas of study, other places he had lived. His old girlfriend in Berkeley, who had left their apartment one day and never returned. His thoughts about what might lie ahead were often short-circuited by the fear that Osbourne had forgotten about him or changed his mind about the whole project or was disappointed that he had heard no expression of support from John, even though he had left no way to get in touch. They were well into the spring by now, and there was no telling what, if anything, Osbourne might want from him.

Then one day Roman, John, and a few others were sitting on the sofas in Canning's empty office. Their boss had left early to go to a Knicks–Pacers playoff game at Madison Square Garden.

"I don't think he even likes basketball," Dale said. "I think he just goes because you have to be so rich and plugged-in these days to get playoff tickets at all. He's displaying for the people in the other corporate boxes."

Mick, staring into the rain through Canning's glass wall, said, "And the weird thing is, you can always see it better on TV anyway. It's like going to the taping of a TV show."

"That's all pro sports is now," John said, "is television programming."

"Oh, I'd go further than that," Roman said. "Pro sports is nothing but an advertising delivery system. He" – gesturing to Canning's empty chair – "took me to the Virginia Slims tennis tournament last year, and I have no idea who played who but I remember that sitting in my seat, without turning my head, I could see thirty-two different ads. And that's not counting what the players had sewn on to their shirts. Thirty-two."

"What do you mean, ads?"

"Well, you know. Placements. Logos. Fila, Chase, Rolex."

"Brute ads," Dale said. "Chinese water torture ads."

"Exactly. More negotiations than ads. Man, imagine if that was your job? Haggling over the size of the X in Ex-Lax on some sign behind a tennis court?"

"Talk about your mental static. Talk about your—"

"Oh my God!" Andrea yelled. "That reminds me!"

They all looked at her, taken aback by this show of genuine excitement.

"All that talk about ugly advertising gave me this sudden Mal Osbourne flashback—"

Everyone in the room who had been on the Philadelphia trip winced and laughed.

"— and I can't believe I forgot to tell you guys this awesome bit of gossip I heard! You know Elaine Sizemore, at DDB Needham?"

Roman nodded. "Nice girl," he said. "Did those Jerry Brown spots."

"Well, apparently out of nowhere she gets a letter, at her home, from none other than Osbourne, inviting her to quit her job and join this new agency he's starting in Charlottesville fucking Virginia."

The silence in the room was uncertain and polite, the way people are silent when they hear of a misfortune that has a comic element to it which no one wants to confess to seeing.

"Osbourne is starting his own agency?" Mick said.

"Yup."

"Partners, or just himself?"

"Apparently just him."

"Where does the money come from?"

"Who knows? He could have it himself, I guess. It's not impossible."

"Does he know this Elaine Sizemore?"

"Not from Eve. He just said he'd been following her career and admired her work. I guess he's just headhunting. No one here got a letter?"

Everyone shrugged. John could feel his face coloring; he considered leaving the room but thought that might be even more conspicuous. And when Roman looked directly at him, he shook his head no.

"Man," Dale said. "I can't believe I didn't hear from him."

Those who had witnessed Dale's humiliation at the Doucette pitch smiled appreciatively at the joke.

"Why Charlottesville?" Roman said. "Does he think he's Jefferson or something?"

"You laugh," Andrea said, even though Roman hadn't laughed, "but wait'll you hear this. The new agency has a mission. He wants to take the irony out of advertising. He wants it accepted as an art form. He wants to make it a force for social good."

Again they sat dumbstruck for a few seconds, unsure whether to laugh – not because it wasn't funny, but because the humor seemed at the expense of their former boss's derangement.

"Kinky," Roman said finally.

"So," John said, and they all turned to look at him. "This Elaine Sizemore, then – she's not taking him up on his offer?"

Andrea snorted. "She's a god damn star at Needham, and she's going to leave that and move to Virginia to work at the Osbourne Institute for the Painfully Sincere? What would you do?"

"You talked to her?"

"No, to another guy there. But if she was considering leaving I think she would have kept this letter to herself, don't you?"

Within a week a copy of Osbourne's "Dear Colleague" letter – not from Elaine Sizemore, but from some other unnamed source – had flown via fax to every agency in Manhattan. A cruelly annotated copy went up on the Canning & Leigh bulletin board for a day until Canning himself tore it down. The following week *AdAge* ran a small article about Osbourne's quixotic reemergence, full of diplomatic quotes from other agency heads; Osbourne himself, the article said, could not be reached for comment.

In bed one night, in the minute after the lights were turned out and the shadows of the window frames angled across the ceiling, Rebecca said suddenly, "You do understand that if I left my job we'd be turning our backs, potentially, on a lot of money. I mean a lot."

"I know that," he said, as if they were in the middle of a conversation.

"There are things we could have, things we could do, that we wouldn't be able to do. Because we couldn't — at least I couldn't — ever get back to the point I'm at right now, in terms of career prospects. We'd have to do without those things. We can't have it all, is what I'm saying. We can't pick up and move away from this life and still enjoy everything that happens to be good about this life."

His heart leapt to hear Rebecca even discussing it, to know that she had gone to the length of imagining what she might sacrifice in order to stay with him; but he felt instinctively that the wise course here was emotional caution. He turned on his side and laid his forehead in the space between her shoulder blades. "I don't care about money so much," he said gently. "I care about doing work that satisfies us both, in a place we're actually pleased about living in."

She didn't say anything more, and in a few minutes her legs jerked in the way they always did in the moment just before sleep.

That weekend, another postcard — this one picked out of the mailbox by Rebecca: "Lawyering and advertising: impartial advocacy. Of course, even in defending someone you hate, you're really defending something you love. Or that's the idea."

Rebecca waved it at him. "Postmarked Charlottesville," she said. "Have there been other cards like this?"

John nodded, his eyes stubbornly on the TV.

"Have you been in touch with him?"

"No. There's literally no way to get in touch with him. Unsigned cards just keep showing up in the mail."

Rebecca stood still for a moment, as if expecting him to say more. Then she laid the postcard on the arm of John's chair and left the room.

As the trip to Omaha approached, Roman kept churning out spots for the Beef Council with a spiteful prolificacy. Every morning he smiled coldly as he transcribed on John's sketch pad the ideas he'd had the night before: What are the chances you'll ever visit the rainforest, anyway? Name one tough vegetarian. Cows are too stupid to live. You only go around once; might as well go around fat and glossy. Tofu is for girls. It's the law of nature. With a week to go, they had nearly twenty ads dummied up when they only needed six; oddly, though, in spite of this, and in spite of the fact that some of his copy was clearly over the top, Roman angrily refused to edit any of it, and when John tried to get him to narrow it down to ten Roman accused him of censorship.

John came back from lunch one day to find "Who wants soft, squishy arteries?" written on his pad. He scowled.

"Do it," Roman said.

"Come on. We have more than we need."

"Do it."

"It won't work. It can't work. Can you really picture yourself flipping through *Newsweek* and coming across this?"

"It'll work, god damn it. All of it will work. I've never been more sure of anything in my life."

They stayed late at the office, getting ready for the pitch; Rebecca was working long hours those days too. John more or less took it for granted that no one would be home in the evening when he returned. The apartment looked half-decorated and impersonal. John didn't cook at all; sometimes he would order Chinese food and save some for her, but more often he would just have his dinner delivered at work. With a sense of romantic diligence they hadn't felt since the early days of their relationship, they met each other for long lunches at elegant restaurants, L'Espinasse, Arcadia, and they never paid for a thing.

The answering machine blinked with unanswered calls, from their parents, from alumni associations, from investment firms, and then finally, one evening before John, untucking his shirt as he walked in the door, had even turned the lights on, from Osbourne.

He was in Manhattan; he was free for lunch the next day. He wondered if John had had time to consider his proposal. He was sorry to bother him at home like this, but considered that a call at the office might have caused some awkwardness.

John was already asleep by the time Rebecca came home; but struggling mightily he raised himself on his elbows and said, "Mal Osbourne called today. I said I'd meet him for lunch tomorrow."

Rebecca, her back to him, made no hitch in her motions to betray that she had heard. In the urban half-darkness to which his eyes were accustomed, he watched while she stood in front of her closet and slowly undressed. She looked like someone else, like a stranger with whom he wanted to have an affair.

He told Roman the next morning that he had a dentist's appointment.

Osbourne sat at a banquette at La Réserve, staring into space, his back to the mirrored wall. He looked rather put out — nostrils flared, fingers tapping — just as if John were late for this appointment, when in fact he was five minutes early. When he sat down, Osbourne brightened somewhat, but only for a few seconds. He wore an expensive-looking gray suit, and his hair was now cut very short, in the fashionable Caesar style.

The waiter poured John a glass of mineral water from the bottle that sat on the table. Osbourne rested his chin on his hands, stared at John in the fully intent yet charmless way a surgeon might have stared at him, and said nothing. John, who was nervous enough anyway — he could never seem to get the wardrobe right with Osbourne; he wore a simple black sweater today, with no jacket or tie — became flustered and forgot the whole script by which he had intended to steer this meeting.

"How have you been, sir?" he said finally.

"Busy." He smiled perfunctorily. "So have you come here to accept my offer?"

John laughed. "Well, not exactly, sir, no." Osbourne's gaze did not waver. "There are . . . there are a lot of variables. I have to admit I'm intrigued by all you have to say about what you want to do. But it's a risk. I have — I have commitments here."

Osbourne sat back into the banquette and began nodding sagely, as if he had heard what he was listening for.

"And if I were on my own, if I were a younger man, with no one else's wishes to consider—"

Osbourne held up his hand. "Listen, before I forget," he said, "how much money do you make now?"

John reddened, but he saw no reason for squeamishness. "Seventy-five thousand," he said.

"I can match that. If there's a bonus involved, I don't know about that, but I can keep paying you that salary."

"For how long, though? I mean, forgive me for—"

"I have no idea for how long," Osbourne said, in a friendly manner. "The point is, the risk is minimized in that sense. And if we should fail, I know you could come back to New York with your book and get another job in a day, if that's what you wanted to happen."

The waiter, who had been not there, was suddenly and discreetly there; but Osbourne waved him away. Only John's menu was open.

"Have you ever been down to Charlottesville?" Osbourne went on.

"Several times. I had a cousin who went to UVA."

"Then you know what a beautiful place it is. You might not know that the housing market is also very reasonable down there. I don't have any idea what your wife earns or how much you might have saved but it might even prove feasible to hold on to your place in Brooklyn, as a kind of hedge, if that's what you . . . So you didn't want to go to UVA yourself then?"

John shook his head.

"You went all the way to California, as I recall? Wanted to get away, was that it?"

John swallowed. He couldn't remember when he might have told Osbourne this about himself. "Yes, sir, I suppose so."

Osbourne, this time, was doing nothing to discourage John's addressing him as "sir"; possibly he just didn't hear it. "And now you'd like to go back?"

"Well, Virginia isn't really my home, but in a way yes, I suppose you're right."

"Fascinating." Osbourne shook his head abruptly. "Anyway, the financial risk, to you at least, seems pretty minimal. What does your wife do?"

"Girlfriend. She's a trusts and estates lawyer."

"Well, they've got rich people down in Charlottesville, too, you know. Lawyers, too. Law firms even."

John finished his water; he was starving, but didn't want even to start in on the bread until Osbourne relaxed the pace of his interrogation a bit. "She has a job here she likes, and she feels she's put a number of years into it, toward partnership, years that I guess she would feel were wasted if she quit."

Osbourne nodded again. "She doesn't want to start her life over again."

"Well, maybe just not in Virginia," John said, laughing.

"And what about you?"

"Sorry?"

"I mean, we've been here awhile and I haven't heard anything about you, about what you might want. So how about it? Do you want to start over again?"

Osbourne's back was to the mirrored wall, and, as if by some trick, John, sitting across from him, could see simultaneously both his face and the back of his head, like the barmaid in Manet's *Folies Bergère*. The restaurant was full, and where silence might have been there was the gentle ring of silverware and the low burble of unfamiliar voices.

"Yes," John said. He was surprising himself now. "I do want to start again."

"Because I'll tell you what it sounds like to me. If you don't mind my interpreting your personal life. I'm not unmindful of the risks for you here. But it seems to me that, for your girlfriend, the real fear is not that our idea will fail. It's that we'll succeed."

The waiter appeared again, his face betraying nothing that would indicate he had been there before.

"Actually, I'm starving," Osbourne said. "John, do you like cassoulet? They do a fine one here."

"I've never had it," John said.

Osbourne raised his eyebrows. "Well, I can tell you you're never going to get a decent one in Charlottesville, so I'd suggest you try it now."

"All right," John said.

While they were waiting for their lunch, Osbourne suddenly said, "Listen, while we're in this territory, let me ask you another personal question: is that all right?"

John nodded.

"How long have you and – I'm sorry, what is her name?"

"Rebecca Sanders."

"How long have you two been together?"

"Three and a half years," John said.

"And you've been living together for . . ."

"About eighteen months."

"I'm guessing," Osbourne said, "there are no children then."

"No, sir."

"No, of course not. It's not something you would have left unmentioned."

John smiled.

164

"She's not pregnant, then, is she?"

Blushing uncontrollably, John said that he was sure she was not.

"Okay," Osbourne said. "Forgive me. I can see I've overstepped my bounds. Let's change the subject then. What are you working on now?"

John told him about the Beef Council campaign. Osbourne's expression did not change.

"And is it work you're proud of?" he said simply.

John thought for a long time before answering, mostly because he was afraid to say no out loud. "I don't understand it," he said. "I mean, we're doing basically the same thing we've been doing, for years, but lately I feel like I don't get how it all works. Which would be fine if I was sitting at home watching it all on TV, but I'm the one *making* it, and I still don't understand how it gets made. It's a weird feeling."

"Have you shared this feeling with your partner? What's his name?"

"Roman Gagliardi."

"Roman? Or with anyone else there?"

"No."

"You feel you have to act a certain way, don't you? In your work environment? You have to take a certain less-than-honest attitude, not just about colleagues' work, but about your own?"

John nodded.

Osbourne winced sympathetically. "Don't you get tired," he said, "of all the lying?"

Back at the office, light-headed, lazy from the rich food, John stared without seeing for what remained of the day; then he took the subway to Brooklyn. The apartment didn't seem comforting either. He sat by the window until Rebecca came home. He expected her to take a sarcastic tack in asking about his lunch; instead she was quite grim and serious, and he didn't know whether to take that as a good sign or not.

"He's invited us down to Charlottesville, not this coming weekend but the next," John said in a breezy, high voice that didn't sound right to him. "He has the offices about finished, and we can just, you know, tour the town, see if we like the feel of it or not."

Rebecca was squatting in front of the open refrigerator, washed in the white light. Her heels came up out of her shoes.

"So is that a problem for you, next weekend?" John said.

She straightened up. "Is that a problem for me? In what respect?"

John swallowed. "Do we have anything that would conflict with that, I meant."

"No. I'm sure we don't." She stooped and looked again through the empty shelves.

"So will you come?" John said.

"I don't think so." She shut the fridge and began opening the cupboards; she seemed not to want to look at him, and John, still in his chair, wondered if she was crying.

"Can you tell me," she said, "why it is we never have anything to eat in this fucking place?"

THE PERPETUAL PRESENT tense of a college town. Always in the foreground, lively and faceless, the student body remains forever between eighteen and twenty-two; only those who accrue around their needs – the shopkeepers, the landlords, the tenured professors – are allowed to watch each other grow old. On the South Side, on Telegraph Avenue, the Bubble Man was out again, in his purple suit, playing the kazoo and banging cymbals strapped to the insides of his knees; Molly saw him through the window of the Soup Kitchen, a self-consciously down-and-out diner where she went most mornings for her coffee and toast with apple butter, a simple pleasure which, strictly speaking, she could no longer afford. Signs on the lampposts for a rally to protest the Gulf War, noon under the Campanile, three days ago. The UC campus lay in a sort of natural bowl; around it, the terraced streets, the eclectic homes set close together, the enervated brown of the hillsides.

Fall in California. The money from her father had lasted a long time, but now it had run out, though Richard and his seven roommates in the house on Vine Street had recently told Molly she was welcome to stay on there rent-free until she found a job. They told her this collectively, the way they did everything, all eight of them in the living room, facing her and smiling. Their earnestness, their cheerful uniformity, was disquieting and easily mocked (or would have been, had she any friends outside the house to talk to about it): but over the weeks and months their genuine kindnesses to her had accumulated into a charity that was not so readily dismissed.

Molly had tried diligently to find some work; she had never held any sort of job before, other than babysitting, but her lack of experience wasn't the problem. The problem was that she hadn't started looking until the end of September, after ten thousand students in need of beer-and-pizza money had flocked back to Berkeley. Everywhere she tried –

bookstores, restaurants, thrift shops, laundromats – the spots were all filled. Her only income at the moment came from an odd job in a fancy North Side home, reading the San Francisco *Chronicle* for an hour or so every weekday morning to an old man who wasn't blind by any means but who claimed that small-print reading gave him migraines. Mr Whalen was eighty and rich and that meant he could be unembarrassed about self-indulgences. He paid her ten dollars an hour, which was generous, but it still came to only seventy or eighty dollars a week. Nor did he reimburse her for bus fare; he was a kind enough man, but his scattered thoughts never for a moment came to rest on the question of just how Molly arrived in his living room on a given morning, or where she went to afterwards. She was too embarrassed to ask for it.

Inadequate as it was, the job had come her way only through subterfuge. She had gone into the UC Student Employment Center on campus, where they posted jobs on a bulletin board. You were supposed to make an interview appointment through the center, but that was out of the question for Molly, since the first thing they would have asked her for was a student ID number. Instead, she memorized the information from the sheet on the bulletin board, walked across Sproul Plaza to the student lounge, and called from a pay phone. Mr Whalen didn't seem to notice or care that she hadn't been referred by anyone from the university. In fact, he hired her over the phone; he liked her voice, he said, not too loud, so many young people were so loud these days. She hung up, chanting the address to herself, and ran to borrow a pen from one of the students playing Donkey Kong in the din of the lounge.

Molly haunted the university in much this way throughout the fall, living on the margin of student life, taking what she needed, unnoticed in the crowd. Her age made her inconspicuous; it was reason enough for her presence anywhere. There were always rallies in the plaza to protest something or other, huge effigy Bushes, signs condemning the Livermore Lab, which operated in contemptuous silence just a few hundred yards away, "the people united will never be defeated," and Molly liked to attend now and then, not at all insensible to the rightness of the cause, but more immediately energized by her bogus affiliation with the crowd, by the simultaneous thrill of belonging and not belonging. Boredom was a danger because it was so easy to get used to it, to forget to want to escape it. She would flip through her brother's course catalogue – he lent it to her the first week of classes and never asked for it back – and sometimes when a class looked good to her she found out where it was meeting (lists were posted in the student lounge) and dropped in just to listen.

It was only possible in the lecture halls, of course; once or twice she got to the door of a classroom, saw that there were only fifteen or twenty desks there ranged in a homey circle, and had to leave the building.

She saw the Bubble Man on Telegraph again and thought about the contradiction at work in him: life had pushed him to the margin, to the very lip of invisibility; he did not appear interested in escaping that region, and yet he had literally made it his life's work just to be noticed, to be seen.

A sense of an interval in her life, a suspension. It might have been possible to enjoy these months of secret aimlessness on those terms, but for the fact that there was nothing on the other side of them. No prospect, no plan, no eventuality: she supposed that if Richard ever managed to graduate (he was only eight credits short, but lately he seemed to have stopped going to classes at all), he might move out of the house, and then something would have to happen. But he might not. So the most she could hope for, in the way of peace of mind, was to forget the future for a while.

Occasionally, into her life as a ghost with all a ghost's privileges, came a kind of vestigial awareness of the fame, the cautionary status, Molly's very name must have back in Ulster: the obverse of her existence now. She found the lives of the people there hard to imagine, even though she had never lived anywhere else until five months ago.

As for her parents, Molly hadn't spoken with them since the hour the cab arrived to take her to the airport in Albany. They called from time to time and spoke to Richard, who reported that Molly was doing wonderfully, had a job, went to classes in her spare time. He said she had even put on some weight. (In fact she had grown thinner, without meaning to, and had lost some of her color as well; Richard wasn't directly covering this up, since he hadn't really noticed it.) Their father – it was always their father who made the call – spontaneously invented and then stuck to the implicit fiction that Molly was out, or asleep, or working, every time he called, and thus could never come to the phone.

"Well, give your sister our love," Roger would say fondly, "and tell her we're glad she's doing well."

"I sure will," Richard said. Molly sat at the kitchen counter five feet away, blank-faced, as if trying not to be heard. "Bye now."

From the day of her arrival, Richard had seemed untroubled,

cheerful in an introverted sort of way – almost placid; it wasn't that Molly was unfamiliar with this face of his so much as that she was conditioned to read it as a danger sign, as highs like this generally presaged an angry sulk of some sort. But his calm remained unbroken, and after the first few months she began genuinely to believe in it. Through July she had slept on the living-room couch; once it was clear to everyone that she would be around for a while, the group decided she could share a bedroom with a graduate student in cultural anthropology named Sally. Sally had had her own room in the house for two years, and this new arrangement came with no reduction in her rent. She took it all quite cheerfully, even enthusiastically. She went with Richard and Molly in the van – the house had a van, to which everyone had keys; it must have belonged to one of them, but Molly never learned to whom – to a used-furniture store in Oakland and came back with a foldaway bed. Sally was twenty-four, petite, hipless; she wore cat's-eye glasses and 1950s thrift-shop fashions – Capri pants, pillbox hats. On some days she looked unnervingly like old snapshots of Molly's mother.

It hadn't taken more than a week for Molly to figure out that everyone in the house was a Christian. She wasn't sure if they could all be classified under the term "born again" (though certainly Richard would have to be); some of them might have lived this way their whole lives for all she knew. But they never talked about it, at least not in front of her. It didn't exactly fit her stereotype of young college Christians; she would have expected them to be all over her. Whatever they did was done in secret, with the exception of Sunday dinner, when they put the leaf in the dining-room table and matter-of-factly held hands to say a long grace before eating. It was the one time during the week when they were all together. Otherwise, what with part-time jobs (they pooled their salaries, along with whatever money some of them still received from their parents), classes, volunteer work, they were all on different schedules; if Molly returned for a nap in the afternoon, when she knew Sally would be in the library – Molly slept a lot now, often for two or three hours in the middle of the day – she never knew who else would be at home. There were few visitors.

She sat in a European History lecture and learned about the assault on the Bastille. Afterwards she went to a coffee shop and sat at an outdoor table, without money to order anything, and watched the scenes of student life at the too-small tables, the uneven stacks of books, the couples stroking each other's arms, the students with their heads in their hands stubbornly reading Lacan or Derrida, not imagining themselves a part of the general pageant of unburdened youth.

Sally came from Massachusetts. Her parents disapproved of Berkeley and wouldn't pay any of her tuition or living expenses there; she had a TA job and some financial aid. She talked to Molly about all this when they were in their beds with the lights out, like twelve-year-olds at a sleepover.

The student film societies, screening old movies in lecture halls and auditoriums, were one of Molly's few affordable pleasures. She spent two or three evenings a week there. Admission for students was a dollar, and of course no one there ever questioned Molly's status as a student; still, mindful of her finances, she snuck in without paying when she was able. She saw *The Sweet Smell of Success* for the first time that way, and as the credits rolled she still felt so exhilarated by all that hyper-verbal moral viciousness that she decided to stay in her seat for the second show. The guy at the door saw her trying to hide, but he smiled discreetly and didn't make her pay a second time, or perhaps he knew she hadn't paid the first time either. Watching a movie straight through just minutes after seeing it before, with everything so fresh in your mind it lost its capacity for surprise, produced, Molly discovered, a new sort of awareness of the people who *made* a movie: an awareness of the actors on screen as actors, of the technicians and assistants who must have been standing disinterestedly just outside the frame as the stars emoted, an awareness of everything they said as words on a page coming out of someone's typewriter in a room somewhere. It only made the emotions themselves seem more remarkable to her. People right there at Berkeley, she considered, studied the art and the science of making movies. Of course those were small, intensive, hands-on classes, not the sort of classes you could sneak into undetected. Molly felt a little sorry for herself and her outsider status.

After the lights went up again, she saw someone moving against the tide of departing film buffs, deeper into the auditorium, toward her. It was the guy who took the tickets.

Panicked, her face became still. He sat down beside her and smiled. He wore black jeans and a bowling shirt with the name Dave stitched over the pocket.

"Great flick," he said. "My name's Eric. I've seen it like ten times. Have you seen that Barry Levinson movie, *Diner?* There's a character in it who does nothing but quote lines from *Sweet Smell.* Plays a character who never breaks character." Molly listened carefully through all this banter for any concealed irony which would end with his busting her for sneaking in without paying. But when he finally asked her if she wanted to go get a cup of coffee at Geppetto's, she realized he was on the level; she let her guard down and said yes.

Eric talked a lot about himself, about movies she hadn't seen and theoretical journals she'd never heard of, and even though this might reflect badly on him, Molly wouldn't have wanted it any other way. Any effort to draw her out, to get her to fill in her own history, would have spoiled the evening for her. He had long black hair but even though he was no older than twenty his hairline was receding. Molly found this satisfying; she liked to see as much as possible about a man when she looked at one, and in that respect at least you could see fifteen years into his future. His glasses were tinted yellow.

"So you're not in the film–studies major," Eric said. "I would have recognized you. Are you a freshman?"

Molly nodded – not because she had thought out this lie beforehand, but because it was the response which least obstructed the flow of his talk.

"Live in the dorms?"

"No," she said, "in a house on the South Side. My older brother is there."

Eric lived in the dorms, even though he was a junior. Couldn't stand those roommate situations, he said – eight people, one refrigerator, no one ever cleaning the bathroom.

He started talking about his efforts to get the film society to arrange a guerrilla screening of *Titicut Follies*. Molly kept her eyes on him while listening discreetly to the conversations at the tables around them, intimate and vehement, couples and circles of friends. Eric's presence was what made her a part of all that, for the moment. It didn't feel so bad, though she was puzzled as always by the general practice of going out at midnight in order to have private conversations in public places. Maybe it was a California thing.

"So what I'd like to do now, Molly," Eric said, "is take you back to my room and make love to you."

Molly, her attention divided, smiled for a moment before she thought to be startled. Men. Usually you could learn everything there was to learn about them in around five minutes; she knew instantly, for example, that Eric had never used this particular line before, that he'd been waiting, his whole uneventful sexual career, to meet some stranger so he'd have a risk-free opportunity to try it. And whence the idea that this was what women wanted – a frank, take-charge, no-time-for-games man, a man too evolved for pretensions? Was it grounded in anything that had ever happened to him, or in too many evenings in his single dorm room reading Penthouse Forum? She wondered about all those things so sincerely that she very nearly said yes just to see if he would fall over dead with surprise; but she collected herself and said, demurely but unambiguously, no.

"That's too bad," Eric said without missing a beat, as if following a script. "Can I have your phone number, then?"

She gave him a false one. But it got her thinking. Not about Eric, but in a more general way about how her invisibility wasn't as complete as she thought. You didn't move through the world without being watched. She liked the idea that boys like Eric, boys who just happened to see her on the sidewalk or in a classroom or a store, wanted to take her home and fuck her, conceived fantasies, instant fantasies in which maybe she would melt at a line like "I'd really like to take you to my room

175

and make love to you," or fantasies involving bringing Molly home to meet their parents for all she knew. The randomness, the variety of these projections was what she liked. They thought they knew her, but they didn't. She might surprise one of them one day.

Some days she took BART into San Francisco and hiked the windy streets there, panting at the top of each steep block and tasting the salt in the air. There wasn't much to see. It was more the bracing sense of hurry she liked to feel, the wealth and coldness, knowing she would only be feeling it for a little while. Street life in the big city was much less ironic than in Berkeley. Once near the Haight she came face to face with a group of girls, her age or younger, runaways with a hard, self-reliant glint. Their experience was not that far removed from hers, she realized; but the notion that she had anything in common with them, not an altogether welcome notion to begin with, was killed by the glare they gave her when they decided she had been looking at them too long.

Thanksgiving came; two of the housemates went home for the five-day school break, but that left seven of them, with a faded thrift-shop tablecloth thrown over the same table they ate at every night. None of them really knew how to cook but they threw themselves into it with a slightly hysterical glee, cooking a turkey in the oven whose thermometer was always broken, trying to re-create from a kind of sense memory various side dishes they remembered from their childhoods – creamed onions, candied yams, Roquefort string beans – with no access to any recipe and no reasonable prospect of calling their former homes for the secret. Molly made a Yorkshire pudding which failed to rise in the temperamental oven but tasted all right anyway with enough gravy. They screamed like children as they cooked, and even with a few dishes which turned out so badly they had to go straight into the garbage uneaten, there was still twice as much food as they needed. It seemed like a perfect opportunity to demonstrate for each other the reality of their own constitution as a family. Richard said grace, and it went on for almost three minutes, with plenty of murmured "amens" from the others; Molly, head down, eyes closed, holding Sally's hand on one side and her brother's on the other, didn't mind it at all this time.

Christmas was going to be harder to manage. The house and the city would empty out to a much greater degree, and her sense of her own marginality would be heightened.

Molly had lost fifteen pounds in her months there, without intending to. It wasn't a matter of poverty. Living away from home simply meant a different relationship to food; meals came not according to relentless schedule but only when you felt hungry enough to get up and do something about it.

She stood up from her table at the Soup Kitchen, late one morning in December, and fainted on to the floor. She came to after a few seconds with a cook wearing a filthy apron and a hairnet gingerly lifting her arms over her head. The waitress put a paper napkin to Molly's brow and when she pulled it back Molly saw it was saturated with blood.

"You need to get this looked at," the waitress said. "What happened to you? Did you just stand up too fast or something?" She was probably a student herself, Molly thought, working her way through college, toward whatever was on the other side of college, her hair in a clean ponytail. Molly wanted to go home with her.

"I guess that's it," Molly said, though that wasn't it; she didn't want to let on that she was at the point of tears herself.

"Do you think you can get to UHS?"

University Health Services.

"I'm not a student," Molly said, taking the handful of balled-up napkins the cook held out to her, apologetically handing him the old, blood-soaked ones. Her head was throbbing.

She started to feel dizzy again. The cook and the waitress exchanged a look.

The cook, who was almost off his shift anyway, wound up driving her to the free clinic in Oakland, about twenty minutes away. She did her best to keep her blood off the upholstery of his battered car. This was her first impulse, to gather up any evidence that anything had happened to her at all. He offered halfheartedly to wait with her; she thanked him profusely for the ride and he drove away.

Inside the waiting room, where she would spend the next two hours, Molly got a clear picture of her situation, a picture made clearer – the ways dreams are sometimes startlingly clear – by the feverish wooziness that came over her in waves even after she was certain the bleeding had stopped. Twenty-one people waited ahead of her, or approximately one for each of the turquoise molded-plastic chairs ranged in immovable rows before the receptionist's empty window. They were people for whom waiting was obviously a condition of life; apart from two children who noisily passed a Cabbage Patch doll back and forth across their mother's motionless lap, the place was deathly silent. Even the two men who were clearly deranged did little to disturb the atmosphere of timelessness, mumbling quietly, directing their animated gestures to the air. And the smell:

alcohol and disinfectant and some other familiar smell like wet wool weaving in and out through the frank human stench. Each person's complaint was invisible to the disinterested; Molly was the only one there actually bleeding. No one took any special notice of her, though, and she waited for her turn.

The doctor was Malaysian, and he was the unfriendliest medical professional Molly had ever encountered: not simply brusque or overtired but outright hostile, seemingly adrenalized by sarcasm. He sewed five stitches into her head and told her that she was seriously anemic. She needed to eat more, he said, and on top of that to take some sort of iron supplement, at least for a month. He said these things in a spirit of self-justification; it was clear he didn't expect his instructions to be followed, nor did he care if they were. The stitches were the dissolving kind, he said; no need for him to see her again.

Molly was all the way out to the parking lot before it occurred to her that she had no way to get back to Berkeley. She wasn't even really sure where she was. She didn't have enough money for a cab; the only thing to do was to call the house and have someone come over in the van, but even if someone was home, and the van happened to be there, how could she provide directions so that she could be found? In her pocket she found change for a phone call; the coins, somehow, had blood on them. She caught sight of a phone booth on the sidewalk a few hundred yards away, but when she reached it she saw it had been stripped, down to the colored wires. No other phones in sight. Molly walked back to the clinic, stuck her head through the window and asked if she could use their phone to call for a ride. The receptionist banged the phone down in front of her without a word.

No one was home.

It was cold and sunny, the sky a cloudless icy blue. Molly went back out to the parking lot, sat on the rear fender of a nice car that must have belonged to one of the doctors, and cried. She cried forcefully, looking at the pavement, her head pounding, for fifteen minutes or so. Then she stood and returned to the clinic waiting room and asked the broad woman with the two children for directions to a bus stop. The first bus she got on took her in the wrong direction, but the driver told her where the transfer point was for a bus back to Berkeley. She got off at Shattuck Avenue, and by the time she made it back to the house on foot it was well after dark.

Everyone fussed over her when she came in, standing up from their chairs, bursting out of their rooms, helping Molly on to the couch, and she let them do it. Richard even led them in a prayer. Molly took four aspirin and went to bed early. She wasn't sure how late it was when Sally came into their room, undressed quietly, and got into Molly's bed, folding her knees behind Molly's and lightly draping one arm around her stomach, just above the curve of her hip. Molly was amazed but still too exhausted to let it keep her awake for long. Nothing happened; they lay there like an old married couple. In the morning when Molly woke Sally was gone.

Molly was sitting in the big red chair with a bowl of cereal, watching television, lightly touching the bandage on her head, when Richard walked in. "Can we talk a little?" he said, smiling; he turned the set off without waiting for an answer.

Molly put the bowl on the floor and struggled to sit more upright in the enormous chair. Her brother stood in front of her, still smiling, his hands folded. His hair was cut very short now; in fact, Molly was pretty sure he was cutting it himself.

"Molly, I'm worried about you," he said.

"It's just a cut. And the fainting thing, the doctor said I just needed some more iron," she said, even though she knew that wasn't what he was talking about.

He shook his head. "I'm worried about your soul," he said.

The room was filled with sunlight at that time of day, and the carpet showed so threadbare in the glare that you could see through to the heavy skeletal weaving underneath it.

"My soul?"

"You're drifting. You're drifting badly."

"And this is because."

"I think you know why."

"Because I'm not saved?"

Richard said nothing.

"And who's going to save me? You?"

"Who does it is not the question. The question is how. And there's only one way."

"What way is that?" Molly said angrily. "What are you, Jimmy Swaggart?" She didn't understand the defensiveness she felt all of a sudden.

Richard's smile weakened. "Molly, you have to admit I've never broached this with you before. I've never pressured you. You've been living in our house for six months and I've let you go your own way. But you're my sister and I can't watch you drift toward damnation like this and not do anything about it. Look at what happened yesterday."

"Yesterday?"

"Are you going to tell me you didn't feel some despair? That you didn't feel lost? Don't you think there's some sort of message for you in all that?"

"I fainted," Molly said, exasperated. "I fainted and hit my head. A nice man took me to the clinic, and I had a hard time getting home. That's all."

Richard shook his head. He seemed close to tears now. "Don't you see the connection?" he said.

In People's Park, overgrown and unmowed, piebald with bare earth and strewn with bottles and condoms, there was a pro-democracy rally during exam week. Molly stopped to watch. The day was overcast and cold; under the familiar bright-red flag on a homemade banner tied between two trees, students took turns standing on a milk crate and declaring their support for their fellow students suffering under martial repression in China. A Chinese-born exchange student briefly interjected a note of authenticity with a speech about the conditions in the smelting plant where his uncle worked; but the speech went on quite long, and people began moving away. All of a sudden three students from the Berkeley Communist Party pushed through the small crowd, shouting their support for Zhao and claiming CIA involvement with the Tiananmen Square occupation. They were quickly shouted down by the others, energized by this suddenly visible opposition, and the three Communists marched off again, red-faced.

Molly lingered at the back fringe of the gathering, hands in her pockets. After a while she noticed another man standing on the fringes, twenty feet away; and when she noticed him, he quickly turned his head away from her.

It wasn't just his age that made him look out of place there – he might have been thirty, but it was not unusual to see grad students around the city that age or older. He had red hair cut to a kind of military bristle; his face bore some old acne scars. He wore a pristine white turtleneck under a long windbreaker, and creased navy-blue pants, though *slacks* might have been a better word for them. Even under the windbreaker he had the overdeveloped arms and shoulders of someone who spent a lot of time in a gym. When Molly turned back to face the speaker she could see the man's face turn again toward her.

"We will not waver," said a young woman in a green field jacket whose head was shaved on the sides, "in our mission to topple the fascist lords of China, and tyrants everywhere." There was such an element of longing in their anger, a frantic dismissal of the idea of inconsequence.

She turned to look at him again; and this time, when she turned away, the red-haired man ambled over casually and stood beside her.

"I will now read the text of a letter the committee has drafted to Premier Li Peng and to Boutros Boutros-Ghali."

"You a part of this?" the red-haired man asked her.

Molly shook her head.

"I didn't think so," he said.

After the letter was read and its contents approved, the meeting ended. Molly continued looking at the empty space above the milk crate.

"What's your name?" the man said.

She turned to look at him.

"Why should I tell you that?" she said.

He stared at her for a long moment as the others filed past, out of the park. Then he stepped closer to her, quite close. With a quick glance to either side, he unzipped the windbreaker and held one side of it away from his body to reveal, clipped next to the buckle of his wide belt, a policeman's badge.

He zipped up the jacket again, and stared at her.

"You shouldn't be hanging around here," he said. His voice was inflected to suggest that he was indulging a rare desire to do someone a favor. It was his cop voice, clearly, or at any rate the one he used to indicate his moral remoteness from non-cops. But in his small eyes, behind this affected benevolence, Molly detected some more genuine cruelty; and she determined to get at it.

"Where should I be hanging around, then?"

"I don't know. A beautiful girl like you. Where do you normally hang around?"

She could see right into him, that was the best part. She knew that all she had to do in order to cut herself to his idea, his fantasy, of what college girls were really like was to not go away – just stand there, as he became more forward, stand there and not be repulsed. He thought he was seeing the essence of her, of all women really. Well, maybe she was showing it to him but he still wouldn't see it, blinded as he was by his vision of himself. She didn't need to make herself say something complimentary about his physique, which would have been hard to do without laughing; he took it for granted that she would admire him, and nothing in her silence violated that idea.

The park was empty now, except for a few derelicts who had been there before the rally began.

"You're married," Molly said flatly, looking at his hand.

"Very observant," he said. Look at that, Molly thought, with a kind of detached awe. Look how he hates me.

His clothes were perfectly spotless and pressed – which pretty much spoiled the undercover effect he was apparently going for – and Molly wondered for a moment about the spirit in which his wife did this for him; but then she jerked the thought of this pathetic woman's existence out of her mind.

"You need a ride home, or anywhere?" he said. Every remark pushed him further into a zone where his own fantasy and what he took to be the real nature of men and women grew indistinct.

"Yeah," she said. "I do need a ride."

"Well, good. I'm sure you'll tell me where you want to go."

They walked to his car, a boxy black American midsize, no siren or police radio visible. In the dust on the trunk someone had written with a forefinger the word PIG. He ignored it.

He drove slowly across Telegraph, pedestrians striding past the car at all points, not waiting for the lights. Molly was looking out her window at the Bubble Man when she felt the policeman's hand at the top of her thigh.

"Not in the car," she said.

Of course he knew a place. It was down by the Marina, near the old Fantasy Records plant. The scarier things got the more satisfied Molly felt. He walked ahead of her up three flights of stairs; he knocked, then pushed open a door to a room with nothing but a fold-out sofa in it. He started kissing her, to get that over with, and when she put her arms around him she felt something in the small of his back, underneath the big ugly windbreaker. It was his gun.

He flinched a little, but he let her keep her hand on it, through the fabric. Maybe he'll shoot me, Molly thought. Maybe after we're done he'll shoot me and leave me here.

She tried to think of what would stop him from doing that. They could trace the bullet to him, she decided.

He didn't want to see her body, didn't want her to take her clothes off, except for what was absolutely necessary, which in this case meant pulling her jeans and her underwear down to mid-thigh. She guessed it was some kind of rape fantasy for him. He bent her over the arm of the sofa without folding it out. It did hurt her a little bit – though probably not as much as he hoped – partly because he was a little larger than she had encountered before.

He mumbled something.

She turned her head and said softly, "What?"

"Say something."

"What do you—"

"Just say something," he mumbled, a kind of stage whisper, his thighs banging into hers.

"Do it to me," she said flatly.

"Shut up! Shut up, bitch!" he screamed. "Fucking cunt! Shut up!" And he shouted wordlessly as he came inside her; if he hadn't had his fingers dug so tightly into her legs, she would have lost her balance.

Afterwards, he wouldn't look at her, though now it seemed more a matter of embarrassment than contempt. When he dropped her off on Telegraph, he didn't even put the car in park. But she wouldn't let him off that easily; she stared at him as she backed slowly out of the car, smiling coldly, and as he drove away she continued to stare at his rearview mirror to let him know that she could not be intimidated out of her understanding of him.

Molly had the next few weeks to worry that she was

pregnant (she wasn't) and to revisit what she'd done. Sex was what it was to her, an act unconnected to any other and a way of forcing men to reveal their secrets, but she knew too that it was not these things to most other people. To them, sex was intimate; to Molly it was extremely intimate as well, but never mutually so. She could imagine meeting a man (though she never had) who would hold this same kind of power over her, who would leave her crying and exposed and feeling fraudulent afterwards; what she couldn't imagine was a balance of power. That wasn't what sex was about. She wondered if she should be worried, though, about the increasing kick she felt from being objectified.

For Christmas her brother gave her a Bible.

On a gray morning, in a steep lecture hall, Molly slipped through the door after the lights were turned out for slides. The class, which she had been to once or twice before, was called Modernism and its Discontents. The chairs in back were filled; even in a class with a hundred students, their instinct was to put as much distance between themselves and the seat of authority as possible. So she walked halfway down the steps and took the first empty spot she could see once her eyes adjusted to the dark, three seats in from the aisle, between a girl wearing a Madonna-like T-shirt ripped to fall off one shoulder and a boy wearing jeans and a white Oxford shirt, his long hair pushed behind his ears, who watched the screen with his hands in front of his mouth, fingertips pressed together.

The hall flashed into darkness for a second, then back to the dim magnesium glare from the giant screen as a new slide appeared.

"*The Disturbing Muses,*" the professor said. He was fat and wore a multicolored sweater. He sat on the front of the broad desk, looking up at the screen, his back half turned to the class. He held the control for the projector in his left hand. "1917. Remember for a moment Malevich from last week, the concern with movement, dynamism, the restlessness of the industrial age. Here, at virtually the same moment of history, Chirico counterposes an art of almost deathly stillness, not motion but contemplation, reverie, quiet."

Another flash.

"*The Song of Love.* 1914. Incidentally, Magritte called this painting, which he saw as a young man on a museum visit in 1922, one of the most important events in his life. Because, he said, in a world of Cubists and other self-conscious manipulators of the flat plane of the picture, here at last was someone who dreamed not of *how to paint,* but of *what must be painted.*"

Molly heard the scratching of pens, and indeed it was the kind of resonant remark she liked to write down herself, not for any purpose other than as a way of making the remark pass through her. She patted softly at her pants pockets, then at the pocket of her shirt.

"Need a pen?" the boy next to her whispered. She started. His voice was soft, and had, of all things, a Southern accent; he looked at her simply and with his index finger pushed the hair back behind his ear.

"No thanks," said Molly. The moment of admiration had passed, and the slide was gone. "I don't have any paper anyway."

He smiled. After a minute, not looking at her, he leaned on the armrest between them so his head was closer to hers. "Can

I ask you something?" he whispered. "Are you even a student here?"

Molly's heart raced a little in the near-darkness; she said nothing.

"Because," he said, whispering now, still not looking at her, "it's almost midterms, and this is only the third time you've been in here."

She considered getting up to leave, but there was nothing threatening in his manner – just curious. The professor went on talking.

"No," she said finally, in a whisper. Their heads were almost touching in the darkness, though they didn't look at each other. "My brother goes here. I live with him, and I read through his course catalogue, and sometimes I go to classes if they look interesting."

"Well, I admire that," he said, and sat back.

A half hour later the lights went up, and Molly tried not to look at the boy to see what he would do, with this new advantage he held over her.

He stacked up his books, exhaled as if satisfied, and smiled at her.

"May I ask your name?" he said.

His manner was almost courtly. But there was no exaggeration in it; she could tell that he wasn't about to ask her out.

"Molly," she said.

He put out his hand. "John Wheelwright," he said. They shook hands, which made her laugh a little. He blushed, and stood up to go.

"Molly, will I see you again?" he asked.

★ ★ ★

OSBOURNE OFFERED TO send a car to the Washington airport, but seemed delighted with John's offer to rent a car and drive the two and a half hours to Charlottesville himself. At the last minute he upgraded to a convertible and paid the difference in cash. He didn't know what he was expecting to feel: the airport was like an airport anywhere, Highway 29 like all highways; the damp heat was the only thing that gave him any sense of geography at all. In a town called Culpeper he turned off the highway for lunch, and there in the dining room of some forgotten country inn he felt a little touch of the South again, the voices like his inner voice, the dark interiors and ceiling fans, the old locals who regarded his long hair and fancy car with a hostile opacity no one from Manhattan could ever have understood. He would have driven the back roads the whole rest of the way, but he had told Osbourne that he would be there in plenty of time for dinner, and he didn't want anyone to worry.

Charlottesville itself, from the car at least, was a disappointment. Every midsized city he went to nowadays – Columbus, Lexington, Eugene, no doubt Omaha just a week from now – looked the same, the chain hotels and chain stores, the strip malls and overused local roads, the grotesque boosterism that led to the too-expensive Center for the Performing Arts. Only the sight of the Rotunda, as he inched along Ivy Road on the way to the Courtyard Marriott where he would be staying, fulfilled any longing for a sense of the verticality of time. He had visited his cousin at UVA two or three times as a teenager, and the way the empty lawn stretched out before that imposing dome was all he remembered of the whole city.

The jammed roads, the strip bars, the prefab apartments: John

190

kept thinking, almost in spite of himself, how Rebecca would hate it all. He acted with faith in the best possible outcome, which was that the trip would go well, and Rebecca would be surprised and converted by John's own enthusiasm, and they would move down South to restart their careers together without any sense of pessimism or martyrdom. This vague, sentimental refrain was really a way of keeping at bay a more surprising and threatening feeling: which was not simply that it would be possible for John to start over by breaking it off with her, but that there was a dangerous appeal – an element of subversion, of role reversal – in being the one who leaves.

The Courtyard Marriott was a long two-story corridor by the highway; beyond the windows, a neatly kept grass embankment and then nothing. John dropped his bag in his room, locked the door again, and headed down the hall to Osbourne's suite. Candy machines, ice machines, the Rube Goldberg-esque maid's cart, the antiseptic, shadowless light. Osbourne had been living and working in these rooms for months, not to save money but because he didn't care where he lived, beyond the idea that he didn't have to waste minutes thinking about emptying his own trash or changing his sheets. When the door opened it was clear from the mess that he was indeed in Osbourne's bedroom, this despite the fact that the table, dresser, and even the walls had huge sheets of drawing paper taped to them. A laptop sat in the middle of the unmade bed.

He acted as if John had just come from the other wing of the Marriott rather than across the Mason-Dixon Line. "You're here," he said, and turned to walk back into the room. "Good. Let me just find some shoes. We'll go take a quick tour of the house and we'll head over to join the others."

"Others?" John said. Osbourne didn't answer. He kicked gently with his stockinged feet through the piles of carefully executed architectural drawings on the floor until he uncovered a pair of black suede shoes.

Osbourne owned a loud little Triumph; John followed in his own car as they drove well out of the city center, into the older districts far from the highway. John couldn't help smiling with pleasure just at the sight of the sprawling, colonnaded antebellum houses, with the great chandeliers hanging above the portico. Some had small historical markers, too small to read from the road, mounted on the wall beside their oversize front doors. John was lost in admiring the sheer arrogant beauty of them, barely paying attention to where he was going, when he noticed Osbourne's turn signal was on. He followed, amazed, as the Triumph turned left on to a long driveway which led to one of the mansions.

They passed beneath a porte-cochere to a parking area in the back. Tarpaulins covered some construction debris, and a stack of windows leaned against the steps to the kitchen door.

"This is it?" John said, in a higher voice than he would have liked.

Osbourne was already out of the car, his eye roving critically, but smiling all the same.

"Built before the war," he said. "But the previous owner messed with some of the original interior about sixty years ago, which is a break for us actually, because it's usually impossible now to get permission to touch anything in the really genuine antebellum homes." He opened the back door with a key, and they walked into the empty kitchen. Osbourne must have noticed the look on John's face. "You know the story of Motown Records?" Osbourne said. "They operated out of a row house in a residential neighborhood in Detroit. On a typical day you had people recording backing vocals in the bathroom, people in the living room typing press releases, people working out bridges on the porch. That's the feel that I want here. Not to make us all feel like we're a family or any corporate bullshit like that. But work that you do in a place that doesn't really look like a workplace always has that improvisatory feeling. You know?"

They went through all four stories, room by room; John stopped counting after twenty. Most of the rooms were still empty except for paint cans or stacks of wallboard. A few drafting tables were already set up, and a walk-in closet whose door had been removed was packed with unopened boxes of video equipment. But despite what Mal had said, it seemed that little of the house's interior structure had been touched, and even unfurnished it was easy to recognize in each room what must have been its old incarnation: a child's bedroom, a den or study, a servant's quarters, a pantry. Apart from the profligate size of it, it looked, in a ghostly way, as if it were the result of a careful excavation, like any number of rich people's homes John had been in as a child; and he briefly entertained the feeling – absurdly paranoid, yet at the same time not altogether unwelcome – that Osbourne had known all this somehow, that he had had John researched in some way. No one else was in the mansion. The sun poured through the uncurtained windows.

John felt simultaneously excited and jilted by the news that there would be others at dinner; the likelihood of this had never occurred to him, just as he hadn't imagined, though of course it made perfect sense, that Osbourne would be lunching other prospective employees on that brief trip to Manhattan last week. But in order to think about any of it – or about the five strangers and potential colleagues who met them at the restaurant, on the pedestrian mall downtown – he had to fight his way through a haze of much more elemental and blissful associations. Ham with gravy, sweet tea, cheese grits, fried chicken served as a side dish: it was exotic to everyone there but him, and while they all made jokes about diminishing their life expectancy if they moved down here, John tried to be discreet about lowering his head nearer to the table and just smelling it all.

Around the small table it was easy for Osbourne to rule the conversation. No one was inclined to interrupt him in any case. They had all come down here to consider their futures, but for now Osbourne seemed much more at home talking about the past. He told them the story of the creation of Apple's "1984," the spot that revolutionized their form. He talked about a weekend spent in Woody Creek with Hunter Thompson, trying unsuccessfully to get him to write some copy for them; in the end they all got high instead and test-fired automatic weapons in the meadow behind the ranch. And of course he had a great many stories about the artists of the 80s boom, Schnabel and Fischl and Borofsky and Jim Dine, whose reputations, he implied in a modest way, he had done much to create. Only through these art-world anecdotes did John learn, to his amusement, that the moody young man on Osbourne's immediate left, wearing black denim in the ninety-degree heat, was Jean-Claude Milo, the artist who had stood them up at his Manhattan loft on that first Saturday morning, almost a year ago now.

Osbourne wasn't drinking, and so no one else dared have more than one; still, it was late – past ten o'clock – and their spirits high when the hostess appeared and told Osbourne he had a phone call. Acting as if nothing were amiss about this, he excused himself; and the six of them whom he was courting began to ask shyly about one another.

Four were from New York (including John and the artist Milo); one was from Minneapolis and one had met Osbourne, she said, in the San Francisco gallery where she worked part-time as a receptionist. One was a published novelist, though John had never heard of him. A former copywriter from Ted Bates said he had quit that job a year ago to write speeches for Al Gore; he was the one who pointed out to the group the self-evident fact that they were all white.

"The provocateur," whispered the woman sitting next to John, at the end of the table. "Stirring up trouble on the shop floor, when we don't even have a shop floor yet."

"Have you seen the place?" John asked her quietly. She looked at him in surprise, and he realized it was because of his accent.

"Yesterday," she said. "It's gorgeous. Nice to work in a place you're not appalled by, I guess, but I'm a little worried I'll be too afraid to leave a McDonald's wrapper lying around. Or even leave it in the garbage, for that matter."

"So you've already agreed, then? I mean to come down and work here?" The others were engaged in a different conversation.

She blushed. She wore circular glasses, with plumb-straight blond hair and the strong, slightly bottom-heavy build, as John thought, of someone who'd excelled at field hockey as

195

a girl. "Last night," she said. "About six hours after I got down here from New York, actually. It's kind of embarrassing how quickly I caved. I hope I know what I'm doing. What about you?"

John shrugged. "I've been here about six hours myself now, I guess," he said, laughing.

"Where'd you come from? You sound like you came from across the street."

"Manhattan, same as you. I'm John Wheelwright, by the way. I work at what used to be Canning Leigh & Osbourne."

She wiped her fingers on her napkin before holding her hand out to him.

"Elaine Sizemore," she said.

He wouldn't realize until much later that that was the moment that decided it for him. In fact, by the next morning, when Osbourne stood with his hands on the doorframe of John's rented car, he still hadn't given his answer yet. Osbourne didn't push.

"You go on home and talk things over with your wife," he said. John didn't correct him. "I know you want your future to include her. Anyone would understand that. It was a pleasure to spend some time with you down here."

John walked back into his apartment and dropped his bag. It was eight-thirty on a Sunday night; Rebecca wasn't there. He had told her, he was sure, what time he was returning.

When she came back some two hours later, she smiled weakly at him. "How was your trip?"

"Fine. Where have you been?"

Their voices weren't angry; they were cautious, simulated voices, to ward off silence.

196

"The movies. I went to Film Forum to see *Mr Death*. You said you weren't interested, so."

She hung her jacket in the closet. The silence was like a buzzing. "How was it?" John asked.

"Great," she said tonelessly. "You should see it."

She went into the bathroom, and he waited for her to come out; but when she did she went directly to their bedroom. After a minute he followed her in. She was already under the blankets, reading.

"Do you not want to talk about this now?" he said, standing over her.

"I'm scared to talk about it," she said. But then, when he didn't leave, she said without looking up, "So are you going down there? I mean to take the job?"

"I *want* to go. Yes. I'm not making any demands here."

"Oh, come off it," she said.

In five days he and Roman were off to Omaha. Their work was already done. Canning must have discussed it with some of the others, because that week Dale, then Mick, then a few more of the creatives stopped by John's desk and asked to see a preview.

"Is it true?" Dale said.

Roman jumped up and lifted gingerly from a wooden crate a board with a huge, soft-focus beauty shot of a hamburger behind the words "Come on. It's in your genes."

"Oh my God," Dale said, grinning. "You know what it's like? It's like you're trying to out-Osbourne Osbourne."

Roman stuck a pen between his teeth, cigar-style. "Honesty, baby," he said. "That's the play."

John didn't force the conversation with Rebecca; in fact,

they were barely speaking. He had made up his mind he was going to Charlottesville, somehow, without making up his mind that he was willing to go without her. On Thursday evening Rebecca walked out of the bedroom, eyes red, and told John he had a phone call.

It was Osbourne. "My," he said. "Is it a bad time?"

"No, Mal, not at all." Rebecca, in her nightgown, was out of the room again.

"If you're sure. Your wife sounded somewhat . . . cold. Were you fighting?"

"Avoiding fighting, I suppose." He had a thought, and with everything so fraught it seemed an appropriate time for boldness. "Have you ever been married, Mal?"

"Me? Yes, once. So look, I'm anxious to hear your decision. I'm willing to go as far as I can to accommodate you, but on the other hand we're approaching our start-up date and if you're not with us I need to make other plans."

John stared down the empty hallway.

"If it affects your decision at all, the others you met this weekend have all signed on, with one exception, the speechwriter for Gore."

The hard part wasn't deciding; he had already decided. The hard part was saying it, letting that decision start to ramify. Turning his back on everything.

Hurting her.

"So what do you think, my boy?"

"All right," John said. "Yes."

Osbourne moved immediately into a plan of action, urging him to fly down again as soon as possible to find a home, offering to cover half his moving expenses. The venture, as John had seen, wasn't up and running yet, and wouldn't be for another two or three months; since John would of course get no severance for quitting, Mal suggested that he not mention anything at Canning & Leigh about his plans for at least another month.

In the bed, reading a magazine in the half-light of the lamp, her face set, Rebecca looked startlingly old.

"That was Osbourne," John said. She let the magazine fall and started crying. He stood beside the bed in silence.

"You won't do it, will you?" she said angrily. He wasn't sure what she was talking about. "You won't break through it. You'll make me do everything. Right up until the time you leave me you'll be talking like fucking Ozzie and Harriet, trying to make everything seem like it's someone else's fault, someone else's decision."

"Who said anything about leaving you?" He hated himself now.

"Come on! You just took that job with him. I heard you! What, do you think there's two of you or something, is that it?"

John knelt beside the bed. "Please come with me. I want to stay with you. I'm in love with you. I want to start a family with you. You act like Mal Osbourne is some lover or something, some third party that's come between us. It isn't like that. It's in me. I love you and I can't be happy here anymore. Maybe that sounds like two people to you, but it isn't, it's one."

Rebecca pulled him into bed beside her, weeping; he took her in his arms, kissed her lips and her face, stroked her hair; then, to his surprise, she was pushing his pants down and pulling at him furiously, hungrily – in tears but with desperate speed she came loudly and then so did he. It was probably the best sex they had had in years. John had no idea what to make of it.

Canning accompanied John and Roman to Omaha, the most featureless, depressing city John had ever spent a night in. Nothing in it looked like it could have been more than fifteen years old. Only the cowboyish attire of some of the men and women they saw in the lobby of their hotel made them feel the influence of a past, even an ersatz past. Roman – who was acting more and more unpredictably lately, on a kind of creative high which seemed ready to collapse at any moment – all but refused to leave his hotel room. He was in the alien Midwest of his imaginings, and he couldn't imagine that they wouldn't know him and hate him on sight.

Roman ran the pitch. The men from the Beef Council wore expensive suits with boots and enormous belt buckles. They were ludicrous; Roman spoke to them in a voice that was almost belligerent. He was not about to explain his work to them. John was worried that these industry giants weren't used to being talked to that way; but Canning seemed calm, even pleased.

They gave the agency their business on the spot. The campaign was the best they'd ever seen; cutting-edge, they said, avant-garde, just what they were hoping for to change their image. Eighteen million dollars in billings a year.

Three weeks later John took Roman out to lunch and told him he was quitting Canning & Leigh to move to Virginia and join Osbourne's new agency. When he had finished the whole story – the letter, the postcards, the trip to Charlottesville – Roman nodded thoughtfully; but he kept on nodding for too long. He tapped his fork on the tablecloth.

"It'll fail," he said finally. "It'll go belly up, and everyone will have a good laugh. And you'll deserve that. Fuck you. Fuck you for lying to me."

And at that point John would have expected him to get up and storm out: but he didn't, he went on sitting there, staring at John with a hostility that was really unexpected. John could think of nothing to say. He signaled for the check.

He was shaken enough by this that he put off giving Canning his notice until the next morning. Canning took it gratifyingly hard, though much less personally: he asked John to reconsider, told him how much his work there was valued, even offered him a raise of seven and then ten thousand dollars on the spot. John wouldn't be moved. The boss was surprised but didn't seem to take the position, as John had half expected, that he was insane. Canning said he had heard of one or two other defections from within agencies in the city.

Around the office, John was of course subjected to a few sarcastic remarks, but in the end there were no hard feelings, and no one – except for his partner, who wouldn't stay for long in the same room with him – treated him any differently in his final weeks at work. After his last day they even threw a little bon voyage party for him at the Landmark Tavern. Only Roman didn't attend. John got drunk enough to forget about that for the evening. In fact, by the time they had to relinquish the banquet room and move downstairs to the bar, they were all as drunk as John could ever remember seeing them.

Rebecca had moved out two days earlier. Her anger had mostly passed. They talked about staying in touch, but it was hard to see how their involvement could survive the discovery that there were attachments in their lives more important to them than their attachment to one another. As for John, the one thing he couldn't admit to her was that he was glad, in the end, that they had never married. Because a divorced man would always have that failure on his record; whereas for them it would presumably be easier to move on, to forget the past, to start again as if starting at zero.

Dale came up with two double scotches, and handed one to John with an air of great ceremony.

"I propose," he said, "that since this may be the last time we ever see each other, we get drunk enough to say what we really think."

John clinked glasses. "Seconded," he said.

"Here's something I've always wanted to tell you," Dale said. "That Rebecca. I've always had such a thing for her, I've always been so jealous of you for getting this amazingly beautiful, smart, hot woman to fall in love with you. So what do you do? You ask her to move down to Deliverance country, to piss her life away in the middle of nowhere. She says no. You dump her. So now my whole opinion of you has changed. You stand before me, revealed as a total fucking idiot."

John put his hand gently on top of Dale's head and smiled. "You're not in her class," he said. "Go on, ask her out after I'm gone. You'll never get near her. Besides, there is a whole nation south of Battery Park, you snob. You stay here on your little island ironizing yourself into early heart trouble. I know where the future is."

"Fuck you," Dale said affectionately.

"Fuck you too," John said.

Canning came up behind them, drunk as a lord, and put his

arms around both their shoulders. "Isn't this great?" he said. "All this *candor!*"

THEIR TIME TOGETHER, over the next month or so, passed predominantly in silence, in half-darkness, looking at slides in Modernism class. There was no real impetus to take things to another level; already Molly spent more time around John, two or three hours a week, than she did with anyone else in her life. It was a relief, actually, to have someone in on the secret of her presence there. Molly would arrive at about ten minutes to eleven and take a seat in the back row; John, whose ten-o'clock class was all the way across campus, would show up a little red-faced, trying not to breathe hard, and sit beside her. This arrangement was never discussed. They had four or five minutes to talk before the lights went down and Professor Leonhard came around to sit on the front of his desk, holding the clicker. Molly watched the screen, watched Leonhard, watched John taking notes as he listened; she felt slightly jilted when he would shut her out in this way, but then the midterm was coming up, which he had to worry about and she didn't.

Four or five minutes a day, three days a week, for a month, was time enough to learn a good deal about each other. Molly answered his questions partially. She told him, for instance, that she was not on good terms with her parents, and had come to live with her brother for a while. John never pushed her for more; he politely accepted every answer as complete, even when she was obviously holding something back. Nor was he the kind of boy – the only kind she knew, when she thought about it – who listened to your speech hoping to hear something in it which would remind him of a tangentially related experience of his own, which he would then explain in full, as if this were evidence of empathy of some sort. Maybe it was only because his experience was so very different from hers.

John just looked at her when she talked. It was a look whose intensity she knew he was not aware of showing. She knew what was going on. Still, he never asked her out.

Leonhard turned the lights off, and directed two TAs to pull the enormous shades down. In the sudden darkness and slightly laggard silence, the first slide, already on the screen, brightened into view.

"Kandinsky?" Molly whispered to John. She could feel him nod. He took out his pen and his notebook; she folded her arms, put her feet on the back of the empty chair in front of her, and stared.

The best way to deflect his interest in her background was to ask questions of her own. Thus she learned that John was from Asheville, North Carolina; that he was the only child of his father's second marriage; his father, a lawyer, was forty-eight when John was born, dead now for eight years, and John's two half sisters were both more than ten years his senior. His mother was very Old South, old money, a great thrower of parties and arbiter of other people's reputations. As he grew older he had an inkling of how small his parents' world really was. It was a desire to shock them out of being who they were that led him to enroll at Berkeley, which they and all their friends had considered – even in 1985 – to be a virtual outpost of Comintern. John had never seen the school, had never seen the state of California, before he arrived for his freshman orientation, three and a half years ago.

Spring break was approaching, just after exams; John would fly home to endure more questions about the ruin of his future prospects, a ritual which would end with his stepfather Buzz guiltily handing over a big wad of money as John waited for the cab to take him back to the airport. But it was the imminence of those two weeks, during which they wouldn't see each other, that finally emboldened John to ask Molly on an actual date.

"You know the LaValle's on the South Side?" he said, his nervousness showing. "Will you meet me there Thursday at about eight?"

Pizza and beer, jukeboxes and shouting; Molly didn't love it, but she suspected that John didn't, either, that he took her there because he didn't want to demonstrate for her the fact that he could afford something nicer. He was waiting for her in a booth, and, unsurprisingly perhaps, for the first few minutes they couldn't find much to say to each other.

Around them few of the tables were full; there were some solitary diners, people who had probably studied through the serving hours for dinner at the cafeteria, and one round table crowded with what looked like freshmen who evidently had no exams tomorrow and were celebrating by playing drinking games – Quarters, Thumper, Boom Schwartz. The waitress who avoided them wore a shirt and tie and one of those mini-aprons.

"So what will you do," John said, "over the break?"

Molly shrugged. "Not really a break for me," she said, "strictly speaking."

"Yeah, but no classes to go to during the day, no . . . Are your roommates going home?"

"A couple of them," Molly said, but this was not true, not one of them was leaving the house.

"Your brother?"

"My brother hasn't been back home since he came out here. It's a long way to fly for just a couple of weeks," she said, a little defensively.

The waitress stood on her toes to lean through the serving window. One of the girls at the table full of freshmen chugged a beer while the others chanted her name, the boys with particular vigor, a drunk female being a special kind of desideratum for them.

"Is it okay," John said, leaning forward on the table, with his eyebrows low, his hair falling into his face, "if I say to you that I worry a little about you?"

Molly stared at him. The thought that rolled through her head — to her instant amazement — was that he was a guy and so she should just take him home and fuck him as a way of killing whatever it was that was growing here, a way of not being taken in by the seeming genuineness of it; and that thought was quickly supplanted by something even more surprising, which was an aching desire to be normal, to be a part of every stupid thing, a desire to play Thumper with a table full of idiots in a public place spending pocket money Daddy sent from home, a pain, in fact, at the idea of being worried about.

John sat back in his chair. "I'm sorry," he said. "I've said the wrong thing. Please forgive me. Sometimes I don't know what to keep to myself."

Molly started to tell him it was all right, but at the same time she didn't want their conversation to go any further along that particular path; so she said nothing. Politely, he began talking about himself again.

An hour later, they were done, and the place was becoming noisier. He asked if he could walk her home. But things had been getting strange at the house lately. It was irrational of her, she knew, since he would only be taking her as far as her front door; still, for whatever reason, she didn't want him to see it. She asked him if she could walk him home instead.

He lived with a roommate in a three-story apartment complex on Bancroft. On his face, when they reached the door to the lobby, was a little amused smile, a look of comic dignity; Molly realized it was because the simple role reversal involved in being walked home after a first date made him as mirthfully self-conscious as if he were in drag. "I had a great time tonight," he said. "Would you like to come up, have another beer or some coffee or something?" And right then she thought she saw, like a shaft of light coming from under a closed door, all the dates he had ever been on in high school, how conscious he was of what was expected of him, and how much, if she got him into bed, he would enjoy being controlled, being over-whelmed; she could do it, she could lose herself and what she was feeling for him in that clinical administering to him of what she knew he would want, even if he didn't know it himself.

But she didn't want to have sex with him. It was a bad and confusing sign. Of course, when she said, "I think I should just get home," he took it for simple restraint. "I guess I won't see you for a couple of weeks, then," he said. And he reached out very gently to where she stood with her arms folded against the chill and touched her very lightly on both elbows as he kissed her.

Something about it, the tenderness of it, upset her; and she thought about what this might signify the whole way home, on the overlit side streets, past the parking garages roofed with artificial turf for soccer games. She was glad she hadn't slept with him, and she was glad she wouldn't see him for a while, but she didn't know the reasons for these feelings. When she got back to the house there were six people, none of whom she had ever seen before, in sleeping bags on the living-room rug. She stepped over them, went to her room, and closed the door.

Some kind of seismic shift, the nature of which she was not made privy to, had taken place in the last few weeks in the house on Vine Street. It now resembled less a home than a sort of base of operations, though what sort of operation it was impossible to say. All day long there were meetings in the house, some involving all the housemates and some composed of just a few; they would stop talking when Molly passed through the room.

Two nights before her date with John Wheelwright, she had come home late from a film-society screening of *Knife in the Water*. No one seemed to be awake. She tiptoed into the bedroom she shared with Sally, carefully closed the door, and began undressing in the dark. Slowly, as her eyes started to pick out shapes in the dark room, Molly began to feel that something was wrong. Her anxiety spread until finally she reached out to the wall and felt around for the light switch. Sally's bed was stripped to the mattress; the closet doors and dresser drawers were all open, and every one of Sally's belongings was gone.

Next morning four of the strangers were at the breakfast table, eating as if late for some appointment; Richard sat at the head. Molly waited until the others had left before asking Richard, her voice scratchy, what was going on.

"Sally's gone," Richard said offhandedly.

"Yes I can see that, but—"

"We took a vote, which was unanimous, and asked her to leave."

"Without any notice?"

Richard shrugged.

"Did she do something wrong?"

Her brother reacted as if this were not a simple question. After a long pause, he said, "It was . . . I guess you could say more on an ideological plane, but I don't want to say any more, we all agreed not to discuss it. In fact, I'd appreciate it if you wouldn't make reference to it in front of the others."

While Molly, who still lived there rent-free, could hardly afford to feel slighted by her brother's continual use of the word "we," she began to wonder how safe her own place there really was. As long as she didn't start antagonizing them – bringing men home, doing drugs, things like that – she supposed they would continue to ignore her as she flew, so to speak, below the radar of their Christianity. Of course, her only real protection was afforded by her kinship with Richard, who seemed more and more, if also obscurely, in charge. If something should happen to cause the others to turn on him, or if he should turn on her himself, then she would have no place to go. She went back to her barren room and thought about it. Not quite twenty years old, she found herself without an attachment in the world she could rely upon, not even within her own family. Calmly she turned over the question of whether or not something was wrong with her.

On the Friday that marked the midway point of spring break she cut across the empty campus to Mr Whalen's house. She read him Herb Caen's column in the *Chronicle*. Friday was payday; on the sidewalk, once she was out of sight of his windows, she tore open the envelope in which he always put her cash: seventy dollars. It wasn't enough to protect her from anything. On Telegraph she walked past a group of five or six blank-faced kids sitting under and on top of some army blankets, passing around an open can of peaches with a plastic spoon in it. She felt everything she came across cutting through the veil around her now, the veil that separated her from what was real.

Outside the BART station she found a copy of that day's *Chronicle*, the same one she had just read to Mr Whalen, on top of a trash can; she took it to a bench by the parking lot and opened it to the want ads. It was like a catalogue of the ways in which her own short life had quietly defamiliarized her with the customs of the world. When she saw an ad for phone sales, she remembered that she had always been told she had a good voice. But when she called from a phone booth the woman on the other end of the line rejected her on the spot. "Sorry, sweetie," she said. "You're too timid. I can hear your voice shaking. I mean, come on."

Phone sex operator: she could do that, she thought, and she liked the idea that her working life would consist of fantasy, that she would be another person entirely. But the "girls," she learned, were expected to take these calls in their homes, at all hours, and that, at least for now, was out of the question.

At some point during the week she had begun to think about John Wheelwright. The form this took, at first, was a series of startling realizations that wherever he was at that precise

210

moment, he was very likely thinking about her too. There was no one else in the world about whom she could say that right now.

Still, she fought against the feeling of missing him, or of looking forward to his return. She didn't believe that these feelings were authentic on her part. John's kindness, his concern for her, was genuine, she had no doubt about that. Her vulnerability to these things was what bothered her. By virtue of their very intensity, she thought, her own feelings couldn't be trusted.

At home she found Richard doing the dishes, wearing a red polo shirt and khaki pants, which didn't strike her as unusual until she walked through the dining room and saw two of her housemates, Steve and Guy, typing into laptops at the table, also wearing red polo shirts and khaki pants.

The weather was growing warmer, and as a consequence the streets, even before the students' return, were more and more crowded with people who weren't going anywhere: preachers, entertainers, schizophrenics, bums. Molly had never given John her phone number or address. On the weekend before classes resumed she realized this meant that, since he had no way to contact her, she never had to see him again if she didn't want to. While having a cup of coffee at the Soup Kitchen she saw a blue spring-term course directory on the table beside her. She asked the couple sitting there if she could borrow it for a second; quickly she flipped through the Art History section until she found a course called The New York School which met Monday in Sprague Hall — it sounded like something John might be enrolled in. She borrowed a pen from the waitress and wrote the room number on a napkin.

Monday morning she went to the first floor of Sprague Hall and took a seat in the back row. John never came. After half an hour she left to go to work. She read Mr Whalen an editorial about the sale of the Empire State Building to the Japanese.

On the way home, on the corner by the secondhand clothing store, Molly caught a glimpse of a red shirt, and was a few steps past before she turned to see her brother, Richard, standing on a wooden stepstool, reciting the Bible from memory. She felt a kind of constriction around her lungs. No one was listening, and yet he did not acknowledge her when she retraced her steps and stood in front of him. He did not acknowledge anyone – he stared into the bricks halfway between the first and second stories of the buildings across Telegraph. On some level, Molly thought, she must have seen this coming, because, though thoroughly frightened, she was not exactly surprised. She noticed a stack of leaflets on the stool beside his feet and took one. "Ten Righteous Men?" it read.

That night she had a hard time getting to sleep. She now believed it was imperative that she see John Wheelwright again soon, but not just for the sake of seeing him. The larger his absence grew, the more he came to stand for everything missing from her life. He was becoming inhuman in her mind, and she longed for the disillusionment of seeing him again, of being reminded of some compromising thing about him which she had apparently managed to forget.

Awake almost till dawn, she then slept past eleven. Deliberately she showered, dressed, and ate a bowl of cereal, before walking to John's house and sitting on the front steps. She did not ring his doorbell. After three hours she saw him walking up the street, alone, in and out of the shade of the elm trees. By the time his face came into focus for her he had recognized her, and he was smiling broadly. He took out his keys as he reached the steps.

"Molly," he said, a little too jovially. "Come on in."

"No, thank you," she said.

They stayed like that for a little while.

"Can you come for a walk with me?" Molly said.

They went to the Soup Kitchen. "Will you buy me some coffee, please?" she said. Then she told him the story of her fainting spell here and her trip to the clinic in Oakland. She regretted having started the story – it sounded too much to her like a plea for sympathy – but she followed it through. When she pointed through the serving window to the cook who had driven her to the clinic, he waved at them. She looked hard at John, who was holding her hand now, for any sign of fear or insincerity. Not that she would have been put off by such a sign; in fact, she would have been reassured. She didn't see any.

John said he had to go to the registrar's office to drop off his tuition check, and Molly went with him, standing silently in line, feeling a little foolish. By the time they came out on to the plaza again it was after four o'clock. They bought a six-pack and went all the way up the hill to sit on a bench outdoors in the empty Greek Theater, to drink and watch the evening fall.

Then Molly told John the story of how she had come to live in Berkeley, of how she had been estranged from her parents, of her affair with the man whose children she had been hired to care for. She left nothing out. She did it so he would hate her, because she felt quite strongly now that if she couldn't

213

do something to change his mind about her she was going to lose control.

They looked across the top of the stage at the sunset lighting up the hills. John waited a long time; then he said, "Do you think it was a mistake?"

"What?"

"Sleeping with this guy, this Dennis. Looking back on it, do you think you made a mistake, doing that?"

Molly nodded; then, realizing he was still staring off at the hills, she said, "Yes, I guess so."

He sighed. "So then you were seventeen," he said, "and you made a mistake. I tell you, I hope you won't hold it against me, speaking badly of your family. But I just can't understand how your mother and father could turn their backs on you like that. I can't understand how anyone could turn on their own child."

Molly burst into tears. John took her hand and kissed it. "I'm guessing that you haven't told too many people that story before," he said. "I did nothing but think about you the whole time I was home. Don't ever think that there's something about you I wouldn't want to know."

They lapsed into a long silence on the downhill walk home. John, who still had no idea where Molly lived, stayed half a step behind her, guessing they were going back to his apartment but afraid that saying anything would break the spell. When they reached his door he took out his keys and they stepped inside without a word. His roommate could be heard in the shower; so they went straight to John's bedroom and closed the door. The walls were covered with hundreds of postcards, all reproductions of great paintings, like a museum in miniature.

There was nowhere to sit, apart from one desk chair, so they both sat on the bed.

When they kissed she felt a shudder go through him, an actual shudder, and after that there was nothing she didn't want to give to him. They stood to undress each other; once her pants were off John remained on his knees for a few moments, his hands on her back, kissing her stomach, kissing the red impressions left by her jeans at the belt line. They sat cross-legged on the bed again, facing each other; Molly took John's cock gently between her hands and looked as intently as she could into his eyes, doing nothing, feeling him grow hard in her palms.

He was so patient. She leaned forward, kissed him, and let her weight push him down on to his back. She straightened up, reached between her thighs, and guided him into her. She was trying to move as slowly as possible – not because that was more enjoyable for her, nor in response to any sign from him. She didn't really know why she was doing it.

Still, it didn't last very long. He closed his eyes and she felt him contracting inside her. She lay down on top of him; he laughed a little, then, still inside her, he began running his fingertips along her back, touching her as lightly as possible, from her neck down as far as he could reach, just below her hips. "You're so beautiful," he whispered, and it went right through her, painfully enough that she hoped he wouldn't say anything more.

In the silence they heard the bathroom door open; John's roommate walked past them on the other side of the wall and into his own room, where he shut the door and put on some music. Molly got up from the bed and carefully opened the door to the hallway.

"Everything all right?" John asked softly.

She nodded. The bathroom was shrouded in steam; she couldn't see her own face in the mirror. She sat on the lid of the toilet, inhaling the heavy air, her palms up in front of her face, and watched her hands shaking.

By the time three weeks had gone by, Molly had pretty much moved in with him, though she now had so few belongings that she wasn't altogether sure John even knew this was the case.

"HERE ARE SOME words that I never want to hear again," Osbourne said. "Edgy. Postmodern. In your face."

Nervous laughter around the table. They were gathered in the dining room — or what was formerly the dining room; no one ate there, and John kept waiting for it to be given some new name, but it remained "the dining room" — for their first staff meeting. The table around which they sat was a magnificent cherrywood oval; at each place was a china cup and saucer. Apart from that, the sunlit white room was free of any decorative touch, for a few more hours at least. Some workmen had been in the first stages of the delicate, complex process of installing one of Osbourne's own brushed-steel Frank Stellas on the long wall opposite the windows, when Osbourne had walked in, trailed by his new staff, and told the installers to take an early lunch.

"We are here to make art. We will make it in a communal setting. However, that doesn't mean you're going to hear a lot of that team-first bullshit that you might have been subjected to in some of your old places of employment. I believe in cooperating, but not at the expense of the emergence of individual genius. No great work of art has ever germinated from some committee decision. Greatness is a pure product of the individual consciousness."

There were nine people, including Osbourne, around the table, six of them holding pens and notepads. No one had written anything down yet. The pads and pens were supplies they had brought from home. No one knew where to find them inside the mansion, because no one had been given an office yet. Osbourne's hair was still wet from a shower; he wore a bright-green polo shirt with the collar turned up and chinos, and his feet were bare. He swiveled restlessly in his chair as he spoke, as if he could hardly wait for this meeting, which he had spontaneously convened, to be over.

"What else, what else. In the west wing there are several bedrooms, just about all of them furnished by now, I think – I'll have to go take a look. Those are for you, as you want or need them. The kitchen can only stay open until eight p.m. Rose – that's the housekeeper, for those of you who haven't met her – is here twenty-four hours. As am I, by the way. For those of you who haven't figured it out" – he held up one bare foot – "part of the east wing has been kept as a living quarters as well, and right now that's where I live. Ah, Benjamin!"

Benjamin walked in from the kitchen entrance, a stout man somewhere in his sixties, John guessed; nodding at the mention of his name, he went around the table pouring coffee from a silver pitcher. A few of them held their hands over the small china cups and smiled apologetically.

"I hope you'll all take the opportunity at some point today

to introduce yourselves to Benjamin, who heads the kitchen staff, and to Rose as well. Now, a couple of you have asked me, in the last two days, when your various job descriptions will be spelled out. The answer is that there are no job descriptions. Titles, same answer – you have none. As for where your own individual office is located, you don't have one." He gaped, good-naturedly exaggerating their looks of surprise.

John had not yet met all seven of his colleagues. Interestingly, they all had the same expression, as far as he could see: gameness, he would have called it, a willed overcoming of the skepticism that every casually dropped bit of information about their new workplace instinctively produced.

"But the real reason I called you all here," Osbourne said, "is to announce some happy news. Which is, we have our first client."

A murmur of relief, and then some soft, somewhat sarcastic but good-natured applause spread around the table.

"Yes, it's true. It's a local client, a bank in fact. The First National Bank of Charlottesville. Now I'm going to try a little something here. Which is, I'm not going to tell you another thing about them."

He stood up and went to the windows, which overlooked the dogwood trees behind the kitchen.

"No research, no market information, no looking at previous campaigns. No history. None of you are from here, and so I'm assuming you have no idea if this is the number one bank in the city or the number twenty-one. I want to keep it that way."

Elaine Sizemore, who was sitting across the table from John, threw her little notepad on the table, where it made a louder noise than she had intended.

Osbourne didn't turn around. "No idea what this client needs. No idea what their self-image is. Because they don't know what they need. We're the ones who know that. We know it already, and market research would just cloud our judgment about that. And if any of you have any experience doing campaigns for banks – well, I can't do anything about that, I suppose, but really what I'd like is for you to forget all about it. Banks want to be humanized, and humanizing banks leads to lying, and lying leads to irony as a way of dissociating yourself, and your audience, from the lie. That's no good. That's the chain we're trying to break.

"So we don't relate the campaign to the bank at all. We don't associate our work with the bank; we do our best work, and then we allow the bank to be associated with it."

He looked around the table. "That's all," he said brightly. "I'll be around. I look forward to seeing what you come up with."

Osbourne walked by the table, stopped to drain his cup of coffee, and disappeared into the hallway. The others, smiling and perplexed, stood slowly. They didn't speak to one another. What was in their minds was doubt, and no one was willing to express it – not out of fear of being reprimanded or informed upon, but because everyone had a significant stake in the success of this enterprise, and right now that success seemed to be largely, if not entirely, a matter of personal faith.

The installers came back in, one holding a carpenter's level and drill and the other reading a pamphlet of some sort; they resumed preparations for the enormous Stella. John, grateful though he was for Osbourne's generosity regarding starting salaries, had all along been expecting a much more shoestring-type operation than the one that was so far in evidence – the china cups, the full-time domestic staff, the sleeping quarters. Where was the money going to come from to pay for all this? With local banks as clients, how could Osbourne run the place at this level for more than a few weeks?

But these reflections were swallowed up in the instinctive fear that had been reinstilled in all eight of them by the familiar vague directive to get to work, to come up with something. John went into the south parlor and sat on one of the couches, trying to think about advertising without the impurities of an actual product to advertise. He sat and thought in earnest, but with nothing to build on his mind began to wander, toward what he might be able to order from the kitchen in the way of lunch, toward the amenities he still needed for his new apartment, toward Rebecca and what she might be doing now; and when Daniel, the novelist, noticing the blank look on his face, asked him if he wanted to go down to the basement and play some pool, John said okay.

IN THE MIDDLE of June came graduation day; but John, whose thesis on Goya was incomplete – abandoned, actually, at least for the time being – wasn't ready for it. He called his parents and told them not to come. They did not react calmly. At the end of the month, John's roommate, diploma in hand, said goodbye and moved south to Los Angeles. John renewed the lease in his own name, this despite the fact that his parents had told him to expect no more money from them. He took a word-processing job in San Francisco at a law firm, to cover the extra rent; and he and Molly had a home together, a home they couldn't really afford, a home with one empty room in it.

Sometimes in the mornings, after John had left for the BART station, Molly would sit in the kitchen and cry for a while, without really knowing why. It wasn't because she missed him. It just seemed like a good idea, at that point, to set aside part of the day for crying, and that was the part of the day she chose. She asked John once what his post-graduation plans had been, before meeting her that is, and he said he hadn't had any; she knew this was a lie. The exodus of students for summer vacation made a certain type of job much easier to come by: Molly now worked as a waitress at Fondue Fred's, a forlorn little restaurant in a mini-mall on Telegraph, four dinners and two lunches a week. Between them they made enough to pay the bills. Neither of them had much of an inclination to learn to cook, but they ate as cheaply as they knew how, frozen dinners, rice and beans from the taqueria. Weekends, unless Molly talked him out of it, John still went to the library to do some research for his thesis, which he now hoped to complete in time to graduate in December. All his friends were gone from Berkeley, either for the summer or for good, so the two of them spent every evening together. In February he would turn twenty-three years old.

Molly felt scared most of the time, particularly when she woke up. Her fear was exacerbated by a sense that she wasn't entitled to it, that by all rights she should have felt safer now, in the embrace of someone completely devoted to her, than she had ever felt in her life. If she awoke before he did she would try to forget things by seeing how aroused she could get him without waking him up. But the early mornings were usually passed in that way in any event; it was a way of blocking out everything. They could hold each other's eyes for a long time while making love. She'd never really thought of it before, but now, when it came easily, she realized what an unusual thing that was to do.

They never answered the phone anymore because chances were the call was from his parents, unless it was from a bill collector. They had no TV; it had belonged to John's room-mate, who had taken it with him, and their financial margin was too narrow at the end of each month to afford one. Neither of them could call on family, at this point, for any help with money, or with anything. Molly wondered to what extent true love was properly bound up with one's feeling of having nowhere else to go.

She bought a cookbook from a Krishna selling odds and ends off a blanket beside Euclid Avenue. Since their incompetence in the kitchen was so general, they tried fancy things as readily as the most basic: vichyssoise, steak au poivre, crème caramel. The latter was doomed from the start, since Molly thought "egg white" meant the white part of the egg, i.e., the shell. John made fun of her; she picked up the phone, ordered a pizza from Domino's, and bet him that she could make him come twice before the pizza arrived. Hours later they were still laughing at the way they had had to pass the money around the corner of the door to the delivery boy; later still, though, as Molly lay awake thinking about the ways in which these evenings were binding them together, there was less and less funny about it.

She was the one taking him through everything, trying everything, acting experienced even when it came to things she had never done before. Trying, she supposed without really acknowledging it, to lose him, to leave him behind, to shock

222

him or to test the reality of what he seemed to feel for her, which was total loyalty, an unwillingness to let her cast herself for him in any light other than the light of his love.

She all but goaded him, for instance, into anal sex, even though it was something she had never tried before. The thought that it might hurt her went against every instinct he had. Ultimately, the pain of it, while not as severe as she might have thought, wasn't balanced out by any great corresponding pleasure, other than maybe an abstract, intimate sort of pleasure born of mutual transgression. But the whole thing, though they never repeated it, was worth it for the look on his face, tenderness bordering on alarm, as he held himself frozen uncomfortably in one position, balanced on one elbow, waiting for her muscles to relax, the other hand stroking her hair.

They did go out, of course. The city was hushed, depopulated, yet strengthened in its character somehow, like something boiled down to its essence. When they could afford it they went out to a movie. On the occasional Thursday – half-price day – they took BART into San Francisco and went to the Museum of Modern Art. John talked her through the dim rooms, modestly, reluctant to offer any evidence of his expertise unless he was asked. Molly was warmed by the pleasure he took not just in knowing a lot about the paintings but in the paintings themselves; and she was even a little jealous of the years he had spent in classrooms, lecture halls, auditoriums, developing this interest. Jealous because it all seemed to have passed her by, impossible now, like a trip back in time, even though she was just twenty years old.

September arrived, and then October. The life of the university renewed itself; neither of them was a part of it now.

Her brother Richard had become, on an irregular basis, part of the street life. He wore his red shirt and announced the damnation of everyone who passed in front of him, damned them without looking at them, his gaze leveled above their heads. Molly stopped to listen to him on her way to work. She didn't have to worry about being exposed. He knew where she was living now, and so he did not even acknowledge knowing her, much less being her brother. Students who stopped to listen for a moment, she noticed, usually broke the connection by laughing, or imitating him, or pantomiming great fear. Their irony was something to which Richard was completely impervious; but it was no less mighty an instrument for that.

Sometimes she encouraged John to dominate her a little bit, to be a little less gentle, less considerate, both because she liked it and also to jolt him out of what he thought he knew about women; but he couldn't really do it, that wasn't who he was. Once he made her gag slightly and he apologized so many times she finally started to laugh at him.

She thought a lot about her brother and what had happened to him, and about whether, apart from the fact that she missed him, what had become of him was something to be mourned. Unabashed eccentricity; a desire for a sense of family, a sense of mission in the world, to rescue life from the pointless and the sham; a longing for something real in the midst of everything that seemed insubstantial; a need for something besides oneself to fear. Were these reasons to doubt the authenticity of a man's religious feeling, or the strongest evidence of that very authenticity?

When they had no money to go out, John and Molly sat at home and read, looking up from time to time and shaking their heads at the picture of premature domesticity they presented, or would have presented if there were anyone looking at them. Once she caught him looking up at her rather more than she was used to.

"What are you doing?" she said.

"Nothing." He had a pen in his hand. She got up and walked to his chair, and saw that on the flyleaf of his book he had drawn a picture of her face.

"It's good," she said.

"I'm not very good with portraits."

In the depths of one night in their bed – out of breath, unaware what time it was – John said, "I don't know what to do. I can't remember what I used to feel like before this. I'm worried all the time that something will happen to change it."

She curled up against his chest. "You've just never gotten laid like this before," she said.

She felt him tense up. When a minute had gone by, and he hadn't said anything, she raised herself on her elbow, so that he could feel she was looking at him.

"Don't do that," he said softly. "Don't joke about it."

Some days Molly would feel, without any particular cause, that it was all bound to end badly, and when that happened she wanted to turn herself off, to make herself stop thinking, usually by trying to flood out with lust these pockets of despair. John didn't really understand what was going on at such moments. She would suddenly engage him in some kind of pointless sexual dare: sitting on his hand on a crowded BART train, blowing him, at three-thirty in the morning, in the brightly lit lobby of their building, sitting astride him, her feet braced against the wall, in a men's-room stall at the San

225

Francisco Museum of Modern Art. She wanted to find his limit, because knowing that limit would drive a wedge between them; but in his mind, the question was not how far he would go but how far he would follow her, and she couldn't find the limit to that.

The chef and the maître d' at Fondue Fred's were constantly asking her out. They knew she was living with someone, but they took it for granted that an attachment like that in someone so young – they were both at least ten years older – was not solid enough to withstand the right pressure. For some reason they preferred to harass her in each other's presence; they were emboldened, or maybe just put at ease, by the knowledge that when they said something outrageous to her they could look for each other's reaction rather than just Molly's. Manny, the maître d', had a small ponytail and wore shiny, ventless suits, of which he seemed to own only two. The difference between his deportment with the customers – practiced, a little too unctuous to be as classy as he thought he was – and his amazingly profane manner among Dylan and the other kitchen staff was so broad that Molly found herself wondering about the circumstances of his life outside of work. But she didn't ask any questions; curiosity about Manny, she knew, would be instantly and eagerly misinterpreted.

Dylan had been in the navy, or so he said, and had no obvious connection to this part of the country at all, having grown up in New Jersey and apparently resolved never to go back there. He had a series of Japanese ideograms tattooed on his biceps, which he always kept exposed. One evening Molly dropped a tray and broke a few glasses just on the kitchen side of the swinging door. She swept the shards into a bread basket and went out back to the alley to dump them in the trash. Dylan was out there, smoking a cigarette. Black trash bags were piled against the stucco walls on three sides; the fourth was the narrow open end of the alley, with a streetlight just beyond it, where every few minutes someone would walk past.

Molly's eyes met Dylan's; she turned away to dump the glass in a garbage can, but the first two she opened were full to the brim.

"You didn't have to smash those glasses," Dylan said, "just for an excuse to meet me out here."

Molly laughed halfheartedly. "I guess I could have taken up smoking," she said.

"Want one?"

"No." She dumped the glass, straightened up, and looked at the pillar of night sky visible at the end of the alley. It was quite a peaceful spot, apart from the smell, which was powerful. She felt Dylan's eyes on her again, and she turned around. Through for the night, he had taken off his apron; his chef's jacket was stained with sauces and animal blood. His hands were scalded red. He mistook her curiosity.

"You and me should party sometime," he said.

"Party?" she said, with distaste.

"Your boyfriend wouldn't have to know."

She had already taken a step back toward the door; no doubt he was growing bolder because of it. No doubt he didn't really expect she would turn around again. So she stopped. Your boyfriend wouldn't have to know. The light from the street-lamp seemed to swim as a wind blew through the leaves. The air smelled of eucalyptus and fish.

"Hey Dylan," she said in a new voice, a voice that was like

a sneer. Her eyes were locked on to his. He said nothing, but threw his cigarette away.

"How long does it take you, Dylan?" she said.

His eyebrows went up; even his surprise looked more like a simulation of surprise.

"That's up to you, I guess," he said. "Little girl."

In the grip of some powerful urge – not self-destruction, exactly, since what Dylan said was true: no one would have to know – Molly reached out and lowered the zipper on his blue-and-white-checked chef's pants. Stepping closer to him, she wove her hand through his jockey shorts until she could take his cock out and hold it in the air between them. She didn't look at it. It was jumping slightly in her fingers. Though he tried not to, he kept looking over her head at the door to the kitchen. He took another half-step closer to her.

Something was wrong, though, inside her, and she fought against it. Then the fighting took the form of her resisting the pressure of Dylan's one hand between her shoulder and neck as he tried to push her down on to her knees. She let go of him and stepped back.

"I'm sorry," she said.

Quickly he pushed his cock back in and zipped up; with the outline of it so conspicuous, he seemed more self-conscious than he had when it was out levitating in the night air. He laughed, without smiling, not at all in a promising way.

"You little cunt," he said evenly.

"I can't, I'm sorry," Molly said, and she pushed her way through the door and into the kitchen. She stayed in the dining room until her shift was over; then, telling her busboy that she felt sick, she left the restaurant without cashing out. Halfway home she sat down on a bench at a bus stop; the buses didn't run at that hour. She sat and thought and didn't come home until one-thirty, hoping John would be angry at her for it. But he wasn't.

The struggles just to get by, to meet the rent and have enough left over for a couple of nights out of the apartment, were a blessing in a way; it kept them, for the most part, from lifting their heads to see the vast amount of time that lay before them at that tender age, time they had no plans to fill, time that represented an unfathomable test of the love that got them through the here and now.

The student film societies started up again, and Molly and John paid a dollar (he refused to sneak in) to see *The Magnificent Ambersons, Downhill Racer, Meet Me in St Louis*. On the walk home, Molly told John the story of Margaret O'Brien's snowman-whacking scene, how Minnelli got her to throw a tantrum by telling her that someone had killed her dog.

"How do you know that?" John said.

"I read the textbook for one of the film courses I was auditing," she said. "It was before we met."

"Read it how?"

She looked at him, as if unsure of the tone of his question. "I would go to the UC bookstore," she said, "and sit in the stacks in the textbook section, and read it there."

They walked on in silence for a little while.

"What do you want to do?" John said.

From the stress on the word *do*, Molly knew what he was talking about; but she pretended not to.

"For a living, I mean," John said. "Or a career, or whatever the word is. What kind of work would you most want to do?"

Molly shrugged, unhappy with the question.

"I don't remember how long you have to have lived in California to establish residency, but if you had it you could enroll here really cheaply, you know. Of course, even a really cheap tuition, at this point we don't have the money."

"I couldn't ask you to do that," she said.

"Of course you could. I mean, maybe not right now."

The streetlights flooded the leaves as they walked in step on the empty sidewalks toward home. Molly simultaneously loved and resented John for his optimism. She couldn't have found the words to explain how hopeless it actually seemed.

Two weeks later Molly was walking up Telegraph, on her way to work, wearing her uniform, when two of her old housemates from Vine Street, Steve and Guy, appeared on either side of her. At first she was happy to see them, especially since they acknowledged her, or at least made no conspicuous effort to get away from her. Then, at the corner of Telegraph and Dwight, Guy took her arm and directed her away from the restaurant, in the direction of the house. "Richard wants to see you," Steve said. Molly laughed at their serious expressions, but before she had even stopped laughing things had ceased to seem comic. They were acting so strangely that Molly had to remind herself that these were people whom she had shared a home with, people who had been quite charitable towards her, that there was nothing to worry about.

Richard was seated at the kitchen table; surprisingly, unlike Steve and Guy, he was not wearing his usual red polo shirt. Over his shoulder Molly could see that the furniture was now gone from the living room, replaced by six or eight foldaway beds. Richard nodded at the other two and they left the kitchen.

"I'm sorry to surprise you like that," Richard said. He seemed to have acquired the ability to sit for long stretches without fidgeting, without moving at all. "But Steve and Guy didn't want to cross your threshold, knowing how you live, and honestly I can't blame them. Your father has attempted suicide. Through God's intervention this attempt has failed. He's in the hospital in Albany. Your mother has asked that you return home for a while."

Molly felt her jaw trembling. She didn't speak. There was something in Richard's manner that made her fear the consequences of crying. He looked at her without any tenderness at all – only with a kind of professional conscientiousness, as if he were delivering a telegram and took care not to give any indication he had looked at it to see what it said.

"If you call and give her your address," he continued, "your mother says she will wire you the money for an airplane ticket."

Molly, try as she might, couldn't really make vivid for herself what she had just been told, and his flat tone wasn't making it any easier. "What about you?" she said finally.

"What do you mean?"

"I mean aren't we both going back?"

His expression did not change; which is to say, his face did not resolve itself into any recognizable expression at all. "She asked me. I told her it was of no consequence to me, and that in any case as her husband had now sinned mortally and without evidence of his repentance I could not be in his company."

"How – I mean, did she say how he—"

"I don't have any idea."

"Tell me what else she said, anything at all."

"She asked me to pass the message on to you, since she didn't know where you were living, and I've done that. If you want to know more, I think you should call her. In fact, I think you should call her anyway."

Molly scrutinized her brother; confusion was making her squint. "You're really not coming with me?"

"I have business here," he said.

They sat across from each other for several more minutes, until his patience with her began to seem like a form of ostentation. But when she stood up to go, she suddenly realized what she wanted to ask him.

"Can you do that?" she said. "Can you just decide that your family is simply no longer your family?"

She could see him soften a bit. "My family is right here," he said gently. "The Howe family lived by nothing, for nothing. You are all reaping what you have sown."

Molly expected to find John home from the library when she got back, but he wasn't there. She called in sick at the restaurant. Then, after breathing deeply a few times, she called the house in Ulster. Her father's voice was on the answering machine. "Mom, it's Molly," she said quickly; after a pause, she left her phone number. Then she hung up.

John didn't get back for three more hours, much later than expected. Kay had not called back by then either. When he opened the door, after dark, and switched the lights on, he was frightened to see Molly glaring hatefully at him from the center of the living room, red-eyed, silent, and nearly hysterical from loneliness.

★ ★ ★

232

EVERY MORNING, ON his drive to work, John passed two of the five billboards that constituted the First National Bank of Charlottesville campaign. Three different times he had actually witnessed motorists drifting to a stop on the shoulder and getting out to look at the images more closely, which surely wasn't something you could say about a lot of billboard campaigns. John hadn't had a hand in them, personally. They were site-specific; one, on a stretch of county road that ran through some undeveloped rolling hills, was a trompe-l'oeil picture of a house under construction. The other, right across from the main gates of the university, showed a mother and daughter hugging beside the open hatchback of a car loaded to the roof with stereo equipment, duffel bags, and cardboard boxes full of books: first day of freshman year. Both contained no type – only the bank's familiar logo, Monticello with a 1 in the center of it, in the upper left corner.

Initially Osbourne had loved them. The site-specific idea appealed to him right away; the fact that the ads were integral to the city's very landscape – not something bought on local airtime during *Friends* or falling out of the Sunday paper with the Arby's coupons – made them more exciting as ads and also reinforced the idea that the client was a hometown product, not some national chain whose monthly statements showed up from a PO box somewhere in North Dakota. And the clients, skeptical at first, had been won over as well. Their business had seen a slight upturn; more significantly than that, though, they kept reporting to Osbourne that everyone, everywhere they went, was talking about those First National ads. They'd never had such a buzz.

But within a few weeks, Osbourne had soured on the whole

campaign. Though he kept stressing that he blamed himself, it was hard not to feel for those whose work was now the object of his undisguised contempt. "Billboards," he'd say, shaking his head. "What the hell was I thinking? You can call it site-specific or whatever you want, but the fact is a billboard is a billboard is a billboard, people only expect to see one thing on it and that's advertising. Their relationship to the work is poisoned from the start." Nor did he care for the ads' content; the approach was fresh, he said, but the message was still the same old message, your friendly neighborhood bank, look at this beautiful home we'll help you build – the same old shit, everyone genially accepted it as a lie whether it was a lie or not. He seemed deeply troubled, and they saw him in the working part of the mansion less and less often; it was assumed that he was secluding himself somewhere in the east wing.

In retrospect John was glad he'd had nothing to do with the First National campaign; at the time, though, he had been frustrated, even a little panicked, by his inability to come up with any decent idea at all. Osbourne had resolutely refused to do any partnering among the staff; nevertheless, John found that when he had an idea or a question or else just needed some company he was spending more and more time in the third-floor maid's room where Elaine Sizemore had her desk. Elaine always wore her little round wire-rim glasses, and she didn't seem to have brought with her from New York any sort of casual clothing: she wore skirts, loose dressy pants, blouses with fancy collars, while others walked around like skateboarders in baggy calf-length shorts and Limp Bizkit T-shirts. She wanted that maid's room precisely because it was the smallest room in the main part of the house; the enormous cherrywood secretary she had found at a local antique store (in the end they had needed professional movers just to get it up the stairs and through the maid's-room door) made the room even more formidably her own. John respected this bold maneuvering for solitude, even as he violated it by lingering in her doorway, blowing on a latte from the first-floor kitchen, asking her what was new.

Both of them were spending more and more time at the office. They didn't have a great deal of work to do; but with the presence of a full-time kitchen staff, and TVs, and a pool table, and Internet access, it was easy to begin to feel estranged from their own small, still-unfamiliar homes. And home, no matter how John might wish it otherwise, was not terribly appealing right now. Eager to avoid the student-dominated apartment houses near campus – where the hours were crazy, the noise was tremendous, and where he would have been the oldest tenant by nearly ten years – he had taken a place out by the 250 Bypass. His two rooms were cramped, half-furnished, with no view; but the primary source of his depression on evenings and weekends there was his fellow tenants. Who, after all, in a small city like Charlottesville, would be living in a furnished one-bedroom apartment with a kitchenette? Drunks; men who had been kicked out by their wives; men who were keeping mistresses and could afford a cheap place set aside for that purpose.

And the walls were not thick. The noises of sex were common; John felt that his inability to ignore them only reflected badly on himself. Much more upsetting were instances like the Friday evening he overheard his next-door neighbor on the phone; the words were muffled, but from the singsong voice the man was using John could tell he was talking to his children. He heard clearly the sound of the hang-up, followed a few seconds later by a wave of uncontrolled sobbing. The next morning John passed this man – maybe in his forties, with a puffy face under a blond beard – on the back stairs leading to the parking area; the man smiled and asked John if it wasn't a lovely day. Six weeks of this sort of depthless interaction was about all John could take before he began spending some of his nights in the west-wing bedrooms at the office.

He wasn't the only one. A custom developed whereby one would hang some personal item – a shoe, a bag, a sweatshirt – from the doorknob of a given bedroom to signal that it was occupied. One or two rooms were usually so reserved at any hour. In some cases, most verifiably Milo's, this was because he worked best in the middle of the night; when he heard the kitchen staff banging around shortly after dawn, he would put down his brushes and go upstairs to sleep until lunchtime or so. But there were rumors that the bedrooms were being used for other purposes, at night and during the day as well. Olivia, the former gallery assistant from San Francisco, and Daniel, John was urged to observe, were often out of sight at the same time, usually just before lunch.

There wasn't a great deal of work to do just then. One Friday, with Osbourne's permission, John left early and drove down to Hilton Head to spend a weekend with his parents. It was September, and the air smelled like cherries as he drove with the top down in the darkness toward his mother and stepfather's development. He got lost, briefly, inside the main gates, before finding the right condo; he had been there only two or three times before. The last time had been with

Rebecca. When he walked in the unlocked door he saw his stepfather, Buzz, in pajamas and bathrobe, reading in a chair inside a circle of lamplight. Buzz smiled and closed his book. "Your mother couldn't wait up," he said. He hovered, beneficently, until John had his bag moved into the guest bedroom; then he announced he was going up to bed himself.

After Buzz was gone and his door closed, John reemerged from the guest bedroom and paced through the house in the darkness. The place had been redecorated again; there was nothing in view now that he recognized from his childhood home. Nothing, even, from the post-Buzz years; so it didn't have to do with considerations of that sort, an effort not to haunt her new husband with relics from the life of the first one. Perhaps even in their seventies they wanted to feel that everything was before them – they didn't feel comforted, but rather threatened, by objects which reminded them of all the years that now loomed behind them. It all seemed worth sorting out to John only because of the nagging sense of failure he had begun to feel every time he entered his own apartment back in Charlottesville. The rented room, the haphazard furniture, the books still in boxes, the neighbors who weren't really neighbors. It didn't seem to him the way a man now in his thirties ought to be living – no connection to anybody, no sense of personal history.

Not much else happened of note on his weekend visit. In the morning his mother made biscuits with sausage gravy, just as she used to do on weekends when he was a teenager, and then while he ate she talked to Buzz across the table about how much she missed Rebecca, what a wonderful girl she was, would it be too awkward now if she tried to stay in touch. John played a ritual round of golf with Buzz and two of his friends — he never touched a golf club except on these visits home, a fact which never seemed to register with Buzz — and John did not begrudge the three old men their undisguised pleasure as a boy their sons' age struggled to keep up with them in this pseudo-physical contest.

Back at his apartment a message from Elaine warned him of a meeting Osbourne had called for first thing Monday morning. "New client," Mal said, as a few of them were still finding their seats. "This one is national. Four TV spots, three thirties and a sixty, and two print campaigns, one one-page and one for an eight-page insert."

He sat and stared at them for a minute as they drank their coffee.

"That's it," he said finally. "Meeting's over. Go, get to work."

They looked at one another. "Who's the client?" Elaine said.

Osbourne scratched his chin. "As you know," he said, "in the end I wasn't entirely thrilled with the First National campaign. I've been spending a lot of time these past weeks thinking about why that is. I believe the answer is that as talented as all of you are, certain ideas are so deeply ingrained in you that it's going to take some sort of shock to root them out. I'm not just talking to those of you with a background in advertising, either. I'm talking about certain very elemental, cultural ideas. We need to find a new approach to get around those dead ideas."

Another silence ensued.

"So," Elaine said finally, "then, I'm guessing you're not going to tell us who the client is."

"Correct. Nor am I going to tell you anything about what sort of business the client is or isn't in. I do not want advertising. There are no reference points for you. Any inspiration here has to come from somewhere inside of you. Four TV spots, nine pages of full-color print, but we don't need it all in one shot. Give me the keynote, the starting point. Don't worry about budget. All the questions you're going to ask me when I stop talking? Don't ask them. You have until the twenty-seventh of October. Amaze me."

JOHN AND MOLLY got to the San Francisco airport and discovered her flight had been delayed an hour; so they had a couple of drinks in the tiny, unenclosed bar nearest her gate, followed by a standing makeout session which had the other passengers staring. At the Albany airport, there was no one there to meet her, only a line of four taxis just outside the door to the baggage claim; the driver of the second said he would take her to Ulster for twenty-five dollars. The eight hours in between, except for the quick change at La Guardia, was time airborne, time nowhere: it gave the slowly sobering Molly a different sense of time entirely, the ways in which it passes and the ways in which it can fold back upon itself again or collapse unexpectedly. It was like flying backwards in her own mind. Even so, she was not anxious for that flight to end.

John had wanted to come with her, but she said no. The less there was to deal with, the better, and Kay's reaction to something as unprecedented as a new boyfriend was too hard to calculate. It was dark when the taxi decelerated off the thruway, too dark to start picking out landmarks, but once they got to the center of Ulster, where the traffic light was, Molly became reoriented and she started feeling each turn of the steering wheel deep in her body. The lights in the house at Bull's Head were blazing. Unseen, Molly walked up the path and opened the front door. Everything was instantly itself again, after more than a year. Kay was not in the kitchen, nor in the living room. Molly did not call out. She caught herself walking almost on tiptoe, not wanting to be heard. The one conspicuous thing about the house was that it was immaculately clean.

"Mom?" Molly called finally.

Every upstairs light was on, and the doors to all the rooms, including hers and Richard's, were standing open. As Molly passed her parents' bedroom, she saw her mother's feet, in high heels, on the bed. Knocking softly on the wide-open door, Molly stuck her head inside.

Kay was asleep on top of the bedspread, her hands folded on her stomach. She wore one of her best dresses, deep blue with a thin white stripe above the hem, stockings, a string of pearls, and full makeup, as if she were getting ready to go out somewhere. A kind of chill went through Molly and, without really thinking about it, she walked furtively over to her mother's side of the bed to satisfy herself that Kay was still breathing. Just as she was sure she had seen her mother's ribcage go up and down, Kay's eyes fluttered slightly and she woke up.

Mother and daughter, their faces inches apart, pulled back in fright. A second or two passed in silence; then Kay laughed and put her hand to her chest. "My, you scared me!" she said, sitting up, touching her hair. "I must have dozed off."

She embraced Molly, without hesitation but not especially

warmly either, as if they had seen each other just a few hours ago. Then she patted Molly's shoulders and looked past her, around the room, as if trying to remember something. Her eyes seemed to Molly unusually bright.

"Were you going out somewhere?" Molly asked.

Kay looked once more around the overlit room.

"It's just that you're so dressed up," Molly said.

"Thank you!" said Kay.

They went downstairs, where Kay insisted on finding Molly something to eat. Molly nibbled listlessly on a tuna sandwich while her mother stood leaning against the counter, arms crossed, and stared at her.

"Where's Richard, by the way?" she said suddenly. "Did he go straight to bed?"

Molly wished very strongly that Richard, or somebody, was in the house with them. "No, Mom," she said gently. "Richard's not coming. I think he told you that."

"Well, of course he did," Kay said.

That night Molly lay in her old bed, listening to the sounds of her mother moving around restlessly downstairs. When Molly saw her in the morning she was still in the same blue dress with the white stripe. Visiting hours at the hospital in Albany began at nine; it was nearly eight-thirty now.

"You go on," Kay said. "I have a lot to do here."

Molly stared. "I don't know the way," she said.

Kay's mouth quivered a little bit, before she abruptly recovered her bright demeanor. "Okay, then," she said. "Are you ready?"

The whole way there Kay narrated every turn they made. "Now a left on to Route 4," she'd say. "Left off the exit on to

241

Mortensen Road." Molly realized that she was expected to pay attention to these remarks so that Kay wouldn't have to make the trip with her a second time. Kay pulled up before the main entrance and put the car in park; but she did not turn the engine off. Molly put her hand on the door.

"You're not coming in?" she said incredulously.

Kay smiled. "Oh, I don't think that's necessary," she said. "Your father will be so happy to see you. And I have some errands to run. It's not easy being left alone, you know. I have a lot to take care of." She pushed the button that raised the power lock on Molly's door.

Molly was too flustered to remember to ask Kay for her father's room number. She gave his name to the woman behind the high front desk, who typed it into her computer.

"Room eighteen–oh–eight," the woman said, her face lit from below by the computer screen. "Left off the elevator, then left again, then right through the double doors."

"Right through, or straight through?" Molly asked.

The woman looked at her in confusion. "Just follow the signs marked Psychiatric Ward," she said, in a softer voice.

That's where he was. Molly went through a metal detector and was buzzed through a set of steel doors which locked behind her, electronically and loudly. By the time she had gone past the dayroom — where grown, sometimes elderly men in exam gowns sat in front of a TV or talked into the air or stood in a corner, touching the walls — she was ready to weep with terror, even though no one she saw so much as noticed her. At the nurses' station, losing her nerve, she asked first to see her father's doctor; Dr Kotlovitz, she was told, was with an emergency patient but was expected back within the half hour.

In the meantime, she could see her father if she liked.

Molly waited just beyond his open door, breathing deeply and flexing her fingers, for a full minute before stepping into the doorway and knocking.

It was her father, sitting up in the motor-driven bed, reading a magazine with his glasses on. But he wore a hospital gown, the thickness of a paper towel, tied together loosely at the back, a garment of shocking immodesty; his hair, grayer than she remembered, bore the unkempt, angular shape of someone who had not been out of bed for a long time, days, even; and because of this, the familiar, untroubled, oh-there-you-are smile her father offered as he dropped the magazine and struggled to swing his legs off the edge of the bed was not only unreassuring – its very familiarity was profoundly frightening.

He remained seated as they hugged; she tried not to look at the pale alarming expanse of thigh he showed as he slid forward on the bed. In a scratchy but cheerful voice Roger suggested that they take a walk. "To the dayroom, anyway," he said. "That's as far as they'll let me go." He held out his arm, and it hung there for a few seconds until Molly understood that she was now to hold on to it, to support him as he struggled to stand and then walk without losing his balance. It wasn't pride, exactly, that made him pretend this infirmity was something the two of them took for granted, as if she had helped him out of bed a thousand times before – more a fear of seeing her hurt or disappointed, a fear so extreme he would carry this pretense of infallibility to the most ridiculous and tragic length, which length, Molly realized, they had now arrived at.

The dayroom was a long drab rectangle, about one-third of it, at that hour, flooded uncomfortably by sunlight through the blindless windows. In one corner, eight feet or so above the floor on a kind of triangular shelf, sat the TV; a dozen black chrome-and-plastic chairs were ranged in front of it. At the moment no one paid attention to it, though the sound was turned up; the four or five patients in the dayroom sat or stood isolated from one another, not talking unless to themselves, having come here, Molly imagined, mostly out of an atavistic craving for some sense of space. She took her father to a padded easy chair at the end of the room furthest from the laughter of the television.

Roger seemed awfully thin, though this may only have been an impression produced by the clinging paper nightshirt. "So," he said to her. "How was your flight?"

Molly wished desperately there was some third person there to tell her what not to do – a doctor, ideally, though she would have settled for her mother or her brother, which is to say that she would have been happy even with advice that was clearly wrong. For now, she let herself be lulled into her father's construction that everything was fine, that the setting of their talk had no bearing on the talk itself. It masked the symptoms of their fear.

"Fine. Very smooth. Mom wired me money for the ticket."

"Did you see a movie?"

Molly swallowed. "Yes. It was . . . it was called *Sleepless in Seattle.*"

"Never heard of it. What was it about?"

"I really don't remember," Molly said. "Dad, can I—"

"Not *Sleeper?* The Woody Allen movie? Because I remember

that one. Lord, that was a funny movie! Gene Wilder with the sheep." He shook his head, remembering, and with unfathomable abruptness his head fell forward and he began crying.

Molly looked all around the dayroom, afraid she was going to need help; but no one, not the other patients nor the one attendant in the room, so much as glanced in their direction as her father struggled noisily to catch his breath. She turned back and took his hand, took both his hands, even as she felt him trying to pull them away from her.

"It's all right," she said. "It's okay. Everything's okay." The words meant nothing. She said them because they tended to produce a certain tone of voice, which she hoped was worth something, as if she were speaking to a horse.

Roger kept trying, with astonishing feebleness, to pull one hand away, until finally Molly understood that he only wanted to wipe his nose. She had no idea why she had been restraining him. When he finally looked up at her again, sniffling and smiling, she could see in his confident expression that he had no idea what he looked like. His gaze shifted past her, around the eggshell-colored walls of the dayroom.

"Would you look at all these lunatics?" he said.

When Molly had him back in bed she returned to the nurses' station and asked again for Dr Kotlovitz. He was a fat doctor, genial and perspiring, and did not react at all to Molly's angry tone of voice when she asked why her father was on the mental ward.

"Standard practice with all attempted suicides," he said. "On top of which it worries me a bit that he still won't talk about what happened."

"He's a very proud man."

"Well, I don't just mean he's being reticent, or doesn't like having his privacy violated. I mean he insists it never did happen at all. Didn't you ask him about it?"

Molly shook her head.

"He insists, and I think he really believes, that this was an accidental overdose. He took something like fifty Seconal. Obviously no accident. If he hadn't vomited in the ambulance, I think we might have lost him."

"Seconal?"

"It had been prescribed to your mother. Whether she was hoarding it or whether she'd stopped taking it and he was refilling the prescription himself, I don't know. He won't talk about any of it with me, or even admit it happened. You should ask him yourself. I don't know what your relationship with him is like – maybe he'd talk to you."

"He's asleep now," Molly said nervously.

"Next time, then?"

Kay was sitting in the car in the hospital parking lot with the radio on. Molly knocked on her window.

"Is he feeling better?" she asked distractedly. Her attention was directed to the radio program, a call-in show, hosted by an angry, intemperate psychiatrist.

"He looks okay," Molly said. "Listen, why don't you slide over. I'll drive." They returned home without speaking; the car was a bubble within which swirled the voice of the woman psychiatrist, berating her invisible patients, broadcasting her contempt for their problems, intimately and nationwide.

Kay did not accompany her on any more trips to the hospital in Albany, though Molly went every day; in fact, Kay, though she dressed up smartly at some point each morning, never left the house at all that Molly could see. Her mother betrayed no awareness that everything was not as it should have been, or as it always had been. But for once Molly wasn't eager to pull at the mask of normality settled upon the visage of life in the house, because she no longer wanted to see what was behind it. So when Kay put on her makeup, laid a towel over the pillow on her tightly made bed, and lay down and napped for five or six hours, Molly just got in the car and drove to town to pick up some food, because someone had to do it.

The IGA was one of the few stores still unshuttered. It was only a matter of time before Molly saw someone she knew; three of them, in fact, her former girlfriends from Ulster High School. One of them was Annika. They passed her on the sidewalk as she loaded bags of food into the trunk of her mother's car. It was plain from the looks on their faces that they had had no warning Molly was back in town. They looked right at her, as if she couldn't see them too, as if her misfortunes had made her into some sort of figure on a TV screen whom you could stare at unobserved; they had all been something resembling good friends little more than a year before. Molly didn't have the time or the mental energy to make sense of it. She had another stop to make – at the drugstore, a sensitive errand, at which she was relieved to go unrecognized – before returning to Bull's Head. Being away from the house, leaving her mother there alone, filled her with a vague dread now, a dread which grew geometrically as she got closer to home.

When she walked through the door, her mother was awake, doing laundry, wearing pearls. "There was a phone message for you," Kay said. "John someone. He didn't leave a number. It's on the machine if you want to hear it." She didn't say why she hadn't picked up the phone when it rang.

"Thanks," Molly said impassively. She went upstairs to her mother's bedroom, played the message back, and let it erase itself.

For the next week, in fact, the phone never rang at all in the Howe household unless it was John calling. All their old friends, or those still left in town, were apparently scared off by the family's new level of misfortune. Kay let the machine record every call, and so did Molly. The pitch of John's voice rose incrementally with each unanswered message; he begged for some confirmation that Molly was all right, that she had arrived there at all. Molly played back and erased the messages on the machine in her parents' bedroom when she was sure Kay was out of earshot. She could hear, in John's voice, the strong suspicion that she *was* there, standing by the phone, that she was fine, and was thus not speaking to him by choice, a choice which was a complete mystery to him. But he would not accuse her out loud.

In the dayroom, her father made small talk as his fellow mental patients muttered grievously against the shadowed walls all around them. In fact, it was the normality of his own demeanor, compared to theirs, that made the dayroom a comfortable place for him. He wanted to know about Molly's year in Berkeley, all about how her brother was doing; drawn into some vortex of dishonesty, Molly revealed to him only the most salutary aspects of her and Richard's lives, such as her attendance of classes on art and literature. He admired her pluck without once broaching the matter of why she didn't, or

248

couldn't, just enroll in the college in the first place. Most days she was engrossed in keeping him happy; but one morning, more out of curiosity than antagonism, she couldn't resist asking him, "Dad, do you know why we're here?"

He laughed, an embarrassed laugh, and then, holding together the lapels of the robe Molly had brought from his closet at home – the nurses had taken the belt away – he blushed.

"I feel so foolish," he said.

Molly waited.

"I just didn't read the label," he said, holding up his hands. "How stupid is that? I was having trouble sleeping, so I got some of your mother's medicine out of the bathroom cabinet. It was late, and I was too lazy to go downstairs and get my glasses, so I just took a couple. I got the dosage wrong."

Molly started crying, silently. Roger didn't seem to notice.

"And now all this," he said. "So much trouble for everyone. You had to interrupt your studies and fly all the way across the country. I just feel so stupid. Can you ever forgive me?"

That evening Molly sat with her mother in the living room. The TV was on; they were watching *Cheers*. It was dull, thought Molly, but it served its purpose, which was to spare them from having to talk to one another. Then Kay said, "That John Wheelwright called again. I saved the message for you."

"Thanks," Molly said.

At the next commercial break, Kay said, "So who is he, anyway?"

"Sorry?"

"This John. He likes you?"

Molly ran her hand through her hair. "I guess so, yeah," she said.

"Nice boy?"

"Yes," Molly said.

There was a silence. "Well," Kay said, "if you're not interested in him, he's obviously not getting the picture. Why not just call him back and tell him to leave you alone?"

The first time she had left Ulster, it was understood that, in however characteristically passive a fashion, her parents were throwing her out. Leaving a second time, Molly knew, was going to mean abandoning them, giving them up to the monstrosity of their marriage. Without a third person there, as a kind of emotional groundwire, the general air of psychopathology was going to thicken until at least one of them wound up dead. The transparently phony aspect of normality that her father had always maintained – and which, in his absence, her mother now seemed committed to – was now, even with one of them in the mental ward and the other at home watching *Cheers,* all that stood between them and a wholly genuine life of terror and hatred; Molly, for one, wished only that that false front might somehow still be preserved. She understood how smart her brother was not to come back here, never mind how elaborate and confining the mindset he needed to construct in order to permit himself to stay away. She also understood that she had never had any real idea, as a child in this house, of the true range of self-deception – the role of lying in survival.

Upstairs, in Kay's bedroom, the laugh track still audible below, Molly played back John's message.

"It's me again. Mrs Howe, if you're picking up these messages, please, maybe you don't know who I am, but I'm begging you, let Molly hear them, or let her know I called.

Molly, I can't sleep, I won't leave the apartment in case you call. What is happening? I don't understand it but I can let it all go if I just could hear that you're all right. Please. Please. If there's something I've done to make you angry with me . . . I've thought and thought and I can't think what it could be. I'm just at a loss, I'm at a loss. Please get in touch with me somehow. I don't have your address out there but I'm thinking of coming anyway. Have pity on me. I'm so in love with you, and until I can figure out what's happened to you I'm in agony. I love you. Please call. Please call home."

Still on the bureau in Molly's room was the bag from the drugstore. She took it into the bathroom the next morning, and when she came out again she had a simple, symbolic confirmation of what she already knew, which was that she was pregnant.

IN THE BASEMENT pool room, or waiting for lunch on the stools beside the pantry, or walking together on the brick path through the orchard – as if afraid of being overheard – some of Osbourne's employees stalled for time by trying to guess the nature of the client whose identity he was withholding from them. Elaine said an eight-page print insert could only mean a fashion concern of some kind; I mean, she said, can you ever remember seeing anything like that that wasn't about fashion? Daniel, though, insisted there had to be more to it than that, there had to be something objectionable or controversial about the mystery client, or else where was the benefit in keeping the name from them? The agency wasn't thriving, and Osbourne felt forced to make some sort of compromise in order to bring in some money – it was easy enough to understand. But John, though he was feeling sure about less and less, knew Daniel was wrong; he himself accepted with no skepticism at all Osbourne's definition of his motives as purely on the level of aesthetic experiment. He wanted the issue of influence taken off the table, so to speak; he wanted their next efforts shaped by no sensibility other than their own. John defended this idea – or not the idea, exactly, but the transparency of the motives behind it – with such unconscious vigor that by the time he finished they were all nodding sagely at him, as if he were only confirming what they already knew.

But the more clearly John understood what was wanted of him, the less equipped he felt to produce anything. With his pads and his pens, a drafting table wedged under the window in the west-wing bedroom where he had begun spending more and more of his nights, he looked out at the cherry trees, at the delivery trucks as they spun through the gravel in the driveway at the back of the house, and he came up with nothing.

It was a great relief to him the day Milo tracked him down in his bedroom. Life in a Southern college town had only made Milo more eccentric, even though, so far as John knew, he seldom left the mansion these days at all. Gaunt, his face and arms ridden with beauty spots, his peroxided hair making him look less like a *fashionista* than like his own father, he wandered the halls distractedly at all hours; John knew for a fact that he had not yet learned everyone else's name. Milo knocked on John's door and walked in without waiting for an answer. He had some questions about materials, he said, just audibly. He hadn't had a lot of experience with the world of print, and he wasn't sure if what he had in mind was possible.

John heard him out, and told him that what he wanted was probably doable, technically; he added, reflexively, that it would at least double the cost of the client's buy.

Milo nodded and looked somber at this news, though it clearly meant nothing to him.

"But you know what," John said. "I'd take it to Mal anyway."

Two weeks later, they did. Milo's idea was to bind into each magazine one double-sided sheet of a kind of Mylar derivative that John, a couple of years earlier, had been shown in conditions of great secrecy by a printer acquaintance in New Jersey, a guy who wanted to know if John's girlfriend, Rebecca, had any expertise in patent law. Now John got in touch with him again. The stuff still could not hold any kind of type, which was the one bug the printer had been trying to get out of it. It was, however, perfectly reflective, almost without distortion – which was all they were now interested in. In other words, the advertisement Milo had in mind was a mirror.

Osbourne sat looking into this mirror, holding it before him at his antique desk as John and Milo stood nervously to one side, for two minutes or more. His face grew redder and redder. Then he asked the two of them to leave his office, and to close the door behind them; which they did. A short while later the door opened and their boss brushed past them; they trailed behind as he blew through the main rooms of the mansion, tapping everyone he found on the shoulder and summoning them to the dining room. When they were gathered there, he thanked them all for their hard work, told them the search was over, and gave them all the rest of the week off.

The client, it came out in the end, was an Internet search engine. They did not balk at the increased costs, nor at the notion that the name of their company would appear nowhere in or near the ad. It ran in *Vanity Fair,* the *New Yorker, Details,* and five other periodicals, all within the same ten days. Osbourne himself took to hanging out in the ballroom at all hours, staring at a computer screen, trolling the Internet for rumors as to the identity of the advertiser – even, when he couldn't stand it anymore, entering various chat rooms anonymously.

That was the beginning of everything. The mirror ad was a sensation, denounced in newspaper editorials, clucked over on the evening news, the subject of jeremiads not just in advertising trade publications but in art journals as well. *Artforum* even ran a special section about it, a kind of roundtable collection of short essays by art historians and museum curators. Then it was selected for the Biennial at the Whitney Museum. Osbourne, though he professed to hate awards, personally entered the mirror in every competition, in the ad industry and outside of it, he could think of. By the time those awards were given out, the search-engine company's stock had split twice, and Osbourne had so much new business that it became necessary, against his wishes, to expand the staff.

And the bright future of the agency – Palladio, as Osbourne had named it months ago, though his own staffers were too superstitious about pretension at that stage to use it – seemed increasingly to belong to the artists, like Milo, whose own ascendancy after the mirror campaign was unquestioned. There was not an ounce of ambition in him. He smoked and wore white T-shirts and appeared – though the others were too embarrassed to ask him about it – to cut his own hair; and if he spent more nights in the west-wing bedrooms than the others, it was not out of a desire to put in (or be seen putting in) long hours, but because he lived in his work, his life did not seem quite real to him outside of it, and thus the apartment he rented in town did not serve as any sort of escape from anything. Osbourne had once mentioned to them – in an early, starry-eyed bull session back when they had very little work to do – that he was torn between wanting to break the practice of not crediting individual artists for their work in ads and wanting to uphold the concept that widely disseminated images, particularly if they were successful, mooted questions of authorship in the first place. But Milo said he didn't want any credit for the mirror anyway. In fact, his suggestion was that it be credited "from the studio of Malcolm Osbourne," as with Brueghel or Rembrandt. Osbourne rejected that idea, but John could see how pleased he was with it.

In house, Milo got full credit for the mirror idea anyway – John saw to that. He made no effort to play up his own role, which was merely technical. In general, though he had never received any signal that the boss was displeased with his failure to produce any actual, usable work, John found it impossible – even in the wake of good feeling generated by the agency's booming success – not to worry. Osbourne seemed more and more to covet art produced from a strictly personal wellspring; one of John's new colleagues, for instance, a New York performance artist named Tara, had had great success with a spoken-word television spot about the death of her father. John had lived as long as any of his colleagues – indeed, he had lived through the death of his own father – but he couldn't seem to dredge up anything on that level. Or, if he could, then he couldn't hit on some way to transform the personal into his particular art. He thought, for instance, about Molly; all that had been painful enough, to be sure, but it was also ten years ago, and what remained of the private intensity of those memories was no help at all to him as he sat on the end of the bed, with a marker in his hand, in his staked-out west-wing bedroom.

So when he received a message – on his home phone, no less – telling him that Osbourne had scheduled a meeting with him, alone, the following Monday morning, John's first thought was that he was going to be fired. Osbourne's secretary sent him up to the fourth floor, where he was surprised to see his employer eating a cinnamon bun in the muted glow of a skylight, alone at a small table with a silver coffee pitcher at its center. He waved John into the seat across from him.

Osbourne smiled apologetically as he finished chewing; then he said, "How have you enjoyed your time here?"

"Very much. It's exciting to be around this, to see it take off like it's doing." He cursed his own choice of words – it sounded like he was more of a spectator here than a vital part of it.

Osbourne wiped his sticky fingers on a linen napkin. "I see two things happening," he said. "One is that you don't seem heavily involved in the actual creative work that's being done downstairs. Perhaps I misjudged you in that respect. Not that there's any shame in that, of course. The sources of inspiration are always mysterious. The second thing is that the type of work, the range of work, we do here is about to change. I've had contacts with other types of enterprises which are very much interested in harnessing our methods here. Not just commodity-sellers, you understand?"

John nodded, though he didn't understand.

"Municipalities," Osbourne said cagily. "Coffee?" John shook his head no. "Universities. Charitable organizations. Political campaigns. Jury consultants – I had a jury consultant call me the other day; frankly I'm not totally sure what they even do. Governmental agencies. So that where I find myself needing help just now is more in the area of long-term planning, and also in the area of people skills. Meeting people, potential clients, charming them, learning from them, heading off their complaints, forming relationships. This is an area where I think you'd excel. So, John, I'd like to offer you a promotion. I don't know what to call it, vice president, senior executive vice president, rear admiral, we can call it whatever the hell you like. The point is I want you working more closely with me. I have a vision, and I think you share that vision. I want you by my right hand, so to speak: my liaison to the outside world."

John collected himself and accepted the offer with all the gratitude he could display. When he went down to the pool room, and told the others the news about how he had just been kicked upstairs, there was no resentment at all – the happiness was unanimous. Everyone liked John, for one thing; and ever since the first partnership benefits had kicked in, two months earlier, everyone was getting so rich that there was no inclination to care if one of them might suddenly start getting a little richer than the others.

ON MONDAY, ROGER Howe's doctor – who spoke only to Molly now, since Kay never came to the hospital or returned phone messages, and who had begun to look at Molly, even as

257

he diagnosed her father's mental state, with a father's furrowed brow and posture of concern – told her that there was no longer any compelling reason to keep Roger in the hospital, a fact his insurance company had called to the hospital's attention. Roger's physical recovery was complete; his emotional status was shaky but not so unstable that he could be held against his will, and he had lately been expressing his desire to return home to his family. Dr Kotlovitz thought he could be released as early as the weekend.

On Tuesday, Molly stood beside the phone in her parents' bedroom and listened impassively as John left this message: "I'm coming out there. I don't know if you're still there. I don't know your address, but I know what town, it's a small town, everyone's bound to know where you are. I don't know whether to be angry or worried or what, but I can't stand not knowing anymore. I'll be there this weekend."

That afternoon Molly sat on her childhood bed with the county Yellow Pages. After trying unsuccessfully to guess the pertinent euphemism – Child Services; Pregnancy Counseling; Family Planning – she called the local chapter of Planned Parenthood and got a list of abortionists in the greater Albany area. Later, when she made the short drive into town, she went to the bank – they were used to seeing her now – and withdrew, with one of the blank slips her mother had signed for her, two thousand dollars.

She opted for a smaller clinic, forty miles away in Canajoharie, thinking there would be no protesters there, and she was right. It wasn't that she feared the protesters or the remorse they might try to fan in her over what she was doing; her only desire was to clear her own path of other people to as great a degree as possible. If she could have performed the procedure on herself, rather than have to endure the benign looks and remarks of a doctor and a nurse, she would have done it. She told the woman at the desk she had called yesterday to schedule a D and C. Without a word the woman passed through the window a clipboard with a form attached and a capless pen dangling from a string.

"Do I have to fill all this out?" Molly asked. Stout, unsurprisable, the woman in the window said, "Yes," flatly, without looking up. Molly took a seat.

There was no one else in the waiting room. Molly filled out both sides of the form, giving a false name and address but otherwise answering truthfully. She checked the box to decline counseling. She checked the "Cash" box next to "Form of Payment."

The first thing the woman did, when Molly handed the form back, was to ask for the cash in advance; Molly then waited for half an hour. On the table was an old issue of *Glamour;* she ignored it. The time passed slowly, with no distractions, and Molly struggled to make her mind a blank.

Finally she was shown to a changing room, just large enough to turn around in, and given a surgical gown. The room had two doors, one on each side; on one tiny wall was a Monet print, and on the wall across from it a sign read "Not Responsible for Personal Property." That reminded her that she was carrying nearly eighteen hundred dollars in the pocket of her fatigues; she put it in the toe of her shoe and pushed the socks in after it. When she opened the door opposite the one she had entered, she was face to face with a nurse, and over her shoulder, sitting on a stool, was the doctor. The doctor held a clipboard in his hand. He smiled at her as if crossing the word "smile" off a list.

"Okay, Ms Wheelwright," he said. "If you'll lie down on the table, please."

Molly saw where her feet were intended to go. The doctor sat on a small stool between her knees. At his feet was a small metal garbage can with a lid.

"Just to double-check, Ms Wheelwright, you're here for a D and C, is that right?"

"Yes."

"Your last period was when?"

"About nine weeks ago."

"And you've declined an offer of counseling on the alternatives to abortion, is that right?"

"That's right."

"Okay then." He signed something on the clipboard and handed it to the nurse, who placed it on the metal table behind her. She handed him a pair of rubber gloves.

It took about twenty minutes. The nurse had no duties to perform; it dawned on Molly that she was there because she was a woman, simply to bridge the gap in some mysterious way between Molly and the man who squinted as he scraped the inside of her uterus with what looked like some sort of sewing tool. The silence was broken only a few times by his saying, "Now you'll feel a dull ache," or "Now you may feel a sensation like cramping." He was never wrong about it. Molly wasn't aware of any particular look on her own face, but at one point, without warning, about halfway through the procedure, the nurse reached out and took her hand.

Jesus, thought Molly, struggling not to lose it; what a terrible idea. Let go of me.

She could hear the opening and closing of the garbage-can lid. "Garbage can" must not be the right term, she thought; but that's what the opening and closing sounded like.

She had no idea how long such a thing should take, five minutes, an hour, so she was surprised when she heard the snapping sound as he removed his gloves. "And we're through," he said, not unkindly. Molly propped herself up on her elbows. "If you have any questions, Renee here can answer them, but if you need to talk to me for any reason, of course I'll still be around."

Renee took Molly's elbow as they walked the few feet back to the changing room. "Now you may feel some cramping-type pain in the next few days," Renee said intimately. "That's normal. A little bleeding is also nothing to worry about. If you get a heavier flow, call us here, or go straight to the emergency room if you feel it's necessary. Use a pad for the bleeding – no tampons. You may want to take it easy today and tomorrow."

At the door, Renee handed Molly a piece of paper. "This is a prescription for some Tylenol with codeine. I'd advise you to fill it on the way home. With most people, especially as young as you, the pain isn't that severe. But sometimes it is. Now," she said as she closed the door, "you just take as long as you need to in here, to collect yourself. Nobody's going to hurry you." She closed the door.

Collect myself? Molly looked around the tiny room for a minute, having numbed herself to such a degree that it was difficult to think at all. She dressed quickly and left. The exit did not take her back through the waiting room; she pulled open a fire door and was back in the bright sunshine of the parking lot.

On the long drive back to Ulster the pain commenced. Soon Molly's fingers were white around the steering wheel. No bleeding, though, which was important, since this was her mother's car. She fished the prescription out of her pocket. Without slowing down, she crumpled it up, rolled down the window, and threw it into the weeds along the highway.

"There you are," Kay said absently when she heard the door open. "I didn't know where you'd gone."

"Visiting friends."

"Oh, lovely. I saved you some lunch."

"No thank you," Molly said, not breaking stride. "I'm not feeling that well."

"What's the problem?"

"Cramps," Molly called from the stairs.

"Poor thing," Kay murmured. Molly went into her room and shut the door.

She lay on her side, facing the wall. Each wave of pain squeezed the tears from her eyes; they rolled sideways across the bridge of her nose and on to the pillowcase. Good, she said to herself. Good. It should hurt. She did not have to think of John, or of their aborted child, in order to feel that where she was right now was where she deserved to be. She wanted, but couldn't quite bring herself, to wish it would last longer than just one day.

IF JOHN WAS unsure at first what his duties might be as Osbourne's adjutant he didn't have the luxury of wondering for long. The new business that poured their way after the mirror ad necessitated expanding the staff; Osbourne insisted on no more than three new employees (though they could have used and afforded twice that number), and he left John in charge of the hiring. They didn't have to recruit – the office was besieged by job applications, by phone, by mail, by Internet, at the very door of the mansion – but John, eager to impress, recruited anyway. In the end he hired a graphic novelist from Cleveland, a faculty member from the American studies department at Yale, and a video-installation artist whose work he read about and subsequently traveled to see – with Osbourne's blessing – at the Biennale in Venice. He kept raising the stakes for himself, wondering when he would contact some- one who would refuse to consider his offer. But no one ever did.

John also ran all the client meetings now, which was sometimes a touchy business – in spite of the agency's escalating fame – only because Osbourne had decreed that they were not to take part in any pitches. If a client wanted them, then the client could hire them, but Palladio would not expend its creative energies in these demeaning closed-door competitions. This rubbed a great many executives the wrong way, and John – flying around the country, usually working alone – needed all of his unthreatening charisma to convince these executives that, considering the agency's brief but unblemished record, they really weren't taking any undue risks; and that Osbourne's refusal to pitch their account was not a slap directed against them, but a measure of the lengths he would go to in order to insulate the best creative staff in the world.

That staff was indeed working at peak inspiration. They had

internalized Osbourne's message, which was that only the art mattered, that clients and their interests were an aesthetic crutch which was hereafter kicked out from under them, that the world of commerce would subsidize them endlessly in return for a portion of the reflected glory of the work they happened to do within the walls of the mansion. The more personal, the better. They were dependent on no one; and John, free of the stress now of competing with them, was able to take pride in the greatness of the work they were producing.

Inevitably, as Osbourne's name – despite his efforts to stay out of the spotlight, to credit only his employees – grew more and more revered, offers began to materialize for him to write a book. John flew to New York to negotiate on his boss's behalf. Private cars took him everywhere, from the hotel to the publishers' offices, from the offices to the restaurants, yet he was still surprised to find himself a little keyed up at the prospect of running into someone he knew in the city – from his days at Canning & Leigh, or possibly even Rebecca herself, who still worked in midtown, as far as he knew. In his daydreams about it he concentrated mostly on how not to appear condescending, in light of the success none of them had predicted. But in the end, he saw no one but strangers and new acquaintances, and he flew home to Virginia with no such experience useful for measuring his old life against his new one, only a contract for his boss to sign, for 1.1 million dollars.

Though it was late when he got back to Charlottesville, he drove straight to the office. Osbourne would certainly be there, and might even be awake, since he kept strange hours; but John would wait to see him first thing in the morning. He went to his own bedroom – the one now generally recognized as his –

in the west wing, and he opened the door. The bedside light was on; but Elaine, though she had tried to stay awake, was sleeping on her side, one knee drawn up, under the sheet. John smiled; he undressed, turned off the light, and, sliding in as noiselessly as he could, moved his fingers lightly across the solid curve of her hip, to see how far he could get without waking her. It was a game they had.

The next morning, when John handed Osbourne the book contract for his signature, his boss looked it over and shook his head appreciatively, then offered it back to John and said that, after thinking it over last night, he had changed his mind and decided not to do it. John, though somewhat put out by this, had to admit he was also not terribly surprised. For months now Osbourne, via his instructions to John, had turned down one by one every request to be interviewed, or photographed, for print or TV. He turned down public appearances of all kinds, in all countries. Even inside the office, in fact, he was less and less visible, though he was usually, as they were all aware, in the mansion somewhere. No one knew if this reclusiveness was calculated or not, but if it was calculated, it couldn't have been working out any better for them.

WITH EIGHTEEN HUNDRED dollars held in a tight roll by a hairband in her front pocket, and a heavy bag with a shoulder strap on the seat beside her, Molly drove Kay's Honda to the Albany airport and left it in long-term parking. Inside the terminal she bought a postcard with a picture of the airport on it, wrote a note to her parents which said only that the Honda could be found in long-term parking (Lot G-2) at the Albany airport, bought a stamp at a newsstand, and dropped the card in the mailbox near the terminal's police station. Back outside the doors to baggage claim, Molly hailed a cab to the Trailways bus depot on Foundry Avenue. She staggered down the narrow darkened aisle of a half-empty bus, slouched in a seat by the tinted window with her knees pressed high up on the metal seatback in front of her, and with the cold, antiseptic-smelling air conditioner blowing on her forearm, her other arm resting on top of the bag stuffed shapeless with her clothes, she began to disappear from the lives of the few people who knew her.

Like the bus ride itself — torturously boring, until the moment she emerged from the Lincoln Tunnel and understood how completely her life had just changed — the years of Molly's life that followed seemed to pass at two speeds simultaneously: interminable and abrupt. Inside Port Authority she called information for the address of the youth hostel, which turned out to be all the way up on Amsterdam and 105th Street. A few nights there, sleeping on a woven mat, in with the backpackers and the foreign boys who kept encouraging her, as baldly as if she were an idiot, to go out and get drunk with them; then she answered an ad in the *Voice* and took her place as one of six roommates in a three-bedroom apartment on Gansevoort Street. The third bedroom, which Molly now shared with a tall, sallow aspiring actress named Iggy, was actually a dining room with a Japanese screen placed in the entrance. Molly could look out the window nearest her futon and see, on one corner, the unmarked entrance to an S/M club, and on the other the trucks backing in and out of the meat wholesalers, the thick men, none of whom seemed any younger than middle-aged, in their absurd white coats like surgeons, covered with sawdust and blood. Molly came with enough money to cover two months' rent and a lie she had prepared about a publishing job she was up for, but in the end the other tenants of the apartment never even asked her if she was employed. She had enough cash for a security deposit and that's where their interest ended. They were used to people coming and going.

All of them in the slovenly apartment were involved in the arts in some peripheral and materially unsuccessful way. They passed around their part-time jobs the way they might have borrowed each other's clothes; Molly found work first at a Kinko's, then at a video store, then as a waitress. They sometimes went, in groups of three or four, up to Columbia for jobs as human subjects – drug experiments and the like. These jobs were so unrelated to who they felt they were that the changes, the hirings and firings, meant nothing. But Molly could meet her measly rent and her one-sixth share of utilities in this way, which was the only accomplishment in which she felt she could afford any interest. Everyone else Molly met took it for granted that she was an artist of some sort herself; she was living the life, she had the demeanor, and after all she had come to the city with no prospects in the first place. But if Molly was involved with creation of any kind it was only to weave herself so seamlessly into this life that she might not stand out from it at all.

Friends introduced her to friends. So many people she met now, men and women, were gay that she couldn't always anticipate when some friendly figure at a club or a party in someone's apartment would suddenly try to get over on her.

She took up some offers and not others; she did make herself a rule – one which her roommates had long ago discarded – that she wouldn't sleep with anyone else who lived in the shared apartment; she didn't want to endanger her spot, since, should she find herself homeless now, she really had no safety net at all. If, in theory, Molly had suddenly changed her mind and decided to have sex with any one of them, she would have known in advance what kind of sounds they tended to make when they came; with the Japanese screens and the temporary walls and the excess of people, there was no privacy to be had at home. No one minded, because you couldn't overcome the closeness of the quarters in any other way than not minding.

In the end they lost their lease anyway, when James, who had been at NYU film school for something like seven years, got drunk and set fire to his mattress after his dissertation was rejected. Molly and Iggy moved into a tiny one-bedroom on Seventeenth Street; the guy Iggy was sleeping with came over the first weekend they were there and put up a plasterboard wall in the middle of the one bedroom, with a gap cut on one side for a door. This meant that Molly had to walk through Iggy's room to get to her own bed; but again, the pretense of privacy was best forgotten if you wanted to live sanely in such a situation. The boyfriend was married and he never knew very far in advance when he could sneak away and come over; if Molly walked in on them, he made no attempt to cover himself, and once in a while asked frankly if Molly would care to join them.

"Maybe some other time," Molly said. Iggy just laughed.

She went to readings, she went to clubs, to gallery openings when there was the prospect of free food. The art that she saw everywhere was an art of personal expression; most of the theatrical productions were monologues or one-man shows, if only for budgetary reasons. This kind of highly confessional art, when it was bad, seemed false, insincere, yet Molly wondered if you could fairly call it inauthentic when the artists themselves (they were usually friends of hers) were sacrificing everything for it – comfort, money, security. Rarely did any kind of failure incline them to question these sacrifices. They would do anything to get their confession on the record.

Every time Molly met a new person, in a social situation, the fourth or fifth question out of their mouths was, What are you working on?

Iggy got a job playing a Mexican hooker on a soap opera, but then the character was killed off and she went on unemployment for a while. She tried to take a job at Starbucks but was fired for cursing out the manager before her training was even completed. Accustomed to such setbacks, Iggy continued going out at night, and refused to admit the possibility of real disaster.

"There's always whoring," she'd say brightly, shrugging her shoulders. It became a running joke between them, every time a bill collector would call or the landlord would wait for them on the stoop.

Years were going by. What was she working on?

She had what might be called an artistic temperament, yet she had no inclination toward art itself. Art was communication; she wanted only to be silent. Music, acting, anything that involved getting on a stage was outside the realm of possibility for her. Even writing seemed to her much too demonstrative. It wasn't fear so much as distaste. In talking about a thing, you automatically forgave yourself for it. She didn't want to transform her own experience, to pretend it was anything other than what it was.

So she started taking any sort of available job in the film business: as an extra, in craft services, redirecting traffic when directors were shooting on location (legally or otherwise) on the streets of Manhattan. Carrying tape, carrying screens and stands, when it wasn't a union shoot: offering her labor in the service of someone else's vision. She didn't think of it in terms of advancement – only in terms of hopscotching from one job to another, without too much of a nerve-racking break in between. There was a whole society of young people who lived in this way, and their sense of self-importance was tremendous, though, to be fair, most of them went into it with more of an ambition than Molly did.

She did some stupid things, some crazy things, from time to time. This was why she tried to keep her personality tamped down now, because when she didn't, what tended to emerge was a vengeful sort of self-effacement. Mostly it involved a reluctance to take herself out of the path of dangerous men. Once she and Iggy had to change their phone number; for Iggy, who had that number on the back of countless 8 x 10s sent to casting directors, this was a great inconvenience, but when Molly made her listen to a few of one particular man's answering machine messages, she said okay. Most of Molly's sexual experiences were pickup situations, in clubs or at parties, once on the street with an Israeli man who asked her directions to the Circle Line. She gravitated toward (or allowed herself to respond to) the ones who verged on some sort of emotional extremity; but it was no longer about wanting to see what they had to show her. Nights like that were like tearing the veil, like mounting little productions of her opinion of herself. She wanted to see what she would look like having sex with a coked-out Dominican who could only stay hard if he was holding a knife to her face. She wanted to see what she would look like afterward.

She had no news of her family. She had no idea if they wondered where she was, or if they knew. She felt she had forfeited her right to have her curiosity satisfied about these things.

There was never a shortage of men who wanted her. She was beautiful, self-effacing, open in her manner and yet completely unreachable; thus she had become the kind of woman a certain kind of man will want to wreck himself against.

One such man was the director of a film she worked on, a documentary about poetry slams. Molly made herself useful, handing out and collecting releases, taking care of the parking permits for the crew. His name was Dexter Kilkenny. He was tall and unhappy, the kind of man whose legs bounced whenever he had to sit down for too long, and he was driven by a career ambition which shone through any cynical disguise he tried to drape over it. Molly did not miss any of the looks he gave her on location, even though he only looked when he was under the impression she didn't see him.

When the finished film was accepted at Sundance, eight months after the crew had broken up at the end of shooting, Dex made sure to call Molly and invite her to the celebratory party at Nobu. She had no idea how he had even gotten her phone number, but she didn't ask. She went with Iggy to the party. Next day, Dex called her at home again.

"Sorry I didn't get to talk to you much last night," he said, as if they were old friends. "The guys from Miramax were there, so I had to, you know."

"Sure," Molly said. "So how are you doing?"

"Hung over."

"Drunk with success."

"Yeah. So I had wanted to talk to you about, about working together again. I really enjoyed what you, what you brought to, uh—"

"You have another movie lined up?"

"Well, no, but from what everyone tells me, the offers should start pouring in after Sundance."

He paused.

"So," Molly said.

"Yeah?"

"So really this is more like a call where you want to ask me out on a date."

"Well, yeah, except, except I don't really do that. Date. No experience in that area."

"So you thought what you'd do instead is hire me," Molly said, smiling. She teased him, but she liked how comfortable he seemed with his own eccentricity.

"No, no, I mean don't misunderstand me—"

"It's okay. Listen, I have an idea. We'll go to the movies. It's dark, no talking, then afterwards we can go to our separate homes if we want to. Sound good?"

Four months later, when he went to Sundance, Dex didn't take her, which was disappointing. While he was gone, though, she moved her stuff into his apartment on Ludlow Street. He was right, too. The offers came pouring in.

AS JOHN'S BANK account mushroomed, he grew to feel that the two featureless rooms of his rented apartment, even though he rarely set foot there anymore, were an unnecessary drag on his personal sense of well-being. He let his lease expire and moved his few belongings into his room at Palladio while he contacted a few local realtors. But the first few places he saw were not right – too new; too garish; too big for one man living alone – and then, after he'd been forced to cancel two or three real estate appointments at the last minute for emergency business trips, the whole house-hunting effort ran out of the steam of its initial enthusiasm, swamped by the more pressing short-term concerns of work.

This contributed to a peculiarity of John's new relationship with Elaine Sizemore, a romance about which he was growing very optimistic: they had never had sex outside the office. John, for now at least, had no other home, and Elaine (she, too, had rented a cheap room upon moving to Charlottesville, half expecting the whole thing to go belly-up in the first six months) insisted that her "home" was so embarrassing she would never let anyone who knew her from the office lay eyes on it. So she and John, on the nights they had been able to spend together, often went out – to dinner, to parties, to the movies – but they always returned to Palladio, unlocking the door quietly and moving on tiptoe through the hallways, even though the west wing was usually unoccupied at that hour, and even though their relationship was an open secret anyway.

That was the way the whole thing had started. After a fancy dinner with a group of executives from Pepsi, John and Elaine had left the restaurant in separate taxis, and had laughed tipsily when his taxi pulled up right behind hers in the mansion's driveway.

"Don't you have a home?" John teased her. She had unpinned her hair in the taxi, and now she kept nervously pushing it back behind her ears.

"I do," she said, "but after a meal like that, one should spend the night in a nice room with a fancy bed, don't you think?"

"One agrees," said John.

Feeling like he was in college again, he invited her to his bedroom for a drink. She said yes with a kind of mock wariness, and the two of them giggled their way through the dark kitchen until they found a cupboard with liquor in it. For some reason he was now finding her round, wire-rimmed librarian's glasses terribly exciting in a sexual way; though this feeling was born in drunkenness, it never went away.

Elaine had a graduate degree, it turned out, in comparative literature, from UC Santa Barbara. It was hard, intriguingly so, to imagine her in the context of southern California, but in fact that was where she was from, and where her parents still lived. John told her that he had had plans to go to grad school in the history of art; he didn't get into why those plans had fallen through, and she didn't ask. No one, he reasoned, wants to hear old-girlfriend stories, particularly traumatic ones, so early in a new relationship. The time for more detailed and honest presentation of their respective pasts would come sooner or later. In the meantime, they were at home in each other's company. The unlikely success of the venture that had brought them together seemed to draft them along in its wake. Elaine had that opaque quality, that air of hidden resources, he liked in women, though she was funny at the same time, alert and undemonstrative and not at all neurotic. Twice she had stopped, in the middle of sex, to ask him – with no trace of insecurity, only a kind of amicable curiosity – what the hell he was smiling about.

In March, Osbourne was informed – by John, over breakfast, in the fourth-floor alcove under the skylight – that he had been awarded the Provost's Medal by New York University's Tisch School of the Arts. The award came, traditionally, with an invitation to deliver a public lecture on a subject of the honoree's choosing. John mentioned this in the spirit of thoroughness and obligation, to his boss and to those who extended him the invitation; after all, Osbourne had turned down every public engagement offered him in the last two years.

Now, though, he put down his espresso cup and looked out the window at the gray sky.

"Let's do it," he said mischievously.

John leaned forward. "Give the speech, you mean?" he asked foolishly. "Go to New York?"

"Yeah. Yeah. I feel a lecture coming on." Osbourne laughed. "When is it?"

The date was set for May. The Tisch School dean sounded something close to frightened when John informed him that his offer had been accepted, with gratitude.

Until then John would remain, as he had been since his removal from the creative staff, Osbourne's public face. Often this consisted of offering short, cryptic, punchy statements to reporters; when possible, John liked to sit and craft these statements with Osbourne himself at the small table beneath the skylight. Though they each had their own east-wing office (John's was on the second floor, Osbourne's on the third), their meetings almost always took place at that small dining table, as if the sight of John were itself a reminder to him of his own alimentary needs.

John's role as Osbourne's voice even extended, more and more of late, to the inner workings of the office itself. The boss almost never came downstairs, at least not during conventional working hours. He had his meals served to him on the fourth floor, and the east wing had a separate entrance which allowed him to come and go without being seen, though anyone working in one of the upstairs rooms could see and hear his Triumph grinding down the long gravel driveway from time to time. Anytime he had a message he wanted conveyed to the staff, he had John do it. If this was a curious aspect of John's duties, it was still, from John's point of view, by no means an unpleasant one. The news was almost always good.

They had lately had inquiries from UNICEF; from the Chicago Art Institute; from two different city governments in the United States, looking for ways to raise revenue through advertising in public places without attracting too much negative press; from the committee to reelect a prominent senator; from a consortium which wanted to build a historical Civil War theme park in nearby Manassas; from Major League Baseball. John felt like laughing with wonder each time Osbourne gave him news of this sort – the scope of their success and their influence seemed to be surging past the boundaries of even their fondest original hopes. But in the time it took him to descend to the first floor and assemble the staff, he tried conscientiously to expunge any of that giddiness from his voice and his manner. The client doesn't exist: this was Osbourne's guiding principle, and John, in the interest of their continued success, tried hard to emulate his boss's thinking.

DEX WAS DOING nothing; he lived in a world of offers. At night he and Molly went out, to clubs, to premieres, to after-hours clubs, to restaurants where no one ate; Molly was usually ready to go home at least an hour before they finally left, in the overlit quiet and the bad smells of Manhattan at 4 a.m. She knew one sure way to get his attention – flirt with another guy, or even just allow herself to be flirted with – but the few times she had tried that, she didn't like the way it ended. She woke up one morning, surly and hung over, and was amazed to see the fully articulated marks of Dex's fingers still visible on her upper arm.

Dex got up at about 1 p.m., when the Federal Express man came. He sat at his tiny kitchen table – big enough for only one, really – under the huge poster of Jean-Paul Belmondo, drank coffee, and read scripts. After a few minutes, he would begin flipping through the pages rapidly, as if looking for a particular word, a scowl of restless contempt stealing over his face. Molly, under orders to keep quiet while he read, would read something herself, or look at the TV with the sound down. Eventually Dex would stand up, listen to his answering machine messages, step into the shower, and ready himself indolently for another night out.

This went on for months. Dex accepted every invitation, in a kind of frenzy, not because he felt he had arrived but because he understood that his window on this kind of life might close at some point unless something else as substantial as Sundance happened to him soon. Molly got to meet her share of famous people, the fatuous and the moody; every evening she swore she didn't know why they went out every night, and every afternoon she became restless to go out again, if only to escape the confines of the tiny apartment on Ludlow Street, which Dex, with twenty-one thousand eight hundred dollars in the bank, refused to give up because it was rent-controlled. Drunk and exhausted every night, hung over every day, their sex life had receded nearly to nothing.

Dex, having told his agent he was eager to look at feature scripts and escape the documentary ghetto, was trying hard to sell out; but something inside him, some kernel of self-regard for which he himself had grown to have a real dislike, was keeping him from doing it. The scripts were all so terrible. He would read aloud to Molly from them.

"Why does everything have to be so awful?" he said, blowing out a thin violent stream of smoke. "And I wouldn't mind if it was awful in some new way. I wouldn't mind being the originator of some new awfulness the world has never seen before. You know?"

Then one day Molly came home from D'Agostino's and played back the messages; after the usual calls from Dex's agent, party planners, film-school buddies, the last one was from Dex himself, talking excitedly over the street noise, asking Molly to meet him at the southeast corner of Houston and Broadway. Immediately. It was just a ten-minute walk, and she found him standing there, neck tilted back, staring up at the exposed side of a ten-story loft building. Atop it was a water tower, just like the towers atop many of the older buildings left in the city, except that this one had been painted, monochromatically, a shocking, bright, metallic red. There was something else off about it, too, and it took Molly a minute of looking before she understood what it was: a mold had been taken of the original water tower, then recast with some sort of plastic in place of the original wood, so that the lines of the object before her, while instantly recognizable, were smoothed out as well, softened, diminished, like a three-dimensional echo, a death mask, of the everyday object it had supplanted.

Molly touched Dex on his shoulder; he looked down at her for a second and smiled – unusual enough, those days – before he went back to staring. Molly realized that she had been brought here to look at it, too.

"I like it," she said. "Has it been here long?"

Dex shrugged.

"Kind of eccentric," Molly said. "What's it doing there, I wonder."

"It's an advertisement," Dex said quietly.

"It's what?"

"An ad," he said – smiling again. "A commercial."

"For what?"

"I don't know." He laughed, without changing expression.

Molly thought about it. "Oh!" she said suddenly. "Is it that guy, that . . . what's his name, the ad guy—"

"Malcolm Osbourne."

"Yeah! It's one of his?"

Dex said nothing. A kind of sneer was creeping over the lower half of his face. It was a look that was attractive only to Molly, who knew the true engagement it signified.

"Is this", she said, "a movie idea?"

He nodded. "I guess it's that," he said. "I mean, I'm standing here looking at this thing – the incredible phoniness of it, the way this guy is held up as a great artist, a revolutionary – the emptiness, the pretension – and I just want to take this guy Osbourne, I want to take a scalpel and cut his throat down to his belly and pull him open and show him to everyone, I want to fuck him up the ass, I want to rip his head off and shit into it, I want to pop his lying eyes out with a spoon and skullfuck him. So yes," he said, "I guess you could say that's a movie idea."

Dex wanted to go back home and call his agent. On the way, he kept turning back to stare at the painted water tower from different perspectives, to hold it in his mind's eye, knowing he wouldn't be able to see it from the windows of their apartment. Molly mentioned, as they waited for the light on the Bowery, that she had just read somewhere that Osbourne was due to appear at NYU, to pick up an award and give a speech, some time later that spring. Dex's face lit up at this news. "We'll go, then," he said. "You can get us tickets. That's excellent, that's ideal, that's why I need you," and he took her face between his hands, grinning broadly, in a loving way, though a little harder than necessary.

JOHN FELT AS if he were carrying some sort of explosive secret with him on the trip from Palladio to Richmond, Richmond to La Guardia, La Guardia to the St Moritz. It was just the two of them, himself and Mal, and Mal didn't say much. No one would be likely to recognize his face, of course; and John, like some employee of the Witness Protection Program, kept restating to himself the importance of acting normally. They sat in their adjoining rooms at the St Moritz for three hours, even ordering separate room service dinners. At Osbourne's direction, John had turned down a dinner invitation from the Tisch School's board of trustees; he needed more time, he said, to go over his remarks. He had seemed agitated all day – not worried exactly, but suffering from a kind of surfeit of physical and nervous energy. Now, when John muted the TV in his room, he could hear Osbourne rehearsing his speech on the other side of the wall. John ate his salmon en papillote from a tray and looked out the window at Central Park, feeling strangely subdued. At six forty-five he put on his suit jacket, went out into the hallway, and knocked on Osbourne's door.

In the tiny anteroom just behind the auditorium stage they could hear the swelling murmur of the crowd. The event, the dean said proudly, was sold out. Balding, in a black suit which he picked at so unfamiliarly it might as well still have had the price tag on it, the dean sat in a folding chair, smiling affably, trying to keep his knees from touching Osbourne's or John's. He did ask Osbourne, hopefully, if he would like to hear his introduction in advance, just to make sure there were no inaccuracies, nothing objectionable, unfortunately there was no written text to show him, it was all in the dean's head. Osbourne smiled and said he was sure it would be fine.

It was fine; John and Mal stood in the wings and listened to it. The dean went on a bit long, working in Tocqueville and McLuhan and Jacques Ellul and Sonic Youth, but it was all quite thoughtful. Then Osbourne walked out to the podium, clapping the dean on the shoulder as they passed, and waited for the applause to die down.

It didn't die down for quite some time.

"Let me tell you something about myself," Osbourne began. "What I do is not advertising. Advertising is all about moving product. Or it's all about envy. It's all about sex, about lust, about instant gratification. Advertising is the beast. Well, I came here tonight, the first public appearance I've made in about seven years, because I have news to bring to you. The beast is dead. I have killed it."

John couldn't see Osbourne's face. A shifting took place throughout the hall, making a rolling sound like something you might hear at night if you lived near the sea; then gradually, thrillingly, it turned into more applause.

"The good news is that advertising has left behind the husk of its form – as mighty an apparatus as the world has ever seen – and as with any form the question of content is wide open. Limited only by the imagination of artists. And yes, I said artists, because the idea that the commercial world may function only as a place where real artists, quote unquote, come to whore themselves – this is an idea upon which everyone agrees in advance, a ready-made idea, an established idea. Hence, a dead idea.

"It comes joined at the hip to another dead idea, namely that art which reaches the greatest possible audience is by definition bad art, because badness, by which is meant simplicity, must be the *means* of reaching that broad audience. This, to speak plainly, is bullshit. The work that we produce at our new institution, Palladio – great work, important work, from an artistic standpoint alone – what should we do, put it in a drawer, take it out and show it to our friends when they come over? No. As an artist I believe that I have something to say, and if I have something to say I use the greatest means of expression available to me. This seems obvious, to me. And yet we are vilified for it. The reason our art reaches millions and millions of people is because *that's the nature of the form*. No matter how good or bad it is, how simple or how obscure, it will enter the consciousness of many, many millions of people. All the elitist defenders of the notion of high art — well, you'd think this would be a cause for them to flock to advertising, say hosannas in praise of it. 'What a wonderful thing is advertising. A haven for great artists, where they don't have to struggle, where they can say what they please with a built-in audience of millions.' You don't need me to tell you that this isn't happening. The great thinkers of the academy haven't figured it out. The business community hasn't figured it out.

"I have figured it out."

Laughter: for the first time in his life, John experienced the intoxicating effect produced by the laughter of a living, breathing, present audience. He took a step and tried to look out across the stage, to see some of the faces of those who had gathered to hear Osbourne's address. But the stage lights were right in his face; he couldn't make out anything past about the second row.

"I worked for years in the ad world, all through the seventies and eighties. I rose to the top of that profession. And I'll tell you, the more successful and respectable I became, the more I was treated like a star, told I was an innovator, the more disgusted I became with myself. I knew that what I was doing was really just a kind of endless theme-and-variations, and that theme was the status quo. There was nothing new about it. Believe me, there was a period of a few years there where I considered just getting out of the ad business entirely. And yet, even when things were at their worst, I knew somehow, in my heart of hearts as they say, that advertising wasn't failing me. I was failing it. There was an enormous, an *unprecedented* sort of potential there, if only I could figure out a way to get at it."

Osbourne paused to sip from a glass of water. The hall was silent, and John, without realizing it, was holding his breath along with them until his boss started speaking again.

"I was also an art collector for many years," Mal said. "Not out of a profit motive: I mean, the motive was for the artists to profit. I loved art, contemporary art, and if I was in a position to help subsidize these struggling young artists, to help them financially and to help them find a wider audience, then that's what I wanted to do. But what happened was, the two sides of my life began to come together, philosophically, in a way I hadn't anticipated. The art I saw was increasingly . . . well, I don't want to say bad, it wasn't bad. It was *frustrated*. It was hobbled by a sense of its own irrelevance, by a sense of the impossibility of mattering, of doing anything new. They were working for each other, really. It became totally, irremediably self-referential, and the basic paradox was that in order to gain acceptance as an artist, you had to make sure that you were working with precisely that small, knowing, insular, incestuous, ever-shrinking audience in mind. No wonder the artists were frustrated! To do what they were born to do, they had to enter a virtual monkhood, aesthetically speaking. They had to forgo any possibility of really mattering.

"At the same time, in my role as a partner and creative director at a major, quote-unquote cutting-edge advertising agency, I saw a number of highly gifted, ambitious, intelligent artists, artists with, in some cases at least, all the good intentions in the world and a lot to offer the world, I saw them doing work that was just awful, mind-numbing, destructive, reactionary. And they were doing it for a staggering, massive, global audience – an audience so starved for a great popular art that these hacks were hailed as geniuses. Okay, not hacks, they weren't hacks at all, but their *work* was hackwork, that's the point. They were locked into a certain intellectual framework. Nothing they did was at all innovative, everything they fobbed off as new was in fact borrowed, tested, safe. And safety is the death knell for art. And these guys thought they were rebels. So I got to thinking if there wasn't some way this seeming cultural wall, separating art and its audience, couldn't be breached somehow. I went looking for artists who I thought would be open to this radical idea as a kind of unconventional avenue to fulfilling their *own* vision.

"We live in a period when the avant-garde has ceased to exist, where nothing shocks any longer because we've seen, done, violated, overthrown it all. What I discovered is that in order to find that avant-garde power again, you have to move into, paradoxically, the most banal of all media. The one place left, it seems, where certain kinds of ideas are forbidden to be expressed. Where the two partners in communication, called editorial and advertising, cling to the Enlightenment-age fiction of their irreconcilability with one another. It's pretty late in the game, right now, if you're an artist; if you want to do something interesting, something new, you have to forget books, forget painting, sculpture, theater, journalism, movies. You have to take on advertising. You have to enclose its incredible powers of destruction.

"In the year and a half that Palladio has been in operation, that is what we have tried to do. We have launched a revolution. We have blown up advertising. We have broken open the frame – aesthetically, and, to a lesser degree, politically. Still, this revolution is a modest one. I feel we are just starting to do what Modernism did, in its revolution – that is, launch the debate.

"Every client of ours – every client – has seen an upsurge in sales as a result of our work. I don't care. Our work will continue even if that circumstance should change. Our whole aim in starting Palladio was to remove the element of cynicism from advertising. And yet what are we most often accused of? Cynicism.

"Actually, the complaint I hear most often may be one most of you are not privy to, because it comes from within the ad business itself. Constantly, I overhear this kind of professional sniping, this scoffing, to the effect that when you see a Palladio ad, you have no idea what it's selling. This 'complaint' is in fact, to me, the highest possible compliment. Because advertisements have *nothing to do* with the quality or value or character of the product they advertise, and haven't for a long, long time. That relationship is a fossil. The thing to concentrate on, ladies and gentlemen, is the quality of the messages these products – which is to say, their makers – agree to propagate. How one can maintain one's cynicism in the face of the enthusiastic public response to this idea is simply beyond me.

"What's next for us? Well, we're looking for more outlets,

by which I mean different sorts of outlets, places where you don't expect subversive messages. I mean, TV, radio, magazines, billboards, it's so stale, really, so limiting. We have recently begun discussing, for instance, an initiative to develop educational materials for schools. Of course we will be damned for this effort before we even begin. But these materials will contain no product references of any sort. Let me tell you, the truly dangerous people are those who insist that there is no such thing as doing good in the world, on a broad scale, without some ulterior motive. And anyway, what of it – the ulterior motive? What exactly is wrong with the desire to sell? If no one's freedoms or rights are violated in doing so? But the question is finally irrelevant. What is important is that we have proven that advertising, our age's greatest form of expression – whose worldwide annual budget, incidentally, is greater than that for public education – can communicate something greater than the masquerades of happiness, the fables of envy and lust and instant gratification, that form the whole worn fabric of Western life, Western dreams. What *meaning* does money have, when balanced against the good that's done? Who ever said that changing the world ought to be a low-paying job?"

The hall was motionless. Osbourne, his jaw set in a hard line, took out a red silk handkerchief and wiped the sweat from his head.

"I believe," he said, "we have time for a few questions."

JOHN WAS LATE getting to work because of an appointment he was too embarrassed to reveal, to his assistant or even to Elaine

– a trip to the Porsche dealership in Charlottesville. For a while he had saved his paychecks, even as the amount on them leapt by fantastic margins every other month or so. But after seeing Osbourne's reception at NYU, John was starting to shake the nagging feeling that all their success might be some evanescent cultural bubble. He felt entitled to a few indulgences.

His secretary, Tasha, was on the phone when he walked past, so he waved and went into his own office next door. After a minute he buzzed her on the intercom, to see what messages had come while he was out. No answer. He buzzed again, waited a few moments, then got up and went to the door of her office; from her desk chair she glanced up at him, surprised. She appeared to be reading a magazine.

"Didn't you hear me buzzing?"

"No," Tasha said, and rolled her eyes. "It must be broken again. I'll call Benjamin."

"What do I have today?"

"The movie people, in about twenty minutes."

The movie people. They were there to see Mal – in fact, they were Mal's guests – but John suspected their motives, and in any case it was a rule of thumb around there that no one saw Mal during the business day without going through John first. John also happened to know that Mal wasn't in the house at the moment, having gone off for a recreational drive, a pastime that sometimes kept him away for hours.

In the meantime, John shut his door and looked over two items he needed to discuss with Mal when they next caught up with one another. The first was how to handle a feeler that had come in from the Committee to Reelect the President. The President was said to be a great admirer of Osbourne's work, or at any rate the principle behind it – the banishment of cynicism from public discourse, and the attraction of the culture's greatest artists to its most accessible of arts. And Osbourne was unlikely to be able to resist an opportunity to influence public discourse on that kind of a scale. The potential problem, as John saw it, was that the President's campaign staff was virtually certain to want some say when it came to the question of content – an anathemous notion around there, one that was off the table from the beginning when it came to other clients. As for the question of whether or not Osbourne was a supporter of the President, John hadn't the slightest idea. Mal never discussed such things.

The second item came to John in the form of a newspaper clipping from the Denver *Post*. In the accompanying photo, what had become one of Palladio's most familiar images, a text-only billboard (it ran in magazines and, as a still image, on TV as well) with the words "The End Is Near" written on a white background, had been defaced by spray paint with green dollar signs, a stenciled American flag (also all green), and the addition of two letters, so that the text – originally Elaine's design, as it happened – read "The Trend Is Near". That this wasn't a routine bit of vandalism was testified to by the fact that it had been repeated in different cities across the West, with a good deal of attendant press coverage. A group calling itself CultureTrust had taken credit for what they termed, as the *Post* unfortunately echoed, a "guerrilla action." Two of its members had been arrested in a similar act in Spokane, vandalizing with green spray-paint work hanging in a gallery show called "The Palladio Phenomenon," and were demanding a jury trial rather than pay a simple fine. The wise course, John felt, would have been to ignore all this; yet he felt a sad premonition that this was not the course Osbourne would favor. Still, you had to tell him everything. God forbid he should find out through some other source.

There was a knock, and Tasha opened the door just enough to stick her head in. "Intercom's still broken," she whispered apologetically. "The movie people are here."

"How many movie people are there, exactly?"

"Just two. The director and a woman he claims is his assistant."

"Claims?"

Tasha shrugged her shoulders. "Girlfriend, assistant, whatever."

"Okay," John said. "Send them in."

She pulled the door shut. John pushed his chair back from his desk, and ran his hands through his hair. They were only coming in to talk; still, they were the movie people, and that made him more conscious of being seen. Another knock.

"Yes?" he said, and the door opened again.

2

I STOOD UP behind my desk as they walked in. Through Tasha's introductions I remained standing, my fingertips splayed out and pressing down on the desk, and honestly that's because I thought there was a real possibility I would fall down.

And this is his assistant, Tasha said, Molly Howe. Molly, John Wheelwright.

We shook hands, that's what kills me. We didn't let on right away what was happening. A door that has opened eventlessly a million times opens one day to reveal Molly standing on the other side: there was a time in my life, believe it or not, when such a moment wouldn't have found me unprepared, when I burned with the unreasonable belief that just such a thing would happen, that she would simply turn up one day, as inexplicably as she'd vanished. But that was years ago. On this day, my astonishment was profound. I put out my hand; Molly reached across the desk and held it for just a second; then our arms fell back to our sides and we went on staring into the mirror of our own disbelief.

It didn't last but a second, though; maybe it was the touch, the physical touch, that snapped me out of it.

Actually, I said, smiling a little, we've met before.

No kidding? I heard Dex say. I don't think I'd so much as looked at him yet.

Molly said nothing. We had a secret; but if I thought we were going to share the private gravity of it somehow, even silently, I was mistaken. She did not return my smile; in fact she seemed immobilized by her amazement, fighting it for control of herself, like someone who comes face to face with a dead person, or a bear, or the Virgin Mary. Her eyes seemed to dilate as I stared at her. She was afraid of me. It was unsettling to see.

Not that I want to put it all on her; I wasn't about to get into explanations anyway, not then, not in front of my assistant and some tall overeager guy I didn't know. Actually, we've met before. Actually, we've slept together. Actually, we were in love. Actually, she left me, and I haven't seen her since.

Years ago, I said. So anyway, Mal is tied up for a little while longer. Why don't I show you around?

IF I SAY it was dreamlike, I'm not just talking about the unlikelihood of it, or about wish fulfillment. There's a helplessness to dreams: things take their unstoppable course, no matter how bizarre, and even if your dreaming mind is allowed to smile at the absurdity of it, still you have no real choice but to go through your paces, speak your lines. Dex walked between us down the broad hallway, hands folded under his arms, doing all the talking. I could see why Mal had found it so hard to say no to him. He's just the sort of highly motivated young eccentric Mal can never resist. About six-three, comically skinny, with short, loosely curled red hair; even on his best behavior he gave off a kind of poorly restrained restlessness, as if events, or other people, were never quite moving at his pace. Just standing next to him was like being in New York again. He'd crashed an opening at Mary Boone to petition Mal to be allowed to shoot a documentary about the remarkable rise of Palladio and its founder; and Mal, while making it clear he would never allow any filming to go on inside the mansion, was smitten enough to invite Dex down to Charlottesville anyway, just for a visit.

What I felt right then, I suppose, was the desire to be able to say to someone, as we walked past, Hey, look; look who just showed up from nowhere. But no one in my current life knew that about me – who Molly Howe was, I mean. The only one with whom I might have shared this revelation, that the sheer unlikelihood of something happening was apparently no guarantee that it wouldn't happen even so, was Molly herself: and she kept turning to look out the little hexagonal alcove windows in the hallway, or wherever she needed to look in order to keep her face discreetly averted from me.

I led them down the broad front stairs and through the main entrance hall, with its original wooden chandelier from 1842; through the tiny, belfry-like east parlor, with the glass-fronted bookcases and the window seat where Alexa, the land artist from Los Angeles, sat folded up in the sunlight, looking up irritably from a copy of *Elle;* through the long parquet-floored ballroom, curtains drawn, animated by the hum of two dozen computers, in which a lavish all-night dance was held in 1861 to celebrate Virginia's secession from the Union. These days we keep most of our video-editing equipment in there.

It's hard to say how she's changed. Her hair is darker now. She doesn't dress much differently, that's for sure: a baggy black sweater, fatigue pants, no comb or pin that would hold her hair in anything other than its most artless position. She's put on some weight. Her face is fuller, the curves of her body somewhat more pronounced, but that's by no means a bad thing: she always was too skinny. I don't just mean that it makes her more attractive. I mean one can take it as a sign of stability, that she's eating, that she's not too depressed, that her life is settled at least to the degree that she can look after her own health. I used to worry about that. She was never someone who took great care of herself.

Awkwardly abreast, we passed through the dining room and kitchen to the back stairs that led down to the basement. It's like a warren, all brick and low ceilings and the occasional inconveniently placed steel support beam the contractors made us put in. I thought I'd show them the soundproofed artists' studios we'd installed down there, but they were all occupied, or at least locked, by the artists themselves. Milo, not content with a sign, had painted the words 'Do Not Disturb' in Day-Glo orange across the door itself. The whole basement had the thrumming, busy silence of a library, and I found myself whispering as we passed through. Just to the right of the stone steps leading out to the driveway is the so-called basement lounge, a doorless rectangle where for decades firewood was stored; Fiona (the artist I hired in Venice), Daniel the novelist, and my girlfriend Elaine were huddled together in there on an old thrift-store couch, watching what I knew must be some of Elaine's work-in-progress on a laptop.

I started past the doorframe, but Dex, for whatever reason, took a few steps into the room. The three of them looked up. Elaine noticed me and smiled uncomfortably before returning her attention to the screen; I have an idea what she's working on, but she doesn't want me to see it yet. Daniel and Fiona glared darkly at the strangers – at the very idea of strangers.

Sorry to disturb you guys, I said. This is Dexter Kilkenny and Molly Howe. Guests of Mal's. Dex directed *Throw Down*.

We're working here, Daniel said. You want to stare, go to the zoo.

Somewhat embarrassed, I led them from there up the basement steps and around the southwest corner of the house, to where you could really start to get a sense of the layout of the grounds. Palladio used to be a plantation home; the greater part of that land was sold off nearly a century ago, but we still have about two hundred acres. The hedges make a kind of smooth geometry of it as it rolls up and down, folding over and over itself like chop on the ocean, toward the Blue Ridge Mountains to the west. It was a beautiful Virginia spring day, hot, breezy, and fragrant.

That orchard, Dex said, sniffing like a hamster. What is that?
Cherry.
Beautiful.

I kept trying to fall a step behind him so I could catch Molly's eye, but then Dex would deferentially try to fall a step behind me again. The wind was blowing, and she kept pushing her hair back from her cheek. She still wears it long enough to blow over her face, into her mouth. She hasn't changed it at all.

So when was this place built? Dex said. Before the Civil War, right?

1818, I said.

Were there slaves here?

We're pretty sure. They didn't keep such careful records. We've never been able to find any record of the slaves themselves, but we did find some old architectural drawings of an outbuilding back by the orchard, with bunks in it and an outhouse nearby. It only makes sense as slave quarters.

Can we see it?

The outbuilding? It was torn down in 1866.

Oh. Well, naturally, Dex said; he seemed disappointed.

I walked them through the cherry orchard, with its brick footpaths and ornate iron benches, some more than a century old. I showed them the child-sized topiary maze the original owner had introduced to spoil his granddaughter, who died of tuberculosis in 1889. I mentioned his relation, admittedly a distant one, to Thomas Jefferson; I even threw in a quote from Jefferson's famous essay on the beauty of Virginia. Somewhere in there, I heard the unmistakable throaty sound of Mal's little Triumph turning off the main road and speeding up the driveway. Mostly to give him a few minutes to get settled, I called their attention again to the Blue Ridge Mountains, naming the ones whose names I was sure of, and in truth it's rarely clear enough to get as beautiful a view of them as we had that day. Dex and Molly were politely awed.

That was the end of their tour. I walked behind them up the stairs to the third floor, and as I did I saw Dex put his arm around her, saw him whisper something she didn't respond to and then kiss her on the top of her head. Colette, Mal's assistant, was just closing the door to Mal's office behind her; she saw me and nodded discreetly.

You can go on in and see Mal now, I said. Where are you staying, by the way?

The Courtyard Marriott, Dex said.

I know it well. Listen, I'll come by when you're done with Mal and walk you back out to your car.

Molly was standing like a dog outside Mal's closed door, her back to me. She couldn't wait to get away.

Oh, that's nice of you, Dex said, but I'm sure we can —

I insist. You'd be surprised how easy it is to get lost in here.

Colette opened the door and ushered them in. A few seconds later she reemerged, pulled the door shut, and looked quizzically at me still standing there in the middle of the hall.

Buzz me when they're done, would you? I said.

BACK IN MY office downstairs, the last of the initial shock wore off, and the truth is, I found myself feeling a little angry. I'm not talking about residual anger, anger over what she did to me ten years ago: ten years ago is ten years ago, and however all that might have fucked me up at the time, I'm well over it. We were kids then. I'm talking more about wondering where she got off acting so petrified.

I mean, what do you suppose she thought I'd do? Scream at her, throw her out, make a huge scene? She knows me better than that.

Of course maybe on some level it was gratifying too, let's be honest; after all, the worst, most humiliating part of any failed love affair is the suspicion that maybe it never meant as much to the other person as it did to you. So if I still had the power to upset her, just the very sight of me, I can't pretend that didn't mean something. But still, to act afraid of me, to the point where she wouldn't look at me or speak to me, that's just over the top. She owes me more.

HALF AN HOUR passed before Colette summoned me upstairs.

Mal's ready for you, she said when she saw me.

From her desk I could see that Mal's office door was standing open.

Where are they? I said.

They left about ten minutes ago. I offered to buzz you but they said they could show themselves out.

In a state of disbelief, I walked into Mal's office. He was in a lively mood. He sat on the front of his desk, in a white tennis shirt and jeans, his black hair still blown back from his recreational drive. John, John, he said. What news?

So you just saw Dexter Kilkenny and his, and his assistant?

I did. He's kind of a character, isn't he?

They cleared out of here awfully quickly. You guys didn't get into any sort of . . .

God, no. Just talked about movies. He still wants to make a documentary about Palladio.

You told him no?

Just like I told him no two months ago. He's a very single-minded guy. I told him to take a drive on Route 20, just get out to where the farmland starts, take in the beauty of the place.

What a day! You get maybe ten days like this in a year.

Did he say he'd do that?

I don't think he even heard me. You know he actually brought release forms for me to sign? The self-confidence of the guy! You have to respect that. I'm tempted to let him try it.

Are you?

Mal stopped bouncing his feet and looked at me; something in my voice, I suppose. Not really, no, he said quietly. The artists would never go for it in a million years. No upside for us in doing it anyway. Why, what did you think of him?

I had the strongest urge, right then, to tell Mal the whole story. But I didn't.

I don't know, I said instead. There's something about him. Not that I think he should make a movie about *us*. But he's young and very talented and he's got a certain focus, doesn't he? Maybe we should try to keep him around for a while, see if we have anything for him. I know Elaine needs some help. She asked me about directors just the other day.

Mal smiled fondly at me. Always on the job, he said. Where are they staying?

The Courtyard Marriott.

Christ. Okay, well, let's at least call them up and invite them to stay over here for a few more days. We have room for them, right?

THAT WAS THE first lie I ever told him. In my defense, it was entirely spontaneous. I simply can not believe that she could run into me like that and then just leave town again without a word to me, as if all the history there is between us, everything that connects us, just plain didn't exist at all. I have no plans to demand some big explanation from her. I have no plans at all. To me it's more like a matter of simple courtesy.

I had Colette make the call. Well, Dex said, I don't see how we can say no.

BUT ALL THAT was ancillary to what my meeting with Mal today was really about. I told him about the call I'd had from the President's people, and also about the trial next month of the two guys from CultureTrust, the ones arrested for defacing our artwork in a gallery out in Spokane. In retrospect it was a mistake to tell him the two things at once, because he seemed to forget all about the first matter as soon as he heard about the second one. I should have seen that coming. It's resistance, rather than the promise of reward, that always gets Mal going.

I don't get it, he said. These are, what, activists of some sort?

College professors, I said. I mean, there's a group of them, but these two particular guys are a couple of middle-aged professors from Eastern Washington University.

What's their objection, exactly? To me, I mean?

I was at a loss as to how to answer that one in a way that wouldn't rile him up further.

Maybe you should go out there, Mal said.

Out to Spokane?

Well, yeah.

And do what?

Mal held his hands apart. Do what you do, he said, smiling confidently, having disposed of the matter now in his mind. You're the fixer.

LIES RAMIFY; I didn't need another lesson in that. But they also raise the level of your alertness in a way, put you in more electric contact with your surroundings. Elaine and I went out to dinner that night at Il Cantinori. All her excitement over what she's working on, the thing she won't tell me about – all I know is it has something to do with Jack Kerouac, because *On the Road* has been sitting on the windowsill next to her side of the bed for the last three weeks – was sublimated into her eating; she went through her saltimbocca and started in on my risotto Milanese before I was halfway through it.

You're not pregnant, are you? I said.

She rolled her eyes at me, and put down her fork. Very funny. Sorry, I'm just hungry. Listen, here's a question, maybe you would know something about this. What's the deal with copyright and dead people?

How do you mean?

I mean, a dead author, do you still need permission to quote from their work?

I took a bite of my reclaimed dinner. Depends. I think it passes into the public domain fifty years after the death of the author.

Oh.

Has – has the figure you're talking about been dead fifty years?

Not nearly.

I mean, I can't see that it matters, permissions aren't that hard to work out.

Well, Elaine said, estates are funny sometimes. Plus I don't want the cost to get out of hand.

Don't worry about that stuff, I said. You know Mal doesn't want you to —

I know, but I worry, I can't help it. It's in my breeding. And then the thing is, I spent the last three days looking at all the stock footage I could find of cameras shooting out of airplanes as they take off? Out the windows, or from the cockpit, from the wheel well, whatever? And it all sucks. None of it is what I need. So I have to find some way to do it in-house. Just like sixty seconds' worth, but I know a shoot like that costs a fortune.

You know, funny you should mention it, I said, feeling the blood rise into my face. You know that guy you saw me with today?

Elaine nodded.

He's a director, and he's staying in the house for a while. His name is Dexter Kilkenny. Mal and I were talking about trying to find something for him to do. He made this documentary about poetry slams in New York, it went to Sundance, he got a deal with Fine Line.

She shrugged. Haven't seen it.

You want to talk to him?

Sure, Elaine said, trying to act blasé. The busboy came over to remove the bread basket; Elaine laid a finger on it and waved him away.

He's from New York? she said.

Sure is.

302

Because I was thinking that would be perfect, actually, La Guardia or Newark, for what I need. Something right next to a whole web of highways, lots of cars. Newark would be perfect.

I'll get you guys together tomorrow.

So who was the chick? Elaine said.

Sorry?

Who was that with him?

Oh. Her name's Molly. She's billed as his assistant. I think they're sleeping together, too.

Huh. Well, he must be quite a talented director, then, she said. Because he's way too ugly to be sleeping with her otherwise.

We both had dessert, and I signed for the check; then we drove home with the top down. The night was as beautiful as the day had been; the smell of jasmine at every stop sign was enough to put you right to sleep. Back at the house there was a light in Milo's window, but there's always a light in Milo's window: he's like a vampire, he can only sleep when the sun is out. Otherwise the place was silent. I didn't know if Dex and Molly had yet arrived, nor, if they had, where in the mansion Colette might have put them. Elaine and I took our shoes off and tiptoed up the back stairs, laughing. We didn't even make it to the bed. It was just one of those nights, where all seemed right with the world and a locked room seemed like the most remote place on earth.

★ ★ ★

THERE ARE NOW a total of fourteen artists on staff at Palladio. Most of them live in-house, functionally if not officially – I suppose it's too hard, especially for artists whose memory of material struggle is still fresh, to resist the maid service and the full-time kitchen staff. Even so, there are empty rooms. We certainly could do more hiring, but Mal has always resisted that, the idea of growth for growth's sake: he never wants to take someone on unless he feels that person's work has made itself indispensable.

This morning, I took my time traversing the ground floor on the way to my office, poking my head in every room. I saw Jerry Strauss half-lying on the couch in the parlor, powdered sugar still in his beard, reading the *Wall Street Journal* and writing on it with a Magic Marker. Jerry seems to like me but I know that with others he can be exasperatingly touchy, self-centered, messianic almost: he works best alone because while he's punishingly self-critical, one word of criticism from somebody else and he flies off the handle. He came to us as a graphic novelist. Jerry is actually not his real name. It took me the better part of a year to find that out. In high school they thought he looked like Jerry Garcia.

I stopped in the main dining room to get myself a latte and there I saw Dex and Molly, eating breakfast, sitting somewhat sheepishly in the high-backed wooden chairs. Dex was at the head of the table, Molly to his right. I sat down across from her.

Welcome! I said, feeling my own smile. You got in last night?

Dex's mouth was full, so he nodded.

Colette got you all set up? Where did she put you?

In a room up on the third floor in the . . . is it the west? (Molly nodded.) The west wing.

Right upstairs from me, I said. And everything was comfortable? Molly?

She looked a lot less agitated now, having had twenty-four hours to get used to my resurrection. Her panic had subsided, and in its place was a kind of injured stoicism, as if some joke were being played on her which she didn't find funny at all. I didn't care.

It's lovely, she said.

Beats the hell out of the Courtyard Marriott, Dex said, maybe a little anxious that Molly's tone wasn't sufficiently polite.

So you guys can of course just do what you want today, take it easy, be our guests; but listen, Dex, if you're interested, there's someone here named Elaine Sizemore who's familiar with your work and she wondered if you had a few minutes this morning to give her some help with a film project she's working on.

Film project? Dex said, wiping his lips. She's a director?

She's not, that's the thing. She's a scriptwriter. So there's a visual element she's having trouble with in this short film she's doing.

A short film, Dex said. So you mean a commercial.

Well, that's not a distinction we make around here. It's something she dreamed up herself, it hasn't been commissioned by anyone, it has no commercial content.

He sighed. Yeah, okay, he said. All right. Why not. I'd love to get a look at the way things work around here.

That's terrific. And Molly, I was thinking that would also give us a little while to catch up. I'd love to hear what you've been up to.

Silence. Rose brought my latte from the kitchen in a mug with a lid on it. I stood to go.

You guys went to college together, Dex said, is that right?

That's right. So Molly, that sounds good to you? In maybe an hour or so?

She looked at me warily. Not much fear left in those startling blue eyes now: just resignation, a kind of dignified resignation, like you'd show your executioner. Sounds good, she said.

Great. I'll come find you.

ONCE, YEARS AGO, in Manhattan, I thought I saw her. I was with Rebecca, and we were walking across Spring Street after the movies, on our way to Fanelli's for a beer before heading back to her apartment. Through the windows of the bookstore I saw the back of someone's head. Her hair, her build. I didn't stop. I made sure we were all the way to Fanelli's and had already ordered.

Oh my God. My wallet is gone.

You're kidding me, Rebecca said.

I bet it fell out when I was sitting in the theater. I had my feet up on the seat in front. Listen, you stay here, I'll run back and look.

It's okay, I don't need –

No, it'll just be a minute; and I ran out the door. It's like the more insane you get, the more instinctively crafty your lies become. At the bookstore, panting, I went through every aisle, and unbelievably, she was still there: head down, behind the curtain of hair, sitting cross-legged on the floor between the shelves with a William Burroughs novel. She looked up at me.

It wasn't Molly. Still, strange to think that somewhere in the world there walked a woman who had that sort of power over me.

DEX CAME TO my office promptly an hour later. I escorted him downstairs to the parlor, where Elaine stood waiting by the window, and I shut the door behind me again as the two of them were shaking hands. I went looking for Molly, in the dining room, in the ballroom, in the basement, upstairs in her and Dex's bedroom. She wasn't there.

Quietly I unlatched the front door and stood on the lawn, making sure I couldn't be seen from the parlor windows. I stared up the driveway, and off toward the mountains. Finally I thought to run around to the back entrance to see if their car was still parked there: it was.

So I walked into the orchard, and that's where I found her, sitting on one of the iron benches. She had cleared a spot to sit, but it was no use, really – spring is here; more white blossoms had already fallen in her hair as she sat there. I try now to imagine seeing her as if for the first time, and I can't, but still, there's no getting around the fact that she's a beautiful woman, more so, actually, than she was as a twenty-year-old. I felt a twinge of the same inappropriate sort of pride I used to feel when I'd be out with her, or even alone with her: that a woman such as this would go out with me. That not unpleasant feeling of being watched, even when it was just the two of us.

I tried to slow my movements.

You might have left word where you were, I said, sitting beside her. Or were you hiding from me?

She shook her head. If we're going to talk, I thought we

307

might do it somewhere where people aren't walking through the room every two minutes.

Well, here we are, I said. I brushed some blossoms off my shoulder.

You engineered all this, didn't you? she said.

All what?

You knew where I was. You brought us down here.

I was taken aback that she might have considered this. Absolutely not, I said. You saw my face when you walked in, right? I'm not that good an actor. The only thing I engineered was inviting you to leave the motel and stay with us. You said yes. Hardly anything sinister about it.

She held her arms crossed tightly in front of her, hands clasping her elbows.

I guess, I said (the edge on my sense of martyrdom dulling already, at the sight of her unhappiness), that I just couldn't accept that after everything that happened, that you could run into me somewhere . . . I mean, I know it was a long time ago. But that's all the more reason. Probably you hoped you'd never see me again. But you did see me. And you acted like you didn't. You would have turned right around and left again. I can't understand that.

Had you been hoping to see me? she said.

Sorry?

She looked down. All these years. Did you ever want to see me again?

I'd stopped thinking about it, I said. There was a while there. I mean, I actually flew out to Ulster to look for you. You knew that, right?

Her head sank lower, so that the hair – that reddish-brown

hair that I'd once held in my hands; each memory was like a little pinprick now – curtained her face entirely.

I went to your house, I said. I'm amazed that you seem not to know this. I spent the night. I drove to the hospital to bring your father home. He didn't know who the hell I was. He was waiting there for you.

Stop it.

Why are you scared of me? I said.

What is it you want? Molly said. She turned in her seat so that her leg was folded on the bench between us, and laid her hand against the side of my face, and I'm sure I jumped; I was the one who was scared now. What, an apology? What would be a proper apology, for what I did to you? If I killed myself, maybe? Of course I'm scared of you! You're my nightmare! In my whole life that was the cruelest, most selfish thing I've ever done. Running away from you like that. Do you think I've forgotten any of it? And so now it's all come back. Well, I deserve it. You're right. It was cowardly to run. I deserve what I get. You must hate me.

Molly, I said, pulling my head back. Molly. Settle down. Keep your voice down.

Her eyes were shining now, but mostly she just looked dull, defeated. She let me put my arm around her. I don't know what I'd imagined would be the outcome of this little meeting, but by now I had just about lost my taste for it; the stakes seemed too high. I wanted some remorse but I didn't want her in pain like this. I tried to reassure her, it felt like an instinct to do so; at the same time, I couldn't help but push on a little bit, gently, because I found there were still a few things I wouldn't mind knowing.

When you would tell me you were in love with me, I said. Were you lying?

No.

Then I . . . I don't get it. I don't understand what happened. What do you mean by selfish?

She sat up a little straighter, composing herself, and slid out from under my arm. You saw my parents? she said, wiping her eyes.

I did.

She shook her head. I couldn't watch them, she said. They're monsters. All those years of living together turned them into monsters. You can't join yourself to another person like that.

I would have married you then, I said.

I know that! I couldn't . . . I might have said yes. I was getting to the point where I'd lost all confidence in my ability not to say yes. I was losing myself to you because your, I don't know, your talent for intimacy was so great. Think where you and I would be right now. Think what would have happened to us. I was barely twenty years old. It would have destroyed us.

Is that what you thought? I said. You thought I wanted to destroy you? I wanted to save you. You seemed so damaged. I wanted to make the space that would let you just be who you are. The problem isn't that love would have destroyed you. The problem is that you don't see yourself as someone worthy of being loved. So you throw yourself away.

She raised her head and blinked away the last remaining tears. She stared into the branches for a long time, as the breeze came along every few seconds and slowly stripped them. Then, without looking at me, she told me the story of our unborn child.

★ ★ ★

PALLADIO

ALL THOSE YEARS, I'd been wondering what I'd done. She knew what she'd done. She was afraid of me because I was the only one in a position to forgive her. If I didn't quite understand why she'd done it, well, I don't suppose it was important that I understood. Of course I forgave her.

I don't know how long we were in the orchard; but when we came out, I know I felt that there was nothing left unsaid. It was upsetting, but it was purgative, and though I haven't exactly spent the last ten years pining for closure, still, it was nice to get it so unexpectedly. That was probably the greatest heartbreak of my life, Molly abandoning me like that. But I was twenty-two, she was twenty: it's the age of heartbreak.

We went into the house the back way, and in the kitchen we hugged for a long time before she went back up to her bedroom to wash her face and I returned to my office to see what calls I'd missed. I walked in and there was Elaine, sitting across from my unoccupied desk, her mouth set in a tight line.

Well, *that* was a fucking waste of time, she said. Where have you been, anyway?

DEX, ACCORDING TO Elaine, was no help at all. He flat out refused to go to New York and do the filming for her; she made it clear he'd be very well compensated for it, but he said the money wasn't an issue. Then, as much as she tried to keep him on the topic, he kept asking her biographical questions, what had she done before this, what sort of writing had she always dreamed of doing, how did Mal recruit her, etc. He wanted to know how much control Mal exercised over her work, over everyone's work; he wanted her to divulge the identity of the client who was paying for the production of this so-called short film she was working on. When she answered him – Mal doesn't control content; there was no client – he said he didn't believe her.

I placated her by promising we'd spend the next morning on the phone lining up a crew to get her airplane shot for her. Then I went off to find Dex, really just to apologize to him for any misunderstanding. Colette told me Mal had taken him out in the Triumph for a drive to see James Madison's house; Molly, too.

★ ★ ★

IT MIGHT SEEM odd that when Palladio is as busy as it's ever been, at the apex of its influence and success, its leader feels free to go off on these joyrides through the Virginia countryside. Mal's traveled a lot this spring, too, sometimes on a kind of quasi-official business (he's now on the board of the Guggenheim in Bilbao, for instance), sometimes just for the hell of it. He bought a house in Umbria, and he's been over there twice to supervise its renovation. He's doing less and less work these days, it's true; but that's all by design, a design he discusses only with me.

Not that he lacks for things to do, or at least for opportunities. For a period in the aftermath of that speech at NYU, half my day was spent sifting through and then politely rejecting all the offers that came his way. My sense of it is that there's a kind of ego conflict going on within Mal right now. He's well known, on a national, maybe even an international, scale, and he gets a lot of what's generally classified as star treatment. People ask for his autograph; total strangers show up on the Palladio grounds to take his picture or to try to talk to him or put in his hands something they're working on. Magazines arrive in the mail with articles devoted to him, some of them on a scholarly level, some treating him as just another element of the pop-culture firmament, wondering who he's dating (nobody, is the answer to that one), reprinting his high school yearbook photo.

Having that kind of talk in your ear, I don't care who you are, has to have an effect. There's a part of Mal that sees this space being cleared for him, this space in the national psyche, and he wants to take his rightful place in it. He *wants* to respond, though up until now he hasn't, whenever some reporter calls up to ask for a quote on the awarding of the Pritzker Prize or the role of propaganda in Castro's Cuba or how he would have advised Bill Gates before his testimony on Capitol Hill.

But the true Mal, to me, is the facilitator, the one who stays behind the scenes. Real power is secure enough not to feel this constant need to show itself. I can understand that kind of feeling, actually. He doesn't want the focus on himself. It's counterproductive. It goes beyond simple modesty; I wouldn't call Mal a modest man, exactly. He wants praise, but he wants it for his work, and so, in order to prevent people from making the reductive mistake of worshiping him, he hides himself from view. That's one reason why he has me.

Anyway, in a nutshell, what he tells me sometimes is that his greatest achievement when all is said and done will be his own obsolescence – the withering away of the state, he calls it, which I subsequently learned is a phrase from the Communist Manifesto. In the early days, he had to ride the artists constantly, try all kinds of tricks to get them thinking out of the box, to break down the culturally imposed barriers between their own ways of thinking (about art, about advertising, about money, about form, about originality) and his vision of the way things might be, ought to be done. But once they get it – once they understand, and internalize, that new way of thinking – they don't need him anymore. The more they work, the more they establish a tradition, one from which the next generation of artists will spring. Mal is laboring to make himself disappear. If he also seems ambivalent about this idea at times, I think that's understandable.

★ ★ ★

MAYBE I HAD an original agenda in asking Dex and Molly into the house for a few days; but if so, Dex certainly had his own in accepting, and he hasn't lost sight of it. He goes right around me, it seems, and through Colette to get to Mal, figuring, I suppose, that all he needs is enough time in which to ingratiate himself before Mal will relent and allow himself and all of Palladio to become the subject of some hip indie nonfiction film.

In one respect he's been successful: Mal seems infatuated with him and with Molly, to the point where the three of them have spent much of the last few days together. Mal took them out to Monticello, he took them out to Il Cantinori and also to his favorite barbecue place out on Route 20; he arranged for a screening of *Throw Down* in the ballroom and of the Matthew Barney *Cremaster* films; he's even had them up to the sanctum sanctorum, Mal's own living quarters on the fourth floor of the east wing, where usually only I'm invited – and even then only in the little dining alcove, never in his bedroom at the opposite end of the hall. (Not that Mal makes me feel unwelcome – just out of respect for his privacy; besides, I'd have no reason to be in there anyway.) Of course there were times during the day when Mal was unavailable to them for one reason or another, and during those periods I'd sometimes see Dex just strolling through the ground floor, down to the basement, peeking into the different rooms, trying, somewhat insensitively I thought, to engage the artists in conversation about what they were working on, what they thought about Palladio itself.

Then today Fiona came to see me in my office. She'd seen *Throw Down* the previous night, by herself in the ballroom, and she was powerfully impressed. She'd been thinking recently about a video installation, a sort of after-Warhol piece in which she'd be filmed while sleeping, only every time she fell asleep, she wanted the person doing the filming to wake her up again, by poking her, making a loud noise, whatever was necessary. She envisioned this going on for ten or twelve hours; she wanted a record of her reactions. This is actually a somewhat chaste-sounding project for Fiona, who's about five feet tall, a voluptuous and deadly serious young woman whose work usually involves a strong, some would say discomfiting, element of sexuality. Would Dex, she wondered, be interested in collaborating on it with her?

Let's find out, I told her. I looked around for him or for Molly but they were out somewhere. So I wrote Dex a note and slipped it under the door to their third-floor bedroom.

He turned up in my office a few hours later. We talked idly about the virtues and the downsides, for an artist, of living in New York, while my assistant Tasha went downstairs to round up Fiona. When everyone was seated, Tasha left and closed the door behind her.

Fiona started by complimenting him effusively on his one film, a ritual Dex made no effort to hurry to a close. Then, leaning forward in her chair, she described for him the project she had in mind. It was just as she had described it for me with the exception of the added detail that she'd be sleeping naked. She knows how to sell herself, that's for sure.

So I'd love it if you'd be my partner in this, Fiona said. Are you interested?

No, Dex said tonelessly, as if she'd asked him if he'd mind if she opened the window.

She was brought up short. No? she said. I mean, maybe I didn't make it clear enough that I don't intend for this just to be a camera on a tripod; there's lots of room, hours of room, for all kinds of creative approaches to shooting the bedroom, the bed, my body.

Sorry, no, Dex said again. I'm not interested.

I felt a little awkward about having brokered this meeting, which seemed on its way to engendering some bad feeling.

Does it have to be video? I said. Because maybe Dex is partial to film, or hasn't done a lot of work in—

I've shot video before, Dex said. I have no prejudice against it.

He looked down and started scraping with his fingernail at some sort of stain on his shirt. Fiona and I watched him.

Well then, she said. What's your fucking problem?

Dex looked distractedly around the walls of my office. He winced a little, as if thinking something over, but at the same time he was pretty unruffled.

I'd rather not say, he said.

The room buzzed with silence for a few seconds.

316

Yo, Bartleby, Fiona said. Why are you even here?

You know what? I said, smiling, rising from my seat. I think maybe it's time to bring Mal into this.

WE MET IN the fourth-floor alcove at the small oval table where Mal has breakfast – where he and I sometimes get together to discuss things before the business day has started. Benjamin was just putting coffee out when Dex and I arrived. Mal had told me to leave Fiona out of it. He knows what kind of a temper she has.

Mal's own face was slightly red, but not out of anger – his manner was quite friendly, expansive really, as if he were pleased to come upon this situation where his intervention was required. He also seemed a bit out of breath. You would have thought he'd just come from some sort of exercise, were it not for the fact that Mal – trim as a twenty-year-old – never exercises in any form. Maybe he ran up the four flights of stairs.

Dex, Mal said, I'm going to get right to it. You're our guest here, you're not an employee, and of course you're as free to do what you like inside this house as you would be out of it. But even in all the time we've spent together the last week or so, I've sensed that we're doing a little dance – not just you, understand; you and me both – in terms of what we discuss and what we don't discuss. That's kind of exhausted itself by now. Wouldn't you agree?

Dex pursed his lips. I suppose it has.

I know Palladio has its detractors. And I know that, as a general rule, when an angry young man like yourself wants to make a film about something, it's not to praise it, but to

317

discredit it, to knock it down. See, I'm torn here; because the very thing that makes me admire you, as a person and as an artist, is also the thing that I have to protect this place against.

You have to be protected against me? Dex said. A smirk, of sorts, was beginning to emerge on his face.

Well, no, I guess that's not it exactly. I mean, I love it that you continue to hang around here because you think that if you can just manage to snow me about your true intentions, I'll relent and let you film here. But your presence is starting to disrupt the equilibrium of this place, and for that reason, I'm honor bound to tell you that there is absolutely no way I will ever allow you inside this place with a camera, ever.

Dex nodded. He picked up his china coffee cup and put it down again without drinking.

So I think your visit here has to come to an end now. And that makes me sad. For one thing, I think you could have done some excellent work here, we have all the facilities and you could have had carte blanche in terms of what interested you; but more than that I mean that on a personal level I'm going to miss having you around. Anyway, I've had my say. It's only fair that before you go I let you have yours as well. Because I get the strong sense that you've been censoring yourself all the time we've been together, and the strain of that is beginning to show.

Dex tapped his fingers on the polished tabletop for a while. When he looked up, he did, in fact, as Mal predicted, appear to be in some way relieved.

My own view of this place, he said somewhat breathlessly, is that it is the absolute epicenter of corruption, and I would never do any work for you guys in a million years. You know? I mean, back before you got started, whoring was whoring; if you had to abandon your art for a while to go shoot a Coke commercial at least everyone knew what that was all about, and even understood how maybe it was necessary from time to time. But look at these people you've hired. They're brainwashed. They don't even know what it is they've been brought here to do. My film wouldn't have condemned anything. It would have exposed this place, that's all. That would have been enough.

Exposed it to whom? I said. We're not exactly keeping ourselves a secret. We're more popular now than we've ever been.

Dex shrugged, as if to say that he was baffled too.

Mal, I said, looking at my watch. What time's your flight?

Shit, Mal said, and stood up. He was on his way to Bilbao for a board meeting. Dex and I stood with him. On the landing, he turned and put his arms around Dex and hugged him – a backslapping hug, a quick, masculine sort of hug, but Dex could not have been more surprised – before continuing down the hall to his bedroom, to finish packing.

Dex and I walked in silence down the stairs. Halfway down the hall toward my office, he started talking to me, without turning his head.

You know, he said in an intimate tone, you're the worst of all. You're the perfect toady. You bring nothing to all this that I can see except your eagerness to please. You make it all possible, so they never have to deal with him, and he never has to deal with them. So everyone stays in the dark. You would have made an excellent Nazi.

I just kept pace beside him, until we came to the door of

319

my office. *I sure did enjoy fucking your girlfriend* was one thing it occurred to me I might have said to him. But that's not me.

I CHECKED THE window on the third-floor landing periodically until I saw them loading up the car. I hurried downstairs; out in the driveway, there was nothing to help them with — they'd only packed enough, originally, for a stay of two or three days — so I waited until the trunk was shut and then I put my hands on Molly's shoulders. She smiled at me, warmly, not concealing anything from anyone; her eyes did look a little red, but I didn't know what that might be about.

I felt like I knew just what I wanted to say. Dex was on the other side of the car, staring at the mountains, but I didn't particularly care if he overheard. I knew this would happen, I said to her. I knew I'd see you again someday. I did want it. I'm glad we had a chance to talk.

I'm sorry, John, she said. I'm so sorry for hurting you. You didn't deserve it.

I shook my head. You don't need to say that, I told her. That's history. It's all forgotten. I'm just glad I got the chance to see that you're (I almost said *that you're still alive,* but I caught myself), that you're doing well.

She put her face against my chest, and I held her for a minute. Dex looked over at us with a modicum of interest. I can't say it felt like old times, holding her like that; but there was something, some kind of phantom reminder of what had more or less enslaved me to her way back when: that shroud of silence, that incommunicable need, that sense that you could do whatever you could think of and still never get close enough. We said our goodbyes. I nodded to Dex, who ignored me, then I watched until their car had disappeared up the driveway.

That was that. I meant it when I told her that I knew we'd see each other again, and get the chance to fill in the blanks, solve the mysteries, hash it all out at a sane distance from our own youth. Fate is a word I don't like; it's more like logic, an aesthetic sort of logic, the logic of beauty. The logic of the story of us.

NOT MUCH NEW this week. Elaine found her director, chartered a plane, got about a half-hour permission window from the Port Authority to take off and land at Newark Airport – every time I see her she's shouting into a cell phone. Mal was supposed to be back from Spain by now, but he called Colette to say he was staying over in New York for a couple of days: someone put him on to the fact that there's an auction of Thomas Jefferson memorabilia at Christie's on Tuesday. He says maybe he can pick something up and donate it to Monticello. He's donated a bunch of money already; they love him over there.

Then this afternoon there's a knock on my office door, and it's Jean-Claude Milo. I hadn't seen him in two or three weeks, even though we're living in the same house. He doesn't look well: he's pale, and exhausted, a little more spectral than usual, though all of us around here are used to seeing him like this during periods when he's working hard.

I have a favor to ask, John, he says. It's a money thing.

Have a seat. Listen, you want anything to drink or anything? I can have Tasha go downstairs—

He waved me off. Thanks anyway, he said. No, so there's this thing I need.

Silence.

How much does this thing cost? I said, trying to prompt him.

He held up his hands. No idea.

Well, so what is it?

He shifted in his chair, staring at the Jim Dine that hangs behind me. It's a deep-red-and-white abstract (I've always thought it looks a bit like a bloody heart), and for a moment there Jean-Claude seemed so engaged by it that I thought maybe he hadn't heard what I'd asked him. Then he gave his head a little shake and returned his attention to me. The thing is, I need a refrigerator, he said; not like one of those huge ones but a small one. To go in my room.

I put my hand over my mouth so he wouldn't see me smiling at the solemnity of this request. Jean-Claude truly seems to have no grasp of money and how it works – the kind of item he described could have cost five thousand dollars for all he knew. As it was, he could easily have gone to P.C. Richard right in town, brought one home, plugged it in, and expensed it. I wouldn't have cared. This way, though, at least I got to have my curiosity satisfied.

What do you need it for? I said.

What do you mean?

I mean, just for eating in your room? I know the kitchen staff goes home at eight, I'm sorry if that doesn't fit with your own hours—

No, it's not that. It's for work.

Work?

For this thing I'm working on. I need a place to store some of my, uh, my bodily fluids I guess is the expression. Oh, and it needs to have a freezer, I forgot to mention that. Is that okay?

Sometimes I wish I had someone around to help me make sense of stuff like this. But in the end, all it came back to was the question of justifying an expense of maybe a hundred and fifty dollars for artists' supplies; and I didn't even have to think about that one. I told him I'd have it delivered to him tomorrow.

★ ★ ★

ELAINE WAS OUT for a late-night run; I was lying on my bed, still fully dressed, trying to read a collection of new and selected poems by a reasonably well-known poet (if I've heard of her, she can't be too unknown) who's applying for a spot here, when I heard footsteps in the hall, footsteps that came closer and then halted. No knock; instead, the whisper of a folded piece of paper being slipped under the door. It was a note from Colette. Mal was back from New York; he wanted to let me know that he was in his office right now, in case I had anything urgent for him.

I didn't, but I went anyway. The rooms on the ground floor were so dark I guided myself across to the east wing by the red lights of the burglar alarms. There were voices floating up from the basement, fading to silence as I took the stairs up to the third floor. Mal's office door was open; the light spilled into the hall.

You're back.

323

Mal smiled. Master of the obvious, he said.

He was looking through the drawers of his desk for something. On his desk was a small packing crate, from which he had removed the lid.

How was Spain?

Dull. But on the plane back to New York someone tipped me off about this Jefferson auction, at Christie's. I couldn't resist. I had to stick around for it.

You bought something?

Mal straightened up for a moment from his search through his desk and slyly folded his arms. He pointed at the crate. Have a look, he said.

I took a step forward and looked inside. Nestled in the straw-like packing material was a small pot, with a very narrow opening, set in a rectangular marble base. I wasn't sure what it was.

Can you believe it? Mal said. That's Jefferson's actual ink-stand, originally from Monticello. Been in private hands for more than a century. He wrote part of the *Notes on Virginia* with that inkstand. Lift it.

What?

Pick it up.

I did; though easily grasped in one hand, it was extra-ordinarily heavy.

Amazing, I said, replacing it in the crate. And I wasn't just indulging him; it actually was amazing, to be in the presence of an original object like that, to think for a moment about the past from which it had emerged, the other hands that had been where mine now had been.

But in the meantime Mal had found what he was searching

his desk drawers for: a roll of scotch tape. He picked up a stack of paper from his desk and set about taping individual sheets to the walls of his office, at eye level, a foot or so above the molding. They were color xeroxes. I only had to look at a few of them before I realized they were all works by or about that group out on the West Coast, Culture Trust.

I got them off the Internet, Mal said, following my gaze. I had some spare time in Bilbao.

I saw The Trend Is Near, of course, along with their appropriation of our famous mirror ad: a similar Mylar sheet, only with the word SUCKER and an arrow pointing downward, written in a kind of faux-lipstick, across the top. Apparently the Mylar technology had improved since we popularized it. I couldn't help but smile.

It's not bad stuff, is it? Mal said. I've been reading up on these guys. They actually have a lot of good things to say.

I sat down in the chair opposite his desk; he finished his circuit of the room, his back to me, rounding out the miniature gallery satirizing us, among others.

I mean look at this one, Mal said excitedly, taping it to the wall and standing back from it. It was a CultureTrust parody of one of Apple's Think Different ads: the image was a photograph of Karl Marx.

The only problem here, Mal said, is how different is this from one of the real ads?

Not too different, I admitted.

So I was looking at it and I thought, you know, if they really want to parody this campaign they should use the same words over a picture of Steve Jobs with a knife sticking out of his head.

And that's when it hit me: I could help these guys! In the end we're really all after the same thing!

And that rather startling idea hung in the air between us for a minute, until Mal stood and lifted the inkstand out of its crate again. Seeing him glance around for a spot to put it down, knowing how heavy it was, I jumped up and moved the crate on to the floor. He set the inkstand down and settled back into his chair again, with a happy sigh; and we sat there contemplated the solidity of the thing, its disinterest, its promise to outlast us.

★ ★ ★

CALL CAME TODAY from the Committee to Reelect the President. That's fallen through, it turns out; I'm told they opted for a more traditional approach. I thought Mal would be disappointed, and maybe he was, but he said that, fun as it was to think about, it was the outcome he had expected.

They're not willing to turn over the control of content, he said, putting jelly on a bagel. They've got all these high-paid consultants, those are the guys doing the hiring, not the candidate himself, and those guys are unwilling to take risks or cede control because then their boss might suddenly wake up and ask what they're doing to earn all that money.

As if content really mattered here, I said.

He nodded vigorously, still chewing. It matters less in this instance than most, he said. At the same time, because the differences between the candidates are so negligible, so superficial, the ads, the quality of the ads, is really all that matters. And when you take into account that every public appearance, speech, convention, whatever, is all so heavily scripted, it

326

amounts to advertising as well. You could make the argument that people are really electing the makers of the ads.

We were sitting in that little breakfast alcove up on the fourth floor. It was about six forty-five in the morning.

You should run, I said.

He laughed. Why not? he said. It makes perfect sense.

But I could tell he was joking. Mal just isn't that comfortable in the limelight.

★ ★ ★

SO I FLEW out to Spokane; and when I got there, the CultureTrust defendants refused to see me. Their lawyer was more polite; he called my hotel room with addresses, times, room numbers so that I could at least attend the opening day of the trial. A quick jury selection, he said, then state's witnesses probably right after lunch. His name was Bill Farber, he was right around my age, and I was kind of touched, actually, by his excessive friendliness; I got the sense that he didn't meet a lot of people in Spokane who came from the outside world, and he was reluctant to let me go. He had been just two months out of Penn law school, in his first job as an associate with some white-shoe firm in Philadelphia, when his parents were killed in a car crash. He took a three-week leave from the firm to return home to Spokane and take care of affairs, make arrangements to sell the house, et cetera. That was five years ago.

Spokane is another one of those cities where you might as well be anywhere. Starbucks, the Gap, some sort of ugly new convention center — it all looks like some sort of traveling exhibition that might pack up and move on the day after you do. And yet if you were to jump in your car in the middle of downtown Spokane and drive twenty-five miles in any direction, you'd be so deep in the woods as to be pretty much off the grid: in fact, you're not too far at all there from the Idaho border, militia country, Unabomber country. Bill Farber offered me a tour of the Spokane River Valley after court was adjourned for the day; though I was sorry to hurt his feelings, my mind was on the business at hand, and so I begged off.

Even the courthouse looked like it had been put together after a recent trip to Home Depot, what with the dropped plasterboard ceilings and shadowless fluorescent lighting. There were six or eight people scattered along the benches behind the rail; one young woman held a notepad. If she was indeed a reporter, I just hoped Bill in his gregariousness wouldn't tell her who I was. The judge was a thin, imposing woman of late middle age, with sparse, teased white hair, and she sat on a riser beneath the seal of the State of Washington, facing me across the heads of the lawyers and the two defendants.

They were older than I had expected; the one named Liebau is fifty-five if he's a day. They wore tweed jackets and looked the part, as I'm sure their lawyer had the good sense to hope, of endearingly eccentric college professors.

The judge brought in eighteen prospective jurors and announced she expected to cull from that small group the whole jury of twelve, plus two alternates, in time for lunch. Everything went without a hitch for the first eight people: what's your name, where do you work, do you have any connection with the advertising business, a few other questions, and done. Seven of them were empaneled on the spot, and the eighth was excused by the judge on the grounds, as he announced with near-belligerence, that he had irritable bowel syndrome.

The woman in the gallery I assumed was the reporter had her pen between her teeth. Across the aisle from me a man who looked like he could have been Liebau's younger, more successful brother had his knees up against the bench in front of him and his mouth open, sound asleep.

Then the ninth citizen questioned, a guy wearing jeans with a crease ironed into them, who looked to be about forty and said he was a dog obedience trainer, said something about how he vaguely remembered having heard of this case on the local news, but he hadn't formed an opinion about it; in a spirit of cooperation he volunteered that he hadn't paid much attention at the time and couldn't recall any of the details. Jack Gradison, the second defendant, scribbled a note on a legal pad and pushed it toward Farber, who was doing the questioning from his seat. The lawyer ignored it and asked the juror how long he had lived in the Spokane area.

All my life, the dog trainer said.

Gradison tapped loudly on the pad with his index finger. Calmly, as if he just needed a stretch, Farber stood up and walked away from him, toward the jury box, buttoning his jacket as he went.

Mr Pope, do you have any relatives who—

Ask him, Gradison said. Every face in the room turned toward him. Farber, though he had been stopped mid-question, kept his cool. After a considered pause he turned to the judge and said, Your honor, may I have a moment to—

Ask him! Gradison yelled.

The judge's first response was to put on, with a matronly sort of sternness, a pair of glasses. Mr Gradison, she said, I'm afraid I'll have to warn you not—

Turn off your TV! Gradison shouted at the jury box. Turn it off!

You might have thought Farber would go over at this point and put a hand on his client's shoulder or something; but for reasons best known to himself, the lawyer stayed where he was, leaning with one elbow on the jury box, watching this meltdown with an air of worldly disappointment. Everyone who had been dozing a minute before in the small, overlit courtroom – the handful of spectators, the locals called to jury duty, even the fat old bailiff who was still seated but now had his hand on his gun – had his head up, alert, like a hound. Something out of the ordinary was happening.

Wake up! Gradison shouted at the jury, red in the face. Wake up! Death is coming for us all! Take responsibility for your own life, your own thoughts! Don't let them tell you what's beautiful! Snap out of it! Take a look at the work you're doing!

I was surprised they let him go on in this vein for as long as they did, but when he climbed up on top of the defense table, that was the end of that. The bailiff spoke into a walkie-talkie and almost instantly three guards banged through the door behind me. They pulled the middle-aged man on to the floor and cuffed his hands behind his back, as he continued to shout. One of them finally put his hand over Gradison's mouth. At some point I looked at the defense table and saw the other defendant, Liebau, still in his chair. He was laughing.

The judge called the lawyers into chambers and emerged

about two minutes later to announce that all jurors present, even those already questioned and empaneled, were hereby excused. The case was continued until the following Tuesday, when jury selection would start all over again, this time with Mr Gradison in restraints, if necessary.

The next morning I went down to the hotel lobby and borrowed from the desk clerk his copy of that day's Spokane paper. A three-paragraph story was buried on page A7. Outburst Postpones Ad Vandals' Trial. I went back upstairs, sat on my bed with the laptop, and searched the various wire-service sites on the net for an hour: nothing. So I checked out and went to the airport. I took the puddle-jumper to San Francisco and the red-eye from there to Washington. It was nearly two o'clock by the time I got back to Palladio.

Mal's not in, Colette called out her door as I passed.

No? Where is he?

New York.

What for?

Some kind of personal business. He said to expect him back tomorrow.

A WORD ABOUT process. Companies don't subsidize any work of art directly; they subsidize the place itself, on a yearly or bi-yearly contract, and in return they are permitted, within very strict guidelines, to associate themselves with the existence of the art that's produced here. No company's name may appear on or in any work. Before or after the work, separate from it somehow, as in film credits or a book cover or a gallery program, is technically okay, but frankly even the clients themselves are starting to view this desire as stodgy, old-guard: far hipper to leave their name off it entirely.

As for the marriage of a particular work with a particular patron, Mal still handles most of that; his sense of appropriateness in these things is keen, and while some clients ask more questions than others, everyone trusts his judgment. Occasionally, a kind of buzz will arise about one of the artists here, and when that happens people will naturally start asking specifically for him or her. But the artists are on their own timetable; if someone happens to be waiting for something, Mal and I make sure that the artist never knows about it. The client will wait, or, if they feel they can't wait, we'll provide them with something else.

Nobody's saying it's a perfect system, of course, and sometimes we do get a complaint. Today a nervous young woman from Oracle called me, all in a snit about Milo. I should say that one of Mal's great attributes is how un-dogmatic he is. (Well, now that I think of it, he can be quite dogmatic: it's just that he reverses field easily, in terms of dogma, if that's what circumstances dictate.) So that when Milo's own aesthetic started moving more in the direction of performance art – to close the gap, as he says, the tragic gap, between his own person and his art – Mal went right along with that, even though the sorts of events Jean-Claude began mounting more or less contravened Mal's stand on the whole notion of the technological, the reproducible, as the foundation of popular art.

(Truth be told, I think Mal's hand was forced to some degree on that one. In January the Whitney is giving Milo his own one-man, mid-career retrospective, Charles Saatchi has

332

started acquiring some of his work – his star is rising at least as fast as Palladio's own within the art world, and I don't know that Mal has much of a choice but to make philosophical room for whatever Jean-Claude feels he needs to do. Not that there's any risk of our losing him. But you just don't want even the appearance of turmoil, of some kind of aesthetic conflict, to get into the air where it might start affecting future commissions.)

So I'm looking at this prospectus, the Oracle woman says to me, and I see that this Milo intends to go sit on some mesa, in, in—

New Mexico, I said.

New Mexico, and cut himself? And execute a painting with his blood?

Jean-Claude's been doing this for years, I said. And it's not like he invented it. Look at Andres Serrano, look at—

It's not the medium that's the problem, she said; she really did have a naturally unpleasant, nasal way of speaking. It's that he specifies no reproductions of the finished work?

That's right, I said, looking through papers on my desk for something to refresh my memory about all this. No reproductions, no pictures of the blood, but the blood itself.

Well, that's a problem for us. I know how well-respected he is, but I have to justify to people here how we're spending this kind of money for something that will ultimately hang in a gallery to be seen by a total of what, maybe a couple hundred people?

You want me to talk to him? I said. Because I will, but I can tell you right now that when Jean-Claude gets hold of an idea, he generally—

333

Actually, the Oracle woman said, what I wanted to ask, and it's not at all personal, I know you'll understand that, but I wanted to ask if you would get Mal to talk to him.

I said I would, and we hung up. It was a more delicate matter than she supposed. Because Mal's likely reaction, I thought, would be to fly into a rage about it and cancel the Oracle account altogether, give them their money back, which would not be a great development. Not because of the money. It would mean that a lot of great art we already have in the pipeline with those guys would lose its chance to be seen and heard.

So I buzzed Colette and asked if Mal was back from New York yet. I believe so, was her answer. I walked upstairs slowly, rehearsing how I would present this to him. His door was ajar, so I gave a polite warning knock and went right in.

Mal was there, all right, and next to him was Molly; they were there together, sitting in the window seat behind his desk. They were not looking out the window. I think I can be forgiven for staring, because I had to make sure I wasn't imagining it. When they became aware of me they turned, startled, and took their hands off of each other.

I could feel my own mouth working, but no sound came out.

John, Mal said solemnly. Would you give us a minute or two, please?

Of course, I said. I backed out and shut the door. It was what I wanted, too, at that moment. It's what I want now. Just to erase the sight.

★ ★ ★

PALLADIO

MAL SENT WORD through Tasha that I was to meet him for dinner at Il Cantinori at 8 p.m. Actually, his message, which Tasha read to me off her steno pad while leaning in my doorway, was more politely worded than that — he asked if I was free to join him — but after all I work for the man, my livelihood is totally dependent on him: when he sends a summons like that, am I going to say no?

I drove there alone, top down, and only on the way did it occur to me to wonder if he had asked Molly along to this dinner as well. He hadn't; another thing, though, which might have dawned on me but didn't, was that this was Monday, the one night of the week when Il Cantinori is usually closed. Mal had them open it up just for us. Palladio spent upwards of ten thousand dollars there last year, so I guess he feels entitled to the occasional favor. We were the only two people in there. One waiter and one busboy stood impassively in the shadows against the wall of the empty restaurant, while the two of us ate at a round table in the center of the floor.

It seems odd, would be a polite way to put it, that he would want to confide in me of all people about this — ask me for advice, even. Truth be told, I came there half expecting he had made this date with me in order to apologize, or, what would have been more horrifying, to ask for my blessing. But no. Eating ravenously, talking more loudly than I'm sure he realized, he just needed to tell the story to someone; and Mal doesn't have a whole lot of people in his life he can talk to, on a personal level, outside of me, and now, I guess, her.

First off, he said, I know about you two. I know you have a history. Molly's told me all about it, that you guys were very serious at one time, and I guess things ended badly. It's a pretty amazing coincidence, even though in another way it just bears out what I've known all along, that you and I are so on the same wavelength that we could even fall for the same woman. I don't know why you felt you couldn't tell me about it back when Molly was first down here, but that's another conversation, and anyway, in retrospect I'm kind of glad I didn't know.

Mal drained his wine glass; the waiter was beside us before he had even placed it back on the table.

It's like something you read about, he said sheepishly, shaking his head; he wasn't talking about me anymore. That first day she walked into my office, we hardly exchanged a word, but I just knew, I *knew*. I was completely transformed. I fell in love with her on the spot. There was this instant connection. Then you suggested inviting them to stay in the house; it was all I could do to keep a straight face, because it's exactly what I was hoping for, but I didn't know how to suggest it myself.

So I spent as much time as I could, that whole week or two, in Molly's presence, but of course that meant Dex was always there too. I kept looking for some kind of signal from her, and I never got one, but then I'd think, well, of course not, how much of a signal is she going to give me with her boyfriend two feet away? So finally there was that one afternoon, the day before they left; I called downstairs to ask for you and Tasha told me you were in with Dex.

So I dropped what I was doing and went downstairs, and I found her in the parlor, on the window seat, just looking out toward the road. I closed the door and I just unloaded, I said it all. I told her I was madly in love with her. I told her that she was unlike any other woman I'd ever met in my life, from the moment I met her I suddenly had that feeling of knowing just what I wanted, and that I was sorry if all this put her in an awkward position but I knew if I let her go without declaring myself I'd regret it the rest of my life. It just poured out of me. Usually I have such trouble saying what's in my heart. I don't know where it all came from this time.

He exhaled nervously, reliving it. The waiter impassively poured more wine and withdrew again from earshot.

She didn't say anything; she just turned redder and redder and stared at me. I felt bad for having put her on the spot like that, but on the other hand it was a terrible position for me to be in too, you know? Totally vulnerable. Wide open. I was dying, but I remember thinking, at least she's not turning away. So then I hear these footsteps on the stairs behind me and it's Tasha, coming to tell me that you need to see me about something.

Mal speared and ate the zucchini flower, the last thing on his plate. He wasn't even looking at me anymore, he was so lost in the drama of it all. I wouldn't mind knowing, actually, what I looked like just at that moment.

You know what? he said, sitting back. I think I've figured out what it is about her that's so . . . inspiring. Tell me if this sounds right to you. She's not uncomfortable with silence. If she has nothing to say then she doesn't say anything. In fact, now that I think about it, she goes further than that: she *makes* these silences. She asks you something, you answer her, and then suddenly there's just this silence. There's something about it that's intolerable, really, in terms of how self-conscious it makes you: it makes you want to fill it up. And so you go on to give more of an answer than you thought you wanted to, and inevitably that's where you say your best stuff, you know? She brings it out of you.

I nodded, I suppose, but if I had crossed my eyes and stuck my tongue out at him I doubt it would have changed the course of the conversation. He was talking just to talk, just to get it out. It didn't have to be me there. I could have been anyone.

I wonder if she even knows she's doing that, Mal said. So anyway, I was grateful, really, to be interrupted there in the parlor, because the tension was just too great. And then I had to hear about this whole episode with Dex and Fiona. I knew he had to go after that. I'd known it for a while, I suppose, but I wouldn't act on it because I wanted Molly around. If only there were some way to keep her here and get rid of him: that's what I was thinking. But I couldn't figure out how to make it happen. And anyway, she hadn't said anything! She hadn't given me anything to go by. Of course, she hadn't said no either. But I got to thinking that maybe what I was doing was just too reckless, or maybe it was some sort of midlife crisis starting to surface. I mean I barely knew this woman at all, and here I was ready to sacrifice everything. So I let them go back to New York. But that just made it worse. I thought about her every second. I went to Bilbao and just lay in my room and thought about her. Finally I decided to go back home via New York. I had to do a little detective work. But I found her.

He wiped his mouth. He poured out the rest of the wine himself; from the shadows the waiter raised his eyebrows to ask if we wanted another bottle, and Mal shook his head no. What is it about her? he said. You know what? You're the only one in the world I can have this conversation with. Literally. Except

Dex, I suppose, but that's not awfully likely. But what is it? She's a beautiful woman, but there's something *about* her beauty, something elusive, something withheld from you that you want to get hold of. Not having hold of it makes you crazy. I tell you, most women you meet, most people you meet, you feel like inside the first hour you've learned everything about them there is to know. But Molly, there's so much inside her, so much you have to work to get at. Innocence is the wrong word, it's definitely the wrong word. It's *purity*. It's an unconsciousness of being observed. Like − like the anti-Heisenberg; she's not changed by being observed. Right? Like a work of art. In fact I keep wanting to say Mona Lisa, but of course that's a terrible cliché.

I thought if I stayed silent long enough myself, the momentum of his excitement would just carry him past this pause and he'd start talking again. But he waited, and stared at me, until finally lines of concern appeared on his forehead.

Listen, he said. You're being honest with me, right? That you're okay with this? Because both Molly and I have nothing but—

We're fine, I said hurriedly. She and I are all square. It's ancient history anyway, and anything that was left to put to rest about the way it ended, we put that to rest. The two of you, well, it's a huge surprise, obviously, but I'm very happy for both of you.

★ ★ ★

WE DROVE, EACH in his own car, back to the mansion. Mal, who enjoys driving like a lunatic even when he's not as keyed up as he was tonight, beat me there by several minutes and was

339

already inside when I pulled up behind the kitchen. From the third-floor landing I could see light escaping from under my door – Elaine was back from New York. I stood motionless for a few seconds, looking at that sliver of light; then I turned and went back downstairs. I went to the pantry and got myself a beer, and I drank it as I wandered around the darkened first floor, down to the empty basement, dark and silent except for some indeterminate noises coming from behind Milo's studio door. It wasn't that I was too upset to face Elaine, or anybody else; it's just that sometimes when you have your mind on something, you'd rather be alone than have to pretend that your mind's on anything else. I didn't want to have to act interested in how anyone else's day had gone. So I killed some time.

Meanwhile, Mal goes up to the fourth floor, opens the door to his bedroom, and Molly's in there.

After a few hours I went back upstairs; the light under the door was out. I opened the door and slipped into bed beside Elaine without waking her.

HE HADN'T EVER met her until that day I escorted her into his office; Dex hadn't even brought her along when he crashed that opening, back in New York, in order to introduce himself. When Mal invited Dex down to Palladio for a visit, Dex asked if it was okay to bring his girlfriend along. Mal said sure, whatever.

And those trips to New York the past couple of weeks, those were trips to see Molly. That one I figured out for myself. He had Dex's address from Colette, he told me, so he just concealed himself in a restaurant across the street until he knew

Molly was alone and then called on his cell phone. They went out for coffee, they went out to eat, and he gave her his pitch. Finally she agreed to leave her old life behind.

I never really got a straight answer as to how old Dex took it when she told him. I know Mal came along, which was standup of him, I have to admit – prudent, too, since Dex did always strike me as a guy with a temper. You wouldn't send Molly alone on an errand like that.

★ ★ ★

SAW JEAN-CLAUDE today. He was sitting on the top step of the third-floor landing, both arms around his knees as if he were cold, drinking from a huge bottle of water. Behind him I could hear the roar of the vacuum cleaner; Rose had grown tired of waiting and had kicked him out of his room in order to clean it.

I sat beside him for a moment. I didn't have anywhere else I needed to be. The sunlight on the stairs and the modulating whine of the vacuum cleaner being pushed repeatedly under the bed seemed as familiar, for a moment, as boyhood, as home. I turned to Jean-Claude; he was just staring at the scrollwork on the banister beside him. I nodded toward the water bottle.

So, I said. How's that fridge working out for you?

He smiled at me, but I swear to God it was the smile you give to someone when for the life of you you can't remember who they are.

★ ★ ★

A FULL WEEK now since her arrival and Molly, as far as I know, still has not made an appearance downstairs. Mal says she's self-conscious because she thinks of the place as an office, and she's

341

the only one there with no work to do, no job to perform. Maybe so. It occurs to me, as it may not occur to Mal, that she's avoiding me, that she's embarrassed by this whole turn of events and understands that it may stir up certain feelings in me. She'd get why I might even be angry.

Of course I have no reason to assume Mal's lying, either, when he reports that Molly is satisfied that she and I are all square now, just pals with a history. Fantasizing about how she's avoiding me just takes me further into the vortex of the completely pathetic. At least I'm able to hide it from everyone, how humiliated I feel, how obscure are the sources of that humiliation: there are these two people I love, and now they love each other. A real disaster, right? It's stupid. I'll get over it.

★ ★ ★

A LITTLE SOMETHING to take my mind off it today, though not in a particularly pleasant way. We have more than half a million dollars committed to Palladio by an outfit called Virtech, out in Tucson; they're trying to develop various sorts of virtual reality technology cheap enough for home consumers, and at this point they're not much more than a gigantic R&D department. But they're just two or three years away, from what we're told, and if they hit first, they're going to hit big. So today their CEO calls from out of nowhere, sounding very nervous. It turns out he just got back from some investors' meeting at which a vocal minority, evidently not big fans of ours, wanted to know why these guys have ceded so much of their budget to their ad agency, when they don't even have anything to advertise.

So why was he calling, Mal wanted to know. We were

sitting in his office. He has a picture of her on his desk now, a picture taken one flight upstairs, which strikes me as ridiculous and boyish though of course I'd never say anything.

Because he wants to know what to say to the guy in response.

Jesus Christ. These high tech operations. The CEO is probably like twenty-four, right? Where are they again – Phoenix?

Tucson.

Can you fly out there and calm them down?

I frowned. Let's wait and see, I said. I'll go if it becomes necessary.

Well, let's not wait too long. Mal rubbed his neck; he's developed a sunburn there from spending so much time in the car. Eighty-six degrees yesterday. Spring is just about over.

★ ★ ★

A NOTE ON my desk this morning when I arrived at five of nine. *Can I talk with you? I'm too nervous to run into you in the hall where there might be other people around. I don't know how much you've told anyone and I don't want to put you in a bad position. I'll be in the orchard tomorrow morning at ten. On that bench where we talked before.*

I folded it into my pocket and went back out to Tasha's doorway. Was anyone in my office this morning? I said.

Tasha had the tiniest oscillating fan I've ever seen, and she was trying to get it to work but it kept tipping over. Present from my father, she said. They just came back from Japan. Anyway, no, I haven't seen anyone, but I just got here about ten minutes ago. Why?

I turned and went back to my office, shutting the door behind me, bewildering her, I'm sure. I don't know why Molly feels it has to wait until tomorrow; maybe she and Mal have plans today. Of course, I can't assume that she's keeping this meeting a secret from him either. Why would she?

If she starts to apologize to me over this I may lose it. But I don't particularly want her to treat it like it's no big deal either. I don't know what I want. So I'll go see what she wants.

ELAINE ASKED ME last night if I'm depressed about something. I should say that Elaine's excellence as a girlfriend has its source in her emotional self-sufficiency. If I am upset, she doesn't take that personally, she doesn't assume that she must somehow be either the reason or the solution for it. Her independence lets her be utterly empathetic. She asked me this, as we sat having Brunswick stew for dinner at the big butcher-block table in the pantry (where the house staff used to eat, a century ago; it's less stuffy than the dining room), with respectful concern – not that conspicuous overconcern that's meant to hide the self-interest at its root.

I slept about three hours last night.

Elaine is very smart. I'm always drawn to these brilliant women, women I can look up to. (Rebecca was like that too.) She reads a lot, and I'm always finding these strange highbrow books beside my bed as if some set designer had snuck in there to help me look more intellectually audacious in my spare hours than I really am. She has a thin, slightly adenoidal voice, and a hyper-articulate manner – actually, *manner* is the wrong word there: she's just very articulate – that she hedges with an appealing sort of fondness for self-deprecation. I sometimes wonder how she sounds when she's talking to herself, if that makes any sense. Her latest kick is the weight room: a month or two ago, mostly at her behest, I filled one of the unused basement storage rooms with a few machines, a Gravitron, a StairMaster, a treadmill. She comes up to the room after dinner to change and she takes the back stairs to the basement. She wears a kind of halter top like a jogging bra, and a pair of Lycra bicycle pants which make her ass, not exactly small even under the best of circumstances, look enormous. No one sees her but me, usually; still, I love it that she doesn't care.

I don't know what keeps us together, really. We never have any problems. We've never talked about getting married. Which is fine with me, and with her too I'm sure. Not every relationship has to be about the rest of your life.

We should go away somewhere, is what I said to her at dinner. We should take a vacation together, travel somewhere. I'm tired of our always being here in the house.

It was an unassailable suggestion, strange only because it was coming from me, and so she couldn't exactly say no to it. Sure, she said, let's do that; keeping it, considerately, on that vague hypothetical plane, knowing it would probably stay there. She looked at me when she said it. I hadn't been looking at her.

★ ★ ★

WELL, I CAN still be myself around Molly; I suppose that's one lesson that might be drawn from today. I've spent so much time since that dinner with Mal trying to reason away this feeling I have that I've been wronged, telling myself that there's no justification for it, I certainly have no claim on her, or on him for that matter – but when I saw her, sitting wide-eyed and sheepish on that iron bench in the orchard, there was no more reasoning to be done, it just all came pouring out, directed at her, which is maybe unfair, but really why should I always be the one who gets hung up on these questions of what's fair or unfair?

She looked like she was ready for it. Like she was expecting it, which is more than I can say for myself. Maybe she just knows me better than I know myself, even after all these years. Or maybe everyone sees through me, everywhere I go, maybe I just walk through life as no mystery to anyone but myself.

We sat in silence, side by side, for a while. I could feel that I was breathing hard.

Thank you for coming to see me, Molly said after a while, just to get me going, probably.

Coming to see you? I said. You've moved into my house.

She sighed. You mean a lot to me, John. A lot. I would never do anything to hurt you. You know that, right?

This struck me as incredibly patronizing. She went on.

In fact, I resisted it longer than I might have because I had an idea that you might be upset by it. I—

You had an idea about that, did you?

Molly raised her eyebrows.

But you went ahead and did it anyway. It seems to me you're trying to have it both ways here. What, are you supposed to be so irresistible? So impossible to get over? Is this the same speech you gave to that poor sap Dex, by the way?

She sat back slightly, resting her shoulder blades against the iron railing, and I could see her relax: the stoic bit, the martyr bit. Her patience with me – everything she did infuriated me now.

I mean I understand that it's all the same to you who you fuck, so it might as well be somebody with a few million bucks and a nice house. But you couldn't find anybody like that in Manhattan? You had to come and do it here under the same roof as me?

There; that did it. Finally she looked at me with some anger of her own.

Please don't talk to me that way again, Molly said. Ever. I haven't done anything to deserve that from you.

No?

No.

So you're serious about Mal. You're in love with him.

I – I have no idea whether or not I'm in love with him. It's only been a couple of weeks. I don't fall in love as easily as that. I mean Mal has, I don't know, a certain magnetism. An allure. I know I don't have to tell you that.

From somewhere out in the direction of the road the breeze blew us the faint sound of sirens.

Anyway, Molly said, which answer would you hate more?

What?

Which would you rather hear? That I'm totally in love with him, or that this is all just some sort of sugar-daddy, mercenary-fuck situation so I can live in a mansion?

I just want to hear the truth, I said. (It sounded so lame, coming out of my mouth; I could tell just from the sound of it that it was a lie, just as surely as if I were listening to someone else.)

You know, she said with some heat, talk about wanting to

hear the truth, we sat right here a couple of weeks ago and you told me that everything was okay between us; more than okay, *forgotten,* and I actually believed that, I took that to heart when I was back in New York trying to decide what to do. Plus you're involved with someone else now, with that Elaine, and you told me that was a serious thing and so did Mal.

I wanted to say that the two things – my relationship with Elaine and Molly's indifference toward our old feelings – had nothing to do with each other. But I was starting to sound ridiculous even in my own ears.

Whatever, I said instead, standing up. Fine. You want my blessing or something? You got it. The two of you are perfect for each other.

And I walked back to the house.

It's all happening again. The helplessness of asking these questions (Are you in love with him?) when I know the answers will torture me. The total defenselessness. Laid wide open, completely obvious, unable to protect myself against total honesty, total exposure. Well, that's not so bad, I guess; after all, it's nothing she hasn't seen before. Just so no one sees it but her.

★ ★ ★

I DON'T ACCEPT it. I don't. He doesn't love her. I don't mean he's lying about it: I'm sure he *thinks* he's in love with her, and I'm sure she thinks he is too. They can't see themselves the way I see them; that's the key. She's so full of self-hatred. She holds herself so cheaply, her sense of her own worthlessness is so profound, that she's drawn into situations she knows are bad for her; and then when they don't work out, when things fall apart, she says to herself, See, see what you've done, you knew it all along, you've left it worse than you found it. Then it's on to the next disaster. If someone should come along who's able to see more clearly, more objectively, what's so beautiful and original and valuable about her, she wouldn't believe in it; she'd think there must be some other motive at work.

And Mal: he sees something unique, original, unprecedented, something unbeholden to anything but itself, and he has to have it. That's how he loves. How can I make her see him – see herself – through my eyes? Because if she could do that even for an instant – see herself as I see her – then she could at least see how she ought to be loved. She *was* loved, once, and somehow she's forgotten what that's about.

★ ★ ★

IN BED, ALONE, when Elaine came into the room and flipped on the light.

Hey John, she said. You awake?

I picked up my watch from the bedside table and squinted at it. 3.19 a.m.

No, I said. I am not awake.

She pulled the sheet off me. Please, she said. Please. I finished it.

With some difficulty I lifted my head. You what?

I need to show you something. She started to put her finger in her mouth to bite the nail, but then pulled it away again, smiling.

I put on a T-shirt over my pajama bottoms and we went down to the ballroom. She already had two chairs pulled up to the editing machine.

It's a short film, just sixty seconds, opening with a shot of the tight interior of the coach section of an airplane; one flight attendant acts out the rote pantomime of what to do in case of an emergency water landing, while another, whom we don't see, drones the familiar instruction over the intercom. A slow track down the narrow aisle shows that no one is paying the least attention. Then the track stops, and zooms slowly toward a guy in a window seat reading a book; the book, of course, is *On the Road*.

As the zoom finishes, the voice-over makes a seamless, volume-up, volume-down transition between the practiced, stultifyingly cheery sound of the flight attendant and a reading of a passage from *On the Road* itself.

So in America when the sun goes down and I sit on the old broken-down river pier watching the long, long skies over New Jersey and sense all that raw land that rolls in one unbelievable huge bulge over to the West Coast . . .

The zoom moves slowly toward the tiny window beside the reading man, and as the tarmac moves we see the plane is taking off. (I have Elaine's copy of the book open here as I write this, since it's handy and I want to get it right.)

. . . and all that road going, all those people dreaming in the immensity of it, and in Iowa by now I know the children must be crying in the land where they let the children cry . . . the evening star must be drooping and shedding her sparkler dims on the prairie . . .

The zoom seems to move through the window and it gazes down as the runway ends and the plane banks over the cloverleaves of crabbed highways surrounding Newark Airport; it seems like we're looking at one particular car but as the plane ascends (reversing the zoom itself, in a nice, dizzying way) more and more cars fill the screen, smaller and smaller, until the plane breaks through the twilit cloudline.

. . . *which is just before the coming of complete night that blesses the earth, darkens all rivers, cups the peaks and folds the final shore in, and nobody, nobody knows what's going to happen to anybody besides the forlorn rags of growing old* . . .

I let it loop four times before I looked over my shoulder at Elaine. She had her arms crossed tightly, elated and nervous. Sometimes you can live with people, sleep with them in fact, and still be surprised by their recesses. Her eyes jumped back and forth from my face to the screen; she was too worried about what I would say to be impatient. I smiled at her.

He's going to love it, I said.

IT WAS IN the sex that things started getting strange, that I sensed I might not have my hands on all the ropes, so to speak, in terms of what I was feeling. I was used to all Elaine's likes and dislikes by now. I didn't try anything different, anything that would help me pretend she was someone else or anything along those lines. It was more perverse than that. I just remember thinking that it was like Elaine was wearing some sort of mask that night, a mask she couldn't remove, and the mask was her – Elaine's – own face.

★ ★ ★

IT'S NOT THAT I love Molly, at least not in the way that I used to, that's over, but I still feel protective toward her and respect her and want the best for her. And I love Mal – I guess I can say that. Why should it bother me, then, the idea of the two of them?

I can't deny there's something strange about seeing them together – foraging for wine late at night in the climate-controlled closet next to the pantry, talking in the driveway (his hand under her chin), sitting in their low canvas chairs on the balcony outside their bedroom – something that goes beyond simple jealousy. They don't seem to belong in the same room, or in the same world; they seem irreconcilable. Maybe that was just my mistake, viewing them not as people in themselves but as aspects, as cordoned-off areas, of my own life. Anyway, I'm shocked, every time.

Jealousy: well, maybe. But also, if those two people find what they need in each other, then, I think, I become truly superfluous in the world.

★ ★ ★

I STOPPED BY my office after dinner to check my voice mail and found a long message from the CEO of Virtech. Offering to fly out, any time it's convenient for us, to have a look at our work in progress, possibly contribute some *input,* he says. I sat and thought about it for fifteen minutes or so. The last thing in the world I want to do right now is go to Tucson, but there seems no way out of it now. There was a tremor in this guy's voice that makes me think he's close to pulling the account, if he's not under pressure to do that already. Not keeping Mal abreast of it is out of the question. I'll make the arrangements in the morning.

SHE WATCHES MOVIES by herself in the projection room, she cooks a little bit, she goes off to the university or just out to explore the town – she can't drive the Triumph so Mal has bought her a little red car of her own, a Sonata I think it is. She's the only one who's not here to work. And I think she is self-conscious about that, because she keeps strange hours, she's all by herself up on the fourth floor – I guess; I don't really know for sure where she is, or when she's in the house at all – for long stretches during the day. She haunts the place. I've heard the others talking about her, but just in a fondly catty way, Jerry asking if now would be a good time to ask for a new matte system now that Mal's getting laid, that kind of thing.

The anger that I feel is the reason that I don't want to go to Arizona or anywhere else right now, the reason that I need to know that she's somewhere nearby at all times. The anger's all I have. I write these sentences down as they come to me, even when I don't know what they mean.

JOHN, FIONA SAID. Can I talk to you?

I motioned to her to close the door behind her.

So Jean-Claude is back, she said, leaning against the wall with her hands behind her. She wore a black T-shirt with the word *Pussy* emblazoned on it in rhinestone script, and chunky shoes that really only call attention, I think, to how short she is.

I know. The work's in the front hall for the next few days if you haven't—

I've seen it, she said. It's amazing. But I have this other thought.

I leaned back in my chair.

Have you seen *him?* Fiona said.

353

I hadn't.

He looks . . . I'm worried about him. He's so thin. And he came back and went to his room to sleep and that was like sixteen hours ago.

He's been through something, I said. He's weak and he needs some time to get his strength back.

Well, sure, she said, and she looked nervous, as if concern for him were something to be expressed only in confidence. But my idea was . . . There's a lot of people here who work very hard, I mean, it's their choice, but it takes a physical toll, and I wondered if you or Mal would be receptive to the idea of having a doctor on staff, or on call, or whatever the expression is. Not living here, obviously, the need's not that great, but just on some kind of retainer so if we—

We already have somebody like that, I said.

Fiona's mouth fell open. We do?

We do. His name is Cadwallader, great old Southern name. He's at University Hospital. Do you want me to have him come over and take a look at Jean-Claude?

It took her a few more seconds to absorb, I suppose, this idea that everything around there had already been thought of. Then she shook her head and laughed. No, she said. I suppose not. He'll wake up. Anyway, good to know.

And she left.

★ ★ ★

JUST AS IN some beach towns you're always hearing the low growl of the surf even when you're not conscious of it, so in Tucson your inner ear is always working against a backdrop of constant, unobtrusive noise, the roar of air conditioning. No one wants to take a step outside if they can avoid it. It seems an odd *place* for a city, is what I kept thinking. At the Hilton I took a shower and had the front desk call me a taxi, and I gave the driver one of those five-digit street addresses you find in new cities. Twenty minutes later we pulled up in front of an office tower that rose about five stories off the pavement, not an unimpressive sight when seen against the level desert that began immediately behind it and ran to the horizon.

The special suits, the gloves, the helmets, the sensory-deprivation chairs, all the stuff of today's science fiction: the young people of Virtech go to their office every morning and work on making it real, about eighteen hours a day from the sound of it. The directors who met with me were all men, all just out of college, wearing concert T-shirts to a business meeting; standard dot-com culture stuff. Pulling somber faces, they escorted me into their boardroom, which was nothing but a long table and chairs on a blue wall-to-wall carpet. The furniture looked like it had arrived that day. I said no to coffee, no to snacks, no to bottled water, and got right to the point of my visit.

What would you say it is you're selling? I asked them gently. I already knew the answer to that. The key to confrontation, in these cases, is to make it look like something else.

They glanced at one another. Then one of them, who wore glasses (well, actually, come to think of it, nearly all of them wore glasses), said, Nothing, right now. Not much VR technology is widely available yet, mostly for pricing reasons. But it's all just around the corner, and what we want, basically, is to imprint our name with the public. So that when the time comes, they'll associate us with the whole idea. If they hear of a thing, or dream of a thing, we're the first place they'll look to see if we have it.

I nodded. So the answer, then, is that you *have* no product to advertise. See, most agencies you might go to, that would be something of a stumbling block. (Laughter.) But you've come to exactly the right place. This is what we do. We don't *do* product-related advertising. Palladio is a studio for the production of avant-garde art, and by subsidizing the wide dissemination of that art, Virtech becomes part of the avant-garde as well, in the public mind. Which is entirely appropriate. Because you guys are the vanguard. You are the bringers of the next big thing. We embody that idea, and you are going to borrow it from us.

And so on. It really wasn't hard. They wanted to be sold; they just needed a little stroking. I brought out some autographed copies of Daniel's last novel, and a series of glossy black-and-white self-portraits by Fiona, also signed. I showed them photos, including some amazing nighttime aerial shots, of something no one has seen yet – Alexa's massive land-art project right there in Arizona, where she's transforming a series of natural caves with mirrors and colored neon lights. Mal predicts it will be a sensation. I told them I'd be happy to make a phone call if they wanted to take a day off, drive down there, and see it all in progress.

Right there, in the conference room, they called their banker and had him cut a check for the last of the money they had originally agreed to commit to us. Smiles all around; one of them suggested that some champagne be brought in, but they had none on hand, and then they began to argue about the best place to send out for it. I was already leaning forward in my chair, anxious to get back to the Hilton, maybe eat a quick meal at the bar before phoning the airline to try to change my reservation. But before they would let me leave, such was their enthusiasm, they insisted I go down to the second floor, to the Prototype Room as they referred to it, and check out some of the stuff whose reproduction I was now a part of bringing into the world. Their excitement about it was touching in its unabashed geekiness, its disconnection from any concern about the impression they were making. They couldn't stop smiling.

In the Prototype Room I stood on a sort of round treadmill while a guy in baggy army shorts equipped me with a visored helmet, a sort of breastplate, and two heavy, loose-fitting, elbow-length gloves. Then he gave me a thumbs-up and lowered the visor over my face.

For the next five minutes, I walked through a ruined city, my feet crunching audibly on pulverized stone and broken glass. I could hear the crash as chunks of concrete snapped off of sheared-off buildings and fell into the street. For a while I wondered if I was the only one there; then a voice whispered in my ear, Hey, baby. Pretty wild, huh? I turned my head, my actual head, in its helmet, and was face to face with a lecherous bald man with a goatee. He smiled at me and raised an eyebrow. I hurried away. It doesn't take long, it may interest you to know, to buy completely into a manufactured reality once your senses apprehend it. A block or so further on, a small child popped out from behind the flaking corner of a facade and threw something at me, a rock or maybe a broken brick. I threw up my hand and felt a distinct sting as it bounced, or seemed to bounce, off the glove. The wind whistled in my ears.

Not much else happened, really: I suppose incident is what the people in the Prototype Room are working on. The rest of my virtual tour of this landscape – based on no real landscape, as far as I could recognize; only a kind of imaginary template of ruin – held one other surprise. At some point, I passed a pool of water in the street, fed by a broken hydrant. I stopped and looked down: and there, shimmering but still distinct, was my reflection. I was a tall, muscular, busty red-haired woman, in torn fatigue pants, with a dirt-smudged face, full lips, and bright green eyes. Across my chest were two bandoliers, and hanging at my side was a gun. I reached down to my hip and touched it.

A few moments later everything went black, except for a small pulsing dot in the upper left corner of my field of vision. The guy in the army shorts lifted my visor, and there in front of me again were the three young executives of Virtech, tense with the effort of modesty.

When I walked out the street door of the office building, night had fallen, and the heat was a little less oppressive. It may sound like a cliché, but in that solitary minute before my taxi arrived, with all the city lights burning steadily against the pure indigo backdrop of the desert sky, I wouldn't have been too surprised if the whole thing had just started to shimmer, then vanished, revealing to me that I was really standing in a sealed, undecorated room somewhere, far from where I believed myself to be.

HIGH WINDS KEPT us on the ground in Atlanta; it was well after midnight when I got back to Palladio. The house was silent; no light even in Milo's room. I put down my bag until I could see by the red lights of the security system. Kind of a peaceful moment, actually.

Then I started walking, toward my office, treading on the outside of the steps where they wouldn't creak (a trick I learned as a kid); past my office; halfway up the stairs between the third and fourth floors, where I stopped. There was an edge of light shining from under the door to Mal and Molly's bedroom. It was so quiet that I had to wait there motionless for a few minutes just to satisfy myself that they hadn't heard me. I sat on the step for a while, thinking of I don't know what – of nothing, really; I might as well have been a part of the house – until at some point I looked over and saw that the light was out. Holding my breath, I rose and started down the stairs again toward my own room, anxious not to make a sound.

★ ★ ★

IN MY OFFICE, with Mal, who'd come looking for me just to see what he needed to keep tabs on. Actually, I'd gone looking for him, in his office, around nine, but he wasn't downstairs yet. Now he was barefoot and holding a huge iced coffee from the kitchen. Another scorching day.

Daniel's taken a section out of his novel, I said, a section he said he was having trouble with, and he's turned it into a short story. So now the *New Yorker* says they'll take it.

Outstanding, Mal said, yawning. Good for him. I'd love to see it.

Yeah, well, the thing is, we've worked all this out policy-wise as far as books go, but what about stuff of ours that appears in magazines? They have their own advertisers. They have their own layout, where ads might appear in the middle of a story, ads that maybe our own clients would consider—

I get it, Mal said, smiling, pleased almost. Things like this, unforeseen things, the kind of things that keep me up at night, tend to give Mal a charge. He loves new territory.

So you'll—

I'll talk to everybody. Anything else?

Yeah. I spoke to Jean-Claude.

Mal's jaw set a little bit. Not that he's mad at Milo for any reason – on the contrary, the further out into the ether Milo seems to go, the more Mal treats him like a favorite son. But his fame is snowballing to the degree that clients who used to ask hopefully if Jean-Claude had any forthcoming work still unspoken for are now insisting on him and him alone. They'll wait, they say. Milo or nothing. It irritates Mal no end.

Hey, he said, where's that thing that was supposed to be in the *Times* about him?

Next Sunday. Anyway, he finally came to me ready to tell me about his next project.

It's finished?

No. But there's a reason he's telling me about it now. It's . . . it's site-specific.

Where's the site?

You'll love this, I said, not sure Mal would love it at all. It's here. Palladio. That's the site.

Mal sat back in his chair and thought for a few seconds. He shrugged affectionately. I don't see any problem with it, he said.

Okay, good, I'll let him know. It might actually make things easier, logistically, because at this point we've got so many people lined up waiting to see it when it's done. Banana Republic, Xerox, DaimlerChrysler . . .

Mal yawned again. Sorry, he said. Didn't get much sleep.

This kind of remark from him always shocks me right at first, because it feels like such an unexpected and intentional fuck-you. It takes me a second to remind myself that he doesn't think about me in that way at all, as a spurned rival or even as someone whose feelings might be hurt – that what seems so real to me, where Molly's concerned, usually turns out to be real only to me.

Doing what? I said.

Talking, mostly.

What do you guys talk about?

You, he said. Just kidding. He stared off into the corner of the room. No, actually, I suppose we talk mostly about me. Or about this place. Now that you make me think about it. She asks a lot of questions. She's curious how I got to where I am. I try to ask her about her own life but she has a way of turning it around. Maybe I should be asking you.

Oh, I really don't think so, I said.

Anyway, she listens. That's what's so great about it. Every woman I've ever been involved with, it eventually comes around to her wanting to change me somehow, they want to identify some sort of middle ground for you to move on to so you can be more like them. But Molly – it's not that she thinks I'm perfect, she just takes me completely as I am, she has absolutely no desire to change me. And the paradox is that being around someone like that – that, itself, changes you. It's changing me. It makes me want to be more like her.

How so? I said, sorry I'd brought the whole thing up by now. But he didn't even seem to hear me.

Not that I worship her either, Mal said. I mean, I do but I don't. I know this may sound a little hypocritical of me now, wanting to change something about her. But she stays upstairs most of the day, reading, sleeping, sitting on the balcony and staring at the mountains. I want to take her places. I want to show her the world. She's never really been anywhere. But she just wants to hang out up there in the room. I bet she could be happy like that a long time, actually. No real contact. Just her and whatever goes on in her head.

★ ★ ★

I KEEP COMING back to that moment, that instant, when I first saw her again, in my office, after ten years. I stood up. I shook her hand; I took my hand back. I remained standing, people spoke, I did nothing else. It's easy to say it was the presence of other people that kept me from vaulting over the desk, pinning her to the wall so she couldn't get away again. But what other people? My assistant and some stranger. Who cares if they know? Why should I care if anybody knows? Do I really believe that once you've made a fool of yourself over someone, you can ever go back to not being a fool, as if it all never happened?

Maybe I should have pushed that skinny fuck Dex out the door, locked it, and then had her, right there on the floor, however forcefully I had to do it. Tasha could watch or not watch, it's unimportant.

Because what I'm really scared of, what I would really like another opportunity to disprove to myself, is that some instinct toward self-deceit, some tendency toward whitewashing, has hardened in me to such a degree that it wouldn't have mattered if no one else was there, if I were alone in my office and the door opened and from the mists of oblivion Molly Howe walked in. I would still have smiled and stood up – buttoned my jacket, maybe – and shaken her hand, like we'd never met before, like nothing was real but the present, like the springs of desperation inside me weren't just blocked but had never run at all.

★ ★ ★

COLETTE COMES THROUGH my office this afternoon delivering the message that Mal has called a special meeting of the entire staff, in the first-floor dining room at four o'clock. Usually he would give me some sort of heads-up as to what something like that's about. Instead, though, I filed in along with everyone else and took a seat. At the head of the table, where Mal sits, someone had wheeled in one of our fifty-inch TVs and a DVD player. There was an empty seat next to Elaine, but I sat across the table from her. We don't keep our relationship a secret but we try not to call attention to it either.

Finally Mal appeared, barefoot, in shorts; before taking a seat or saying a word to any of us he went around and pulled down all the window shades. He returned to his seat and stood beside it, looking around the room, whispering something to himself. I realized he was counting heads.

Anybody seen Milo? he said. No response.

Well, that's okay, I guess, Mal said, and sat. He picked up a remote on the table beside him; there was a kind of popping sound, and then Elaine's Kerouac film began to roll.

He let it run through twice, then switched it off. There was

363

a moment of confusion – it's not customary to hold this sort of formal screening of in-house work – in which Elaine stole a glance over at me and cocked her head to ask if I knew what this was all about. I shrugged discreetly to convey to her that no one was more in the dark than I was.

Around the table there was a bit of scattered, tentative applause. Mal was still looking at the blank screen. Finally he spun around in his chair.

Nice, he said, but no. I do like the way it reverses the usual imagery, I mean, it makes the whole notion of driving a car seem old-fashioned, retro. Most car ads you see are basically high-gloss porn.

It was startling – if I understood him right – to hear him refer to Elaine's piece as an ad. He never does that.

The thing is the quote, he went on. The entire aural element of the piece is lifted from Jack Kerouac. I have that right, don't I?

Silence. I don't think Elaine was sure whether or not she was being addressed directly.

We could include an acknowledgment, I said, if that's what you mean.

No, that's not what I mean. The point is we don't do that. My first thought was that Elaine should know this by now. But then I thought maybe not: maybe I haven't made it clear enough, to everyone. So here it is. We don't co-opt, we don't filch value, no matter the source. Advertising has skated by on that method for decades. Any artistic value a piece like this one might have is value established somewhere else, in some other context, established and then bought. That's why people hate advertising, even at the same time as they like the ads themselves. Stealing value. Well, we're putting a stop to that here. We are about original value, about the creation of value. Let other art derive itself from us! No looting, no sampling, no colonizing of the past!

His voice was raised, and he wasn't smiling. Elaine was leaning back in her chair, staring at him, her neck mottled red. His exhortation hung in the air for a few seconds.

The original, he said, more quietly. The unique. The unrepeatable. The perfect magic of the artifact. This is our new creed. That's what I want. That's what we will all, as of now, be consecrating our efforts towards. Our direction has evolved: that's only natural. This just seemed like a good opportunity to make that clear. So this piece you all just saw: we won't be using it. Thank you all for coming.

ELAINE, NEEDLESS TO say, tracked me down in my office within the hour. I shut the door, but still she was so loud that I figured the best thing to do was get her off the site.

Okay, fine, she said, glaring. The least you could do is buy me a few drinks.

I took her to El Sombrero. She sat in silence through one margarita, her nostrils flared.

You know, I said finally, I had nothing to do with all that. I certainly would have tried to change his mind if—

Filching value, is that what he said? She shook her head. Jesus. You know what I think it's really about? Pride. He doesn't like the idea that he'd have to share credit for the provenance of one of these artworks with poor old dead Jack Kerouac.

I don't know that that's it. It's more like, I don't know, a point of dogma with him or something.

Dogma! Dogma bums! So did he think it was *demeaning* to Kerouac, is that it? That I was stealing from him? Did you know that I wrote my whole master's thesis on the Beats? I went on a road trip to fucking *Lowell* when I was in college, for Christ's sake! I visited his *house!*

The bartender looked at us sternly. I held up one hand and nodded to reassure him.

And he said it would be okay if I wrote the text myself, she muttered, quieter for the moment. But that's the whole point. *On the Road* is an artifact of a specific past, a time we can't go back to. What are we supposed to do, create a new past? What is this, Year One? What is he, fucking Pol Pot or something?

I drove home because I was the less drunk of the two of us, but it was still a mistake; I was plenty shaky myself. By the time we turned down the Palladio driveway, I was down to about fifteen miles an hour. Elaine started reciting.

So in America when the sun goes down, she said, and I sit on the old broken-down river pier watching the long, long skies over New Jersey and sense all that raw land that rolls in one unbelievable huge bulge over to the West Coast, and all that road going, all those people dreaming in the immensity of it, and in Iowa I know by now the children must be crying in the land where they let the children cry, the evening star must be drooping and shedding her sparkler dims on the prairie, which is just before the coming of complete night that blesses the earth, darkens all rivers, cups the peaks and folds the final shore in, and nobody, nobody knows what's going to happen to anybody besides the forlorn rags of growing old . . .

Other lights were on, in other rooms, but we saw no one. Somewhere on the road home oblivion had kicked in: in the hallway, walking behind me, she put her hand through my legs and squeezed, giggling delightedly when I jumped. Drunkenness always tends to release something in her, for better or worse. I was impatient with it tonight; but then, as she turned off the light I had just turned on and started fumbling with my shirt buttons, a strange thing happened, strange at least for me: that angry impatience fused with my lust, redoubled it, and it wasn't like my desire to push her away from me just gave way to a desire to fuck her: the two desires were suddenly one and the same.

I put my hands under her arms, lifted her to a standing position again, and spun her around. She took two steps toward the bed in the darkness, but I shoved her the rest of the way, until she fell across it.

Oooh, she said; a little too sarcastically, I thought.

That didn't help. Before long, though, her growls were real, and I closed my eyes and banged into her as hard, as violently as I could. I wanted to hurt her, there's no question about it. But she didn't seem to get it. Then, with my chest against her back, I withdrew, shifted up a little, pushed forward again.

Whoa, she said, with a kind of nervous flutter.

I kept on.

Hey, she said. Hey! Stop! Finally she got her hands underneath her and did a kind of pushup, so that I lost my balance. I rolled all the way on to the floor, and sat there.

You were hurting me there, she said. Jesus, you must be drunker than I thought.

I'm sorry, I said.

We were both breathing hard. She had raised herself up on her elbows and I could feel her staring down at me as I sat on the floor.

That's not like you. I mean, you could ask. Don't bother, 'cause the answer's no, but you could ask, you know what I mean?

I'm sorry, I repeated. I guess I just got too excited.

I just stared at the wall ahead of me. Finally I felt her drop herself back across the bed.

What the fuck is going on around here today? she said.

★ ★ ★

I WENT TO your house, you know. I flew to Newark. I put the ticket on my credit card and flew out there. What a mistake, to have warned you that I was coming: but I had no inkling of that yet. I was spending money we didn't have anyway, so there seemed no sense in limiting myself; I rented a car at the airport, spread out one of those Triple A maps on the passenger seat beside me, and found Ulster.

Nothing much to see. It's the nicest town around there, I suppose, but then the surrounding towns look practically like Appalachia. You'd never really prepared me for it, the bald hills, the scruffy pines, the houses with collapsing porches and front yards full of rusting iron chairs and deer antlers mounted over the garage door; but I suppose you didn't feel the need of it, you didn't think I'd ever see it, or that you'd ever see it again either. At what I supposed was the center of town I parked just short of the traffic light and went into the first open store I saw, a cluttered, shabby Rexall pharmacy with a few of the ceiling panels missing, a few of the fluorescent lights burned out.

Excuse me, I said to the back of a gray head, and a thin, white-haired lady, bird-featured, eyeglasses hung round her neck with a black shoelace, turned to face me with a kind of dull mistrust. I don't imagine they got a lot of strangers coming through that town.

Do you have a phone booth in here?

The stare she was giving me was mostly because of my accent, I realized. She shook her head no, as if the word *no* might not be part of whatever language I was speaking.

A phone book, then? A local phone book? She gazed at me blankly. I just need to look up an address, for a family in town. I've lost it, and they're expecting me.

She cleared her throat. What family?

The Howes.

She cocked her head. Unhurriedly, without ever smiling or making some other kind of sympathetic gesture toward me, she patted down the apron she wore over her flat front, then searched through the mess around the register, until at length she located a pencil and a notepad. She wrote down the address, along with directions to the house, tore the paper off, and handed it to me.

You can thank me by telling them they still owe me two hundred and fourteen dollars, she said. Where are you from, anyway?

But the bell over the door was already ringing behind me.

★ ★ ★

DID I DO something wrong? Back in Berkeley? I mean, I

369

always had the sense, in the year or so that we were together, that I had to be careful, that Molly was poised for flight in some sense, that the balance was delicate in terms of holding her life and mine together. Still, it all seemed to be going well, until one day she left and never came back. What happened? Should I have insisted on going out to Ulster with her? Should I not have followed her out there; should I have been more patient, shown more trust in her? Should I not have left all those phone messages, or announced I was coming, just springing a surprise capture on her instead, as one does with an animal or a mental patient?

I wish the answers were clear. Actually, what I wish is that the answer were clearly yes. Because such a mistake, the mistake of a young man too much in love, would gnaw at me, there's no denying it: still, it would be easier to carry through life than the suspicion of a much more vague, ingrained, broad-based, personal insufficiency. I couldn't hold her, I couldn't make myself indispensable to her, and that kind of personal failure isn't located in any act, one that might at least in the realm of fantasy be taken back or amended. I fell short; and that's much harder to accept.

★ ★ ★

THAT WHOLE EPISODE with Mal essentially rejecting Elaine's Kerouac film as too derivative – I confess I thought of it at the time as a small fire to be put out, a matter of mollifying Elaine, trying to let her know I sympathized with her bewilderment at having been humiliated in front of the entire staff and at the same time to let her know that Mal's decisions, hard to understand though they might be, were basically unappealable.

Well, I underestimated its effect. No work of art has ever been rejected here before. It's all I hear anyone around here talk about: when they talk at all, that is, when they don't clam up because they see me coming.

Jerry Strauss is carrying around what he calls a formal letter of protest, trying rather confrontationally to persuade everyone to sign it. Most have; those who refuse have a hard time with him.

It's about your fucking *freedom!* he says. Does that mean so little to you?

Look, Daniel told him. (Daniel is one of the few people who dares to stand up to him.) A letter of protest, what's that? Will it do anything? Will he reconsider?

If we're all together on it—

Of course he won't. This place is not a democracy. And I'm glad it's not. Has he been wrong about anything yet?

He's wrong about this. Ever since he brought back the goddamn Madwoman in the Attic up there—

He's *not* wrong about it. That film of Elaine's, God knows I love her, but that was a piece of shit, and he was dead-on right about why. I'm not going to the barricades over something like that. It's childish.

You know, Jerry said, holding the typed letter a little too tightly in his hand, this really only means something if every name here is on it.

And why is that, if you value your independence so much? You're just trying to have it both ways, to pretend you're a rebel and still cover your ass. All you'll do is make yourself feel better in the most superficial way. A petition! It's like something you'd do in fucking high school.

Goddamn coward, Jerry said. Just admit that you're too afraid of losing your job.

Admit it? Daniel said, laughing. Of course I want to keep my job! It's nothing to admit! This is the best job in the history of the world. What, Jerry, do you want to go back to publishing zines and working at Kinko's?

Elaine is never a part of these conversations that I can see. I guess the thinking is that she's still too upset. Discretion keeps me from asking them, just as a way of taking part, if they know where she's sleeping now. Her stuff has disappeared from my room.

★ ★ ★

THE HOUSE WAS a simple white condo with a split-rail fence in front, and a withered-looking garden on the side not shadowed by the rim of the valley. It was mid-afternoon but it seemed much later there; all the lights were on inside. No one else was in sight. The sky was a kind of bleached blue, one of those early spring days that seem surprisingly cold, unfairly cold.

I thought you were in there. I rang the doorbell, waited, rang it again. It was possible that all those blazing lights were on some sort of theft-deterring automatic timer, but just as that occurred to me, I saw someone moving, through the filmy curtain over the narrow window beside the door. Someone walked right through my field of vision and out of it again, without so much as a hitch in her step or a glance toward the door.

I knocked, even though I had heard the doorbell ringing in the house. Finally, crazed with the thought that you were inside, I jumped over the railing at the end of the porch and walked around to stand in the garden, the direction in which that figure had traveled. I found myself at about chin level with the sill of the kitchen window.

This was your mother; that much was obvious. Her gray hair was in a bun, and she wore a blue pants suit (maybe she went to an office on weekends, I thought), but she had that same mouth, that same smooth, too-fair skin. I knocked on the kitchen window and this time she heard me, though she didn't jump or scream, as well she might have under the circumstances. She smiled at me as if this were the most natural thing in the world, to find a stranger staring and knocking at you on the other side of the kitchen window. Then she left the room. Maybe she's phoning the police, I thought, chinning myself on the windowsill to try to see further into the house; but then I heard the front door open at last, and a maternal voice chirped, May I help you with something?

With all the good manners I could muster, I walked around the railing and back up the porch stairs, brushing dirt off my pants.

Are you Mrs Howe?

Kay, she said.

Her eyes were very bright, very wide.

Is Molly in?

Molly's out, Kay said. Would you like to wait for her?

If I might, yes, thank you. She held her arm out, and I stepped across the threshold, through the vestibule, into the bright living room.

Do you know when she's coming back? I said.

But Kay had already forgotten about me; with one knee up on the arm of the couch, she was straightening the pictures.

Left alone, I sat politely in the living room for a while. I had my bag in the car but I didn't quite feel right about bringing it in yet. After an hour had passed, during which your mother walked by me four times, humming to herself, without so much as looking at me, I felt free to give myself a tour. At the top of the stairs was, I guessed, your room. It was unmistakably the bedroom of a young girl: the novels and high school textbooks still in the low, two-shelf bookcase, the stenciled mural on one wall of characters from nursery rhymes, the fringed and tasseled spread on the old wooden bed with the half-moon headboard. No photos in there, though, of you or anyone else, which I thought was odd; no trophies or mementos or anything specific to who you were, or are; still, that didn't stop me from breathing the air in there, the atmosphere of you at age eight, age ten, age fourteen, as if I were on the top of a mountain.

I heard Kay humming as I came downstairs again. She was polishing the silver. It was now nearly six o'clock; there was no sign of you; and I was starving. Yet for all Kay's industriousness I saw no sign that she was planning dinner, for herself or for anyone else. I hadn't seen her eat all day.

Did Molly say what time she might be back?

No, dear, Kay said, smiling.

Because I wasn't really . . . I hadn't planned . . . I trailed off feebly, not sure how to say politely any of the things it occurred to me to say. Finally I hit upon:

Mrs Howe, since I'm putting you to so much trouble, I'd be happy to drive into town and pick up something for dinner.

She smiled reproachfully at me, as one would at a small child. Oh, you wouldn't find anything open now, this late on a Sunday, she said. Not in a little town like this.

She went back to her polishing. My hunger was getting the better of me, even at the same time as I was growing a little afraid of her. All of a sudden it occurred to me to wonder if your father had died. Silently I begged you to get back home from wherever you were. Would you mind, I said, if I helped myself to something? I don't want to be rude, but I've come all the way from California today. You know how that airplane food is.

Help yourself, Kay said cheerfully. I think Molly did some shopping.

I got myself two turkey sandwiches and a can of Sprite and sat at the little table in the kitchen. It was dark outside. I thought what an odd thing it was, to find myself in the space of a day transported into your childhood kitchen, and how that oddness would dissipate at once if you would just show up.

Kay was standing in the kitchen doorway. She now wore a nightgown.

Who did you say you were again? she said.

Hurriedly, I swallowed, and wiped my mouth. John Wheelwright, I said. I could have gone on, but I didn't; surely the name must have meant something to her.

You're the boy that's been calling all the time, she said finally, with a terrifying kind of neutrality. From Berkeley.

Yes, that's right.

She nodded. Well, good night, she said. And before I could resign myself to sleeping in my car, she added: If you like you can sleep in Richard's room. I just put fresh sheets on the bed yesterday.

Mrs Howe. Do you know where Molly's gone?

She shrugged. Molly comes and goes, she said. She's always been a very independent girl. Very mature for her age.

Yes, but, I mean, do you . . . Should we be worried?

Her eyebrows shot up, and stayed there, and for a few moments I regretted having tried to puncture her equanimity after all: she looked as if she might be right on the edge of some kind of hysterics. But then her face resolved itself again into that same eerie calm. Nonsense, she said. Molly can take care of herself. We all can take care of ourselves, can't we? Now, you get some rest. If she's not back in the morning, there's something I need your help with.

She disappeared. I washed my dishes and sat in the living room in one of two huge recliners there; determined to stay up all night if necessary, thinking now that you must have been out somewhere with some old high school friends, even an old boyfriend maybe. I lasted only a short while before the stress and the cross-country travel finally overwhelmed me into sleep, right there in the chair.

When I woke, the sun was up, it was Monday, and you were still nowhere in sight.

★ ★ ★

LATELY MAL SEEMS to have lost his taste, in the interstices of our discussions about work, for trying to get me to talk about Molly with him, to share our admiration, to help him put into words what he feels but can't always articulate. Too bad; because as time goes by I find I'm getting better at understanding it myself.

I know that Molly loved me. Even then, though, it was her remoteness, her unreachability, that transparent partition between herself and the outside world that like it or not you were part of, even at the moments of greatest intimacy, that made her so alluring, so thoroughly *involving*. You could reach her, you felt, you could get to her, if only you could figure out how. It wasn't a matter of simply putting in the effort but of finding the key, making the imaginative leap. Impersonating her, in a manner of speaking, as a way of intuiting what she needed. In some ways, it was like falling in love with someone who couldn't speak a word of English.

Her hair is brittle, even I can see that, because she doesn't take care of it, or even pay attention. Her lips are full, but also dry, chapped, uncared-for. My point is that beauty is greatest when it shows through in spite of itself. The more beauty is enhanced, the more it converges toward an ideal, an arbitrary, bland ideal; while every inch of Molly, every aspect of her, is unique, unrepeatable. Her two front teeth are just slightly, disproportionately large, so that they are sometimes visible between her lips when she's listening to you. There is a blue vein that runs more or less straight down the center of her right breast. She bites her nails. These are not flaws. They are the opposite of flaws.

Some feelings acquire a burnish from time, some feelings are swallowed up by time, leached from memory. She was my one great love, that's obvious, but I'm not just saying that, believing that, because that love failed. I'm not being sentimental; I'm not deceiving myself.

Of course it's possible that that's the very definition of greatness in love. A love so great that you fail it, you find your own resources are unequal to it. The problem of how to do it justice, in a sustained way, turns out to be beyond your capacities to solve.

★ ★ ★

MAL WAS PACING around my office today when I came back from lunch.

Elaine has *quit?* he said loudly. I turned around and shut the door.

Is that so? I said. I didn't know.

Didn't *know?* Come on, you think everyone around here doesn't know you're sleeping together?

I don't know what everybody around here knows.

She's gone already. She left me a note, because she said she couldn't face me, and now she's gone, back to New York.

I had an idea something like that might be happening, I said. She moved all her stuff out of our bedroom.

When did this happen?

A few days ago. But I was—

A few *days!*

But I was hoping she had just moved in somewhere else in the house.

Hoping! Mal said venomously. You couldn't be bothered to check it out? She was one of our original hires here. She did a lot of fantastic work, and she'll do more, only now it will be for somebody else. On top of which, I don't particularly want it getting around that people are leaving the place, just when we're hitting our stride. That's a very damaging rumor to be floating around.

You know, she was really angry at you about the Kerouac thing. Did her letter say anything about—

How could you let things get out of hand like that? You have a romantic dispute, you settle it. There are more important things at stake around here. If you're having some kind of problem with her, I expect you to manage it better. This is a very serious fuckup in my book, letting someone like her get out the door just because you can't treat her properly.

Mal, I said, that's a very personal thing. You get to a point where you have to ask yourself how committed you are.

I expect you to manage it better! he said, and slammed the door behind him.

* * *

I DROVE YOUR father home from the hospital. Your mother sat beside me, giving directions, not unpleasantly. All she had said by way of explanation was that she didn't enjoy driving anymore. None of us had any idea where you were, at that point; but since Kay didn't seem troubled by your disappearance, I figured I shouldn't be, either. I guess that was it. I was younger then, and they were grownups, and it's astonishing how the confidence another person displays in his or her madness can just draft you along, for a while anyway. Plus, they were your parents, and I wanted to make a good impression on them at any cost, because my plan at that point was that once I got my degree and a job I would ask you to marry me. That's how I was thinking then.

Kay wanted to wait in the car, but in a moment of lucidity brought on by panic I pointed out that surely they would only discharge her husband to the care of a family member. We walked across the parking lot, myself a step behind her, and into the hushed reception area; she stopped a passing nurse and asked her which way to the mental ward. Just like that. I had only a few silent seconds, in the elevator, to savor that feeling – half fearful, half comic – that goes through you at such a time, the feeling of how on earth could I possibly have arrived at this moment? How could the leading edge of my life now consist of such an errand: in a town I'd never seen, a total stranger to everyone, chauffeuring a middle-aged man I'd never met back to his home after a stay behind the steel doors of a psychotic ward?

All for you, I had time to remind myself as the doors buzzed open. That was the justification for all the strangeness. All in the cause of you.

Maybe you'd disappeared for a day or two just because this particular errand was one you'd find too upsetting. I could certainly see that, now that I was there myself. Maybe you'd be home when we all returned. Or call, at least, to apologize for your absence, and to see that everything had gone as planned. Then you'd learn that I was there.

The look on your father's face was something else I won't forget. Yet for all the horror that registered in his face on seeing me – I was a complete cipher, a bafflement, an insult – I felt an instant bond with him, because, like me, the one and only thing he really wanted at that moment was to see your face. And you weren't there. He stood holding a suitcase, dressed in a casual-preppy style (chinos, deck shoes, a V-neck sweater with some sort of country-club insignia on it) that couldn't have been more inappropriate to that place. Which I suppose was why he had put it on.

Where's Molly? he said. *Who are you* was the companion question that passed over his face; but I was obviously with Kay, and he was too well-bred to ask.

Molly's not here, said Kay. She looked at me expectantly, until I jumped across the gap between us and took Roger's bag. Not without some difficulty: he didn't want to give it to me.

Where is she? Did she have to go back to school?

No, Kay said, nothing like that. (She had already taken two steps back toward the steel door of the ward.) Molly wasn't around this morning, so . . . This is John, a friend of hers from California. He came to visit.

John Wheelwright, I said. Pleased to meet you, sir. Roger shook my hand, with astonishing feebleness.

His mouth fell open, as he struggled with this turn of events, with his wife's apparent refusal to give him the satisfaction of acknowledging the strangeness of it. But what was he going to do: turn around and go back to his bed in the psych ward until everything outside reconfigured itself into the shape he had expected?

Well, he said finally. All right then.

I drove back; like everything else about these few days, the route was already engraved in my memory. Roger sat in the back seat. I'd feel better if I could tell you that not a word was exchanged, that at least there was that sort of tacit recognition of the absurdity and gravity of the whole situation. But in fact I was the only silent one. Your father looked out the window and spoke admiringly about the fecundity of spring, the beauty of the farms, the wisdom of those who laid out our nation's highway system. Your mother spoke in a manner that seemed more concrete but was equally crazy, ticking off mundane household details as if her husband were returning from some sort of business trip. They spoke alternately, but nothing ever had any connection to what had just been said.

My father grew up on a farm, Roger said. Wheat. Wheat and rye. He used to go out, this was as a boy of nine or ten, and scythe before school. Can you imagine it? This would have been . . . well, he was too young for World War I, but his brother, I remember . . .

The porch light is out, Kay said, staring through the windshield. It's not the bulb. I didn't call Norman because I thought maybe it's something simple. But if it's the wiring, we'll have to call him.

Dogwoods! Roger said. He rolled down his window.

We pulled up to the house; I hopped out and took his bag. He smiled at me, purely instinctively, as I imagine he would have smiled at any proper show of politeness; then he continued to stare at me as his smile gradually fell. I think he was trying to figure out if I was something he was now going to have to get used to. I walked a few steps ahead of him into his home; Kay was already inside, turning on the lights.

Is Molly back yet? Roger said.

You were not. It felt like an entire day had passed, but it was still only about ten-thirty in the morning. Roger said he thought he'd take a nap before lunch. I was sure his own bed would feel good to him, but such sympathetic sentiments were impossible to express, particularly when the two of them, husband and wife, seemed locked in an intuitive agreement that nothing out of the ordinary had happened at all. Even my own bizarre presence there didn't cause a ripple in the placid surface of their madness. Kay sat down to watch a talk show on TV. I went out and sat on the porch, in an Adirondack chair facing the open end of the valley.

I had to believe you'd come back. I couldn't figure out where you might be hiding, or why you'd slip out just at the moment when your father was scheduled for his release; you must have known about that. Maybe there was much more, in

382

a sinister way, to your relationship with him than you'd ever told me. Or (I admitted it was possible) you were hiding out of embarrassment over my seeing what your home was really like. Well, if so, I regretted having put you on the spot like that, but really it was your own doing, refusing to answer my calls like that. You had to know I'd come looking for you. I was so stupid with love.

Down at the end of the driveway, just beyond the gate in the low wooden fence, a mail truck drifted to a stop; an arm reached out, opened the box, shoved in a pile of paper, shut it, and flipped the flag up all in one motion worn by boredom into a gesture of unbroken gracefulness. A few seconds later, when the truck was out of sight, the front door opened behind me, and Kay walked out to collect the mail. She flipped through it as she passed me again, without a smile or a glance in my direction. In spite of everything else going on, I felt a little offended that she should treat so casually a guest in her home. My own upbringing showing itself, I guess.

Ten minutes later, when I went back inside to offer to make your parents some lunch, I almost ran Kay down: she was still standing about two steps inside the front door, holding a postcard up in front of her face.

It was from you. All it said was that the Honda was in the long-term parking lot at the Albany airport. I read it a few times over Kay's shoulder, both of us struggling to make sense of it. Then my heart leaped, and I began thinking immediately about how to make my own escape from that place, where in the house your parents might keep a phone book, where I could find a phone out of their earshot in order to call the airport myself.

Because it could only mean one thing. You had flown home to me, to California, and now I wasn't there.

★ ★ ★

MAL SUMMONS ME to his office.

I had a call from Rachel Comstock, he says. You know who Rachel Comstock is?

He looks angry.

No, I say.

Neither did I. She's a producer at 60 Minutes. She apologized for bothering me but she said she had called your office three times and never had her call returned.

The air was heavy with some kind of recrimination. He was sitting behind his desk; the windows were open, and a stack of papers riffled underneath a paperweight. I was damned if I was going to let this turn into a conversation about my job performance. I was damned if I was going to say I was sorry about anything.

What did she want? I said.

His nostrils flared. See, the point is that I'm supposed to be finding that stuff out from you, and not the other way around. But since you're interested enough to ask, 60 fucking Minutes is now doing a story on these CultureTrust guys out in Spokane. The trial's turning into some kind of circus. These two guys apparently think they've inherited the radical-clown mantle from Abbie Hoffman, at least that's what this Comstock woman tells me. You know how embarrassing it is to have to learn this stuff from a total stranger, from a journalist no less? I thought you were on top of this!

I am on top of it. It's a criminal trial. It's the gallery pressing charges, not us. What do you want me to do?

What do I want you to do? I want you to go back out there and take care of it.

What do you mean, go back out there?

Fly back out there, he said, in a somewhat challenging manner, I thought.

When?

When? Right now would be good. What do you mean when? This is a public relations disaster—

There's no point in my going out there. If the 60 Minutes people see me there all of a sudden, that'll just make it seem like a bigger deal, like we're genuinely worried about these –

I'm sorry? he said. Was there something unclear about what I told you to do?

Mal's nostrils were flared, and his mouth was set so tightly it was quivering. It wasn't like him to get this mad about something work-related. This can't be about a couple of self-important middle-aged vandals three thousand miles away, I told myself. This has to be about something else. I folded my arms; the possibility existed that I might actually start crying, and the swell of that feeling in me really made me furious.

Is that what you want? I said. To get rid of me?

What the hell are you talking about?

I stood there staring down at him – he was still in his chair – and I thought, I don't really know what to hope for anymore.

What's happened to you, John? he said. You've really changed. Your behavior has been erratic these last few weeks; I'm not the only one who's noticed it. What's the matter?

What's the *matter?* I said.

Because if this is about Molly then all I can tell you is you're acting like a petulant idiot. Get over it. I realize this is a strange situation for you, it's a strange situation for all of us, but it's just what's happened. I mean you might as well tell me now: do you still have feelings for her?

No, I said. I don't.

Then what's the problem?

We have a history.

Yes? Mal said. And?

And when he said that, somehow all the air just went out of me. Maybe he's right, I thought: what difference does it make? Why should I think that what matters to me would matter to anyone else?

Okay, I said. Fine. I'll fly out to Spokane tomorrow.

Mal relaxed. Well, you don't have to look so glum, he said. It's three days at the most. You have to be back Thursday for Jean-Claude's thing.

Though in fact I wanted to be back for the debut of Milo's Palladio piece, there was something about the way Mal said I had to that caught my attention.

Why? I said. You'll be here for it, won't you?

He smiled coyly. No, actually, he said. I'm leaving tomorrow too. I'm flying to Rome.

Rome?

He nodded. I'll have to catch one of the subsequent performances.

I have to tell you, Mal, some of the clients we have flying in will be pissed when they get here and—

You can handle them, John, he said.

I couldn't see why he was being so cryptic. Did I know about this? I said.

Actually, no one knows about it. I'm going back to Umbria, for the final renovations on the house. A week at the most.

He couldn't keep the smile off his face. He stood up from his chair and leaned forward across the desk. In his tone of voice, in his every movement it was clear that he wanted to find some way to restore the old intimacy between us.

I want to spend my honeymoon there, he said to me. When I come back I'm going to ask Molly to marry me.

★ ★ ★

THERE WERE NO phones on planes back then. I tried once from the Newark airport and got my own voice on the machine. Of course, it was two in the afternoon, California time; you could have been anywhere. So then I spent another six hours, just as I had on the way out east less than a week before, in a kind of furious, helpless anticipatory limbo, knowing that you were below me somewhere, unable to communicate with you without actually finding you and holding you still. I still believed, *I still believed,* that I would find you back in our apartment, waiting for me. What is this power you have, to make me believe? I thought you'd have an explanation, a typically strange rationale for your odd behavior, and that I would have a right to demand that explanation. Not out of anger; never out of anger, where you were concerned. Maybe that was my mistake: you would have loved me more, or at any rate taken me more seriously, if instead of trying to talk you out of your own self-contempt I had shared in it, reinforced it, at least when provoked. But I wanted that explanation purely in the spirit of furthering my understanding of you.

There isn't much else to tell. I took a cab straight from the San Francisco airport to our door, the last twenty bucks I had, by the way. The place was empty. I stood in the kitchen until a distinct visual memory of your leaving popped into my head through sheer force of desperation – a picture of you with a green canvas duffel bag with handles on it. I ran to the bedroom closet, but the bag wasn't there. I looked under your bed, in the bathroom, in the hallway. Nothing was conclusive enough for me.

Then I sat and called your parents, back in Ulster.

Hello?

Mrs Howe? I'm sorry to bother you. It's John.

Who?

I swallowed. John Wheelwright. Molly's friend. I was just there.

Right. (There was a shuffling sound, as she sat up in bed I suppose, and she said quite clearly to her husband, *No, it's that friend of hers.*) Sorry. It's late here, you know. I was sleeping.

Honestly, it hadn't occurred to me, but it was past midnight there by then.

Where are you? she said.

Back in Berkeley.

Oh. (This with some distaste.) Can you put Molly on?

What?

Molly, Kay said. Is she there?

No, I said. I was calling to see if she'd come home yet.

Home here?

Yes.

388

No.

No word from her?

No, Kay said, a little impatiently. I don't know where she is. We went and picked up the car today, it was where she said it was, but beyond that I have no idea. I guess she's left again.

There was a long silence.

All right then? Kay said; and she hung up.

So that was that. You were nowhere, and I had no idea what had happened to change what existed between you and me. Whatever existed, actually, was unchanged; it *still* existed; here it was – our kitchen, our phone, our furniture, our bed. It only needed you to come back and take your place in it.

I say that was that, but of course it took me a long time to come to terms with the finality of it, to admit that to myself. And anyway, before I could even begin those endless skeptical inner repetitions of the fact that you really were gone, start wondering what that meant for me, how I could move forward from there – how I could move at all, in any direction! – there was one more thing to try.

I sat in a restaurant on Telegraph, drinking coffee in a plush threadbare armchair which I had turned around to face out the window, until a young man in a red shirt and khakis appeared across the street, holding a stack of pamphlets in one hand and carrying an old plastic milk crate under the other arm. He plopped the crate down in the middle of the sidewalk and stood next to it for a minute or more with his eyes closed, in what I gradually understood was a prayer. Then his eyes fluttered open and he hopped nimbly on to the crate and immediately went into a loud harangue of some sort (I couldn't hear it – I was still in my chair across the street) with his eyes focused sharply on the empty space before him, a foot or so above the heads of the pedestrians. Those with the bad luck to be passing just as he started to speak could actually be seen to jump in surprise, and to turn around resentfully or curiously as they picked up their normal stride; within just a few seconds, though, the voice had blended into the street scene, and no one paid any attention to the preacher's words at all.

I got up and walked across the street. It was Berkeley, so the cars just coasted to a stop and waited for me even though I was crossing in the middle of the block. The preacher had reddish-blond hair, already beginning to recede from his large, unlined forehead. His features were small and round, piggish you could almost say. He didn't seem to see me, even when I came to a stop in front of him, right at his feet.

Are you Richard Howe? I said.

He didn't so much as glance at me; he must have heard me, I thought, but then again maybe not – maybe he was in some kind of a trance state. Look around you, he shouted, addressing the crowd without really seeming to see it. Is this the life you wanted for yourself? The years on earth are over in the blink of an eye!

Are you Richard Howe? I said again. I have to talk to you. It's important. It's about your sister.

Where are you rushing to? To the office? To a store, to buy things? What are you rushing toward, really? Death, my friends, death! It will be here in the next instant! Beyond it lies eternity! Is there anything more worth preparing for than that? Does money matter, in the end? Do nice clothes matter? Jesus says . . .

And on like that for nearly an hour and a half. No one, I

reasoned, could keep that volume and pace up indefinitely; so I sat on the pavement with my back up against the used-record store and waited. He never turned around. If I'd had a hat, I could have put it on the pavement by my feet and probably made a few bucks, which I needed.

Ultimately he stepped down from the crate, picked it up under his arm, and started up the block. I jumped to my feet and overtook him. It wasn't hard; he was clearly exhausted.

Are you Richard? Please. It's important.

He ignored me. But now, beside him, looking down on him in fact, for he was not a tall guy when off his crate, I could see that he very likely was not your brother. There was no resemblance there at all. So I let myself fall behind him and I followed him down Telegraph until he turned on to Vine Street; I watched him unlock a door and I memorized the address. Then, because I had been away from home for a few hours, I went back to see if you had returned, or called, or maybe written a letter.

Around six I returned to the house on Vine Street. I knocked and then stood well back from the door, in case anyone wanted a look at me. It took a while before the door opened, and two smallish, short-haired, clean-shaven young men stood in the doorway, wearing red shirts. They stood abreast, as if trying to keep me from seeing inside, or from charging in. Not that they were big enough to stop me anyway. It was all pretty strange.

My name is John Wheelwright, I said as levelly as I could manage. I'd like to speak to Richard, as soon as it's convenient. It concerns his sister Molly.

Yes, said the one on the left. We know who you are. I think he meant it to sound spooky, but his high voice and solemn demeanor just made my own impatience with him harder to control.

Shoes off, said the one on the right.

Sorry?

Shoes off, please. Leave them outside the door, if you would.

I did so, and the two of them parted. Nervous in spite of myself, I padded down the hall in my socks, and turned the corner into the main room.

The walls, stripped of decoration, were painted a blinding white – blinding mostly because the room was filled with lamps, maybe ten of them, lighting every cranny of the place so thoroughly that nothing cast any shadow. On the floor, his back against the wall just inside the doorway, was yet another red-shirted young man sitting cross-legged on the floor holding a sketch pad; on it, he was finishing up what for one startling moment I took to be a pastel portrait of your father. But then I saw Richard, and the family resemblance was powerful indeed. He sat in a cracked black leather La-Z-Boy, fully reclined, his hands folded on his stomach. It was the only chair in the room. The other young men, four or five in all, sat on or lay across these huge square pillows scattered around the floor.

The whole thing just struck me as amazing and pretentious: trappings with no discernible purpose beyond gussying up the triviality of their mission, compared to the mission I was on.

I am Richard, he said. He might as well have told me he was Mr Kurtz. He reached down for the handle and returned his chair to its upright position.

Is Molly here?

Of course not.

Do you know where she is?

I have no idea, he said archly, disdainfully, as if I'd asked him what time it was and he'd responded by telling me he didn't wear a watch. I haven't seen her in a long time. Are you the person with whom she is living in sin?

I nodded. It wasn't that I didn't want to offend him. I just had no time to waste on being offended myself.

And now she's gone, Richard said, and you don't know where she is.

That's right. Have you heard from her?

Richard shook his head. If you were willing to defile her, he said, and of course you weren't the first, then you can't really be surprised if another defiler comes and takes her from you, can you?

I reddened at this. The young men on the floor were following our exchange with great interest, smiling, as if nothing more than amusement were at stake.

You don't even know me, I said.

Oh, I know you.

The others murmured their agreement.

I know Molly, too, Richard went on. She has been on a path toward destruction ever since she left her parents' house. She is remorseless. And you have taken advantage of her for a while, and hastened her down that path, when you could have done something instead to turn her toward salvation. But what have you lost, really, from your own point of view? I would imagine that such a sinful relationship is more or less interchangeable with another one.

Dumbfounded, I said: She's your sister.

He shrugged. And you're my brother, he said. What about it?

I'm in love with her.

You are a hypocrite. Your actions, not your words, are what signify, and your actions tell me that what you felt for Molly was not love.

He shifted in his seat, and smiled.

But it's not too late, you know, he said. You've made a mistake, but it's not a mistake from which you can't recover, if you start right now, by pledging your soul to Jesus. Are you willing to save yourself?

I want to save your sister, I said. That's how I will save myself.

Molly is past saving. Who knows? She may have arrived in Hell already.

I took a step toward him, expecting that his little minions would jump up to try to protect him. But they didn't; I kept going across the room, fists clenched, intending to drag him out of his La–Z–Boy and take advantage of his slander of you to make him answer for all the frustration I felt.

Richard flipped up the armrest of his reclining chair, reached into a little wooden compartment there intended by the manufacturers, I imagine, to hold a bag of chips or a TV Guide, and pulled out a gun. He laid it in his lap. The young artist had stopped his sketching; he was shaking his head at me, sorrowfully.

If you change your mind, Richard said, our door is always open to you.

THAT WAS IT. I waited another month, until I was out of money, and gave up the lease on the apartment. I called my

parents, apologized abjectly, and begged for the funds to
continue living out there until Christmas. I took a room in the
North Side home of a man whose wife had just left him and
taken their kids; evenings, while he drank in front of the TV, I
stayed behind my bedroom door and wrote my thesis on Goya
for the completion of my degree. I had them mail it to me in
Los Angeles, where I moved in order to work in the art
department at *New West* magazine. When that folded, I took a
job in the LA office of J. Walter Thompson; after two years a
headhunter found me and I went to Chiat/Day. When they
opened their New York office, they offered big raises to anyone
willing to relocate. I was willing to relocate. There was nothing
holding me anywhere.

There's more I could tell you. But I get the feeling I'm
talking to myself.

★ ★ ★

TO SPOKANE VIA Las Vegas this time; I lost fifty bucks on the
slots right there at the gate. But before that I called Farber, the
lawyer, from a pay phone and told him I was on my way. Same
old guy; he kept insisting I hadn't woken him up when it was
clear that I had.

He was able to see me for breakfast the next day. I told him
that Palladio was anxious to settle the case against CultureTrust
in an expedient and mutually beneficial way.

Settle? he said, trying to flag down the waitress with the
coffee pot; he's just the sort of guy to whom waitresses don't
pay attention. It's a criminal proceeding, not a civil one.

Nevertheless. When can I talk to your clients?

Lots of luck, he said, with a raised eyebrow; but right from the table he called and this time they actually agreed to see me that very afternoon. I don't know why they said yes this time probably for no better reason than that they had said no last time.

The judge had lifted the contempt charge against Gradison and both men were out on bail. I rented a car and drove along the river until I was well out in the boondocks. I had to keep checking my odometer because, according to the directions Farber had faxed to my hotel room, which I held in one hand as I drove, the dirt road on which Liebau had built his house wasn't marked in any way. I found it easily enough in the end. The house was two miles up the road, deep in the woods. It was some beautiful country.

Liebau's house was a huge A-frame, with a small yard area in front and on one side, from which all the stumps hadn't yet been cleared. Underneath the porch steps I could see two generators, one working, one evidently being repaired. I knocked; Farber appeared at the screen door, and let me in.

The great room was dominated by a wall of masks, hung haphazardly, in a variety of sizes and aspects. They were tribal, made of painted wood; more than that I could not say about them. They stared across the room at a wall of sagging bookshelves. On the north side, a vast picture window looked straight into the face of the woods; on the south, a large woodstove with iron doors. Above us, against the south wall and behind the chimney, was a sleeping loft. In the middle of the room, the two men – Professors Gradison and Liebau – sat waiting for me at a low table, cross-legged on a couple of pillows laid on the floor. They wore old wool sweaters, work pants, boots, and their time in prison did not appear to have slimmed them down at all. They did not get up.

The masks are beautiful, I said, lowering myself on to a leopard print cushion across the table from them. African?

From New Guinea, Liebau said, in a reasonable enough tone of voice. I did my doctoral research there.

And Mr Liebau, you built this place yourself?

He gestured to his colleague. Jack and I, he said. With some help from friends who had different sorts of expertise. Hooking up the generator, digging the well, and whatnot.

You're not survivalists, are you?

Not yet, Liebau said.

Gentlemen, thank you for seeing me. I may as well get right to it. You and your organization seem to have locked yourselves in a kind of death spiral with Palladio, the place where I work. It's gone on for a long time now; and it's reached the point where the toll it's taking on everyone concerned, on the work that we all want to do, is enormous.

(I knew I was flattering them with terms like *organization*, but that's just what I wanted to do. I wanted to give them some opportunity to claim victory.)

I'm here to resolve our differences in an amicable way. Your lawyer, I imagine, has already told you that we've gotten the gallery itself to agree to drop the charges against you, but now, what with all the publicity the trial's gotten, the judge says no. So now it's between us. Nothing is off the table.

The door to the kitchen swung open. A young, attractive Asian woman brought in tea, on a beautiful hand-painted tray, and silently departed. She wore slippers. I tried not to let my surprise show.

You're not here to resolve anything, Liebau said. You're here to make us disappear. Mal Osbourne is not troubled by our disagreeing with him. He's troubled by the fact that our *disagreement* (he held up his index fingers, clawlike, on either side of his head) is getting national attention, because of the chord it strikes with the masses.

I'm sorry, I said, smiling. Did you just use the word masses?

Yes, god damn it! So you can come here and simper all you want about cooperation, but we know this is all about silencing us. And we will not be silenced.

You pathetic lackey, Gradison added, in an almost apologetic tone, as if completing Liebau's sentence for him.

There was a chair in the room, by the picture window, and Farber sat in it, his back to the windblown pines outside. Legs crossed, he sipped his tea and studied the scattering of masks across from him.

You're wrong, I said. Mal *is* bothered by the fact that you take issue with him. And no one wants to silence you. Anyway, you're missing the point. Mal Osbourne is not the enemy here. He's fighting the same thing you guys are fighting. The established cultural order is what he hates.

Then Liebau, a man nearly old enough to be a grandfather, a man with patches of white in his neat beard, did an astonishing thing: he stuck his tongue out as far as he could, crossed his eyes, and repeated what I had just said, in a tone of mock earnestness. The estabwissed cuwtuwaw owdew is what he haes.

This was a new one. I reminded myself that my unflappability, my ability not to take things personally, was what Mal prized in me – it was the secret to my ascent. Still, it was clearly time to do away with the niceties; social graces only seemed to antagonize these people.

Fall semester starts soon, I said. You guys ready? For classes and whatnot?

Farber sat up straighter. I don't see how that's in the bounds of—

Liebau held up his hand. He already knows. He wouldn't ask if he didn't know the answer. We've lost our teaching jobs.

How will you find work?

We have our resources.

You put a lot of faith, I said, in the strength of your ideas. I mean, I guess that goes without saying. You'd have to, since all the force, all the money, is amassed on the other side.

Gradison, who had been noisily stirring his tea, suddenly held out one fist to me, turned sideways. Thumbwrestle? he said.

No, thank you. So let me get to the point.

Mal had said I would know what to do, and it was true; it was all coming to me now, spontaneously, as if he were working through me, without instruction, my mind racing to keep one step ahead of my speech, since I didn't think it would be wise to stop talking.

Mal Osbourne actually has a great respect for the work that you two have done. Even when it's been directly at his expense. He can see – he and I have talked about this several times – he can see that it has a great deal of iconoclastic energy, as well as a strong visual sense, a sense of how to get a message across in the least fussy, most memorable way possible. Not just a desire to break molds, but an instinct for it, a knack for it.

I'm moved, said Liebau to Gradison. Are you moved?

Palladio would like to hire you both, I said. Your starting salaries would be two hundred thousand for the first year.

Now I had their attention. In the crack of light under the swinging door to the kitchen I could see two points of shadow; the Asian woman was listening there. Farber was all ears as well.

You want us to come down South, Gradison said, and live in the big house?

Not if you don't want to. You can stay right here if you prefer.

Liebau held up his hand. Hire us to do what? he asked, confused.

To do exactly what you do now.

Come off it.

I'm not kidding. We'll write it into your contracts. No restriction on content. Keep making fun of us, if that's what you want to do.

They stared at each other.

Ask anyone who works there, if you want to, I said. Ask if their content has ever been tampered with, or censored in any way. (I was out on a limb now – Elaine's Kerouac ad had been squashed, of course, on formal grounds – but that was an anomaly, and anyway I had to win here, I had to go back home with something to show. I knew it's what Mal would want, even though, strictly speaking, there was no precedent for it.) Mal is a facilitator; he provides the link between great artists and the means for disseminating great art. All he has to offer is his sensibility. He hasn't been wrong so far. And he thinks that you two have greatness in you.

Liebau tapped Gradison on the shoulder; they stood and

walked to the corner of the room, where, shoulders hunched, they whispered to each other, complete with overdrawn hand gestures. Everything they did seemed to have that overlay of irony to it, of performance. I looked over at Farber, who met my eyes and shrugged, caught up in the suspense of it himself. After a minute or two they came back to the table and lowered themselves on to the pillows again.

Two million, Liebau said.

Sorry?

Two million. Each. The first year.

I scratched the bridge of my nose. Well, I can talk to Mal about it. We can work something out. Nothing's outside the realm of—

Twenty million, Gradison said. For me.

Yeah, me too, Liebau said.

I didn't change expression. I'll talk to Mal about it, I said. It was clear that they were just trying to get me to say no to them, and I would not.

Liebau leaned forward, stuck his bearded face at me over the table, with an expression of great curiosity in the crow's feet around his eyes. You are an amazing creature, he said to me. An evolutionary marvel. Do you know that?

This isn't about me. It's—

Oh, I beg to—

It's about the two of you. It's a sincerity check. Because I think that your idea of yourselves is predicated on failure. You enjoy making these destructive gestures precisely *because* no one's listening, because you know no one cares what you think. Well, here's a chance for you to take the ideas you hold so dear and make the whole world listen to them. What's your answer?

No, Gradison said, not smiling now. Our answer is no.

See, I don't understand that. You define yourself through these ideas, that, I don't know, that Mal Osbourne is Satan, that nothing he says is sincere, that his art is about commerce even when it has no commercial content, whatever. I don't know. But now it seems to me that these same noble ideas would, to you, not be so noble – they'd be changed entirely – if instead of being unemployed middle-aged leftie dinosaurs you were actually succeeding in disseminating them widely. It's the trappings that really concern you, not the art. I think it's all a pose, I really do. I think you don't really believe in yourselves at all. It's a pose.

Liebau beckoned me closer. I leaned my head across the table. He cupped his hands around his mouth as if he were getting ready to shout, but when his voice came out, it was a whisper.

Dissent is the art, he said.

He sat back, and, in his normal voice, repeated himself. Dissent is the art. And crushing dissent, Johnny, in case you haven't twigged to this yet, is the business that you're in. Swallowing it, bastardizing it, defanging it, eliminating it. The reason you think our art's meaning wouldn't change if we sold it to you is that you don't think it means anything anyway. Art comes from somewhere. It has a provenance. Changing that provenance changes the art. Denying that provenance denies the art.

He sighed. And now, he said, in conclusion: get out.

I thought they were kidding. I smiled.

Get out, he said. I mean it. Get out of my house. You defile it by sitting here.

Get out! Gradison said.

Get out! Liebau said, louder. The two of them got to their feet. Get out! Get out!

I looked at Farber. Do you think you could encourage your clients to—

Something – a pencil, I think – whizzed by my head. Get out! They were shouting now. Gradison ran over to the wall and took down a mask – long, scowling, with open mouth and large wooden teeth. Holding it over his face, he ran back across the room and stood inches from me, hopping from foot to foot.

Booga booga booga! he shrieked. It was ridiculous. Then he picked up my half-full cup of tea and proceeded to throw it on me.

They followed me out on to the porch, still screaming, Get out! I hurried into my car. Gradison and Liebau, overweight men, college professors, climbed up on the hood and banged on my windshield with the flats of their hands. Their faces were stretched by a fury so outsized I couldn't really be sure it was genuine. When I put the car in reverse, slowly, they rolled off the hood and landed on their feet in the driveway; but when I got out on to the dirt road and stole a glance into the rearview mirror, there they were, still huffing after me, shaking their fists, before they finally stopped, leaning over with their hands on their knees, trying to get their breath.

★ ★ ★

IT WAS ALL in the nature of a demand, I see that now, but why shouldn't I make demands of her? An impartial observer, I think, would say that I was owed, that I had a claim originating in what she had done to me, in the cruel aimlessness she had brought to my life just when I thought I knew what my life would be devoted to. But forget impartiality, I don't want to be impartial. That's the last thing I want. Nothing in my life since has been as real as our love, and I can't see anything in her life right now that strikes me as particularly genuine, either. And before that? A glorified PA for some half-talented Hollywood wannabe, for whom nastiness was passed off as integrity, as evidence of a tortured soul, when really the only thing torturing him was ambition? I'll show him a tortured soul.

All the way across the country I thought about what I would do. Mal was out of the country. I couldn't make up my mind what to say to her, but saying nothing was out of the question. The inevitability of it propelled me; resisting it would have been like trying to break a fall by flapping your arms. So I dropped my bag in my half-empty room and made my way across the ground floor to the east wing. The ballroom doors were closed, to protect the surprise of Milo's installation: other than that, a normal day. I did stop in my office, on the way upstairs, to see what messages there were that needed returning. It was nearly seven o'clock, and so Tasha had already left for the day.

On the fourth-floor landing I felt a wave of nervousness, but I kept on going. I knocked, for the first time, on Mal's bedroom door. No one answered. She may well have been out; I hadn't thought to check for her car. Suddenly it began to seem like an opportunity of a different sort. I tried the door, and, as if in a dream, it was unlocked.

I'd never been in there before. I don't know what I expected. He's done it in white, all white, the bedspreads, the curtains; only the brass railing at the head of the bed

404

shone gold. No artwork on any of the walls. No books, no mirrors. A door to the bathroom, a double door leading to what must have been a walk-in closet, and a door to the balcony, which was open; the breeze pushed at the skirts of the long white curtains.

There was someone in the bathroom, and she seemed to hear me at the same moment I heard her. The faucet turned off.

Who's there? she said.

I stood still, and held my breath. I made myself so silent I could hear the blood in my ears.

John? she said.

Molly walked slowly into the room and smiled at me, with a lack of alarm that I thought was really inappropriate under the circumstances. What are you doing here?

I came to tell you something, I said, my voice shaking a little in spite of myself. You have to leave this place. You have to get out of here.

She looked concerned – not for herself, though, for me: as if there were something so odd or disturbing about the expression on my face that she hadn't even heard what I'd said.

Listen to me, I told her. I swear to you this isn't about me. It's about you. Well, it's about this whole place, really, every-thing around here is fucked up, it's falling apart, and that's because you're here. I'm not sure why that's true, exactly, but I'm sure it's true.

Molly pulled her head back in amazement. John, she said, I haven't done anything. To you or to anyone else. I do my best to stay out of everyone's way. It's a huge house and I live in it, that's all.

I nodded. I'm not accusing you of anything, I said. But ever since you got here, I can feel things going downhill. For all of us. And now he's going to ask you to marry him.

She actually laughed.

What? she said. You're dreaming. What makes you think that?

He told me so. He's going to ask you when he gets back.

Molly's eyes widened.

It's a fucking joke, I went on. He doesn't even know you. He doesn't know how to love you. He doesn't have any idea who you are. He can't understand you, and so he wants to have you. And if he has you, then that's it, it's all over. I'm sorry I can't say it any better. But I remember you, Molly. I know how you need to be loved. And it's better not to be loved at all than to be loved in some inauthentic way. I mean, for most people any kind of love is better than nothing, but that's not you, you can't have less than you deserve. It wouldn't be right. Can you understand what I'm trying to say?

Molly was looking at me strangely. Unfocused. Like she didn't really see me; but her eyes were right on mine.

Because if you can't, I said, then God knows no one else will. Let me just ask you one thing, okay? What do you see in him, anyway?

She took a step closer to me. I've stopped seeing things in men, she said. If you wait long enough, they show you everything anyway.

Her voice was odd. She was staring at me carefully, like you'd stare at a mirage, like you half expected it to disappear if you just looked at it hard enough, and as she did so she reached up and ran her fingers gently along my collarbone.

I didn't move.

What's left for me, John? she said. I have a lot of time left to get through. All I want is to be comfortable. Shouldn't I be comfortable?

You have to get out of here, I said. Inside me the blood was hammering away. My face was turning red.

She ran her hand gently over the curve of my head, like you might do to a child. Why do you care? she said.

Stop it. I'm trying to tell you something.

Everything I touch falls apart. You've come back to me, though. I knew you would. I've been waiting up here for you. Is that what you want to hear?

That's not true, I said.

She was talking almost like someone in a trance. Something's happened to her, I told myself. You can't take advantage. But it was no use. What was the point of resisting? Still, inside, until the last second, I resisted.

Why do you care? she said again.

Because he doesn't love you.

You still love me, though, she said. Don't you?

I could feel her breath on me when she said it.

You have to go.

With one hand around my neck she pulled me toward her, and with the other she covered my eyes.

I'm not even here, she whispered.

I wanted to worship her but it wound up happening differently. Though I wonder about it now, at the time it seemed right that she should be so passive, letting me call all the shots, which I was certainly in the right frame of mind to do. I thought of her passivity as a gift to me, an offering. I went through the whole catalogue of sexual memories, though in truth a lot of the stopping and starting had to do with my trying not to come. I wanted it to last for ever. Literally, that was what I wanted. I made it last a long time.

Did it change anything? Did it make me feel like I'd taken back something that had been stolen from me? To some extent. At one point, when I was behind her with my fingers dug into her hips above the bone, and she was on her knees and elbows, I saw that, with her eyes closed, she was crying. But I was too far gone myself at that point to stop and ask her what was going on. The sight of it at the time, if you want to know the truth, just made me fuck her harder. I used to go out of my way to avoid using that word, actually: *fuck*. But I need it now, it is the anti-euphemism, it describes what cannot otherwise be truthfully described.

But that was well after I laid my hands gently along her jaw and we kissed, for a long time, until at one point I heard a lovely suppressed moan from deep in her throat, as if she had just remembered something. Every instant, in fact, was another memory brought painfully back to life, as painful as it should be to bring something dead back to life again. I'll know it's time to kill myself the day I can't recall even one aspect of it.

At one point we were in a kind of sitting position, with her legs wrapped around my waist. The patchy redness that broke out around her neck was a sexual response: another detail to remember. As we ground slowly together I realized she was saying something, her face buried in the hollow between my neck and shoulder.

What? I said.

She moved her lips from my skin, but left her forehead there.

I'm sorry, she said. I'm so sorry.

Don't say it. Don't. It's forgotten.

Which, actually, was the truth. Nothing could have been further from my mind. Or no, that's not it; time seemed to have collapsed in some way, so that what had happened then was also happening now, only with a different outcome: I was holding on to her, I would never let her get away like that again. We had gone back in time, so that what was in many ways the defining moment of my life was now unmaking itself. Just as if it had never happened at all.

We fell asleep there, in the dead of night, in the white room, a room defined only by our presence in it, sterile, outside time. Sometime before morning I was snapped awake by the prospect of Benjamin's arrival with breakfast, and I dressed and tiptoed back downstairs.

When people – poets, or what have you – compare sex to death, I think this is what they're referring to. Everything builds toward one moment, that moment is the completion of the act itself: just as the moment just before you die is the realization, the sum total and final complex relation, of everything about you, everything you've done, felt, said, heard. Then the moment comes, and you want to put it off, you want to go back. Because you realize the explosive moment you've been spurring yourself on toward is also the end of everything. You want to turn back time, to knock everything apart so that it can reassemble itself again. You want to go back. But you can't do it.

★ ★ ★

TWO WEEKS SINCE my previous entry, which I had imagined would be the last one. Two days since the contents of my laptop

409

— returned to me following its miraculous survival — were subpoenaed. Palladio's lawyer is fighting it, but from what I'm told he won't have a lot of luck. So my most private thoughts, all the things that I considered unsayable, are now about to become part of the public record. Perfect.

Forrest Shays, the lawyer, has told me in no uncertain terms to stop writing things down, but I'm sorry, it would feel pretty hypocritical that way; if it's all going to be out in the open anyway then this little digital record, permanent and ephemeral, may as well have at least the virtue of completion. So I'll end by relating the — what's the word Mr Shays himself keeps using, the word we're all supposed to remember come deposition time? The *incident*. I guess that's to try to establish that not only did none of us see it coming, but no one could reasonably have been expected to do so. Well, they can call it what they want. I do consider myself responsible, though maybe that's just my nature; anyway, the lawyers are all over it now, and I'm relieved that none of it is for me to decide.

Tasha sent a fleet of limos to bring Milo's audience in separate groups from the airport, and I waited outside the front door to greet each car as it arrived in a cloud of dust up the driveway. We haven't had any rain here in at least a month; the mountains are still an unseasonable brown. Anyway, I brought them in, bore stoically the disappointment they didn't bother to hide when I told them Mal was still in Umbria, and gave them the tour. Took them through the front hall, the main dining room, the basement studios; escorted them out the back door and through the orchard, where everything was now picturesquely dead. I saved the ballroom for last because that's where we were going.

The corporate clients' petulance (I'd been on the phone with some of them all week, finding new ways to explain why and how they were being asked to subsidize work that would literally never be seen outside the doors of their ad agency) eventually gave way, over lunch, to the general mood of high anticipation. A Jean-Claude Milo unveiling was a big deal indeed, and there is always something invigorating about being part of the select. All the heads of marketing were there, PR people, art-loving corporate vice presidents and their comely secretaries. Jean-Claude's dealer from New York, her assistant, nearly all of our staff who wanted to see the happening. About forty people in all. At two o'clock exactly, I unlocked the tall ballroom doors and we all ventured in.

In the ballroom all the heavy curtains were drawn, and the computer screens glowed blankly. A larger movie screen hung from just about the exact center of the ceiling. Jean-Claude was sitting underneath it, on a small red carpet, wearing a rough brown robe like some sort of Tibetan monk. I remember thinking that this might have explained the weight he'd lost – some sort of Eastern asceticism, some sort of exploration of Buddhism, maybe. Beside him was a rectangular table skirted with a black curtain: not unlike a table you might see a magician use. Jean-Claude himself was calm, engaged, smiling at everyone who made eye contact with him. When most of the murmuring had subsided, he looked at me and raised his eyebrows.

That's everyone, I said.

Would you shut the door then, please, John? he said.

It was his normal voice – he was not in any sort of character; still, soft as it was, the sound of it silenced everyone even before I had the heavy doors pushed shut.

Jean-Claude stretched out his arms before him, paused a few seconds, then, with an air of great ceremony, clapped his hands twice; whereupon the lights went off. Ironic laughter, at this religious-ceremony-cum-infomercial: laughter that quickly subsided, though, maybe because we were now in almost total darkness.

A smell, a strange sort of artificial smell, sweet but excessive, like an overabundance of air freshener, seemed to rise up from the floor of the room. Then, one by one, all twenty or thirty of the small video screens at the computer-editing consoles flickered to life: each showed a different sequence of still shots of various works of art, some famous, some unknown to me, some I recognized as Milo's own. They ran in a loop, slowly, at about the pace at which an old-fashioned slide show might go, and as they did, a sound arose from speakers Milo must have concealed all around the ballroom, an empty sort of crackling and hissing that had to emanate from an open microphone with no one in front of it, turned up louder and louder – I'm sure I wasn't the only one feeling some dread lest someone actually start speaking into it, for it would have been earsplitting.

The sequence of artworks on the video screens looped a third time. Only this time, each image, after a few seconds, was consumed on the screen by a digital image of fire, creeping from the corners, blackening the center, until it was gone and the next image took its place. A murmur, audible to me even over the taped hiss of the unmanned microphone, went through the assembled. Then, on the larger, overhead screen, a simple white-on-black text began to scroll downwards.

This is what the words on the screen said:

If you were to go into the teahouse today, on execution day, and listen to what is being said, you would perhaps hear only ambiguous remarks. These would all be made by adherents, but under the present Commandant and his present doctrines they are of no use to me. And now I ask you: because of this Commandant and the women who influence him, is such a piece of work, the work of a lifetime, to perish? Ought one to let that happen? Even if one has only come as a stranger to our island for a few days?

At this point, though we could still see almost nothing, and any noise in the room would have been lost in the ambient sizzle of the empty mike, a stronger smell began to permeate the room, a chemical smell, something familiar but not easily identified.

The screens went blank. The hiss was cut off. Then, after a moment, we heard a familiar little trill of electronic bells, followed by another voice, instantly recognizable, the voice of James Earl Jones.

Thank you for using AT&T.

Laughter.

There was a sound, a whoosh like the sound of a tablecloth being snapped, and before anyone knew what was happening the center of the ballroom was lit by a kind of pillar of flame. I heard a couple of screams. Actually, though I say the room was lit, the weird thing was that that light seemed to draw everything into it; I don't remember seeing any other faces or even any shadows; the flame itself was steady, it held its shape, like a cigarette lighter or something. It was the shape of a pear or an inverted teardrop, rising a few feet off the floor and coming to a sort of point, smack in the center of the field of darkness that was the ballroom. A different sort of acrid smell began to reach us.

Turn on the lights! someone screamed. It was Fiona's voice. For just a moment I thought it was a collaboration, a part of the piece. Turn on the fucking lights, somebody, please!

We were a crowd, and we reacted as a crowd, even though we were still invisible to each other. All of us moved at the same time. I turned to grope my way back to the wall where I knew the switches were, and as I did I fell right over one of the corporate visitors, who had probably just stumbled over someone else. I heard the air escape from her with a little cry as my knee went down right into the center of her back. We were in a panic, and I will leave it to others to interpret at what point we were officially outside the boundaries of poor Jean-Claude's masterpiece, if indeed we made it out of there at all.

The stench was unbearable, and it only seemed to feed the animal quality of our fear as we knocked each other down and banged our hands against the walls, searching no longer for the light switch, but for the door. Stand back! I screamed. Get away! Back off! but I have no idea if anyone heard me. By the time I got to the door and opened it – I dared to look behind me only once the light from the rest of the house had flooded in there – the fire had reached the heavy, floor-to-ceiling drapes and from there you pretty much knew that the whole old house was bound to go up.

Someone else called 911. Someone else at least had the presence of mind to run into the pantry for the fire extinguisher, though by that time the ballroom was like a furnace; the door to it couldn't even be approached. Me, I ran like someone being pursued by the hounds of hell across the living room, through the front hall, and up the stairs. Colette was out on the third-floor landing, an inquiring look on her face, waiting, I suppose, for someone to come and explain to her what all the commotion was about. I pushed her out of my way as I turned on the landing and headed for the fourth floor.

Molly! I screamed. Molly! Get out of there! The bedroom door was locked; I pounded on it. Molly! Get out! I'm not kidding! It's John! I pounded once more; then I took a step back, kicked right beside the doorknob, and splintered the wood around the lock. One more kick and I was in.

Molly!

She wasn't there.

Like an idiot I wouldn't believe it, I looked in every room up there and then I looked again: she was gone. By now I had gone through the panic, I suppose, come out on the other side of it. I was calm, but not in a level-headed sort of way. It was a stupid calm, one that caused me to walk rather than run to the fourth-floor landing and peer down the stairs as if I were waiting for the distant light of a train. My eyes smarted. Smoke was already finding avenues to the top of the house.

I went back into the bedroom and pushed open the doors to their balcony. The first fire engines had already arrived. I could see people, a lot of people, standing or sitting or doubled over coughing on the great lawn, staring up at the catastrophe, up at me, though they didn't seem to see me. I wondered if they thought I was planning to go down with the ship. Then a firefighter pointed to me, the others pointed too, and as I stood on the balcony, smoke beginning to frame me as it made its way through the balcony doors and disappeared in the daylight, I watched them run to one of the rescue vehicles, drag what looked like a huge tarpaulin out on the grass, and connect some sort of generator-run air pump to it. In just a couple of minutes it had inflated into a huge soft target, like a pillow, like those landing areas stuntmen use, just outside the frame.

Cracking noises were now audible somewhere behind me, but I couldn't feel any heat yet apart from the strong heat of the day. With my hand as a visor I took a look all around, from this view I had never before enjoyed and never would again, at the grounds, at the tiny featureless figures of the people with whom I had worked and of the people who would save me, at the lawns and orchards and hedges, at the shadows of the clouds pouring over the scorched contours of the Blue Ridge Mountains. When the firefighters finally signaled that they were ready I put one leg, then the other, over the iron railing of the balcony. It's no easy thing to make a drop like that, even when you have no choice, even if you've seen it done before. My fingers were tight around the balustrade. But I wasn't ready to die yet, that's all it really comes down to if you wait long enough, and so I closed my eyes, opened them again, and with one last loud exhalation to calm myself, I jumped.

3

HOURS LATER, SORE and still a bit lightheaded from the impact of the fall, John sat apart from the others on Palladio's broad front lawn and watched the firefighters pounce expertly on each last small stubborn flare-up of the great conflagration. The western end of the house was burned close to the ground; the columns at the entrance were blackened but apparently intact, and the east wing, though gutted to near-transparency on the bottom two floors, had not collapsed at any point. In just the past few minutes the whole ruined structure had seemed to take on, as the twilight smoothed it into silhouette, a more abstract wedge shape. During the lulls in all the shouting, John could still hear the fierce, diminishing hiss of water on embers, and an occasional ominous tick or crack. Smoke – dark at first, then whitening once it reached the heights still lit by the last of the sun as it dropped behind the mountains – rose straight as a chimney in the hot, motionless air.

He wondered if he might have a slight concussion. Red emergency vehicles of every description had torn a rough circle in the manicured grass around the mansion; they were idle now, though their engines had been left running and the flashing lights stuttered more vividly in the growing darkness. The Charlottesville police had set up a barricade at the driveway entrance, primarily to keep out the press. Of course, some of those guests still sitting on the lawn, or lying down or coughing or breathing through portable oxygen masks brought to them by the EMTs, were invited press themselves. John could make out several people talking into cell phones. Part of the general dreaminess that was overtaking him, as he sat on the grass with his arms around his knees, had to do with the knowledge that the whole thing had escaped his control once and for all.

Near his hip he felt an insistent pulsing, and he thought for a moment he might be bleeding; but in fact it was his own cell phone still clipped to his belt – he had set it on vibrate for Milo's premiere. He knew who was trying to reach him. More than he could ever remember wanting anything, he wanted not to answer Mal's call: but though the place was now gone from under him he still had a sense of stewardship about it, and so – after standing and walking a safer distance away from Fiona, who was being held upright under the arms by Jerry as she shrieked (that was the only word for it) into his chest – John answered.

"What's going on?" Mal said angrily. "I call your office I get no answer, I call my office I get no answer. Where are you? What's all that noise?"

John broke it all to him as gently as he could, which wasn't so gently, considering that there were times when he had to shout into the phone just to be heard over all the engines and indecipherable radio calls on the lawn. He told his boss that the mansion had caught fire, a fire set by Jean-Claude, whose art of self-sacrifice had culminated in what was apparently a work incorporating his own suicide. Even when John had described everything as best he could, it was clear from Mal's tone of businesslike optimism that the magnitude of what had happened would not sink in right away.

"Well, the important thing is that everyone's okay," he said.

John had to explain more carefully that everyone was not okay – that, while nothing was official yet, it seemed impossible not to conclude that Milo himself was dead. The fire was now almost out, but the house was beyond saving. And there was one other person still unaccounted for.

Mal fell silent. John then asked if by any chance he had spoken to Molly that day.

"Not since last night," Mal said. "Oh no."

"Now look, I actually think – it's true no one seems to know where she is – but I actually have reason to think she wasn't here at all when it happened. I . . . I went upstairs and looked all through your quarters. Every room. She wasn't there."

"Did you look for her car?"

John winced, and hit his head softly a few times with the heel of his hand. "No," he said, starting to sprint across the lawn toward the house, "I didn't think of it. God damn it! Hold on."

But the firefighters had run another barricade across that end of the driveway and wouldn't let him through. John pleaded, phone in hand, with the commander of the emergency rescue squad, telling him that the safety of one of the house's residents was at stake. Too dangerous, he was told; what remained of the house on the eastern end was still being examined to determine the danger of collapse. As for whether or not anyone was still inside, they had people sweeping the place now.

"Ten, twenty minutes," the commander said, his gray hair flattened with sweat. "Try to calm down."

When John raised the phone to his ear again, Mal was already in the back of a taxi, speeding toward the Rome airport.

"I'm going to lose you," he said. "Keep trying me." Then the connection was broken.

John sat down in the grass beside one of the empty ambulances, between the house and the path to the orchard. Ten, twenty minutes. No one came over to console him or to see if he was all right. They sat and stood in little knots of shadow around the lawn. Maybe they were waiting for some official word about Jean-Claude; maybe they were unable to take their eyes off such an epic disaster and were waiting only for the fire department or someone else more thick-skinned in these matters to tell them when it would be seemly to leave. At the other end of the driveway, out by the road, John saw a portable arc light snap on in the dusk, beside the satellite trucks. He told himself that even if the red Sonata was still in the driveway, it didn't mean anything for certain.

Finally the commander let loose with a startling whistle, as one would to a dog, and indicated to John with a nod that it was now permitted to walk around behind the house. Four or five ash-dusted cars, including his own, were there in the driveway behind the kitchen – one, an airport limo, had even had its hood smashed when one of the chimneys had fallen on it – but the red Sonata was not among them. Molly was gone.

John felt a huge spasm of relief, of physical relaxation, roll through him; in his weakened state, it all but knocked him down. With his hand on one of the dusty cars for support, he stared up at the intact balcony from which he had jumped. Just then one of the EMTs, a younger man, helmet in hand, walked up to him.

"The lieutenant says you're in charge?" he said.

John nodded. "The owner of the house is out of the country," he said.

"Right, okay. Well, we've been through the whole house. I'm sorry to have to tell you that we recovered one body from the western side of the building. But everybody else got out. The rest of the house is clear. We've been through all of it."

"Thank you," John said solemnly to him, and the EMT nodded curtly and backed away. A while later John got on his cell phone and called Mal, still on the ground in Rome, to tell him that the good news was that Molly was still alive.

★ MESSAGE ★

No Empire Lasts For ever.

★

IN A STATEMENT he handwrote in his airplane seat on the way back from Italy, Mal announced to the world that Palladio would rebuild, that its work would go forward despite the tragic and incalculable loss of life and historical property, not to mention the loss of the artwork hung, stored, or in progress in the mansion at the time of the fire, a loss estimated to go well into the millions. John typed it up himself – Tasha, angry and traumatized, had gone home to her parents in Richmond – and distributed it via the fax machine in his room in the Charlottesville Sheraton. He felt simultaneously proud and foolish. The Sheraton had given them two whole floors, that first disastrous night; but today he and Mal were the only ones there. The rest of them had flown up to Boston, where it turned out Milo's parents lived, for his memorial service. As for Mal, Mr and Mrs Milo had tersely requested, through their lawyer, that he not attend. Mal chose to believe that this request was made out of the understandable desire for privacy, since his presence at the service would surely provoke the attention of the media. John suspected other motives, but he kept this to himself. Nor did he share with Mal his premonition – correct, as it turned out – that many of the artists, having taken advantage of this unimpeachably somber pretext for leaving, would not return to Charlottesville when it was over.

Return to what, after all? They couldn't conduct business out of hotel rooms for long, if they expected potential clients to take them seriously. Two weeks went by before they moved their business operations to an office borrowed from their lawyer, a silver-haired Southern gentleman who looked at least a decade younger than his seventy-three years and who owned the two-story office building in which he practiced, in the commercial section of downtown Charlottesville. The move made sense, since most of what was left of Palladio was a matter for everybody's lawyers to pick through anyway. In the flurry of local and then national interest in the half-sinister, half-absurd circumstances of Milo's self-immolation, the Charlottesville DA had even announced he was opening a criminal investigation, but Shays laughed this off, both publicly and privately, and he was right. On the other hand, lawsuits filed by clients seeking refunds (even when the work they'd commissioned had already been completed and displayed — they claimed all the work that had ever emanated from Palladio, except for Milo's, was tainted and devalued now), by a group of former employees claiming emotional distress, and by the Virginia State Historical Commission were all harder to ignore.

John sat at a desk six feet from Mal's, without much to do, having been decorously told by Shays that the best help he could provide right now, in light of all the pending lawsuits, was not to say anything at any time to anybody. Still, he did have a particular responsibility. Several times a day Mal would ask him if there was any word yet from, or about, Molly. There was not. As far as taking a more active approach to finding her, the few things they could think to try had all been tried in the first day or two: the Virginia state police had no luck locating the car; and if she had any credit cards there was no record of her using them anywhere. Nervously, John had called Dex in New York, who affirmed that he had had no contact at all with Molly, though if he did he would welcome the opportunity to hang up on her or slam the door in her face, and by the way John and Mal deserved what they had gotten and should go fuck themselves. Later that same day, John dialed the number of Molly's parents' home in upstate New York. It rang and rang, but no one answered.

He couldn't know whether Molly had taken his advice to heart and fled the place, coincidentally on the day it burned down; or whether she had simply been out on an errand that day, returned to find the house in flames, and taken this as some sort of opportunity or directive to move on; or, as seemed most likely to him, whether there was some other explanation entirely for her disappearance, one that he wasn't equipped to imagine. John's most persistent worry, though, was that it would occur to his boss, in a moment of idleness, to ask about what might have preceded that disappearance, if John had seen Molly, spoken to her, heard her say anything significant in the days just before the fire, when Mal was still in Italy. But he never asked. As with the lawsuits, which he made no effort at all to dispute but only to dispose of, Mal made a point of refusing to dwell on the recent past, because his current mindset was all about the future.

Bulldozers came and razed the walls of Palladio, and with them, so it seemed, went the general air of secrecy that had surrounded the place; anonymously sourced news accounts of its mysterious inner dynamics, of Milo and Mal Osbourne and the woman whose arrival in the mansion seemed to prefigure its destruction, went into their customary upward spiral. Milo's ambiguous legacy proved suggestive to every sort of extreme opinion. To some, the whole episode only cemented Mal's own genuinely messianic status. Then there were those who concluded Milo had been nothing but a sort of double agent all along, bent on destroying the house of Osbourne from within, all for the cause of integrity in art, even at the cost of his own life. And many, to be sure, did not consider Milo an artist at all, but simply a young man suffering from a mental illness, whose suicidal cries for help were turned to account in a Barnumesque fashion by cynics interested only in money.

And then in September, John, too, left Virginia, under sad circumstances. His mother died of a swift and unprecedented heart attack, on her knees in the flower garden behind her condo. Mal, who despite their physical proximity had lately seemed quite withdrawn, frowned at this news but remembered to offer John his condolences. John went out to the parking lot behind Shays's office, put on his sunglasses, and drove to South Carolina to help his stepfather, Buzz, make arrangements.

★ MESSAGE ★

You have to appreciate authenticity in all its forms.

I will peer around corners.
I will see past clouds.
I will get to the source.

"Isn't it *good* to believe in something?" he asks the crowd as he strides on to the stage after an introductory hymn from the choir, his eyes bugging, teeth gleaming, blond-tipped hair holding fast in its swept-up place. "Isn't it *bizarre* to believe in something?"

But there's a twist. The artist is not Garry Gross, who took the picture, but Richard Prince, who took a picture of the picture and then

THE RIGHT RELATIONSHIP IS EVERYTHING

★

THE NANNY CALLED in sick, which was a huge inconvenience; it would shorten Roman's hours at work, and Jo's, and certain things they had come to take for granted they didn't need to know, like what time *Little Bear* was on, they would now have to figure out for themselves. But at least you could be sure, when the nanny said she was sick, that she wasn't faking. This was only the third time, and she'd been with them five years. You couldn't get too angry about it.

"Do we still have yesterday's *Times*?" Roman asked his wife. They were back to back in the small kitchen, preparing the two different breakfasts for the kids.

"I took the papers down to the basement last night," Jo said. "Sorry, I thought you were done with them. Why, was there something in there—"

"That's okay. I didn't . . . somebody emailed me about it just this morning. I'll go look for them."

"I'm sorry."

"That's okay."

After breakfast Roman took the baby on his shoulder and went down to the garbage room in the basement. There were roaches everywhere. This is no place to raise children, Roman thought. He felt Isaac's tiny chin lift up off his shoulder blade and could picture his son's goggle-eyed expression as he strained to look around. One new place was as amazing as another to him.

Roman looked through the pile of recyclable paper, vaguely disgusting even though it was only a day old, until he found the *New York Times* with the little "Joanna Gagliardi" sticker on it. He wiped it on his leg and went back upstairs.

They agreed to split the day – he'd go into the office in the morning while Jo, who had a fundraising job at Columbia University, stayed home with Isaac; Roman would then pick Evgenia up from school at one o'clock (it was Friday, a half day for her, just to make things even less convenient) and take over at home for the rest of the afternoon so Jo could get up to Columbia and at least maybe return a few phone calls. Tag-team, she called it, when these situations came up. Which was quite often: late nights in the office, weekends, school vacations, illnesses. Their marriage had evolved, over the years, into a series of these trivial, unacrimonious negotiations over time, like labor disputes really, between two old, old adversaries who knew each other so well that they weren't really adversaries anymore.

He walked Evvie to school; she kept her hands stuffed in her pockets and her chin tilted up slightly, just like her father. She walked without seeming to feel the burden of the enormous yellow backpack she carried. It was as if she expected to be gone for days, sleeping outdoors. All her secrets were in there. The two of them didn't exchange a word. They hadn't argued, and Roman knew she loved him possessively; she was just getting to that age, that's all, she had her own thoughts and didn't need to have those thoughts validated for her by sharing them with an adult. That age came shockingly early, like everything else, for kids who grew up in New York. For just a moment the scene before his eyes was displaced by a premonition of the handful she would surely be when she was fifteen.

"Goodbye, sweetheart," he said to her outside the classroom. She allowed him to help her get free of the backpack, in order to take her jacket off.

"Is Maria going to die?"

So that's what all the silence had been about. "No, honey. Of course not. Maria is as healthy as a horse, believe me. She just has a cold, like everybody gets. I'm sure she'll be back and feeling fine Monday morning. You can do a get-well picture for her if you want."

On the subway he read yesterday's *Times* article. There wasn't too much in it he hadn't learned yesterday, around the office, on the phone, on the Internet, in the *Post*. John Wheelwright, his old partner, had invited a group of corporate clients and art-world poobahs to watch one of his employees commit ritual suicide under the rubric of performance art. In taking himself out, this Milo character had taken out the whole storied antebellum building as well, though there was some question – some fierce debate, actually, among pundits, lawyers, and art critics – as to whether or not this had been a planned part of Milo's "piece" or an unfortunate and unintended consequence of it. Mal Osbourne had been conveniently out of the country when it happened. At least one of his newly disenfranchised employees was trying to connect all this to Osbourne's girlfriend, some younger woman he apparently kept stashed mysteriously in the attic like Mr Rochester in *Jane Eyre*, and though this seemed even to Roman like a bit of a stretch, the tabloid press was howling in search of her – unsuccessfully thus far, for she seemed, on the very day of the tragedy no less, to have disappeared.

His old partner. Roman wasn't at Canning & Leigh anymore either. Those places tended to grow fat on their own success, fat and conservative, and before long they were churning out junk every bit as revolting as the reactionary giants of Madison Avenue. Success brought money, and money always brought a specific kind of fear – the fear of having to do without the money again, Roman supposed – which manifested itself in a creeping dependence on focus groups, management reviews, probationary management reviews. When the atmosphere turned dark like that you just had to get out of there.

So Roman was now at a new shop on Mercer Street, called the Kollective. Ten people, no hierarchies, no office doors, which was the only aspect of the place, actually, that Roman found a little bit precious. The ten came from agencies all over the city, sensitive, disgruntled, highly creative artists who chafed against any sort of corporate restraint. People who rebelled even when they knew it wasn't good for them, much like Roman himself.

The emergence of these little splinter groups, this rising and thinning and dividing like the branches of a tree, happened all the time in advertising. It was like the Communist Party: all these factional disputes, questioning each other's ideological commitment, cadres spontaneously forming to protect the doctrine from impurities and compromise. It would probably happen at the Kollective someday, too, Roman knew. That was all right. The interesting question was when, or if, Roman himself would wind up becoming the conservative one, sick of moving on, proud enough of something he'd built to want to stay and wither into irrelevance along with it.

In the office they had all heard the story of the burning of Palladio; they'd spent much of the previous night emailing one another with rumors and jokes about it. No one was in the mood to work. They knew Roman used to work at Canning & Leigh back when Mal Osbourne had his name on the door there. But they weren't aware that Roman and John

Wheelwright had been partners. It didn't take long to emerge. Roman certainly wasn't going to lie about it.

"No!" yelled Douglas, a copywriter with a ponytail and a terrible beard; like many of them he was so young he made Roman feel like he was turning into his own father. "No! Partners? Get the fuck out of here!" They all sat forward in their sofas and club chairs. The place was decorated like a million-dollar fraternity.

"You and the guy were *partners*?" said Kathleen, the receptionist, ignoring a ringing phone. "For how long?"

"Two years," Roman said softly. "We worked on Doucette, on Fiat, the National Beef Council, whole bunch of things. We did some good work."

"So what was he like?"

Roman said nothing right away.

"Did he show sadistic tendencies?" Douglas asked helpfully. "Killing small animals in the office, anything like that? Did he ever chase Canning through the office with a cigarette lighter?"

"We were friends," Roman said. The others were cowed momentarily by the evident feeling in this remark; and, feeling exposed, not wanting to appear too sentimental in front of his colleagues, Roman moved along. "I think he has to be telling the truth about it, that he didn't have any idea, that no one did. I don't know. He had this great girlfriend, a lawyer, who he dumped to go take this job with Osbourne. He was a very nice, very polite guy. From North Carolina. Hated to argue. Hated it. I almost always got my way with him because of it. Very kind, very meek almost, but meek in a good way. Naive. I never understood how naive until he was taken in by this whole Mal Osbourne thing."

"Yeah, well, that's in the toilet now," Douglas said.

"I heard they got it on film," Kathleen said. "A snuff film, basically. I heard MOMA's already offered Osbourne a million bucks for it, but Osbourne can't get it back from the cops."

"Hey, who says irony is dead?" Douglas said.

No one accomplished much that day, which suited Roman fine. He kept one eye on the clock all morning long. He was nagged by the knowledge that he had left a lot out of his account: not so much about John, but about John and himself. The bitterness with which they fought at the end – well, with which Roman fought: John, he remembered, was mostly just taken aback. Too startled to defend himself against the force of Roman's feelings of betrayal. And that was how it had all ended between them – the partnership, and there was a friendship there that ended, too.

Roman ate his lunch on the subway. Evgenia greeted him with a solemn look when she emerged from class into the cubby room, as if this were a gravely unusual occasion, having Daddy pick her up from school.

"Did you remember I was coming?" he said cheerfully, stroking her hair.

They didn't even take their coats off at home; Jo, anxious to get going, already had the baby in the stroller and the diaper bag packed. She kissed them goodbye on the corner of Broadway and went off to work, and Roman and the kids walked to the playground.

Isaac was asleep in the stroller by the time they got there. Roman pulled the canopy down to keep the sun off his face. Evvie saw some friends from school and ran off to play. Roman sat on the bench, watched her for a while, watched all the kids enjoy their noisy sovereignty.

He was secretly thrilled, on a kind of secondary level, that this whole pretentious Palladio effort had failed so spectacularly. He felt he had known it all along, though certainly no one could have predicted the form in which this failure would come. But he was also self-aware enough to be unsettled by the depth, the intensity, of that thrill. It had a bitter quality, in fact. Palladio's success, while it lasted, had eaten at him. Not just in the way of jealousy, either, nor in the sense that he felt a private humiliation at being proven wrong (for he never accepted that he had been wrong). It was more that it made him feel alienated, profoundly so, though from what, he wasn't sure. He just didn't want to live in a world that took people like Mal Osbourne seriously.

Still, there had to be something going on down there that nobody was talking about, something that had wrought such a change in everybody. What was it? Maybe it would all emerge in time.

It stirred him up, as he sat on the bench, hands in pockets, surrounded by the penned energy of a bunch of five- and six-year-olds at the start of their weekend. And all emotions, as they escalated, eventually converged in one place with Roman, and that place was anger. He was angry all over again that someone as thoughtful as John could have made such a stupid decision – by which he meant the decision to move to Charlottesville in the first place – and thrown away the promise of his life. He was angry all over again at John for lying to him. And there was Osbourne himself, and the woman, whoever she was, and the reporters who had already started to pick them apart for the sake of the common amusement until there was nothing left of them at all.

"Daddy," Evvie said. She was suddenly standing right beside him. "Did you bring snacks?"

He looked through the diaper bag and found a bag of Wheat Thins Jo had tucked in there.

"Here you go," he said.

She looked at him with that air of detachment, that air of taking his existence, as a parent, entirely for granted.

"Why are you mad?" she said.

Roman, startled, said, "I'm not mad, sweetie."

Evvie lost interest; she took the bag of Wheat Thins from his hand and ran off. Roman saw her sharing them with some girls he didn't recognize. Maybe Evvie had just met them. She formed these instant friendships all the time.

That was the hard part, he found, about spending any extended time with the kids. You had to be so careful not to show them what you were feeling. They could only understand it, at that age, as something either directed at or caused by themselves somehow; and so you had to hide it from them. And then maybe it wound up emerging, hours or days later, with your wife or a telemarketer who called during dinner or some idiot on the street who didn't pick up after his dog; or in some other inappropriate way.

★ MESSAGE ★

As we enjoy today's Super Bowl, let's remember that Americans of all races and ethnic groups are on the same team. Working together we can win.

On Mr Olivo's wish list are Elvis Presley, Dag
Hammarskjold, Jimi Hendrix, "maybe Nelson Mandela"

Self-expression is everything.

In this, the season of giving, the gift of freedom is the
greatest gift of all.

Become unaffected;
Cherish sincerity;
Belittle the personal;
Reduce desires.

SELLING THE GOVERNMENT LIKE SOAP; IT
SEEMS TO WORK

A people who do not dream never attain to inner sincerity, for only in his dreams is a man really himself.
Only for his dreams is a man responsible – his actions
are what he must do. Actions are a bastard race to
which a man has not given his full paternity.

*

JOHN STAYED IN South Carolina, in the spare bedroom of the
condo by the golf course, for a month, seeing to the disposition
of his mother's effects, as well as, quite unexpectedly, the sale
of her home; for Buzz, it turned out, with a lack of decorum
that seemed all the more astonishing given his historically
passive and unflappable manner, announced his engagement to
a widow who lived in the same development. We only get one
life, he told John with a sympathetic smile, and she and I are too
old to lose any more time to appearances. The widow's brother
had a place on Boca Grande which he was too infirm now to

use; and so John found himself standing in the driveway waving to them, his mother's widower and a woman he had never met until a week ago, as they drove off to Florida to live out the rest of their lives.

The condo sold quickly (John, who had always found the place somewhat featureless and numbing, was surprised to learn that there was a waiting list of prospective residents), and when the buyers called him there one evening to ask politely if he would be willing to throw in his parents' old furniture as well, he couldn't think of any reason to say no. He hung up and looked around the place – the sectional sofa, the big glass coffee table, the gigantic armoire with the gigantic TV in it – feeling a strange and ambiguous sort of awe at the seamlessness with which his mother's final home would pass into the hands of amiable strangers in about a month's time.

He would have to be around then for the closing; time enough, certainly, to head back up to Charlottesville and see what required his help. But after putting it off for a day or two, John admitted to himself that he wasn't all that anxious to get back, at least not right now. Things weren't the same. Living in a hotel room; working all day in a tiny spare office that didn't belong to them; and the work itself – there simply wasn't much of it at this point. Long hours that summer had been passed sitting idly at his borrowed desk, trying only to be unobtrusive while Mal, with his fingers laced in his hair and a look of vengeful determination on his face, thought.

Finally John called Mal at Shays's office. Mal was actually somewhat brusque on the phone, even before John got around to the subject of his call.

"How are things around there?" John said. "Pretty quiet?"

"Still pretty quiet, yes," Mal said.

"Well, here's the thing. I guess I didn't really understand, until I got away, that this whole thing has taken kind of an emotional toll on me, and then with my mother's passing away . . . If it's okay with you, Mal, I need some more time."

"That's fine," Mal said evenly.

"I mean, if there were anything pressing then of course I would come back. But, you know, in all fairness, I never once took any vacation time while—"

"It's fine, John, really. I don't need you for anything right now."

John was brought up short. He couldn't tell, over the phone, if there was any sort of bitterness in Mal's tone or if he simply meant what he said.

"I have Colette here to answer the phone," Mal went on. "And the rest of it, right now, is all pretty much inside my head anyway."

John felt an unfamiliar surge of pity. He needed to say something just to shake it off.

"No word from her, then?" he said.

"No. So what will you do down there? Keep an eye on your stepfather?"

John didn't feel like going into it. "I don't know. Drive around a little bit, maybe. I haven't been down this way, except to see my mother, in so long. So, maybe just a little motoring excursion through the South."

There was a pause, before Mal said, "You're not going off to look for her, are you?"

"No," John said, startled, feeling his color rise. "No, nothing like that."

436

★ MESSAGE ★

"We had already developed a brand plan that encompasses who I am," Mr Woods said. "American Express isn't going to branch off into areas where we're in conflict. So I'm going to be promoted in the way I hope to be perceived."

Is this a great time, or what?

Ever tuck your baby in from the airport? You will.

Ever send a fax from the beach? You will.

Advertising is not a new thing. We think of the stained-glass windows in Chartres Cathedral as art, but when they were made they were art only incidentally. They were put there to sell theology – they were billboards – and if the people who built the cathedral had had neon they would have gone crazy for it. There's nothing new about any of this. The mosaics in Byzantine churches and early Christian churches are billboards selling Christianity. Tiepolo's ceilings are Counter-Reformation propaganda. Selling is an old

CHANGE EVERYTHING

★

ALL THE WORK was in Los Angeles. But Dex knew – and his friends in the business loved to tease him by confirming – that though he might be capable of surviving a short visit to Los Angeles, there was no way he could ever live there. He was too quick, too belligerent, too much in need of stimulation. It was a moot point, since at this stage no one was offering him work anyway; but it got him thinking, in his many idle hours, that he really was a stranger in his own country, a kind of internal exile, because as far as he was concerned there was nowhere off the island of Manhattan that was adaptable for living. He was stuck there.

And so, while another man in his position – faced with the humiliation of having his live-in girlfriend stolen from him by the one man in all the world he most despises – might have considered leaving town and starting over, for Dex the only truly viable option was to lie about it. He told his friends who asked where Molly was that she had developed a drug habit and he had thrown her out. He felt no guilt about selling her out in this way – look what she'd done to him, after all – and, in terms of being exposed, was comforted by the thought that she had never really kept up a close friendship with anybody in the business. She knew them all through him.

When they had first returned to New York together, after Osbourne asked him to leave, Dex was more energized than ever, full of ideas for making the Palladio documentary even without Mal's cooperation. But no one would finance any of those ideas. They all wanted to see the inside of the place on film; failing that, there had to be something damning, something to subvert the iconic status of Osbourne himself, and in that area Dex had nothing more concrete than his own deeply felt sense of injustice that the man was so popular in the first place. Dex was returning, in fact, from yet another of these disastrous meetings, trying to kowtow before unimaginative money men, on the very evening he came back to his apartment and found none other than Mal Osbourne standing right there in his living room, condescending and triumphant, with his arm around Molly.

Now Dex's savings were just about gone. He tried to get back to work. Out of desperation he even accepted an offer to work as an AD on the third sequel to a teen sex comedy; he tortured himself for weeks over the shame of it, and then in the end the studio head was fired and the whole project went into turnaround before even one day of photography. Then one morning he picked up the paper and read about the burning of Palladio. His very first thought – before he got to the paragraphs that mentioned Osbourne's missing girlfriend – was what a legendary ending this would have made to the film he had imagined shooting there. But his own less hypothetical connection to the events in Virginia had been made clear enough to him by the end of that day, by which time he had unplugged his phone rather than field another call from a reporter wanting to know about Molly, how it felt to have her stolen from him by a famous person, what it was about her that seemed to drive men to such extremes, if he had any idea where she might have gone.

His friends didn't avoid him after that – many of them had half suspected him of lying about his breakup with Molly all along – but he avoided them, hypersensitive to any real or imagined condescension in their voices now that they knew he had been cuckolded and made a fool of. There was no sense in pretending he wasn't humiliated, since he had taken the trouble to lie about it so elaborately in the first place. Fuck them anyway, went Dex's reasoning.

Broke, he finally agreed to accept a gig his exasperated agent had secured for him, directing a commercial for deodorant, on the condition that he be allowed to do it under an assumed name. It only took a day, and by the middle of that day his distaste had been at least temporarily supplanted by the pleasure he took in getting a shot just right or in having a crew to order around. The agency that hired him was very pleased with the result and eager to work with him again. Dex could have as much work of that sort as he wants, in fact, but he only takes enough of it to get by; he doesn't want it to define him. In between jobs he's back to sitting in his kitchen and reading through the spec screenplays his agent's office forwards to him, hundreds of them, looking for the one that doesn't embarrass him, the one that comes anonymously from out of nowhere to bear out and ratify for him his own vision of the world.

★ MESSAGE ★

It will be a free literature, because it will serve not some satiated heroine, not the bored "upper ten thousand" suffering from obesity, but millions and tens of millions of workers, those people who make up the best part of our country, its strength and future.

YOUR COMFORT IS MY SILENCE.

YOU KILL TIME.

I am deeply troubled by the suggestion that the
university has abandoned its historic commitment to
freedom of expression in the process of developing
the contractual agreement.

I SHOP THEREFORE I AM.

> We Democrats need to speak frankly and often about
> personal responsibility, knowing right from wrong
> and being prepared to punish wrong, loving our
> country and the American ideal, hard work, and car-
> ing about those who need help.

Art or Advertising? Either Way, Seoul is Mesmerized

★

HER MOTHER USED to insist on accompanying her all the way
on to the train, fussing over her, talking to the conductor, afraid
Bethany would miss her stop, fall asleep and wake up in
Manhattan. But then one time the train actually began pulling
out of the station with Joyce Vincent still on board and she had
had to pull the emergency cord. The police were there by the
time that one was over. So that put a stop to the humiliation;
now her mother just handed her her overnight bag in the
parking lot, hugged her, and anxiously watched as she took the
stairs to the platform.

It was always nighttime when Bethany rode the train – Friday
night when she left, Sunday night when she returned – and
she liked the insular, underpopulated, anonymous feel of the
sixty-five-minute ride each way. She was fifteen and she did
not welcome being looked at. The conductor took her ticket
and after that she didn't have to deal with another face, besides
her own reflection in the darkened window, the whole rest of
the way.

No one to make fun of how she looked, or to pretend to
ignore it in a patronizing way, which was maybe worse; no one
to judge her or exclude her; no eyes in which to see her own
pitiable nature reflected. It was sweet to get away from her

mother, too, not because she was unsympathetic to Bethany's problems but because she was way too sympathetic. She secretly loved it when Bethany or her brother Kevin fucked up – because it confirmed her own view that the damage done by her ex-husband, the kids' father, was insurmountable and continued to ramify. She wallowed in her children's failures, as in her own. Still, she put them on the train to Rhinebeck every weekend to see him, because that's what the court had ordered.

Kevin hadn't been on one of these trips with her in about three months now. He just didn't want to go. Nothing special against his father: it's just that there was a lot of stuff going on most weekends at home, parties and such, and he didn't want to miss it. What were they going to do, make him go? He was two years older than his sister and was starting to go bad in a serious way. Bethany knew about a lot of things, drugs and stupid petty crime, that her parents would fall over dead if they ever found out about. Mostly, though, he was just so nasty. No compassion for anyone. Boys were different, but Bethany wondered if this state of advanced bitterness was something she herself was about to grow into, considering all she and her brother had in common.

On the bright side, her dad had been a lot nicer to her since Kevin had stopped coming. He felt so guilty all the time anyway. He had this small house he was renting in Rhinebeck, which was kind of a wealthy town, and a job at a different branch of the same bank he had worked at in Ulster, back before everything blew apart. It was easy, in his chronic state of remorse, to get things out of him. Last month he had bought her these Doc Martens she liked, just because she saw them in a store window. Eighty bucks.

Outside, she knew, were trees, and scrub, and the highway, and the houses and cluttered yards of poor people, and from time to time the river. No loss, not being able to see any of it. She got out her Discman and put on the new Kid Rock.

Some of her pseudo-friends, hearing where she went on weekends, told her stories about getting stoned in the train-car bathrooms, which were huge on account of the wheelchair-access laws. Or hiding in them to beat the fare. Or having sex in there, on a bet. Bethany wasn't interested. She was still a little scared of experiences like that. It was one reason she secretly didn't mind missing the various parties on Saturday nights, the keggers in the woods, the gatherings at the elementary-school playground.

"Can't," she'd say. "I have to go visit my dad."

"Oh, right," they'd say. "Drag."

They were pulling into the Rhinebeck station now, and there he was. He stood in the floodlit parking lot, hands jammed in his pockets, next to his car. He wore a big parka over his suit. Too vain to wear his glasses, he squinted at the train, trying to find her face in one of the bright windows. Bethany watched him search for her. The music blasted in her ears.

★ MESSAGE ★

MAYBE LUXURY DOESN'T MAKE YOU SOFT AFTER ALL

COMPROMISE IS JUST A POLITE WORD FOR SURRENDER

"I make images and they make images, so why not put them together?" Mr Rodrigue said. "Would Andy Warhol have done this? Yes."

443

JONATHAN DEE

THE WOMB IS OVERRATED

Self-appointed moral critics throughout the ages have
warned of moral declines when what they should have
hailed was moral change. Today is no different.

May Technology Bring Us Together

"Who wants to call themselves 'Jew'?" Ms. Bleyer asked. "We've been called Jews for 4,000 years. It's played out. Heeb just sounds so much cooler."

In February 1994, Benetton began its campaign for
peace.

★

THE FRANTIC, ESCALATING nature of publicity was such that
people all over the country got sick of the story of Jean–Claude
Milo within weeks, and forgot it in all but outline; still, even
after it all seemed to have blown over, Palladio received no
inquiries regarding new business of any kind, nor even any
expressions of patient support from faithful clients wondering
when and where they expected to reopen. If the connection
between these two phenomena – Milo's death and the
obsolescence of Palladio – seemed at least instinctively obvious
to the world at large, to Mal it remained frustratingly oblique.
For whether one saw Milo as a martyr to his art or simply as an
inadequately supervised lunatic, the fact was that he had never
expressed any dissatisfaction with his life at the mansion, never
made any attempt to dissociate himself from it. Indeed, the
last two years had been indisputably the most productive of his
life. Why should his death, even taking into account its

violent circumstances, reflect on the larger concerns of the place, or on the nature and the quality of the work that was done there?

Mal couldn't fathom it. With little else to do, he brooded on it with increasing bitterness until he gradually lost touch with the idea that the whole episode, to one way of thinking at least, had not been about him at all. In the popular fascination with the story he could see only a calculated, opportunistic effort to bring him down. He was an innovator, a visionary, and there are always people – hordes of people, in fact – who are interested in seeing such a person fail.

At some point he resigned himself to the idea that Molly, wherever the hell she had gone, was not going to come back; but the most alarming aspect of this realization was how little effort it took to resign himself to it. He had never felt as though he understood women anyway. Still, he wondered what had come over him – barely two months ago he had been ready to throw everything away for her, he had been fixing up a villa to surprise her with on their honeymoon. His ex-wife would never have recognized him.

The lawsuits were settled. The artists had dispersed, back to the lives they had forsworn in order to come to Virginia, though the blow was softened for most of them by their considerable savings. Mal let Colette go with a year's severance, money that came out of his own pocket. Every morning he drove from his room in the Sheraton to his room in Shays's office building, where he now sat by himself, answering the phone when it rang. One morning, as he tilted back in his chair with his hands folded on his stomach, staring up at the whorls on the stamped-tin ceiling, his cell phone went off in his pocket: it was his contractor, calling from Umbria. The marble bought at great expense for the small terrace facing the hillside had cracked in the first frost; the quarry was refusing to replace it, insisting that the problem could only be attributed to incompetent masonry. When Mal hung up fifteen minutes later he felt less depressed, his energies less scattered, than at any time in the last few months, and when he thought about it he realized that he had managed to forget that he did still have a home somewhere in the world after all, even if it was one he had never lived in. Then there was Italy itself, a country he had always loved, a country that understood the ancient verities, unlike America, which masked its cultural rootlessness with the constant exaltation of the new, which had, in place of a sense of eternity, perfected the art of forgetting so as to be able to learn the same things over and over again with undiminished enchantment.

Though his contractor assured him it wasn't necessary, Mal flew overseas to settle the dispute over the marble; he told Shays not to expect him back anytime soon. His plan of action is simply to read, manage his estate, live in leisurely obscurity as an expatriate country gentleman. His sense of things is that if he disappears, people will forget him, and when that happens, it's only a matter of time before they start asking for him again.

★ MESSAGE ★

THESE ARE REAL PEOPLE
NOT ACTORS
ABOUT TO FIND OUT IF THEY'RE HAVING A BABY

HUMANITY IS THE STONE

Entertainment is itself an ideology.

My goal is to destroy all my possessions. I have been making an inventory of everything I own, and it comes to 7,006 items, from televisions to reading material to records to old love letters to my Saab 900. These are the things I have accumulated in the 37 years of my life. Some of them are hard to part with, like my father's sheepskin coat, which he gave to me many years ago. But I have made a conceptual decision as an artist to shred and granulate everything.

"You always have to consider that," he said. "But you can't exploit reality."

★

A REPORTER CAME to see them in their cell. They tried not to get excited: they were under no illusions anymore about the intelligence or the political sophistication of most reporters. Still, it was an event. Part of the reason for going to jail was to serve as an example; in order to spread the word of that example, you needed help. And the guy was from the AP.

They were back in jail because the judge had tossed them in there for disrupting the trial again. No negotiations this time. Jack Gradison had lost it during one of the prosecutor's objections, calling him a liar, shouting out statistics about wealth concentrated in the hands of a diminishing few. To Jack an argument was a fight, and he was not going to allow himself to be pilloried without responding just because they happened to be inside a government building. The judge had found Liebau in contempt too, even though he had said

447

nothing, but Liebau had no problem with that. If you were a revolutionary then you should simply consider jail one of your addresses.

It was supposed to clarify the mind. A jail cell was existence stripped to its essentials, and so there were no distractions, nothing to cloud your thinking. Antonio Gramsci, one of Liebau's heroes, had done his best thinking in jail, had written the invaluable *Prison Notebooks* there. Still, Liebau had to admit that this notion of existence stripped to its essentials wasn't totally borne out by his own experience. Jail was, more surprisingly than anything else, an unbelievably noisy place. For hours at a stretch he found it hard to think at all.

The series of buzzers commenced, far away at first and then gradually louder, and by the time the last door was opened Gradison and Liebau, in spite of themselves, were standing expectantly behind the table. The guard watched them with a focus that looked like sleepiness, like an alligator's.

The reporter's name was Suarez. A good sign; minorities often were more receptive to the whole notion of concealed power. He asked them a few basic questions about their background, their court case, questions which, Liebau could see, Jack was a little miffed an AP reporter wouldn't already know the answers to.

"So," Suarez asked. "Let's start then with your first meeting with John Wheelwright."

The first meeting he was talking about was the first day of their first jury selection, many months ago now. Liebau smiled tightly and said that while their lawyer had subsequently told them that Wheelwright had been in the gallery that day, they hadn't met him then. In fact, they had refused to meet him.

Suarez apologized and wrote hastily on his little notepad. But then, for some reason, the questions about this Wheelwright, this bagman, this insignificant lieutenant to the cultural fascist Osbourne, just went on and on. What did you say to him when he saw you. What did he say to you. How did he look. How did he act. Did he mention anything about . . . well, about anything. How did he strike you?

"He struck me as a worm," Gradison said. "Listen, what the hell sort of interview is this?"

Then it all came out, how this insufferable gofer, who smiled at them all the time and offered them the moon if they would just agree to shut up, had flown back to his plantation and watched one of his underlings set fire to himself in the name of advertising. This guy was wound a lot tighter, apparently, than they had thought. Not that they had really spared a thought for him at all at the time, or even now.

"And apparently," Suarez said excitedly, "there was a woman."

Liebau was stunned and dispirited. This was what they had been steeling themselves for? They had gone to jail to await rebirth as minor players in some monumentally irrelevant soap opera about people they didn't even know? It wouldn't have surprised him a bit to learn that Osbourne had contrived this entire thing, to trump the growing public interest in CultureTrust and obscure the motives of these two men who couldn't be bought, to keep them from getting famous for their dissent by making them famous for something else.

Contrived or not, that's pretty much what happened. Search engines were becoming society's short-term memory, and thus the names of the two cultural guerrillas were now bound forever to the name of the flunky who supervised the maniac who thought his own gruesome death would make a nifty Banana Republic ad. The galleries were full now for every day of their trial. Their judge seemed enraged by all the attention. She refused to grant any more mistrials; the defendants wouldn't shut up, though, satirizing their captors, provoking their anger, refusing to legitimize the proceedings by sitting quietly through them. Her solution in the end was to put them back in their cell with a TV connected to a closed-circuit hookup. They sat on their bunks and watched their own trial on television, cursing at it, hurling unheard insults at all the participants, as if they were watching a beauty pageant or a football game.

They were found guilty and fined $500 each. When they refused to pay, the judge waived the fine and commuted their sentences to time served.

They were free, and undefeated; but it wasn't the same without Osbourne on the scene. Their creative edge was lost. The thing they were fighting against seemed too diffuse now. There were ten thousand people doing something like what Osbourne had been doing, only not as provocatively, nor as well.

Six months later, broke, with nowhere else to go, Liebau convinced Gradison that their best option was to go back to the University of Eastern Washington and ask to be reinstated, at least as adjuncts. To their surprise, the petition was granted. Gradison taught English, Liebau anthropology, and Liebau had to admit to himself that he generally felt calmer – Kimiko, his wife, pointed out that his health had improved as well – as a result of this retreat into the world of artifacts, into the realm of dead culture. Still, a retreat was what it was. Like many college campuses these days, theirs sometimes seemed to him like a kind of retirement community for bitter or self-aggrandizing old radicals.

Gradison, though, had more trouble coping with his withdrawal from guerrilla life. The two men saw less of each other for a while. Then one night Jack drove out to Liebau's remote A-frame, which, when they were younger and stronger, he had helped his old friend build, and announced – pacing up and down in front of the picture window, while Kimiko banged things around disapprovingly behind the door to the kitchen – that he had decided to turn himself in for a certain activity he had been a part of in Madison, Wisconsin, in 1971.

Liebau knew the activity to which he was referring.

"Are you crazy?" he said. "That's not some five-hundred-dollar fine. That is the whole rest of your god damn life in federal prison."

"I want to do it," Gradison said sullenly.

"You can't do it!"

"What's the fucking difference!" Jack shouted. "Is there somewhere else I need to be?"

A door slammed, and moments later they listened to Kimiko driving off in the car. The two men wound up crying and getting very drunk. Through the wide picture window they saw the sun light up the forest, before they fell asleep.

A year later, Liebau's tenure was restored. Gradison, according to the minutes of that fall's English department meeting, had asked for and been granted a psychiatric leave.

★ MESSAGE ★

Have you met life today?

Rebel. Express yourself. Take your creativity to a whole new level. Express yourself.

Through the Ad and intent of the Advertiser we form our ideas and learn the myths that make us into what we are as a people. To Advertise is to Exist. To Exist is to Advertise. Our ultimate goal is nothing short of a personal and singular Billboard for each citizen. Until that day we will continue to do all in our power to encourage the masses to use any means possible to commandeer the existing media and to alter it to their own design.

In "A Tale of Two Rooms and a Blind Man," the artist — who spent time in prison in China for making subversive art — invites us to feel, smell, or sense objects in a pitch-black room and then describe them — in a stark white room — to an elegant blind man, who then sculpts them from clay. Through 4/20.

★

FIRST JOHN DROVE up to Durham and stayed in a little bed-and-breakfast he found there, just reading, walking through the dignified campus and past the frat houses with the wading pools and legless couches in the front yard, feeling that particular pang one feels as an outsider in a community of the young. He was happy that way for almost a month, even as the gregarious curiosity of the old couple who ran the B&B turned into a more restrained suspiciousness at his ability to pay every week on time, in cash, without seeming to do anything for a living or to speak of any place he needed to get back to. When the semester ended and the town emptied out he drove — top down, wind roaring in his ears, the Porsche drawing admiring or challenging

452

stares on the highways – to Savannah, where he hadn't been since he was a boy, just to look around; and from there to New Orleans, where he thought he might stay to see Mardi Gras, just because it seemed like one of those things one ought to be able to say one had seen.

He wasn't so naive as to expect he would run into Molly anywhere on the road. Ten years earlier he would have been looking around for her reflexively at every red light. Now, though, if anything he tried not to think about her, not out of regret or resentment but because he felt that his unchecked thoughts of her tended of their own accord to grow increasingly unfair. If you were too focused on yourself, then it could seem like it was Molly's destiny to come into men's lives, give them something to long for, and then withdraw again, with no residue but the longing. But then you started to turn her into a metaphor, which wasn't right: which, in fact, couldn't be done, because to equate her with anything else was to miss the point of her anyway. And meanwhile, she had to go on living her life.

In New Orleans he phoned Shays's office, took a deep breath, and asked to speak to Mal. Shays got on the phone instead.

"John!" he said, his stagy courtroom drawl growing a little shaky with age. "Mal's not here!"

John didn't want to leave the number where he was, a French Quarter rooming house. "When will he be back?"

Shays laughed, entirely inappropriately, John thought. "Don't know!" he said.

More questioning elicited the mystifying news that Mal had gone to Italy to settle some dispute regarding his house in Umbria. He hadn't said when he would return, but John assumed that had to be an oversight on somebody's part – maybe

Shays's, since he was, after all, a little deaf. Mal wouldn't stay away for long. John still had his cell phone number; but in light of this news, he suddenly felt a bit hesitant about using it. He asked Shays to leave a message for Mal, saying only that he had called to check in, and would call again.

In the end, the town he was most charmed by was Oxford, Mississippi, and when he got tired of driving he went back there and rented a little two-story house near the university. To keep busy, and to meet people, he took a volunteer job as an illustrator for the Sewanee Baptist Church. Nothing too Bible-thumping, just illustrations to accompany Sunday-school texts, newsletter design, pamphlets for the troubled about alcohol abuse, marital difficulties, things like that. John hasn't found religion himself; never in his life, in fact, has he felt a particular pull in that direction. But the work is pleasant and un-demanding; John likes to draw; plus, he can't help but be aware that there's a certain integrity to it. He is putting his consider-able talents – talents whose expensiveness his kind employers would never in a million years suspect – to good use, in support of certain strong, sincere, uncompromised beliefs, beliefs he respects, even if they aren't necessarily his.

★ MESSAGE ★

Where do storytellers get their stories?

In some quintessentially Jeffersonian way, *Puppy* renders all who see it equal. With its coat of many colors, *Puppy* straddles a cosmic fault line separating the hilarious and the insidious, the architectural and the organic, the temporary and the timeless. In some Machiavellian way,

There's No Future In Advertising.

In exchange for the $40,000 for the first academic year, they are expected to wear their First USA clothing whenever they make public appearances on their campus or others for the company. Each has to maintain at least a C average (Mr McCabe was a straight-A student in high school; Mr Barrett got A's and B's) and live up to the terms of a moral clause – if they misbehave, the deal is off. But Mr Filak said he fully expected to "re-sign" them for the full four years of college.

★

THE OCEAN SEETHED all day, low waves, too low to attract the surfers even if it had been warm enough for surfing, which it was not. That was the appealing thing about winter in the rambling beach house: the cold weather kept away the trespassers, the partyers, aimless scraggly young people not caring what they befouled on their rambling path to hell. The less appealing thing was that the cold inside the house had to be fought off via heating oil, which meant money, which they didn't have. Lately they had been setting the thermostat at fifty-six degrees, and Richard had overheard some grumbling about it.

He watched the restless back-and-forth of the ocean – like an animal, he thought, like a tiger miserable in its cage – from behind the uncurtained picture windows. He would have opened the door to the porch, just to hear the surf for a moment, were the cold air not likely to antagonize the others even more. The beach house had been given to them, outright, by a former disciple. Gone now. And while the house itself had been his, all its contents, it turned out, had previously been granted to his ex-wife in their divorce. There was nothing in the five bright rooms now except about twenty sleeping bags, and in the dining room a portable altar from which Richard, every evening after dinner, sermonized.

Seven months ago there were twenty-eight of them there. Eleven had left, three new members from the local college had joined. Richard had to remind himself not to get too discouraged about that. When he thought about overall numbers, he worried, but when he thought about each of those eleven defectors as individuals, he couldn't regret that any of them were gone. There was no room for weakness or hypocrisy, to say nothing of downright heresy. True, they were commanded to be fishers of men, but at the same time the purity of the group, the purity of their mission, couldn't be diluted, or else he would ultimately lose them all. It was a delicate balance.

The sea snapped and unfurled. A soup made from lentils would be their dinner tonight, the fourth night in a row. Gratitude for this bounty would be a hard sell for his sermon afterwards, and anyway, he had taken that as his subject two nights ago. The important thing was fidelity to a cause, God's cause: they should glory in their own severance from the wickedness and avarice of the world, glory in all evidence of it, even painful evidence. If you couldn't move through even this brief life with a sense of purpose, then what were you? One of those surfers, maybe, looking for someone else's property on which to build your small fire and get stoned.

Of course, words were hollow if Richard himself wasn't willing to assume a leadership role.

He felt a kind of cramp, an actual hunger pang, under his rib. And in the next moment he decided he would begin a fast, something he hadn't done for a long time, as a way of refocusing himself, and through himself all of them, on the unseen. He would invite, but not require, his followers to join him. It would be a way of separating the wheat from the chaff.

Not that fasting was without its spiritual challenges for him as well. For what he would have to keep secret from them, if the past was any guide, was that the whole experience excited him, in some private and vaguely shameful way. He was not afraid when that point came – the point at which you felt the touch of death. Once he had gone for nineteen days. The others had knelt in a rectangle around him and prayed, sobbing. It was glorious. He could probably match that now, or even do better. But was he really fasting just to purge his mind, or was there some subconscious wish underneath it, the wish to get it all over with, to put behind him the degradations of this life and arrive earlier than scheduled at the feet of a gratified Lord?

This was the sin for which he was constantly examining himself. Lust for death. He decided he would make it the topic of that night's sermon.

* MESSAGE *

Nobody likes a group of angry do-gooders shouting SAVE THE WORLD. That's not what this is about. This is a revolution, but it is a joyful revolution. It is a revolution based on a simple idea: Each of us has something inside that is making a noise. UNDERNEATH ALL OF THE LAYERS, the me-first layer and the get-out-of-my-way layer and the keep-your-hands-off-my-stuff layer, a halfway decent person is in there, waiting to be heard. That person isn't angry. HE JUST WANTS OUT.

THERE IS A GREATNESS WAITING FOR YOU. We are busy, we are distracted, we are cynical, but this greatness waits. Through a speech by Dr King or the story of the Grinch or even a bumper sticker, THIS GREATNESS FINDS YOU IN A moment, unlikely or untimely, and suddenly you find yourself connected to humanity in a way that shocks you. And this greatness will hold you up so high and strong that any previous version of YOURSELF SEEMS FLIMSY.

WE HAVE NO RIGHT to say anything about anything other than boots. We're not ministers or gurus; we're not philosophers or politicians. We are simply bootmakers who have found something to be true. THAT TRUTH IS SIMPLE: Every single one of us has a chance to do something big with our lives, something bigger than any coach or financial consultant or personal fitness trainer ever told us. And by waking up to this potential, and acting on it, amazing things happen: to other people, to ourselves. This has nothing and EVERYTHING TO DO WITH MAKING BOOTS.

*

WINTER WAS COMING again and nothing was going to stop it. Kay wasn't sure what month it was, but in the nights lately she had definitely felt the cold. She couldn't wait for Roger to do something about it. She had always been more sensitive to the elements. One good draft could put her on her back for a week. If he didn't care about that by now, she wasn't going to sit around and wait for him to start.

So she went up to the attic to bring down the storm windows; but while she was up there she found some other things, a box of Richard's old record albums, an accordion file, its edges gnawed away, full of Molly's old report cards from grade school and even her class pictures. Such a serious face! Her teachers all loved her, they knew that town couldn't hold her, they knew she would make her mark. Kay sat on the attic floor and went through every piece of paper. This was an important find: something Molly's own children might want to see. Molly would probably be embarrassed, of course; no mother can stand having her own kids see her as a child. By the time Kay closed the attic's trapdoor behind her again, it was night. The storm windows were forgotten.

But she wrote a note about them in the diary that she kept in her bedside table drawer, so nothing was really lost. She'd only been keeping a diary for a few years. It started out as a kind of exercise in reminiscence, but before long it ceased reaching any further back into the past than the day on which each entry was written – a list of errands completed, mundane tasks performed, a way of accounting for her time. And each entry ended with a reminder to herself of all that was still left to do.

Of course, it was somewhat nebulous now, the whole idea of the end of the day. She wrote in the diary when she felt the need of it. She had no schedule for going to bed, or for getting up; no sense of finishing the day in the evening, nor of starting

459

a new one in the morning. She would simply come to, with an awareness of some sort of gap in her consciousness, and would see by the sudden change outside the window that she must have fallen asleep for a while. Sometimes this would happen in her own bed, other times in Molly's or in Richard's. When she slept in Richard's bed she tried to imagine what he was doing over in Germany. One thing for sure, though, she couldn't fall asleep at all anymore if there was anyone else in the bed.

In her diary she had noted that a trip to the pharmacy would be necessary.

She never moved anything in the kids' rooms, except to clean. It all looked just exactly as it had when they were teenagers. Posters, tapestries thumbtacked to the walls, small photos cut from magazines and stuck to the wallpaper above the desks with Scotch tape that she carefully replaced when it turned brown. It wasn't for her sake. Maybe they would come back home looking for something in particular, something whose private significance she could never guess. Maybe Richard would come back from Berkeley, where he was a professor now, and his wife, hoping only for some hint, some relic, of the upbringing he had talked so much about, would be stunned to find instead everything kept perfectly intact, for her to see. She might start crying at the sight of it – the habitat of her beloved, when he was just a boy. They were expecting a baby of their own now.

It was night again, and she definitely felt the cold.

Molly too might be sitting somewhere, in her office with the incredible view, daydreaming about her childhood, about time lost; she might be recalling the way her room looked in the morning when she awoke, mourning all that as gone for ever. Imagine the rush of amazement and gratitude when she came home to find that nothing had been lost at all!

"Kay?"

Roger was calling. She sat on the bed in Molly's room. "Kay?" She sat, calmly. The doorknob rattled and she realized that she must have locked it. After a while he went away. She could hear him leaving, even though his footsteps were always so soft.

She had no ill will left for him. For a long time they had just irritated one another, she remembered, but now something like the opposite was true, they moved through the house, which seemed plenty large enough for both of them now, in their independent orbits, natural, regular, where their paths might intersect once every few hundred years, as in an eclipse. The only habit of his that annoyed her anymore was the way he would turn off the radio. He'd go into a room, and when he'd leave it again she would enter to find the radio had been switched off. There were little radios in every room of the house, except the kids' rooms. She kept them on the talk stations, all of them tuned to the same one, though she would change her station-allegiance every few weeks. Always talk, though. No music. Music got on her nerves; and there were so many things worth knowing about.

She didn't know why he couldn't just leave them alone. She wanted them on continuously — that's why she'd gotten all electric ones. They weren't turned up loud. True, sometimes she craved a little silence, but when she did she just went into one of the kids' rooms and shut the door. She didn't see why he couldn't just do the same thing.

He had his work to do, and she had hers.

The children were never coming back. She didn't even know where they were. Maybe they were dead. She imagined them dead, imagined the depth of her own agony, so vividly that she started to wonder if maybe someone had told her they were dead, told her that on the phone, and she had just forgotten it.

If you changed around their bedrooms, refurnished them, gave them over to some other use, then they were no longer shrines to the children's having been there: instead they became shrines to the children's having left. Besides, change them into what? If they weren't Molly's and Richard's rooms, then what was that extra space doing there at all?

In the upstairs hall, she put her ear to the closed door of her own bedroom and heard the sound of Roger weeping. She listened for a while; discreet, unmodulated, the sound eventually gave way to silence. She went downstairs. It was morning again.

Time for the pharmacy. She hated to go, actually. She hated leaving the house, even for a short while; the forces of decay made too much headway while she was gone, so that when she did return, it could be overwhelming. And she hated driving the car. Especially now that she had to go all the way to Canajoharie just to get her prescription filled. The Rexall in town was still open but that witch who worked there had too many questions, questions about money, questions about the prescription and whether it hadn't expired. Last time, the woman had put on those glasses chained across her flat chest and held the bottle itself up to the light, trying to insinuate that the label had been altered somehow. That was the end of that relationship; Kay took her business elsewhere, to Troy, to Middletown. She had found a place in Canajoharie that would be fine for a while.

She put on her scarf, her fur hat with the earflaps, her gloves, her long down coat. She got into the car and turned the heater up all the way. Something was agitating her, as was always the case on these trips. She knew they were unavoidable, but still, an hour or two spent in the car just seemed like such a waste of time. She couldn't bear to waste time anymore. When she sat on the bed to write in her diary, she didn't want to look back on the time and wonder where it had all gone. There were the storm windows to put in, for one thing.

And that was just the beginning. There was so much left to do. She could remember, it seemed like years before, talk about selling the house and moving somewhere else. Fine: once everything was finished. But if you started something, and then just abandoned it before it was completed, then what had the point of the time been at all?

* MESSAGE *

Do you keep the promises you make to yourself?

Wash Out Your Mind

Once you put something out there, people can interpret it any way they like – nothing contains a specific meaning; nothing is degrading for anybody.

Communication Without Boundaries

BOOKS ARE OVERRATED.

Only what they do not need first to understand, they consider understandable; only the word coined by commerce, and really alienated, touches them as familiar.

463

Bring Us Your Content

generally avoids such trivial speculation, suggesting instead that business in the new age will be transformed, the salvationary spirit of the entrepreneur will soar and the roving ambitions of individuals will find resonance in an incandescent web of knowledge. Freedom will grow, wisdom thrive and wealth spread. What more could a prophet of a "redemptive technology" possibly desire? Forget the mundane

The Voice of the People Can Topple a Despot.

While We May Fall Short, We Will Not Give Up, Nor Will We Remain Silent.

In order, therefore, to find an analogy we must take flight into the misty realm of religion.

*

MOLLY, THOUGH SHE doubted anyone was looking for her anymore, traveled for a while in an indirect path, in the general direction of the center of the country. Mostly by bus; money was a problem, even after she'd sold the car. She stopped in a state she'd never been to before, in a city she had never heard of. She's been there a while now.

She works for an insurance company, one of the larger ones, in their secretarial pool. She had no real secretarial skills when she went in to answer the ad for the job, apart from scoring 100 on their spelling test. But the woman who interviewed her, an overweight woman (but they were all overweight there) with a towering blond perm, kept looking hard at her.

"And you didn't go to college," she said, for the second time.

"No."

"Where did you say you were from?"

"Virginia."

The permed woman stared at her. Molly could see her weighing the possible effects of asking all the questions she wanted to ask.

"Okay, come here," she said finally, standing up from her desk. Molly's first thought was that the woman was going to hug her; but no, she was only waving Molly briskly into her own desk chair. When Molly was seated the woman spun her a quarter turn toward her computer terminal, and right then and there gave her her first typing lesson. QWERTYUIOP. After about five minutes they stopped.

"Okay, all right," the woman said. "I can see you're going to get it. I'll give you a starting date of two weeks from now. That'll give you time to practice at home, which you'd better do."

"Yes, ma'am, I will, thank you," Molly said, though she had no keyboard to practice on, and indeed, at that point, no home.

But that same day she found a place, a beautiful warped old clapboard house painted yellow whose two third-floor rooms had been converted to an apartment after the owner's husband had run off, leaving her with two young children. The apartment had its own entrance, an outdoor wooden staircase which Molly was responsible for keeping free of snow and ice. When Caroline, the landlord, first saw Molly — an attractive single woman from out of town — she had her doubts, what with the kids sleeping right downstairs from her. But she's proved to be an ideal tenant. Always pays right on time; hardly makes a sound.

Caroline's children were a little shy with Molly at first – a little scared of her, in fact; a stranger, even a nice lady, creaking around upstairs as they lay in their beds in the dark was like a nightmare scenario come true for them – but nowadays, if they're in the yard when she comes home from work, they'll yell to her or even run up to tell her about some triumph at school. If Caroline is having a day where she's particularly depressed, Molly will come downstairs and read to the kids before bed; then the two women sit on the porch glider and drink wine and talk in whispers until they're sure the two children are asleep.

Molly's little secretarial subdivision ("pod" is how they're told to refer to it) contains five other employees, all women. Her supervisor is a woman too – Fern, the woman who hired her. In fact there are only five men in her entire department, only two who work on her floor. No one speaks to them. Molly lives in a virtual society of women, with the sole exception of her landlord's son, Tucker, who is five. This wasn't what she was after, in settling there, but in practice she feels it suits her fine.

There was one time, back in New York – around dawn, drunk, at home after a party at which some contemptibly suave TV actor whose name she didn't even know had kissed her on the mouth in full view of everyone by way of saying goodbye – when Dex had hit her with his closed fist. It was in the chest, oddly, as if he'd changed his mind about it at the last instant. The next day she showed him the bruise and he apologized so long and hard that at one point he had started crying. He had always had a temper, and sometimes in the course of making a point he would grab her arm hard enough to leave a mark, but only that one time had it gone further over the line than that.

The point was not to defend him but to remember how amazed, how genuinely compelled and shocked, she had been to learn that that was in him: the wild possessiveness, the terror of abandonment, the capacity to hurt. That seemed like a long time ago. Now she had no reason not to suppose that it was in all of them.

And there was something in her that seemed to bring it out. She knew she wasn't supposed to think that way, that someone impartial might say she was only blaming herself for things that were not her fault: still, she thought and thought about it (little to keep her from turning over the past, in the evenings in her two-room apartment) and she could not conclude that she was wrong. They all wanted to make her talk, when all she wanted was to stay silent. Silence maddened them. They all wanted to make her belong to them, for no other reason than that they could see she did not want to belong to anybody.

There is a multiplex nearby, and when she needs to get out Molly takes the bus there. Some of the movies seem more promising to her than others, but usually she winds up seeing them all. Some more than once. This has gotten her into trouble on occasion – an unaccompanied young woman at the movies, in a city just large enough for people to lose themselves in. Once a man came and sat in the seat right next to her with just ten minutes left to go in *Castaway*.

The credits rolled. The man – he was her age, or maybe a few years younger – leaned toward her slightly, without taking his eyes off the screen, and said, "That Helen Hunt – what have seen her in before?"

"*As Good as it Gets,* maybe?" Molly said.

"Oh, right, right." The lights went up. "Hey, you know what?" he said, in a tone of playful conspiracy. "You've seen this movie before."

Molly looked at him, alarmed.

"Yeah, I knew it," he said. He had a kind of sallow, slack complexion, like someone who has lost a prodigious amount of weight. "I've seen you in here. In fact, I was thinking maybe you've seen me in here, too."

Molly had lost a mitten, and looked around under her seat for it.

"I mean, come on," the man said, laughing unconvincingly. "I mean, it's not *that* good a movie."

He followed her all the way to her bus stop, and by that time his banter had grown a little less ingratiating, a little more aggressive. But he didn't get on to the bus. Molly next went back to the multiplex about two weeks later, and there was no sign of him.

Life alone, she understands, life without attachments, means that when she dies something will die along with her. But she doesn't find any great cause there for regret – indeed on some nights, in some moods, there's something grimly satisfying about it – and anyway, she still has a long, long expanse of time to get through, a life like a spy's life, never disguised but essentially retrospectively, unseen. At night sometimes she can hear, through the floorboards, the sound of Tucker and his sister Hannah crying in their beds. They are crying, Caroline has explained to her, for their lost father. Those moments only reinforce for Molly actually, the wisdom of her own resolve not to become a mother herself. What comfort could she be to anyone.

PALLADIO

★ MESSAGE ★

You are forgiven

A friend is someone you know about, someone you can trust. A brand's a bit like that. You met this friend through advertising . . . Without advertising, how would you recognize your friends?

You are forgiven

USEFULNESS OF TECHNOLOGY ALTERS ATTITUDES

You are forgiven

And if there is a gimmick in all of this, it is that there is no gimmick. For

You are forgiven

Let us, then, restore to the notion of commitment the only meaning it can have for us. Instead of being of a political nature, commitment is, for the writer, the full awareness of the present problems of his own language,

forgiven forgiven
forgiven forgiven
forgiven forgiven
forgiven forgiven

SKEPTICISM MAKES THE WORLD ACCOUNTABLE.

What's On Your Mind?

THE REVOLUTION IS HERE.

YOU'RE ALL FORGIVEN!

469